Promise Me

Promise Me

ROBIN BIELMAN
SAMANTHE BECK

Entangled Publishing, LLC
2614 South Timberline Road
Suite 105, PMB 159
Fort Collins, CO 80525
rights@entangledpublishing.com

Embrace is an imprint of Entangled Publishing, LLC.

Edited by Stacy Abrams
Cover design by Mayhem Cover Creations
Cover photography by George Rudy/Shutterstock

Manufactured in the United States of America

First Edition April 2019

embrace

To our readers. We hope you love this story as much as we loved working on it together!

Chapter One

Kendall

I don't usually make wishes on stars, but looking up into the late-night June sky, I close my eyes and think, *I want to wake up every morning, full of energy and so excited for the day that I don't need coffee.* Sounds simple enough, but simple and easy are two very different things. I could pretend law school is what I want and spend the summer enjoying carefree days until my house-sitting gig is up and I head to the University of Chicago for another three years of education, but that would be like a giraffe impersonating a koala bear. Wrong.

Opening my eyes, I tug on Snowflake's leash and continue down the front walkway of my aunt and uncle's Hollywood Hills home for a quick stroll before bedtime. "It's not like it will kill me to follow in my dad's footsteps," I say aloud. "But I want to love what I do, not settle. For a long time, I wanted to be an actress. Now, I don't know what I want to do with the rest of my life, but I've got the summer to figure it out." I drag in a deep breath, the scent of jasmine and roses filling my nose. "God, I love the smells here. I'm not going to miss the car fumes and hot asphalt of New York. The hot dogs, though, those I'll miss."

I'm talking to a dog.

Don't judge.

Snowflake is the cutest furball on the planet, but do *not* say it to her face, no matter how adorable she looks prancing across the grass on her short little legs, trying to act all badass. She's a Pomeranian who thinks she's a pit bull. In her tiny little mind she's the alpha, and she will puff herself up and cute you to death with an angry dance and a frenzy of high-pitched barks to prove it. As far as I know, Aunt Sally is the only one who can love on her without unleashing the full force of her Pomeranian fury. The rest of us she merely tolerates. But tonight I choose to take her quiet disregard as a sign of respect. She's deigning to be a good listener.

As soon as we hit the sidewalk she selects a nice patch of grass to do her business. "Good girl," I say. She lifts her snout and looks at me like she already knows this. I laugh. It's been a couple of years since my last visit, and she hasn't changed a bit. The pet sitter did warn me she's been feistier than normal but attributes it to missing my aunt and uncle and said I could call her if I had any problems.

I follow Snowflake's lead up the street, the moon smiling down on us. Compared to my apartment in New York City, it's downright tranquil here. Earlier, music blasted from the house next door, f-bombs dropping repeatedly in many of the songs. My aunt briefly mentioned her next door neighbor, "Vaughn." She texted to say that if I needed anything, he could help, and included his phone number. From the music selection, I'm guessing he's closer to my age than hers.

The noise level has since subsided, but lights shine brightly. Shadowy movement passes beyond the windows. There are definitely people inside. Music suddenly shatters the quiet, the latest Maroon 5 song blaring through the wide open front door. Inexplicably, Snowflake chooses that moment to bark like someone yelled "dog party!" and run toward the neighbor's driveway. I tug on her leash because I'm not one to trespass, but she's crazy for something and isn't about to back off. Then I realize someone's walking down the dark driveway. Someone tall, broad-shouldered, and ambling with a loose-limbed grace that suggests he thinks he has the driveway to himself. Whoever he is, Snowflake can't wait to greet him.

I'm about to call out hello when an engine revs. Red taillights blaze from the top of the driveway, and a vehicle jerks like the driver forgot to release the brake. Oh crap.

The guy stops and turns in slow motion as an SUV rolls down the drive. I'm close enough now to hear his, "Oh fuck no," as the car lurches.

He sprints to the center of the driveway and faces the car like he's the Hulk and can stop two tons of metal momentum with his bare hands. What is he thinking?

"Stay," I command Snowflake and run up the driveway. "Hey!" I shout.

The guy turns around and *oh my God*, the car suddenly picks up speed and heads straight for him. "Look out!"

He doesn't listen, his eyes locked on mine instead. In a burst of super-human strength I didn't know I had, I tackle him and fling us to the side of the concrete before he's roadkill.

"What the—" he mumbles then *oomphs* as we hit the ground. Lucky for me, I'm sprawled on top of him, a slight sting in my shoulder from our initial landing.

Icy fear grips me as I look down the drive, praying Snowflake has stayed put. She has, but being the badass that she is, she's barking for the driver to get out of the vehicle and keep all hands where she can see them. Thankfully, the SUV has stopped, its back end in the thick green bushes flanking the entrance to the driveway.

A tall blond woman in a short blue dress stumbles out of the car, laughing her head off like she didn't almost crash into a human being. "Jesus, Vaughn, your ride is as fucked up as you are." More laughter comes from a second woman climbing out of the passenger seat. Snowflake growls.

Beneath me a low voice mutters, "It is *now*."

I turn back to my aunt's neighbor. A small corner of my mind registers the sound of high heels clicking up the drive and Snowflake's bossy bark telling those girls where to go and how to get there, but the rest of me is totally focused on the man beneath me. Slammed against his warm, hard body I feel small, his broad shoulders and chest cushioning my fall. My gaze slides to defined biceps straining against his short sleeves. His masculine scent is clean, with a hint of something spicy. Whatever it is, it puts sexy ideas in my head. I let out a deep breath, grateful he's still in one piece. My heart stops trying to punch its way out of my chest.

Then I raise my eyes to his face, and holy crap. He's beautiful. The face of a model beautiful. Wait. I think he *is* a model. Like of the gigantic Times Square billboard variety. His light brown hair is a little longer now, but there's no mistaking that square jaw and those dark, olive green, come-closer-if-you-dare eyes.

A slow grin takes over his very nice mouth, making my cheeks warm.

He blinks like I've all of a sudden gone out of focus. "Thanks for saving my life, angel," he slurs. "Are you okay?" The smell of alcohol hits my nose, and my stomach pitches.

I scramble off him. "No problem, and I'm fine."

Maintaining eye contact, I put a hand out to help him up. Adrenaline continues to fizz through my system. I can't believe what almost happened.

His warm palm connects with mine, and I brace to

counterbalance his weight, but he gets to his feet under his own power, teetering just once before gaining his footing and standing upright.

"I hope she wasn't your ride," I deadpan.

Vaughn cracks up like that's the funniest thing he's ever heard. His laugh is contagious, and I'm laughing with him in seconds. It's that or digest the seriousness of what just happened. Snowflake's bark breaks our hysterics. She runs to me.

Make that him.

I watch as he scoops her up and she licks his face like he's wearing bacon-flavored cologne. "How's my girl? How's my pretty girl?" he murmurs. "Did you chase Becca back inside the house?" Snow can't get enough of him. Little dog legs run in the air as he lowers her to the ground. When he straightens, his eyes wander down my body and on the return get stuck at my chest. I glance at my thin white Winnie the Pooh tank and red shorts and cross my arms to block his notice. I didn't think I'd run into anybody, so I didn't bother to put on a robe. "Nice outfit," he says, his gaze finding mine again.

That's my cue to hurry home. I've been around my share of hot, complimentary guys. NYU was full of them. But this handsome stranger makes me more nervous than all of them put together. I grab Snowflake's leash. "Thanks. See ya."

Without a word, he walks with me, his feet bare, his steps not exactly steady.

"What are you doing?" I ask. "Shouldn't you go make up with your girlfriend?"

"She's not my"—he hiccups—"girlfriend. But that is my car she left blocking the driveway. I've got to move it or my roommates will have my balls and hang them as a rearview mirror ornament when they can't pull up to the garage."

There's an image I could do without. I glance at him out of the corner of my eye. He winces as if confused by what he just said. When we reach the car, he fumbles with the door handle before feeling his way into the driver's seat like he's not sure it will hold his weight. I have no idea how much partying he's done tonight, but it's obviously enough that I can't, in good conscience, let him stay behind the wheel, even if it's only to travel up the driveway. Call me overly cautious, but that's how it is. I've gotten behind the wheel when I shouldn't have, and I'm still not over it.

The driver's side door hangs open, so I reach in and pluck out the keys before he can turn the ignition on.

"Hey. What are you doing?"

"I don't think you should be driving. I'll give these back to you tomorrow." I could move his car for him, but I don't want to chance leaving him his keys after I do so. To avoid any argument, I hurry away.

He stumbles over the smooth sidewalk, trying to keep up with my quick strides. I look up and notice his face is pale. Shit. I hope he's not going to be sick. I slow my pace as music blares from his house again.

"Can you slow down, speed racer?"

His uncommon label gets me to stop in my tracks, happy memories pushing aside my haste. "I love that movie," I say, risking coming off as a dork. I was the only one of my friends wowed by the live action film, but whatever.

He smiles. "Me, too. My friends called me Mach 5 when I was younger."

"Because you drove fast?" I am *really* glad I took away his keys.

"Ran fast."

"From girls?" Snowflake tugs on her leash, signaling I need to stop conversing and get us tucked into bed.

"Why would I do that?" he asks in a flirty tone.

Right. Silly me. "I'll return your keys tomorrow," I repeat, closing the distance to home. I contemplate throwing the keys in the rose bushes around the perimeter of my aunt's front yard so he'll leave me alone, but I can't do it. I'd hate to see any thorns leave even the tiniest scratch on him.

He follows me up the walkway, his uneven gait about as far from a runway model's as you can get, but he still manages to tap my shoulder. "Why?" he says.

I stop a few feet from the front door. "Why what?"

He looks down at me with verdant eyes full of uncertainty. He's not sure what to make of me. I'm not sure what to make of him, either. Then he closes the short distance between us. He's not so stable, and his chest brushes mine. "Why do you care?" he asks softly.

I'm afraid if I step back he'll lose his balance and fall, so I hold my ground. It's not easy. I'm nervous. Not that he'll hurt me. That he'll kiss me. Which is crazy with a side of never-going-to-happen. My imagination hasn't run this wild in a long time.

"I don't care about you," I lie. I've known him all of five minutes but don't want to see anything bad happen to him. "I mean, I don't *care* care." What am I spewing? This is what happens when exhaustion hits. Long travel day equals verbal nonsense. "I care about people in general, and it seems like you've had a rough night."

His long dark eyelashes sweep down and stay there, and for a second, I wonder if he's fallen asleep on his feet. I clear my throat.

"People don't usually give a shit about anyone but themselves in this town." He's studying me now, like I'm something rare. I both like and hate it. I don't deserve the pedestal I think he's just put me on.

I put my hands on his upper arms to steady him and take a step back. "I'm not from around here." The space between our bodies is cold, but relief fills me all the same. "Go home, Vaughn. Get some sleep." I give him a small smile before turning around. "Good night." I open the front door. Snow sits patiently while I take off her leash and then she bounds inside.

"Wait. I know this is asking a lot, but…would it be okay if I hang here for a while? Someone's spoiling for a fight and I really don't want to deal with it tonight."

Snow puts on the breaks, the pitter-patter of her paws on the hardwood coming to a quick halt. She spins around and I swear she nods her approval along with a wag of her tail.

Okay then. Looks like we've got a guest. I've no idea what Vaughn's story is, but right now it seems like he needs a safe place to rest and, given he's friendly with my aunt (not to mention Snowflake), I'm willing to provide it.

Until a Nine Inch Nails song practically shakes the foundation. I am never going to get to sleep tonight. Before I can say, "Do you think someone could turn the music down?" he lifts his finger in the universal show of *hang on a minute* and pulls his cell from the pocket of his light blue jeans. I'm impressed when his fingers type a text with ease. Seconds later, the music stops.

The grin he gives me could win an Academy Award. "Done."

Okay, guess we're on the same wavelength. I spin around and wave for him to follow. The light is on in the kitchen and, as I round the corner of the breakfast bar, I discreetly drop his keys into a drawer, closing it quickly so he doesn't notice.

"So you're one of the nieces," he says.

"I am." I reach into a cupboard and pull out the aspirin.

"Sally told me you'd be here this summer." He sits at the breakfast bar. His arms cross atop the counter and his body sags. He looks tired, and I can't explain why, but I get the feeling it's not just from lack of sleep. But from the day-to-day stuff we all have to deal with. It's in his eyes. They remind me of my own when I look in the mirror after a difficult day.

I fill a glass with water from the sink and hand it to him along with the two small white hangover helpers.

His eyes lock on mine. For five heartbeats—yes, I count—he just stares. Finally he looks down at the aspirin in his palm, looks back up at me. I'm curious what he's thinking. I'm suddenly curious about everything that has to do with him.

"Take two and call me in the morning," I tease when the silence makes my pulse pick up. I lean against the counter across from him, grateful for the support.

"Thanks, angel." He swallows the pills with the water and puts the glass down. I'm about to remind him of my name—I'm sure my aunt mentioned it—when he scrubs a hand over his jaw and adds, "Or should I call you Trixie?"

I bite my lip to keep from grinning. I wanted to be Trixie so badly. Speed Racer's girlfriend, played by the awesome Christina Ricci, was the coolest.

"How about Kendall?"

"I've never met a Kendall I didn't like."

"How many have you met?"

"Counting you?"

Good to know his sense of humor is still intact. "Of course."

"One."

I smile, expecting he'd say that. "You're my first Vaughn."

"I'm honored to take your Vaughn virginity."

I laugh. "You should be. Clearly I've been saving it."

Instead of a quick comeback, he closes his eyes and dips his head for a long moment. "Okay, either Sally and Jack installed a carousel in their kitchen, or I'm more wasted than I thought."

"I'm going to have to go with more wasted than you thought. You should probably lie down. Lucky for you, I just happen to have a vacancy on the living room couch."

"Thanks. Sorry for..." He makes an all-encompassing gesture with his hand.

I give him an *It happens* shrug and walk out of the kitchen. He follows me to the family room even though I'm pretty sure he could've led the way. He's got a familiarity with the house I'm guessing stems from my aunt having him over for breakfast or dinner or something. She and my uncle don't have any kids, and she's always taking in strays.

Not that Vaughn is lost. But there's something about him I can't quite put my finger on. I grab a blanket out of the antique wooden chest behind the love seat while Vaughn sits on the couch and puts his feet up on the coffee table. For the second time, I notice he's barefoot. It shouldn't bother me, but it does. Drunk *and* shoeless seems so...so desperate to escape his own party. His own life, maybe?

All of a sudden, my own tangled mess of regret and guilt pulses louder than the beat of my heart. I hate when my past takes over my present, so I bite down hard on my bottom lip to remind myself where I am and that I want this summer to be about new beginnings. It's time I move on from my mistakes.

Vaughn's green eyes are intense and right on mine when my head clears. I quickly walk over to the love seat and grab the throw tossed over it.

"Sit with me a minute?" he asks, moving his feet to the floor and sitting taller as I approach.

I hand him the plush chenille throw while deciding how to answer. He takes it, grazing my arm with his fingertips in the process. The slight, probably inadvertent contact makes me crave more. Nope. There's no way I can sit with him. If I do, I don't know what will happen, and I've lived the past four years knowing exactly what will happen. Since the accident, staying in control has been my lifeline.

"I'm beyond tired." Total truth right there. "I'll see you in the morning, okay? And if someone is still spoiling for a fight then, you've still got me on your side." I turn away, ready to collapse into bed.

"Promise?" he says softly.

I twist around to hit the light switch and say, "Promise."

"G'night," he mumbles.

"Goodnight." I can just make out the outline of his body in the darkened room before I rush upstairs and dive under my covers. The sheets are cool, comfortable. Safe.

For now.

Chapter Two

Vaughn

My mouth tastes like Satan puked in it, and my skull feels a couple sizes too small for my brain, but I can account for both those situations. Cuervo Gold and bad judgment share the blame. What I can't account for is that I have no freaking clue where I am.

I'm pretty sure I'm on a sofa, but it's definitely not mine. Mine's leather and smells like spilled drinks and haphazard sex. I've woken up with my cheek sweat-glued to the Italian hide often enough to recognize its sticky embrace without opening my eyes. This cushion I'm crashed across feels as if it's stuffed with the feathers from cherubs' wings, and it smells like a field of flowers, after a rain shower…in heaven. Waking ensconced in all this disorienting plushness has an unanticipated effect on me. Suddenly I'm hard as a rock. Ridiculously, almost painfully hard, and I see pictures—or maybe flashbacks—in my mind. Pale blond hair. Big blue eyes. A white tank top doing the legal minimum to conceal full, soft cleavage and a bitable ass stretching the limits of a pair of little red shorts.

Angel? Trixie?

Neither sounds quite right, but I could do some seriously perverted things on this sofa while fantasizing about her.

Instead of molesting the furniture, I pry one eyelid open and gut out the pain that lances my brain as the light assaults my sluggish pupil. After a few blinks of protest and a halfhearted groan, I submit my other eye to the same violation. All I can see is some nubby beige low-weave rug with a geometric bamboo print, but it's distinctive enough to tell me I'm in my neighbors' living room.

Shit. Sally and Jack are cool neighbors, but they're not exactly part of my crowd. They're like my parents' age. I strongly doubt they invited me over at midnight to slam tequila shots until I passed out, plus they're out of town, which leaves me at a loss as to what the hell I'm doing here. I push myself upright and rack my mind for details from last night. Nothing swims into focus except the blonde and…a conversation about Speed Racer? But I can't argue with facts. I'm definitely in my neighbors' sun-drenched living room after spending a drunken night on their highly fuckable couch.

While I sit here trying to get my bearings and convince my cock to stop doing its best porn star impression, someone slams through the front door. The next thing I know, a girl wearing a black tank top and microscopic cut-offs sweeps into the living room, lugging a guitar case and an oversized rolling duffel bag that looks like it's been around the world about sixty million times. She stops short when she sees me and fumbles the handle of the bag.

The duffel hits the rug with a *thump*, but the guitar receives more care as she places the case on the floor next to the bag. Snowflake bounds into the room in *Full Metal*

Jacket mode, skids to a halt in front of the new arrival, and defends her turf with a rapid-fire series of yips. It's nothing I haven't heard before—she's seven pounds of explosive canine ferocity and she's not afraid to pull the pin on it—but this morning her display of dominance threatens to make my ears bleed. Then she lets loose with a low, rumbly sound I don't recognize, almost like she's trying out another language. It takes me a moment to realize she's *growling*.

"Hey, girl." I lean over, put my hand at Pom level, and give her a c'mere whistle. She hops between us, unsure she can abandon her captive, and barks at me as if to say, "Intruder, stupid human! I have cornered an intruder!"

"Who's a good girl, Snowflake?" I wiggle my fingers at her, which is our code for someone's about to get a heap of personal attention from her big, furless slave next door. She gives the blonde one last growl and bounds over to me. I lift her up and nuzzle her furry face. "There's my girl. Yes, you are. Such a good guard dog."

She squirms in my arms and licks my face, unselfconscious of her dog breath, and for half a second I'm not sure if I'm going to pass out, throw up, or die on the spot. I settle her on the sofa so I'm out of range of what has to be the most lethal weapon on earth and inhale blissfully odor-free air through my nose. She promptly claims the pillow and sits as if it's her throne. Satisfied I've taken the Pomeranian off high alert, I turn to the guitar player.

She cracks a wad of pink bubble gum before a slow smile curves her lips. "Aunt Sally didn't mention they'd gotten a second pet. But that's okay." She pauses and blows another bubble as her eyes drop to take in the show going on behind the fly of my jeans. "If you're friendlier than that walking hairball, I might even let you sleep in my bed."

I drag the nearby blanket over my lap and meet her brazen curiosity with some of my own. She's not the angel from last night. This girl is tall—legs for days on full display in the little shorts—long, straight, sun-streaked hair, but strangely familiar blue eyes. And she's flirting as naturally as other people breathe. Even loaded, I don't think my memory would be that far off. Besides, going by the luggage and her surprise at finding me here, it's safe to assume she's just arrived.

Her presence tugs a thread of a conversation I had with Sally last week. Her nieces are coming to house-sit for the summer while she and Jack cruise to Australia? Antarctica? Who knows, maybe both.

"Hey. I'm Vaughn. I live next door." More little flashbacks flicker through my mind as I piece together an explanation for why I'm here. I remember walking out of the house last night with some half-assed idea of clearing my head, because I'd lost the mood to party, but then…things get jumbled. I recall the glow of taillights coming at me, and then someone tackled me and I landed on the concrete beneath a sexy blonde with soft curves and quick reflexes. I'm pretty sure she offered up the sofa. "I…uh… My place got kind of hectic last night, so the other girl let me crash here."

Light-colored eyebrows lift at my halting explanation. Instead of introducing herself, Legs folds her arms in a gesture reminiscent of the blonde last night and frowns. "Other girl? What other girl?"

Uh-oh. I'm afraid to say anything else, because more details from Sally are pouring into my consciousness. Her nieces are half sisters, raised separately, and they aren't what you'd call close. And clearly she failed to mention the family reunion to at least one of them when she pitched the house-sitting gig. This girl's looking at me expectantly, like there's no way I'm getting out of here with a smile and a shrug. I stand and prepare to make a fast exit. "Oh, hey, I should take off—"

"*What* other girl?" Mouth tight, she steps up, right into

my space. I have to vault over the sofa if I want to make a hasty getaway. Snowflake musters up a halfhearted snarl from the comfort of her cushion, but the girl in front of me snarls right back. "You want a piece of me, you overgrown rat? Take a number."

In response, the dog who routinely intimidates UPS guys twenty times her size jumps down from the couch and flees the room as fast as her stubby legs can carry her. So much for man's best friend.

"Um." I manage a sidestep and glance around, hoping something I spy will jar a name out of the haze of my hangover. "Blonde. Blue eyes about your shade, and…"

"Fuuuuck," we say at the same time.

I swear because my gaze lands on the mantel clock across the room, which reads quarter till eight. My very punctual, very sadistic trainer will be knocking on my door in fifteen minutes, hell-bent on kicking my ass for the next two hours. If I'm even a minute late he'll make me regret those sixty seconds for the rest of my natural life.

The girl drops onto the sofa and presses the heel of her hand to the center of her forehead as if staving off a headache. "Oh God. Not perfect princess Kendall."

"Kendall! Yes"—I snap my fingers—"that's her name." And that's as deep into this family reunion as I'm getting. If I were any kind of a human being I'd stick around and try to defuse the powder keg of a situation taking shape before my eyes. Kendall did me a solid last night and I should return the favor, but I don't know that she'd appreciate my interference, and honestly, I'll have my own powder keg of a situation to handle if I don't get moving.

"So, yeah, tell her bye for me, okay? I gotta bolt." I fold the blanket into a semi-polite drape across the back of the sofa and then pat the front pocket of my jeans out of habit. No keys. I'll have to look for them after I'm done working out. "See you later…"

"Dixie," she supplies.

I flash her a quick smile before I head for the door and let myself out as quietly as possible. Feeling a little like a deserter, I jog toward my place and get another rude awakening. My Range Rover sits askance at the end of the driveway, like an abandoned getaway car. Heat having nothing to do with the jog crawls up my neck and into my face. Becca and one of her friends wanted to go to a club to meet up with a guy and complete a *transaction*, because I wouldn't let her invite the guy here, but I was done—and pissed—so I said have fun and walked out the door before she could drag me into another argument. Apparently she took my departure as permission to borrow my ride. I really don't know what was going through Bec's mind, but I remember now, Kendall risked her neck to shove me out of the way of my own damn car and then confiscated my keys when I tried to get behind the wheel. I owe her epic thanks for what she did and an apology for putting her in a confiscate-my-keys situation in the first place.

I run up the driveway, which is damn steep, and anger builds with each stride. I know better than this. I'm not stupid. Why I'm sabotaging myself when I've got a shot at attaining something I've been working toward for years, I really can't say.

Okay, that's bullshit. I know one reason why. All I have to do is look at a calendar for the diagnosis. I wanted to focus on something other than the sorrow my whole family gets sucked into around the anniversary of my sister's death. I'm not sure we'll ever completely adjust to the loss, but I need to stop dealing with it in ways nobody would approve of—including her—because a chance to take over the hosting duties for a hit show like *America Rocks* doesn't come around very often. Reckless behavior will get me aced out of that opportunity so fast I won't need tequila to make my head spin. So yeah, I'm pissed at myself.

Pissed enough to slam through the front door without considering who I might wake. People might be crashed on *my* couches. I glance around the living room, relieved to see I have no lingering guests. Chances are I wouldn't recognize them anyway. Most of last night's festivities are still one big blur. Becca likes to party. We have people over, and next thing I know the place looks like a hotel suite with an open bar. My best friends and roommates, Dylan and Matt, think Becca's using me—which she is—but they don't object to hosting her and a group of her hot friends every now and again, which I think means Becca hasn't cornered the market on using people. Even if they did object, neither of them was home last night, so whatever went down was totally on me.

Bec wanted to celebrate. She leaves today for a stint in NYC—some modeling jobs plus a meeting with a director interested in casting her for a film role—and she loves a proper send-off. I was happy enough to give her one. Happy for the distraction from my saddest memories. Happy to celebrate her success but also, to be brutally honest, happy to celebrate her leaving, which I know is a shitty thing to admit. She and I have been friends for a while, but it's not the healthiest of relationships.

In case I needed more proof, I have this morning as a perfect example of yet another fun-filled evening that ended with me feeling the need to hit the eject button.

Not my best move, given I almost became a statistic in my own driveway. Were it not for fast action on my new neighbor's part, I might be waking up in the hospital this morning. Or the morgue. I blink back to the moment she threw herself in harm's way for me, a complete stranger, and a clearer vision of her takes shape in my mind. Wide set eyes, a stubborn little chin, and last but not least, Cupid's bow lips curved into the patient smile of someone stuck dealing with a drunk-ass fool.

She showed up out of nowhere last night, just like a guardian angel. I grab a bottle of Advil from the cabinet, shake two into my palm, add a third, and wash them down with eighteen ounces of Fiji from the fridge. Then I head back to the main room and start up the floating staircase along the travertine wall that separates the living area from the office and media room.

I stride into my bedroom and hit the lights, because I can't see shit with the blackout curtain pulled over the floor-to-ceiling windows that frame a kick-ass view of Sunset Boulevard, Beverly Hills, and, on a clear day, the ocean. I have no idea how far the view extends today, because, once the lights come on, all I can see is Becca's ass giving me a sideways smirk. She looks like she spent a month sunbathing nude in the Caribbean. There's no discernible difference in skin tone anywhere on her body. Truth is it's a spray tan. She would never subject the moneymaker to ultraviolet rays and premature aging. I waste a split second realizing I miss the strangely vulnerable look of tan lines—light skin never touched by the sun or a chemical facsimile thereof. I bet Kendall has tan lines. When some lucky bastard sees her pretty little ass, he's seeing something she keeps private.

Not Becca. She lives her life at the other end of the privacy spectrum, and she couldn't have staged a sexy, bed-wrecked scene better, except…her feet are filthy. Black stains her heels and balls of her toes, as if she ran a marathon through hell's gutters last night. I'm equal parts concerned and disgusted by those dirty feet.

I'm also angry with her for pulling that stunt last night. She almost ran two people down and walked away like it was a big joke. Now she's naked in my bed as if the use of her body somehow makes everything all right. I pull the door shut behind me, not especially loud, but her head jerks up. She rubs her eyes, yawns, and settles her cheek on her crossed arms, adjusting the angle until tiger eyes find me from behind a screen of hair. "Hey. Where'd you storm off to last night?"

"Nowhere special." Aside from arguing over drugs last night, I'd confided I'd done an audition for the new host of *America Rocks*, and instead of offering encouragement or asking me how it had gone, she'd said it was good experience to audition, even if the job is out of reach. Of all my friends, I thought she'd be the most excited, but the truth, I'm realizing, is that Becca's main focus is Becca. There's not much left over for anyone else.

My response earns me a pouty frown. "I waited for you, but you never came back, so I figured you were off sulking somewhere. You definitely wanted nothing to do with me. You didn't even return my texts."

I shrug, hit with the sudden realization that our friendship has run its course. We'll always be colleagues, but I don't want to pretend everything is okay when it's not.

"I'll let you make it up to me." She does a leisurely little grind against the crumpled sheets.

"Will you?" I'm closing the distance to the bed before I realize I've decided to move, but it's not desire compelling me forward, it's disappointment at her assumption we're both this easy.

The smile she sends me says she'll let me do all kinds of things. "I've got a confession. Sometimes I pick a fight with you just for the makeup sex." She stretches with the grace of a jungle cat and lifts her hips a few inches—enough for me to wonder what positions she assumes during what must be the most thorough spray tan sessions on Earth.

"Can't." I smack her ass to come off like a good sport, and over her gasp, explain, "Gunnar will be here in ten minutes."

"Oh, baby." She runs a finger over the pink mark left by my palm and then lets it drift lower. "Ten minutes is all we need. C'mon." Her busy finger finds the target, and her eyelids lower seductively as she pleases herself. "I leave for New York this afternoon. Don't you want something nice to remember while I'm gone?"

"Not this time." *Not ever again.* I escape down the short hall leading to my closet/dressing area on one side and the master bath on the other. I veer toward the closet. "Gunnar's not so easy to make up with," I call out. "If I'm late, he will punish me in ways I don't want to contemplate. Not even for you."

"Fine," she huffs just before I pull the pocket door shut.

I hear the shower kick on as I change into workout clothes. The coast is clear. I fly downstairs in time to answer the knock on the front door. My own personal drill sergeant stands there, and the first thing he tells me to do is move my car so he can park in the driveway. I say I can't and make it sound like there's a mechanical problem.

He calls my ride a piece of shit as he turns and jogs down the drive. I know the routine. Five-mile warm-up. I fall into step beside him, but my attention strays to my neighbors' house. I scan the windows as we run past, hoping for a glimpse of my guardian angel, but all is quiet.

A picture of Kendall drifts through my mind. Arms crossed, eyebrows low, she's looking down her small nose at me and struggling to hold back a reluctant smile. It's possible I wasn't a total dick, but I definitely owe her an apology-slash-thanks. I think about ways to thank her while Gunnar puts me through the paces. When he finally cuts me loose, I limp upstairs to my bedroom, relieved to see Becca cleared out sometime during the last two hours.

A shave and shower make me feel halfway human again. I pull on jeans and a blue-striped button-down and check myself in the mirror. Casual but respectable.

I head downstairs to find Dylan in the entryway looking slightly more debauched than usual. He eyes me from above the rims of dark sunglasses, offers an irritated, "Nice parking job, fuck-up," and brushes past me into the living room. He drops into one of the low-slung leather sofas and tosses his Ray Bans on the glass coffee table. His eyes are closed before his head hits the armrest. "Think you could move it?"

"I'm working on it," I answer, and glance at my watch. It's late, even for Dylan. "Did somebody get lucky last night?"

He doesn't bother opening his eyes, but his jaded smile answers for him. "I don't think luck had anything to do with it."

"The redhead from the club?" Dylan recently sank a choke-a-horse chunk of his trust fund into a new club on Sunset. He won't say it out loud, but he wants to prove something to his dad, who has always been too busy running his own empire to give much notice to anything else. I think it's come as a surprise to a lot of people, including Dylan, how personally invested he is in the day-to-day business of operating the place.

His smile stretches and he opens his eyes to slits. "Lisa. Her cousin from Mississippi is in town trying to land a job, so it ended up being a party of three, I guess you could call it." He glances around the room still strewn with empty bottles, glasses, spilled snacks, and various other party detritus, and his eyebrow goes up. He trails a finger through the filmy layer of white powder dusting the table and then rubs it on his gums. "You were a busy boy last night, too."

Not quite that busy, but before I can answer, the front door opens, and Matt walks in looking legit badass in black utility boots, dark-blue tactical pants, and a white LAPD cadet T-shirt with his last name emblazoned across the chest in block letters. Or maybe four years in the USMC accounts for the badassery? Either way, I would not want to pick a fight with officer-in-training Matthew Wright.

Luckily, Matt's the most even-tempered guy on the

planet.

Unfortunately, I was not expecting to contend with him this morning.

When he hauls himself out to his mom's house in Alta Dena on a Friday, he usually stays the entire weekend and heads straight to the academy Monday morning. Change of plans, obviously. He stops beside me and pushes his sunglasses to the top of his head. "What's up with your car?"

"Sorry. I had a little problem last night. It will be fixed in the next hour."

He levels an assessing look on me that causes a bead of sweat to run between my shoulder blades. Criminals of L.A. stand no chance. Finally, he says, "Do I want to know?"

I shake my head. "Nope."

"Okay, then." He rolls his eyes until they settle on Dylan. "What else is going on?"

"Dylan's recovering from a three-way with the hot bartender from The Cabana and her cousin from Mississippi."

"Nice."

"It did not suck," Dylan agrees, "although Mississippi did, like a fucking pro."

"Best of luck to you on the impending sexual harassment lawsuit," Matt adds, mostly just to screw with Dylan. "Isn't that the first rule they cover in Management 101? Don't fish off the company pier."

Dylan isn't the least bit concerned. "Lisa gave notice last week—got a recurring role as Sexy Cocktail Waitress #2 in a new series. Last night was her going away party, and she was no longer in my employ by the time I gave her the farewell bonus. Nothing I did compromised my ethics. Now, I can't speak firsthand for what went down *here*, but evidence suggests"—he drags a lazy fingertip across the table again—"Becca entertained."

Matt winces and shoots another irritated look my way.

"Is she still here?"

"No. She left for New York this morning," I offer up quickly, feeling like an asshole for letting things get out of hand last night.

"Can I assume this place will be cleaned up by the end of the day?"

"Merry Maids are on the way," I say, and make a mental note to call them ASAP.

"All right. Good." He heads to the stairs. "I'm doing a ride-along this afternoon, so let's just say I was never here."

"You were never here," Dylan calls out in agreement, settles deeper into the couch, and closes his eyes. "Now move your land yacht, V-dawg. My Audi's on the street."

Right. I backtrack to my office to call the house cleaners, unsure why I didn't say anything to Dylan and Matt about our new neighbors. Because I'm embarrassed about the circumstances under which my introductions occurred? That's probably it, since there's no reason I should care if Dylan goes over there and tries to convince them a three-way with him would be the perfect sisterly bonding activity or Matt gives them his good-guy smile along with his number and tells them to call him next time our music gets too loud or his idiot housemate stumbles to the end of the drive and can't find his way home.

Or whatever. I'm not the social chairman of the house. It's not my responsibility to make sure they know what goes on next door. With the maid service arranged, I place a call to buy a gift for Kendall. The present ends up being a little over-the-top for a simple thank-you, even with an equally sincere "I'm sorry" added on, but her actions last night were more than simple girl-next-door decency. I'm hoping it shows her how grateful I am for everything.

Fingers crossed.

Chapter Three

Kendall

I tossed and turned all night, dreaming about the hot dogs from Mo's pushcart on the corner of Fifth and East 62nd Street. The Hawaiian dog is my favorite. Honey mustard, Canadian bacon, pineapple, and jalapeno relish. I've been known to eat two, which really annoys my best friend, Brit, because she can't figure out where I put all the food I consume. Hot dogs alone wouldn't have kept me up, though. I dreamed about Vaughn eating one, too. In nothing but his Calvin Klein briefs. In my defense, it's all he's wearing in Times Square. I may have slipped off the crowded sidewalk, twisting my ankle, the first time I laid eyes on the ad. Brit did a full-on face-plant, her four inch heels no match for jumbo sexiness.

I stare at my bedroom ceiling a minute longer, then kick off the bedsheets and use the bathroom. The girl in the mirror staring back has tired eyes. Her hair is a wavy mess. I tie it into a ponytail, brush my teeth, and wash my face with cold water. "Let's see if he's still here," I tell my slightly more presentable reflection.

Nervous tingles invade my body as I head downstairs. Half of me hopes Vaughn is already gone—it is after ten—but the other half hopes he isn't. Normally, I don't think in halves, but Vaughn is...confusing. I don't know how else to label the knot of anxiety *and* interest in my stomach. I'm worried that if he has this kind of effect on me when he's drunk, what is seeing him up close when he's sober going to do to me?

Doesn't matter.

I pause midway to the family room to gather my wits and strengthen my walls. I'm an expert at letting people see only what I want them to see. Brit knows all my secrets, but that's because Miss Psych Major is relentless. When talk of boyfriends came up our first week as roommates at NYU, I managed to give vague answers for only a few days. She wanted to connect with me, and despite being away from home and everyone who knew my story, I found myself letting her in.

So, she understood when I kept my nose in my books, because my grades mattered to me and they were something I could control. Focusing on school kept my mind off boys and kept my reputation sterling. I had fun and socialized, but mostly I stayed the course academically. I graduated with a 4.0 and scored a 170 on the LSAT. The plan is for me to go to law school and follow in my father's footsteps. That I'm not in love with the plan is a complication I'm trying to figure out. As soon as possible.

Sounds in the kitchen get my feet moving again. Vaughn is awake and probably searching for his keys. I've had some time to think about what to say to him this morning, so I round the corner with purpose.

And trip over my own feet.

Vaughn isn't in the kitchen. My half sister is. "Dixie?" Holy shit. Maybe I'm still dreaming. I blink her away, but she's still there. The typical mashup of dread and possibility fills my empty stomach.

She lifts her head from buttering a piece of toast and looks at me like I'm something that crawled out of a drainpipe. "Hello, princess."

Her hollow greeting guts me. We haven't seen or talked to each other in a while and, foolish me, I always think time will bring a level of acceptance to our relationship. I swallow the disappointment, because a show of vulnerability only rewards Dixie's habit of sharpening her claws on me. "What are you doing here?"

Dixie puts the knife down with a loud *clank*. "Three guesses, princess."

"Please don't call me that." It's an old nickname, and it brings back bad memories of summers spent hosting my half sisters. Forced interaction with two sullen girls with features similar to my own and absolutely nothing else in common. Dad cheated on Amber's mom with Dixie's mom, and then married neither. He was having a little problem with alcohol at the time. Three months into recovery he met my mom, and that relationship stuck. My half sisters collected child support and summers with Dad, and resented me because I had the "real" family complete with two parents, a dog, and a pink canopy bed.

Dixie just smirks. "If the glass slipper fits…"

It's been only sixty seconds and I've had enough. I point to my bare feet. "I don't see any glass slipper, do you? I do see my size sevens, and one of them is going to leave an imprint on your backside if you don't tell me what you're doing here."

She shrugs and takes a bite of her toast, chewing slowly while I wait. Finally, she washes it down with a sip of coffee. "What do you think I'm doing here? Aunt Sally asked me to house-sit."

"Impossible. She asked *me* to house-sit."

A staring contest ensues. There's no mistaking we're related if you look at our eyes. We both have our father's baby blues. A characteristic Dixie hates.

I know I'm not wrong about Aunt Sally inviting me here. She said she wanted me to have the summer to decompress and weigh my options before I start school in the fall.

My stomach cramps. My aunt is the only person I've told I don't want to go to law school. She offered me time to be by myself and think about a back-up plan, and, since I hate the idea of going home, I jumped at her suggestion. I don't know if I have the courage to change course and disappoint my dad, but I am sure doing something my heart isn't in will only make me a bigger mess. I stand to lose more than three years of my life to a law degree. I stand to lose my happiness, something I've finally come to believe I deserve after fulfilling my punishment for my drunken teenage offense.

Dixie lifts her phone to her ear.

"What are you doing?" I ask.

"Calling Aunt Sally. She'll tell you I'm staying here."

Meaning staying together is out of the question. I plop down on a barstool at the breakfast bar. Dixie hates me. She hates that our father never thought of her mother as anything more than a few quick fucks—her words not mine—and then he married my mom, and they had me. They've been married for twenty-three years. They haven't all been easy. My parents have had their ups and downs, but he loves my mom. Loves me.

"No answer," Dixie says, putting the phone down.

Our aunt and uncle are on a cruise, so I'm not surprised. And now that I'm looking at my sister, I'm not all that shocked to see her. My aunt has always been the glue to keep my sisters and me in touch.

"It's good to see you," I say, hoping to cut through some of the strain between us. I understand Dixie's animosity.

She's led a very different life than me. But I'm not to blame for my dad's indiscretions.

"How long have you been here?" she asks.

"I got in last night." *Vaughn!* "Umm…I'll be right back." I hurry into the family room, only to find he's gone. Disappointment drags my shoulders down. Which is unsettling. Guys don't disappoint me.

Dixie grins slyly when I walk back into the kitchen and shakes her head. "Only you would leave that on the couch and expect it to still be there in the morning."

"What are you talking about?"

"He left."

Heat converges on the back of my neck as I sit back down. "You saw Vaughn?"

"Saw, lusted over, flirted with."

He flirted with her? Of course he did. Dixie, with her long legs, confidence, and devil-may-care attitude might as well have "Give me your best shot, Stud" tattooed on her forehead.

"What? You didn't flirt with him?" She squints at me. "Of course you didn't. So what gives?"

I bite the inside of my cheek before answering, "Nothing." Heart in my throat, the last thing I'm going to do this morning is discuss anything personal with her.

"Okay," she says easily. She wipes the corners of her mouth with her fingers, her toast finished. At the sound of Snowflake's barks and the front door closing, we both turn in the direction of the foyer. Snow's tough-girl *woofs* nearly drown out the soft voice trying to calm her. The pitch grows even louder as I picture Snow herding the new arrival toward the kitchen. Given the circumstance I've found myself in this morning, there's only one person it could be.

"Ack!" my other half sister, Amber, shouts when she finds Dixie and me. She releases the handle on her suitcase, her hand flying to her chest. "You scared the crap out of me!"

"Hi," I say.

"Fucking hell, Aunt Sally," Dixie mutters under her breath.

Snow, seeing the three of us in strained but quiet compliance, turns on her paws and leaves us alone.

Amber is my dad's oldest daughter by a few months. Growing up, she and Dixie sometimes ganged up on me, but it wasn't because of any camaraderie. They did it because I had Dad all the time and they didn't. Like it was my fault he fell in love with my mom and not theirs. I tried to play peacemaker up until they turned eighteen. After that they visited for only a week here or there and usually separately. Looking at them both now, I understand why they'd harbor ill feelings toward me, but how dumb of them not to love and support each other.

"Surprise," I add. "Looks like you got a plane ticket and house key in the mail, too."

Amber closes her eyes, takes a deep breath. She focuses her blue gaze on me when she says, "You guys are here to house-sit for the summer?"

I nod. "Apparently Aunt Sally wanted us all together again." It's been years since the three of us have been under this roof at the same time. We didn't talk much to one another that summer. I remember lots of glares and sighs of dislike. Even so, I'd been grateful for the distraction. I didn't want to be home in Wisconsin between my freshman and sophomore years at college.

Amber toes the side of her bag. "No offense, but this really isn't what I signed up for."

"You could turn right around and go home," Dixie suggests.

"Or *you* could." Amber snaps back.

"Can't."

"Me either."

Why can't they? I swallow my curiosity, knowing they won't appreciate it. Dixie especially. Amber's gotten a little more pleasant as we've grown older, so maybe I'll question her when we're alone. I study her now. If you ask me, even angry and disheveled, she's the prettiest of us. She's got our dad's light hair, too, but her mom is a redhead, so it's a beautiful shade of strawberry-blond, and her eyes are a deeper blue than Dixie's and mine. But she's thinner than the last time I saw her, and paler, too. "Are you okay?"

"I'm fine," she says, sounding defensive. Or maybe I am, but I hear a silent *Why wouldn't I be?* in her reply. Then she takes a seat next to me as if staking her own claim to the place.

Silent tension fills the room. It's so thick it's a miracle the three of us are still breathing.

The three of us.

My aunt obviously gathered us here for a reason. She's always wanted us to be close, but we're adults now, and that decision isn't hers to make. I've wished it to be. God, after the accident, I wished for it so hard. But I finally accepted it's one of those things that will always stay just out of reach.

Dixie starts opening cupboards. "The three of us under one roof for the summer. Holy shit, I need a drink. Where's the liquor cabinet?"

"I don't think there is one." My stomach churns at the idea of her drinking this early, but she can do what she wants.

"Jackpot!" She holds up a bottle of vodka like a trophy. "Sally loves a Bloody Mary with brunch, so"—she opens the fridge—"Hallelujah, there is a God. I've got all the ingredients I need."

Amber and I silently watch her mix the cocktail. She moves efficiently, like she's done this a thousand times. She has. "Are you still bartending?" I ask.

"I quit to come here."

"Meaning..." Amber trails off.

"Meaning I need to find a J-O-B while I pursue my music career. Aunt Sally said I could stay as long as I need to."

"That's great," I say. Music has been a dream of Dixie's for a long time.

She pushes a drink in front of me. "No thanks." She slides it sideways to Amber. "I'm going to pass, too," Amber says.

"Suit yourselves." Dixie lifts the glass in a solo cheers gesture. She guzzles about half of it, closes her eyes in appreciation, and then opens them and takes us in again. "Okay. That helps. So, what's your deal?"

Amber and I glance at each other. I guess we are going to get things out in the open. "Go ahead," I say. Five minutes in their company isn't enough of a foundation for me to spill my deal. I'm here because Aunt Sally offered me an escape. From a past I still often struggle with, a future I can't pull into any kind of focus, and a dad who firmly believes a law degree is what I need to make me happy.

"Nothing to say, really. I'm on summer break," Amber replies. "I start my master's program at UCLA in the fall, but I can't move into on-campus housing until September."

"You're getting your masters?" Dixie asks with surprise and resentment. She couldn't afford to stay in college. Our dad offered to help, but she refuses to accept anything from him.

"Yes. Speech therapy."

Dixie doesn't bother with an additional comment, instead turning her attention to me. "And is perfect princess Kendall still heading to law school to be just like her daddy?" She couldn't sound any colder or look any more hateful if she tried.

"I'm not perfect." Far, far from it, but she's never seen past my childhood. Past the time and affection I've received from our father. That none of it was my call doesn't compute with her, which makes it difficult to be close, even if she wanted to be.

"No? You're the one who grew up with a pink room and a mom *and* dad who attended all your plays and debate team competitions and watched you blow out your birthday candles and took you on vacations with them."

And there it is. "Why do you always have to bring that up?"

Dixie shrugs one shoulder before downing the rest of her drink.

"Seriously. We're adults now. Don't you think it's time to let that stuff go? I can't change it. You can't change it. Move on already." My words repeat themselves in my head. I should take my own advice. I'm trying to. "I'd like us to be friends."

"Of course you would," Dixie fires back.

"What does that mean?"

"You hate the idea of me not liking you."

"So that's why you don't?"

"Partly. By the way. Winnie the Pooh? Really? You want to be treated like an adult, you might try dressing like one." She steps to the fridge and pulls out a carton of orange juice. "Here," she says to Amber, "drink this. You look like you're about to pass out, and I can deal with only one of you at a time."

Amber takes the carton and drinks right out of it. "Thanks."

My stomach growls, so I jump to my feet. "How about I make us some breakfast?"

"I'm good," Dixie says at the same time Amber says, "I could eat."

"Do you like frittatas?" I ask Amber, ignoring Dixie. Aunt Sally's housekeeper stocked the house with groceries yesterday, and I scoped out the goods last night.

"Sure."

Before I grab a pan, I discreetly open the drawer with Vaughn's keys inside. Now that I'm over the shock of seeing my sisters, my mind skips back to him. I wonder what he's doing right now. He's not in his car, since the key is right where I left it, which means we have unfinished business.

Dixie's phone rings as she takes a seat on the stool I vacated, the interruption saving me from a quick mental pic of my hot next-door neighbor. She notes the caller ID and picks it up. "Hello, Aunt Sally," she says cheerfully.

I stop what I'm doing and give my full attention to my sisters.

"I'm good… Yes, we're all here. Very sneaky of you arranging this… Both Kendall and Amber look fine… I look fine, too… We'll try…"

"Put it on speaker," I say.

Dixie waves off my request. No doubt to annoy me. Whatever. I'll text my aunt later.

"I promise we won't kill one another… And be nice to one another… And yes I'll tell them." She pauses. "Okay, sounds good… Talk to you soon. We love you, too."

That's the one solid thing my sisters and I do have in common. We wholeheartedly love our aunt. She's our dad's younger, bighearted sister. The two of them aren't super close, but for as long as I can remember she's taken a fierce interest in us girls, maybe because she and Uncle Jack don't have kids of their own.

"What did she say?" I ask.

"She said she's sorry for luring us here under the pretense that we'd each have the house to ourselves, but that she thinks it's past time we get over our shit and act like sisters rather than strangers."

"She did not say shit," Amber says.

Dixie rolls her eyes. "That's the gist."

"Think we can do it?" I ask. Maybe, just maybe, my sisters can help me move forward for good. Brit's tried. My mom. My therapist. Dr. Sutton says the only person holding me back is me. But love, guilt, and loyalty form a powerful glue, which is why my heart's still stuck to someone who can't give his back.

Chapter Four

Vaughn

The respectable-looking guy on my doorstep hands me a small, iconic blue shopping bag and a matching envelope containing a receipt. I say thanks for the quick delivery, tip him, and shut the door. Dylan's dragged himself to his room, so I take a seat on the couch to inspect the goods. In the bag I find a blue box, a blank white card, and another small blue envelope. Too much? Maybe. But it's also perfect. I hustle to the kitchen for a pen, then compose an apology.

Thank you for being my guardian angel. And for the sofa. I'll trade you keys. Sincerely, Vaughn.

Satisfied, I tuck the card back in the envelope, place it in the bag, and make my way down the driveway, across our narrow side yards, and up the steps to my neighbors' front door, all the while mentally reviewing the possibilities. *Maybe she's not home? Maybe she's still asleep? Maybe she'll slam the door in my face?* I wipe my palm on my jeans and ring the doorbell. When I hear the click of the lock I dial up my best apologetic smile and get ready to talk fast.

But as soon as the door swings open my rehearsed greeting dies on my tongue, because it's not Kendall or Dixie looking up at me with polite inquiry. This girl's got shoulder-skimming ginger-blond hair and fair skin. Clearly, she hasn't spent much time in the California sun. She's buried her petite frame under boyfriend jeans and a slouchy blue KU jersey that verifies her non-native status. Her eyes widen as she returns my stare, and I'm guessing she recognizes me from the underwear ads, or the cologne commercial, or the music videos I'm featured prominently in, playing opposite a Disney star turned pop sensation.

"Oh my God. You're…you're…"

Not exactly a household name. Not yet. "Vaughn," I say, and extend my free hand to greet her. "I live next door."

"Wow. Definitely not in Kansas anymore," she murmurs, and then realizes she's left me hanging and grabs my hand as a flustered pink invades her cheeks. "I'm…um…uh…shoot. I knew this a minute ago."

I laugh, because she's already laughing at herself. "I know you're not Kendall or Dixie, if that helps?"

"Amber," she supplies, and slides her hand out of mine. "Sounds like you've already met my sisters."

"Yes. Speaking of which, is Kendall around?"

"She is. Sorry, please come in." She steps back and gestures me inside. "She's in the kitchen. Let me get—"

"That's okay." I flash her a don't-trouble-yourself grin and sweep past her. "I know the way." I was raised better, and I can practically feel my mom thwacking me upside the head, but I don't want to give Kendall a chance to have Amber run interference for her. I want to see her. I want to hand-deliver the apology.

"Ohh-kay…" Amber trails after me.

I stride into the kitchen and stop short. Last night is a

bit hazy, but this morning a breathtaking backside in snug red shorts is aimed my way in vivid color and clarity. The owner of said backside is leaning over, checking something in the oven while humming "Bootylicious." Without turning around, she asks, "Who was at the door?"

"Vaughn," I answer.

My voice jars her. She jerks upright and spins to face me in a startled-cat move. The oven door slams shut, and the sharp *bang* echoes in the whitewashed calm of the kitchen. Suddenly, I'm face-to-face with her. Kendall. My guardian angel. A part of me wondered if those blue eyes I recalled from last night would seem as laser-beam intense in the cool light of day, or the curving mouth as unintentionally inviting, but the truth is my tequila-soaked mind didn't do her justice.

"Don't you know it's dangerous to sneak up on someone who's reaching inside a three hundred and fifty degree oven?" she demands, fluttering a hand over her heart as if to calm it. The move draws my attention to the very nicely filled out Winnie the Pooh T-shirt I wasn't sure my dirty mind hadn't dreamed up. It's no dream. She's real—every bitable curve, every lick-able expanse of skin, every exasperated crinkle in her brows.

"Sorry." I know the sincerity of my reply is severely undermined by the fact that I'm checking her out like some kind of pent-up pervert, but the pajamas leave too much on display for me to settle for a view of the floor or the wall. Although she's looking now, too, and her eyes lose a little of the irritation as she inspects my shower-damp hair and freshly shaven jaw. They turn warmer as her stare roams across my shoulders and down my shirt, following the buttons like a path that ends at the front of my jeans. Her attention lingers there as if she can see beyond the curtain of my shirttails to the hard-on twitching to life behind my fly. I wasn't at my best last night—not even close—but at least this morning I'm showing her I clean up well. The way she bites her lower lip tells me she's noticed.

I clear my throat. "I wanted to thank you for the sleepover."

"Oh, hey. Why am I still standing here?" Amber's voice interrupts the awkward silence that follows what might not have been the smoothest opening line. "I have to go…um… make sure Dixie isn't doing any…thing."

Kendall makes an absent little sound of acknowledgment. As Amber's quick footsteps fade away, the girl in front of me drags in a long, deep breath. The kind of breath that tells me she's fortifying herself for whatever's coming next. The kind that fills the lungs to capacity and expands the chest.

Do not look at her tits. Do. Not.

Too late. My gaze goes rogue and settles on her tank top. "Did I mention how much I like your PJs?"

"Are you still drunk?" She crosses her arms over her chest, blocking Pooh from my view.

So much for cleaning up nicely. Apparently I'm not going to qualify for nice guy status that easily, but even so, the accusation leaves me a little defensive. "I'm not the least bit impaired this morning, angel." She's the one lounging around in a tank top and sleep shorts at nearly noon. Is it my fault I notice? I also noticed her checking me out in return a second ago, so I'm not the only one aware of the electricity crackling between us. I take slow and deliberate stock of her this time, letting my gaze linger on her bare legs, the V of her shorts, and the way her crossed arms plump her breasts over the neckline of her top. "But if you want to put me to a test, I'm game."

Her chin goes up a notch, but not before I catch a flicker of uncertainty in her expression. She moves to the other side of the breakfast bar like she wants some extra protection, and I immediately feel like a dick.

"You know what?" She opens a nearby drawer and digs out my keys. "I'll take your word for it. But here's the thing. Next time party central gets out of control, I might not be available to do my famous flying tackle and magic disappearing car key trick. I've got different plans for this summer, and I need to focus on them, so, sorry, but—" She tosses the keys across the counter.

I snag them before they sail off the edge of the granite. "No sorry due to me, angel. We've got this backward." I'm supposed to be here apologizing and thanking her, not getting bent out of shape because she's not offering to share her bed with me like Dixie, or getting so tongue-tied she forgets her name like Amber. I'm very used to both of those reactions, but it seems Kendall's not like her sisters. I look away for a moment to gather my thoughts, and when I look back at her she's not exactly reserving judgment—it's too late for that—but this is my chance to do the right thing. I take it. Placing the gift on the counter between us I say, "I'm sorry about last night."

She blinks at the bag and then slings a questioning glance at me. I shrug and pocket my keys but don't miss how she tracks the movement. Suddenly, I'm hyper-aware of my hand sliding into my jeans.

I can tell by the way she swallows that she is, too, but she shifts her attention to my face and points at the bag. "What's this?"

"My way of thanking you for coming to my rescue last night. A lot of people would have chosen not to get involved and just let whatever was going to happen, happen. Others would have called the cops. You did neither. You saved me from some really bad decisions that could have caused a fuck-ton of consequences, and I want you to know I appreciate it."

For one unguarded moment her face just…lights. There's no other way to describe it. It's not just her tentative smile or the glow of pleasure in her cheeks. It's not even the thrill of the gift. No, it's like what I've said really matters to her. Then, all of a sudden the glow shuts off. She straightens and pushes the bag toward me, and I know she's about to reject the gift. "Forget–"

"It smells really good in here." I cut her off by blurting the first thing that springs to mind. Whatever she's baking smells fantastic.

"Shit!" She rushes over to the counter, grabs the potholder next to the stovetop, and pulls something out of the oven. Something browned to perfection as far as I can tell, but Kendall makes a worried sound and inspects it closely.

"That looks amazing," I say. "You like to cook?"

"Mostly I like to eat," she replies with absolutely no shame, a rarity among the usual crowd I'm surrounded by. It's refreshing.

I can't stop my smile as I come up behind her and lean over to inhale the scent of steaming peppers, onions…I don't know what all, but it's making my mouth water. Then I get more than I bargained for, because I also inhale a sweet, earthy scent, equal parts bubble bath and sex. It clings to her skin and makes me fantasize about her soaking in a steamy tub, getting herself off. That affects me in other ways. The moment she stills, I know her focus has shifted, too. She's staring at the pan, but her thoughts are on me.

"What's on the menu?" I ask, shamelessly fishing for an invitation to today's brunch.

"Back it up, mister, you're crowding the cook."

I guess I am, and I half anticipate an elbow to my gut, but instead she looks up and slays me with an unguarded grin. She wasn't expecting a playful moment.

"Can we start over?" It's an impulsive request. I know I can't get a complete do-over, but if she'll give me a chance, I can definitely do *better.* "Like, I'll say 'Hi Kendall, I'm

Vaughn' and you'll say…?"

The shine of amusement fades. She slides out of my grasp and steps away. "I'll say, 'Hi Vaughn. It's nice to meet you, but I think it's best if we stay on our sides of the fence. I'm only house-sitting until August, then I'll be gone, and our paths will never cross again. By fall I'll be a vague memory of a crazy night you had over the summer. Take care of yourself and have a great life.'"

Her breezy tone doesn't quite match her expression. She's politely insisting there's no point in us getting beyond "Hello neighbor." I'd really like to know why she feels that way, so I settle myself on one of the barstools at the counter and prop my chin on my hand. "You honestly think you're so easy to forget?"

"For drunks, yes."

Seriously? I mean, *seriously*? Last night was me in full fuckup mode. I won't deny it. Hell, I'm not trying to deny it. But I came here this morning for more than my stupid keys. I came to apologize for pulling her into my drama, and rather than accept it, she calls me a drunk? That's some serious shade to throw at someone she barely knows. For several seconds we stare at each other. I wait for her to blink, look away. Give an inch. But she doesn't. I'm not getting anything close to a do-over. Fine. I still know my manners. She's entitled to the thank-you and apology.

I push the blue bag toward her and stand. "This is for you. I'm sorry about last night. Thanks for keeping me safe."

Then I walk out, because there's nothing left to say.

Chapter Five

Kendall

Those three sentences are not what I expected to come out of Vaughn's mouth after calling him a drunk. I say each sentence over in my head. Bringing me a gift is a thoughtful gesture. And it's *the* blue bag. I glance at it, wondering what kind of jewelry he thinks I'll like, considering I'm not wearing any.

He's remorseful. His apology—twice—proves as much.

And I did want to keep him safe. Did I let my mind go to worst-case scenarios and the possibility of others getting hurt if he'd decided to drive somewhere? Yes.

But this isn't just about him. It's about me.

For the first time in over four years, I'm curious. About a guy. One I barely know but somehow manages to stir up emotions I haven't allowed myself to feel in a long time.

With a shaky hand I slide the blue bag closer, but before I peek inside, I'm hit with doubt—and annoyance. Vaughn's apology and gift make me mad at both of us. Yes, it was sweet, but it's also excessive. A simple "sorry" followed by a "thank you" is all I needed. All I can afford, given the last thing I want is to have something that reminds me of him. I can't, in good conscience, accept a gift like this. I pick up the bag and hurry toward the kitchen door to return it to him.

I also owe him an apology for calling him a drunk. I shouldn't have done that. He flustered me and I lashed out because I didn't know how to handle his playfulness.

I run outside, hoping to catch him, but he's nowhere to be seen. I take a deep breath, take a minute to gather myself. The sky is the kind of summer blue and white that makes you wish you could fly from one puffy cloud to the next. The air smells like jasmine and roses. Vaughn smelled like an ocean breeze wafting across clean sheets. The combination made me hot under my skin, and I'd felt an uncharacteristic urge to rub my back against his front when he stood behind me at the kitchen counter. I blink away the unwelcome memory. An irresistible energy radiates from him, and it draws me in even as my past tethers me.

Vaughn is dangerously hard to resist. And he knows it. Of course he does. He earns a living by having that effect on people, right? But the simple notion doesn't stop my stomach from fluttering when I think about the perfect angle of his clean-shaven jaw. Or the panty-dropping smile he wields without even trying. And his eyes… God, this morning they were lucid and such a brilliant shade of green that I feel even guiltier for doubting his sobriety.

If nothing else, I really need to say I'm sorry. I start down the narrow slope of the side yard toward the sidewalk. I'm almost there when the sound of an engine purrs to life. Turning, I catch Vaughn's car maneuvering out of the driveway. I take a few tentative steps forward, not sure if I should flag him down or wait for another time to return his gift. My decision is made for me when he drives slowly by and turns his head in my direction. He's wearing dark sunglasses.

His mouth is set in a serious line. I'm not positive he sees me, or if he's just looking at the house, but it doesn't matter, because a second later he's out of sight.

Not out of mind. I fear he'll never be out of my head, our one weird night together forever stored in my long-term memory. I trudge back into the kitchen with the Tiffany's bag dangling from my fingers.

Amber is cutting into the frittata. Dixie is sitting at the breakfast bar sipping on what I suspect is her second Bloody Mary and paging through a magazine. "Look!" She holds up the magazine open to a page with a black-and-white advertisement that features Vaughn's face and bare shoulders. He looks beyond handsome with stubble lining his jaw and just a hint of a smile, like he knows exactly what a woman wants. *Him*. "He's the Giorgio Armani fragrance guy."

"He did smell good," Amber says.

"I can't believe you didn't fuck him last night." Dixie closes the magazine. "Or at least fool around. Jesus, Kendall, did you take a vow of celibacy after—"

"Stop." I bang the kitchen door shut and lean against it. "Do not say another word."

"Don't have to." The ice tinkles in her glass as she takes a long drink, holding the conversation hostage until she's good and ready to continue "You just answered my question." For a brief second I imagine compassion swims into her eyes, but she makes known my mistake when she adds, "Which means I get to play with Vaughn and any other hot guy who makes an appearance."

"You're that easy, huh?" I say in a weak attempt to get back at her. I've never been able to best her verbal sparring and don't like myself for trying.

She crunches a piece of ice before curling her lips into a bulletproof smile. "Why yes, I am, princess."

There's no wounding Dixie. She doesn't give a damn

what anybody thinks of her, least of all me. "For the last time, *please* stop calling me that." I clench my fists so hard my fingernails bite into my palms.

One dark blond eyebrow wings up. "Is the 'please' supposed to make me care?"

Tears sting my eyes. I didn't do anything to deserve her hostility. For my whole life I've done nothing but try to be a sister, and when that didn't work, I kept my distance. It's not my fault our father behaved like he did, but the truth is, he's a decent man who made mistakes and has tried his damndest to make up for them. If she'd stop holding his sins against him, she might discover what our dad wants more than anything is a relationship with all three of his daughters.

"The 'please' is because unlike some people, I have good manners."

"Princess, you have no idea how polite I can be."

"You're right. I don't know if you can be polite at all," I throw back with as much spite as I can muster.

"You want to go there right now? Fine." Dixie slaps a hand on the countertop, straightens her back. "Four days ago I walked into my bedroom and caught my boyfriend fucking my best friend. My best friend who I helped get the waitress job at the bar where I worked, and my boyfriend who also happened to be my boss and the guy I'd moved in with. So in the span of thirty seconds, boom." She splays her fingers wide to mime a bomb blast. "Bye-bye boyfriend. Farewell best friend. Adios apartment."

"I'm sorry," I say. "That sucks." I can't imagine any guy having the balls to cheat on Dixie. She's vicious when crossed.

"Why are you sorry? You didn't break my trust. They did. But that's not the point of my story. The point is, I could have screamed and thrown shit. I could have castrated him and kicked her ass. I could have done a Carrie Underwood on her car and torched his precious guitars."

"Oh my God. You killed them, didn't you?" Amber asks. "Now you're on the run?"

Dixie glides a hand slowly through her hair and then shakes it out. "No. I walked away without giving them the satisfaction of knowing I'd found them, which is pretty fucking polite, so don't ever question my behavior when you don't know anything about my life." With that, she picks up her drink and polishes it off.

I press away from the door and sit on the barstool beside her, for some dumb reason wanting to offer comfort.

"Don't even, princess. You think we're going to do some sisterly bonding over broken hearts? I don't have a heart, which I'd think you'd have figured out by now."

Okay, then. I dart my eyes to Amber. She's cut the frittata into eight perfect pie slices, her focus on food rather than our screwed-up family. It's not pity I feel. It's care. For the first time in our lives Dixie's opened up with something personal, and it gives me hope.

"Did you really leave without saying good-bye?" I ask, reaching for a piece of the frittata.

"I might have put a boot through his favorite guitar on my way out, but yeah, pretty much." She grabs some of the egg-and-veggie dish with a smile on her face. "I certainly can't explain how his picture and the address of the bar ended up on a site called Knobgobbler, and I have no clue who posted her number on Skanky Bitches."

Amber chokes.

"Easy, girl," Dixie says. "Am I too much for your delicate ears? Better get used to it."

"There's water bottles in the fridge," I say.

She grabs one, takes a big sip, then clears her throat but doesn't say anything. She's always been the quietest of us, but she seems more distant than normal, probably because of our situation.

Dixie licks her finger clean. "So now that you know I'm jobless and homeless, why can't you guys leave and go back to where you came from?"

I roll my eyes as I study her posture, her face. Four years in New York City taught me a lot about people. I'd often do my homework in coffee shops and people-watch for hours. Brit and I would make up stories about the pedestrians we saw through the windows, giving everyone a happily ever after, of course. Dixie is tough, no doubt, but she's also hurting, and that's why she's lashing out.

Amber waves away Dixie's question. "I think one confession is enough for our first day. I'm going to go take a nap."

"You can't run away from us all summer," Dixie says.

"I'm not running away." Amber rounds the breakfast bar. "I'm exhausted from traveling, so I think that earns me a pass."

"It does," I tell her.

She gives me a small smile and leaves the room.

Dixie stands and starts cleaning up the mess I made of the kitchen before Vaughn showed up. "So what's your deal? Shouldn't you be with mommy and daddy on some celebratory trip to Europe or something? You did just graduate, right?"

"I wanted a change of scenery this summer." Dixie has no idea I haven't lived at home since I left for college, staying summers in the city to work and inviting my parents to visit me during holidays.

"Ha! I bet you're wishing you'd chosen someplace else." She covers the frittata with plastic wrap and puts it in the fridge then leans her hip against the granite countertop. "Luckily the house is plenty big enough for all of us if we don't want to talk to one another. Aunt Sally will just have to deal."

Dixie's eyes shift to the Tiffany's bag. "What's that?"

"Nothing." I grab the gift and put it in my lap to hide it from view.

"You suck at"—she makes air quotes—"nothing. It's written all over your face that it's something. So, come on, spill. I'm a good listener. You wouldn't believe some of the stories I've heard while bartending."

"Why would I tell you anything?"

"You know what? You're right. You stay in your corner and I'll stay in mine." She resumes cleaning like I'm no longer in the same room.

The truth is I'm way out of my element when it comes to Vaughn, while Dixie could probably write a book on the topic of men. Maybe this could be the first step toward building a relationship with her. I put the bag back on the counter. "It's a gift from Vaughn."

She tosses the sponge into the sink. "No shit. What for?"

"A thank-you for letting him sleep on the couch last night. There was a party going on at his house, and he needed someplace to crash."

Dixie might not have a college degree, but she's wicked smart. She squints, assessing me. "Let me get this straight. You met the guy last night. Let him sleep on the couch because shit was going down at his house, and he brings you an expensive gift to say thanks."

"Sounds about right."

"Half right, maybe, but I don't really care. Are you going to open it?"

"No. I'm going to return it to him."

"Why?"

"Because a thank-you is all that is necessary." I lift the bag. "I can't accept something like this when I barely know the guy."

"That's ridiculous. You don't even know what it is."

"You'd accept a gift like this and wear it without any

qualms?"

"Hell yeah, I'd accept it. Then I'd sell it. Look, princess, before you strain yourself figuring out how to return the Hope Diamond, open the damn box. They do carry stuff besides fancy jewelry. Maybe it's a pen, or a key chain, or a sterling silver corkscrew to help you pull your head out of your ass."

Rude as she is, she could be right. It's probably just a token. A nice one, because he's obviously got the means, but the kind of thing a person gives as a gesture of appreciation for an associate or a helpful neighbor. A key chain makes perfect sense. I bet that's what's inside and I'm freaking out over nothing. It's still too generous a gift, but possibly one there's no harm in keeping. Vaughn did go to the trouble of picking it out for me.

"I should open it."

"About time." Dixie puts her elbows on the counter and cups her face in her hands to watch me.

I've never gotten a gift from Tiffany's before, so I have no idea if everything comes in a dark blue velvet box, but that's what I pull out of the bag. My heart pounds a little harder as I open the box. Nestled inside isn't a key chain but a sterling silver daisy key pendant necklace with a diamond in the center of the flower. My hands shake. It's delicate. Beautiful.

"Huh," Dixie says. "Looks like you've got yourself an admirer. Word of advice?"

"Yes," I answer immediately without looking at her. Instead, I tuck the necklace back into place and put the box in the bag. It's too much. I'm returning it no matter what she recommends.

"A guy like Vaughn gives a gift like that? He wants to fuck you, plain and simple, so if you're not down for that, princess, you should follow your Hannah Montana instincts and give the *thank-you* back."

I don't bother responding. I'm not sure what the gift

implies, only that it adds a layer of confusion to my bad mood. He barely knows me! I stand up and walk out the kitchen door with the bag in my hand.

Out of view from the kitchen window, I sit on the iron bench next to the gardenias Aunt Sally planted and tends to like children. Lying in the dirt beside the bench are the three large garden rocks Amber, Dixie, and I painted when we were young. Each is different in color and design but painted in similar childlike strokes. I decorated mine with calm blue swirls. Flashy purple lightning bolts zigzag across Dixie's, and Amber's glows with a round yellow sun. Aunt Sally tends to our rocks as well, because they're still shiny.

Now that I have privacy, I pull the small blue envelope out of the Tiffany's bag. I purposely didn't tell Dixie there was a card. It was hard enough sharing the gift with her. I slip a white notecard from the envelope and read what Vaughn wrote.

Thank you for being my guardian angel. And for the sofa. I'll trade you keys. Sincerely, Vaughn.

I slide the note back inside the envelope and return it to the bag.

I'm no one's guardian angel. If that were true, Mason would be okay. We'd be planning our future, maybe even getting married this summer. Instead, I'm alone and desperate to find a job or career path that doesn't include law school.

I get to my feet and walk to Vaughn's front door. He may have meant well, but right now his thoughtfulness is too much for me to bear.

I put the bag behind the potted plant and turn and walk away. For the next couple of hours I search online for local jobs, sending my résumé to a few entry level positions that sound interesting.

That's a lie. They don't sound interesting. I close my eyes and wish for time to stop until I figure things out. Impossible, of course. Just like Mason's recovery.

Chapter Six

Vaughn

When your agent summons you to lunch at The Ivy to meet with an *America Rocks* producer, you arrive promptly no matter how drastically you have to bend time, space, and traffic laws to do it. I'm antsy by the time I pull to a stop at the curbside valet in front of the iconic white picket fence surrounding the patio of the famed West Hollywood eatery. The dash clock reads 2:07 p.m. Not perfect, but respectable. I surrender my car to the attendant and try to steady my pulse. There's no need to look eager. Best case scenario is I've raced from a shoot in Culver City to jump through another hoop. Worst case? This is their way of letting me down gently and offering me a consolation prize, like man-on-the-street interviewer for the open audition crowds. Hours of tape for maybe ten minutes of screen time per season. And fuck it, after I recovered from the catastrophic disappointment, I'd probably take the offer. I love the show that much.

Instead of steadying, my pulse stalls like a rusty clutch

because I spy Nigel Cowie holding court under the shade of a generous white umbrella. Nigel's not just a producer for *America Rocks*, he's *the* producer, and he's sharing the small linen-draped table with John Brenner—one of the associate producers I met during my first audition and subsequent callback—my agent, Nina Felder, and my father. I've never met Nigel before, but the tall, tanned Englishman is instantly recognizable thanks to his habitual five o'clock shadow and signature tight black T-shirt. I stand stock-still for a half second to take it in, savor the moment, and yes, to give my heart a chance to fall back into a normal rhythm.

I get only the half second, though, because Nigel spots me, stands, and extends an arm my way. "Vaughn Shaughnessy. We meet at last."

The patio's not full for a Sunday afternoon, but every head swings from the prominent Brit to me, and every Hollywood insider and waiter-slash-actor in the place starts doing the math on two *America Rocks* producers, one agent, one manager, and the guy from the Armani ads. I plaster a confident smile on my face and stride over like I expected this meeting. "Mr. Cowie," I say, and shake his hand. His grip is firm, his smile surprisingly genuine.

"Nigel," he corrects. "I believe you know this lovely lady and these other gents?"

"Of course." I shake hands with John, who looks like Tony Romo's twin brother, kiss Nina's flawless cheek, and give my dad a quick one-armed hug. "Glad you could make it," he mutters in my ear, letting me know I'm tardy. Nigel gestures me to the single empty seat at the table.

I sit, and conversation pauses while a waiter approaches with a tray of drinks—Ivy gimlets all around. My back is to most of the patio, but I can practically hear texts being tapped out on every phone in the vicinity. When the waiter retreats, Nigel leans in and raises his glass. "Cheers. Apologies for mucking up everyone's schedule with a last-minute meeting," he says in a voice modulated for our table alone. "I'm off to London tonight and I wanted to meet all the talent on our short list in person before I left." He touches his glass to mine and adds, "Old-fashioned of me, I know, but I like a sit-down and a chat. I appreciate you indulging me."

"It's no problem," I manage, which sounds humble and understated when what I really want to do is leap up and high-five Nina. I want to fist-bump John. I want to kiss Nigel full on the mouth. Mostly, I want to wipe the frown off my dad's face. This is great news. Why is he scowling like someone pissed in his cocktail?

"Sorry, John. Nigel," my dad says, "forgive my confusion, but I guess I'm still trying to catch up. Friday, a very reliable source told me your team had drawn up the short list and we weren't on it…"

I stop my head from swinging in my father's direction. He'd had an unofficial thumbs-down since Friday and didn't think to share that information with me?

"…today, I get a call for this meeting and find out we're still in the running. Obviously, we're pleased, but why do I have whiplash?"

John props his forearms on the table and leans in. "Confidentially?"

Dad nods. "Of course."

Total waste of breath. Whatever John's about to disclose will be breaking all over the gossip outlets before this meeting concludes, but we pretend it's just between us. "You're not the only one with very reliable sources. Late last week one of ours informed us Flynn Bateman is about to be the latest name trending with a MeToo hashtag attached. We conducted a quick but intensive investigation into the accusations, and while we are of course not prepared to comment on whether he broke any laws, we determined certain documented behavior fell short of the *America Rocks* ethical standards. He was one of our top contenders, due to his potential to reach the smartphone demographic on the platforms they favor and lure them away from their YouTube channels and Instagram feeds a couple hours a week." John's eyes shift to me. "Now you are. Unless you tell me someone's got hard-to-refute evidence of you doing things that would make it impossible for you to sign a morals clause."

"Of course not," my father replies before I can even open my mouth.

"Brilliant." Nigel sets his drink down, and I realize the meeting is basically over.

"What *kind* of morals clause," Nina interjects, ever the pragmatist.

Nigel rubs his palms together. "Nina, John will have someone send over the gist of it first thing tomorrow morning, but the legal folks tell me it's completely reasonable."

"I'm sure they do," she says without much concern, but I know she'll go over every word and work that shit until she's satisfied it's fair. Beneath her Clair Huxtable facade beats the heart of a tireless detail-wrangler. "I'll give it my immediate attention and let John know right away if anything doesn't read right."

"I'm confident you will." His smile widens to include my father, who has been in on the rounds of auditions, discussions, and negotiations so far. "And I'm sure we can count on your continued discretion regarding this process."

He follows that up with a wink, because we all know this, too, is part of the game. If you're Nigel Cowie you don't sip drinks on the patio of the Ivy with a guy plenty of insiders know auditioned for host of your show unless you want to fuel rampant speculation. Which he does, because having people buzzing about this is good for the show.

I figure it's time for me to get in this meeting and say

something. "Aside from ethics, Nigel, can you tell me what's on *your* wish list for the next host?"

Across the table Nina gives me a tiny nod of approval.

Nigel sips his drink and considers how he wants to answer my question. "I loved Gray. Loved him. Admired him. He was one of my mates. But this process isn't about finding another Gray Ellison. We had him, he was bloody amazing, and nobody can replace him. That chapter of *America Rocks* is closed. It's on the next host to write the next chapter in a style and voice that works for them. Page one, someone with the versatility to appeal to the loyal, longtime fans while at the same time attract a new set of viewers."

"I—"

"Right." My dad cuts me off. "You don't need another Gray Ellison, but you do need someone who can project a similar all-American image. Someone who knows how to watch what he says, what he does, and with whom he says or does it, because this franchise is handing over an audience, and the host's choices have the power to alienate that fan base. Here's the bottom line. Flynn Bateman wasn't ready for prime time. We are. In today's world you have no safe zone. So Vaughn"—he turns to me—"you need to keep in mind that every facet of your life is part of your brand and, by extension, part of the *America Rocks* brand. Does that make sense?"

Yes, but my face heats at my dad's assumption that he needs to spell this out for me, especially in front of Nigel and John. He's treating me like a kid, and everyone at the table realizes it except him. For two people who share DNA, he doesn't know me at all.

"Yeah, Dad. Thanks. I think I've got it."

My tone doesn't invite any further discussion, but my dad doesn't need an invitation. "Most importantly, you've got me." He directs his attention back to Nigel. "I'm here to manage his brand, down to who he makes appearances with, who his name is linked to, and so forth. There will be no missteps."

I tune out. Kendall's angel face forms in my mind, silently contradicting my assertion that I'm not a risk to their brand. Okay, maybe I'm extra defensive on account of my actions last night, because in light of them I may actually deserve to be treated like someone without a fully developed prefrontal cortex, except my father doesn't know a damn thing about what happened. I tune back in to hear my dad insist, "I have a strategy for everything."

Nigel offers a neutral smile then raises his glass. "To strategy." We all toast, and moments later, Nigel thanks us again for working him into our schedules. I give him credit for sounding sincerely appreciative for a man most people in this town would reschedule surgery for if it meant getting a meeting. Chairs are eased back, handshakes exchanged, and then John and Nigel sail off, making brief stops at other tables as they chart a course toward the sidewalk.

Dad and Nina launch into a review of the meeting. I listen as they trade impressions, but a fact keeps circling in my head like a hawk over prey. My dad's control freak tendencies are getting worse as my career advances, not better. I respect his business expertise, and I appreciate everything he's done to help me succeed, but I've got to set some boundaries with him. Before we end up hating each other.

A better man would have done it sooner, I admit a couple of hours later when I'm back in the privacy of my car. But my relationship with my father is complicated. When it comes to my career, I'm not just shouldering my hopes and dreams. I'm carrying his as well, because I'm the only one left to do it. I'm the second-string replacement for his paternal ambitions after the real star of the family—my sister—went dark far ahead of her time.

Even without the fucked-up family expectations, the stakes are high and getting higher. The producers of a massively successful reality show don't often hand the reins over to an unknown quantity. If they do, everyone's taking a risk, but if *America Rocks* goes off a cliff with Vaughn Shaughnessy driving, Vaughn Shaughnessy takes the blame. Failing to get the gig after making it this far will mean I clutched at a crucial moment. I had a real shot, but ultimately they deemed me too something—too inexperienced for network TV, too unfamiliar to audiences, too clumsy with the banter and interviews—and *that* would be disappointing because banter and interviews are my strong points. I can't change my level of experience, or do much in the near-term to increase my profile in Middle America, but I can talk. More importantly, I know how to listen, and I know how to steer the conversation into everyone's comfort zone. Lose your sister when she's nineteen, on the verge of achieving her dreams, you learn how to walk and talk your way through hell and back. I like to think that's why I'm uniquely qualified to land the job. But landing the job comes with a backdraft of pressure. I feel it. My dad feels it, too, and asserting control is his way of dealing with the tension and protecting me from failure.

Understanding where his compulsion comes from doesn't make it easier to tolerate, but nothing's going to change unless I tell him to back off and figure out a way to make it stick. With that promise to myself issued and accepted, I toss the problem into a compartment of my mind labeled "Later" and focus on the satisfaction of advancing toward something I've put a lot of effort into accomplishing. It's a good feeling.

The sun's tinting my rearview mirror orange by the time I drive down my street, reminding me that I have a very narrow window to finish packing before a car arrives to take me to LAX. I may be tomorrow's next host of *America Rocks*, but today I'm a guy with a commercial shoot in Miami. I hit the brake to make the left turn into my driveway and some of my king-of-the-world high fades. What went down on this slab of concrete last night is a prime example of the kind of behavior America, and the producers of *America Rocks*, will not forgive. Thankfully, they'll never find out about that stupid lapse in judgment. Kendall won't say anything. I mean, I'm not naive, and I don't go around trusting people I've barely met, but she didn't even tell her sisters, so I don't see her doing some kind of "You'll never guess whose drunk ass I saved" post all over social media.

On the other hand, she's yet to forgive me. And that bothers me. A lot. Unfortunately, there's not much more I can do. I apologized. I thanked her with words and with a gesture I hoped she'd appreciate. Did she? That remains to be seen, but the next move, if there is one, is hers.

I pull to the top of the driveway, easing off the accelerator just before the slope flattens out into the small parking area in front of the garage. The stripped-down classic black Bronco Matt bought back in high school occupies the far left slot. Dylan's sporty new silver R8 Spyder sits in the spot closest to the door.

The cars fit their owners like personality profiles. Dylan's smooth and fast. Matt's strong and rock solid. I'm somewhere in the middle, I think, as I slide my Range Rover into the space between their vehicles. We're brothers in every way except birth, and I value that even more now than I did as a kid. Being in this business brings a constant stream of new people into my life, and most of them act like they're my friends—at least to my face—but they don't really know me, and they don't really want to know me. They want to project onto me whatever image suits them best. The face of their product, the candy on their arm, a commodity to be exploited for their purpose, and I wouldn't have a career if I couldn't satisfy those demands to some extent. But Dylan and Matt want nothing from me except what any guy wants from a bro. Be cool, show some love, and restock the beer fridge every once in a while.

You have no safe zone.

But I do. These guys are my safe zone. They give me shit when I deserve shit—and expect the same from me—but they're in my corner. They'll be stoked for me when I tell them about my meeting, and they won't lecture me about how I should handle myself. They believe in me. And I know I can trust them.

The knowledge restores my king-of-the-world mood. I walk into the house with my arms spread wide and call out, "Stop jacking off for a second and listen—"

Dylan's pacing the living room, his phone to his ear. He holds up a hand to simultaneously acknowledge me and signal me to shut up. "Hell no. We're not paying Sandoval a dime if they brought us cases of broken bottles, and… Screw that. I don't give a shit what he says. Reject delivery. What do you mean it's too late? Who the *fuck* signed for the order without inspecting it?"

I settle myself on one of the sofas and watch the excitement of life in club-land unfold before me. It's weird and oddly encouraging seeing Dylan invest actual effort into something besides having a good time or getting laid.

He stops pacing and pinches the bridge of his nose. "He's fired. I don't care. I'm firing his ass. Oh, and tell Sandoval I'm not paying for the cases of recycling his guy dropped off. If he doesn't have my order delivered within the hour—intact this time—I'll find another supplier."

With that threat hanging in the air, he disconnects and throws his phone onto the coffee table. "Goddammit."

"Tough day at the office, honey?"

"Holy shit." He comes around the empty sofa and drops

down heavily. “If someone doesn’t suck my dick in the next five seconds, I swear to God my head is going to explode.”

Matt walks in from the kitchen at that moment, bottle of beer to his lips, and I snap my fingers at him. “Got an emergency situation here, Officer Wright. This man’s dick needs sucking.”

Matt doesn’t miss a step as he crosses to the mantel to commandeer the remote. “I’m not sucking that dick. I know where it’s been.”

“I don’t want either of you cocksuckers anywhere near my dick. Hand me my phone, Vaughn. This is a job for your mom.”

Predictable burn, but smoothly delivered. My comeback will involve his grandmother and her obnoxious Chihuahua, but as I reach for his phone I notice a familiar blue bag sitting on the table.

What the…?

I snag it, vaguely aware of Matt turning on the flat-screen and Dylan telling him to find the Dodgers game. I look inside to see the opened card and the little blue box. “What is this doing here?” The question comes out louder than I intended, silencing the conversation.

“I don’t know, man,” Matt answers. “I found it by the door earlier today.”

I’m halfway to the hall before I hear Dylan’s footfalls behind me. “Hey, what did you want to tell us?”

“Tell you later,” I say over my shoulder, not breaking stride. I cut through the kitchen, grab a beer from the fridge, and twist off the top before heading out the big sliding glass doors leading to the patio. My ego’s not fragile. In my business you have to learn to let disappointment roll off without leaving a mark. But having my gift tossed back in my face leaves a bruise. I gave this to her, dammit. Because I’m sorry, and grateful, and I wanted her to know how much

I appreciated what she did.

And now I'm standing on my patio with a stupid Tiffany's bag in my hand and no fucking clue what I'm doing. The calm, glassy surface of the pool mocks my agitation. *Planning to bang on her door and give her crap for returning the gift? That'll show her what a cool guy you are.*

Shit. I lean against the railing separating the patio from the pool and down half my beer. I don't have time to deal with this right now. I should be upstairs throwing the last-minute stuff into my suitcase and making sure I'm checked in for my flight to Miami.

I push away from the railing to do that and catch movement from the corner of my eye. Over the hedges of bougainvillea I watch Kendall step out onto the patio next door. Our house sits higher on the hill, which gives me a bird's-eye view of their backyard. Late afternoon sun sends long shadows across the lot, but there's enough light for me to see she's traded the Winnie the Pooh pajamas for a snug raglan shirt and a little pair of drawstring sweat shorts that ride the flare of her hips. Her hair is swept up into a careless bundle, and I can't help but notice the graceful arch of her neck. She stands there, still and beautiful as a statue.

Then the statue stretches her arms high over her head. Her face tilts toward the sky, and my throat goes dry at the pull of her shirt across her full, upswept breasts.

Matt or Dylan cranks up the volume on the game—something they tend to do when they're in and out of the living room and they don't want to miss anything. Sound surges. Kendall's arms drop quickly, and her head swivels my way, clearly annoyed. Good. That makes two of us. My car's due any moment, but the knowledge doesn't stop me from stalking down the deck stairs, around the hedge, and into my neighbors' meticulously maintained English countryside of a yard. Part of me hopes she retreats into the house.

But she doesn't retreat. Not an inch. She crosses her arms, plants her feet, and faces me as I approach, her chin tilted up at a take-your-best-shot angle. She's braced for a fight, and all of a sudden I have none in me.

"This is yours." The words come out slightly winded, and I hold the blue bag out to her.

She crosses her arms a little tighter and backs up a step. "I can't accept it, Vaughn. I don't know what you think giving me a fancy gift accomplishes, but—"

"It says 'thank you.'"

"It says more than that." She glances away for a moment, and when she makes eye contact again, I'm at a loss for reading them. "You don't have to buy my silence with pretty gifts, you know. I'm not going to tell anyone about last night."

I never doubted that, but apparently she doubted my motives. I tamp down on my cynicism. "Okay. Thanks."

She straightens her spine. "And I'm not going to fall into bed with you because you bought me something pretty." Early evening shade can't dim the pink in her cheeks.

Obviously I haven't corned the market on cynicism. "I'm glad you think it's pretty." I push the bag at her again. "And I'm sorry if I confused you. I'm not trying to buy anything. Not your body—which is amazing, but clearly not for sale—or your silence. Not even your forgiveness. Seriously, Kendall, I just want to say 'sorry' and 'thank you.' You looked out for a stranger. You cared enough to get involved. I like to think maybe the next time you're feeling like no good deed goes unpunished, you'll put on the pendant and remember someone appreciates what you did for him."

All the pink drains out of her face. "It was nothing."

"Not to me."

She bites her lip, and her gaze drops to the bag I'm still holding out like a dumbass dork. What else can I say?

"There's a gift receipt in the box, if you don't like it..."

Her eyes find mine. “No. I like it. It’s beautiful. Thank you.”

“Then take it. Please.” I’m not so off my game that I can’t remember to say the magic word.

Reluctantly, she lifts the bag from my hand. Skin slides over skin in the process, and I endure a quick and dirty fantasy of those hesitant fingers sliding down my chest, over my stomach, and into my jeans.

Not a chance. Maybe not, but the memory of having her back against my chest this morning comes back to tease me, and all at once I have to do better than a simple pass-off. “Wait. Hand it over,” I say, curling my fingers toward my palm.

She stops in the process of taking the box out of the bag. “What?”

“Give it here.” I reach over and pluck the box out of her hand then I crouch and put my beer on the brick patio. “Turn around.”

Her hesitant look challenges my command, but she slowly turns around. I take the pendant out of the box and put the box next to the bottle. Then I stand, step close to her—close enough to smell the clean, herbal scent of her shampoo—and drape the pendant around her neck. The key slips low into the three-button front of her shirt for a moment. The very tip nestles between her breasts, and the poke of her nipples through the cotton tells me I’m not the only one who enjoys the unintentional detour. I lean closer to secure the clasp, and the wispy hairs on the back of her neck flutter in the breeze created by my breath.

“H-have you got it?”

Her body heat scorches through my shirt. She shifts her weight from one foot to another, and her backside brushes the front of my jeans. I force myself to keep my hands on the clasp and not drop them to her hips to hold her in place while

I grind my painfully eager cock into the cushion of her ass.

There are a hundred girls in your phone who will fuck you up, down, and sideways if you say the word, and you're down here rubbing up against one who would probably slap your face for even thinking about making a move.

"Got it." I smooth my hands over her shoulders and slowly back away.

She turns to me and touches the pendant.

"It suits you. Beautiful and delicate, but strong at the core."

I don't know how I expect her to react, but the uncertain look takes me by surprise.

"I'm… You really don't know me well enough to say that."

"I know when somebody rescues my sorry ass." I'd like to know more, I almost add, but don't because I get the feeling she'd run back inside if I uttered the words out loud. Instead I bend to pick up the box and my beer.

She takes the box from my open hand, and her fingertips feather across my palm. Her eyes lock onto mine again, hold, and something more intense than the casual contact passes between us. She tears her gaze away and looks at my house.

"You better get back. Sounds like you've got company again."

I shake my head. "No company, just my roommates watching the game."

Dark blond eyebrows lift. "Hearing impaired roommates?"

I laugh and wander to one of the wrought-iron benches lining the patio. "No. Hardcore Dodgers fans. Sorry. I don't think they realize anyone's here. I'll tell them to turn it down." On impulse I nod my head toward the house. "Come meet them."

She's quiet for a long moment, staring down at her toes

so I can't read her expression, but I can sense her reluctance. "Come on." As if it's settled, I stand and hold out a hand to her. "Let me introduce you. There are only a few people in this world I can always count on, and these guys are two of the best. You should meet them. Get to know your neighbors."

Finally she looks up at me with those big blue eyes, and there's something so torn in their depths I almost look away.

"We're not really neighbors, remember? I'm only here temporarily."

"Kendall, in the grand scheme of things, we're all only here temporarily. Wait…are you one of those people who's afraid to leave the house? No problem. Sit tight. I'll bring Matt and Dylan over here."

She fights a smile now that I've called her on her shit. "Okay. Fine. I'll come say hi," she says just as my phone chimes with a notification. I pull it out of my pocket to find Becca has posted a picture of the two of us from a party a couple of weeks ago. In it, she's rolling a joint on my bare stomach. What the ever-loving fuck does she think she's doing? Yes, weed is legal in California, but it's not legal across the whole damn country. The next host of *America Rocks* is not going to be a pothead.

"Everything okay?" Kendall asks, reminding me where I am. Then a horn blasts from my driveway. "Fuck. That's my car." I glance at my watch. "I've got a flight to Miami for a photo shoot happening tomorrow. And I need to take care of—"

"No worries." She backs away. "You're busy, which is totally cool. I'll meet them another time."

I nod, finish off the rest of my beer as I make my way across the yard, and call Becca to get her to delete the photo. She laughs in my ear, tells me to chill, until I point out it's a bad look for *both* of us. The producers of this film she's got a shot at probably don't want to take on a party girl for a key role. That pushes the right button. She relents. Mission accomplished. Career implosion averted. I can live with losing out on *America Rocks* if I lose on my own merits. But to lose because of a stupid picture of a stupid joint? Not happening as long as I can head it off.

I haven't been an out-of-control mess, but I haven't been a choir boy, either. Are there more compromising photos on someone else's camera roll? I don't know, and it's everything I don't know that could put me at risk.

An inner voice that sounds ominously like my father points out, *You don't know Kendall.*

Chapter Seven

Kendall

With the sun warming my back and the sparkling, chlorinated water of the swimming pool just a few feet away, I leaf through the pages of *Cosmo*, stopping on the article, "The Career Inside You—How to Find the Perfect Job for Your Personality." Could it be that easy? Read a couple of pages and come to a realistic and more importantly, father-approved, occupation? (So far I've gotten zero response from the résumés I sent out.) I scan the bold type, searching for the magic words to help me discover what's inside my head without breaking my dad's heart. Not only am I following in his professional footsteps, I'm attending the same prestigious law school he did. More than one professor at the University of Chicago has my dad on speed dial. The dean knows stories about my father no one else does. And I'm already on the short list for Law School Musical, a group that puts on a law school parody every spring and was founded by a small group of students that included my father. It was video of my dad performing way back then that sparked my interest in theater. As a young child, I watched those annual performances over and over again, not exactly understanding the songs, but falling in love with the energy and spirit of the performers.

So it was no surprise, really, when I announced at six years old that I wanted to be an actress. TV, film, Broadway, I dreamed about doing all of it. When I was accepted to NYU, I knew I was that much closer to making my dreams a reality. Mason got accepted, too, into the film school, and aspired to be a director. We'd planned together, worked hard together, and were ready to take New York and our futures by storm. Together.

Until I ruined it.

That night changed my life forever. I gave up my dream of acting and stopped believing I could be anything I wanted to be. My so-called friends treated me like an outcast, talked about me behind my back, and looked at me with contempt. I'd wished so hard I could trade places with my boyfriend.

The magazine slips out of my hands at the thought. Wished, past tense. It took college, therapy, and an amazing friendship with Brit to help me like myself again. Turns out I'm not the only human being who's made a horrible mistake, and knowing I wasn't alone, that others got through the regret and shame and self-hatred, made living easier.

I reach over to grab the magazine then press up from my stomach so I'm sitting cross-legged on the lounge chair. A bead of sweat trickles down the middle of my chest, sliding underneath my bikini top. This afternoon, I'll resume my job search.

Dixie wanders into the backyard in nothing but miniscule black bikini bottoms, dark sunglasses, and a shimmering coat of sunscreen. She carries a large clear plastic tumbler full of some icy beverage and a notebook with a pen tucked into the spiral. A red-and-white striped beach towel I recognize from Aunt Sally's stash drapes her neck. When she catches me looking, she says, "What's a matter, princess? Never seen tits before?"

I ignore her, as I should have done all along. Silence is our friend.

She, Amber, and I have reached an unspoken truce built on the understanding that we keep to ourselves. We each have our own bedroom and bath, Dixie taking the downstairs guest room rather than her usual room where a Jack and Jill bathroom links to Amber's. Meals have been hit or miss with our own preferences for eating times. Three cars at our disposal mean we can come and go as we please. Without my aunt here to keep us connected, we've found it fairly easy to avoid one another in the six-thousand square foot space and vast city less than a mile down the road.

This afternoon, however, the only two lounge chairs in the backyard force Dixie and me into close proximity. I was here first, I remind myself. She can lug the free chair to the other side of the pool or skip the effort and go back inside the house.

Retreat's not Dixie's style, though. She settles herself on her stomach in the other chair. "You're the only freak I know who keeps her top on while lying out alone in the backyard."

"I happen to like tan lines and preserving the appearance of my skin on certain areas of my body. Especially these babies," I say, cupping my boobs. I'm at least a full cup size up on Dixie and don't mind rubbing it in.

"Bet that's the most action they've gotten since you landed in Cali."

I drop my arms. "Don't burn your nipples," I answer sarcastically.

"I won't, but I appreciate the *concern*."

At the mention of concern, my mind races to Vaughn. I've been the responsible one for four years—the friend who made breakfast for her hungover college roommates, cleared her day to help a classmate study, and stayed up all night to talk when boys behaved badly. It's my comfort zone, being the one to take an interest in others. Not that I didn't always like to take care of my friends. I did. But when you screw up so spectacularly, it becomes even more important. I want to give back a thousandfold, knowing it still will never make me even for my sin.

But last weekend, for the first time in forever, I felt *deserving* of a guy's interest. I'd melted under Vaughn's gentle touch and hard body when he draped the necklace around my neck. Craved more. I was relieved when he had to leave to catch his flight—but a small, long-dormant part of me was woken enough to register disappointment.

"What *is* with the grandma attire?" Dixie asks, interrupting my thoughts.

My white bikini is far from grandma gear. "It's called a swimsuit. You should try one sometime." Insult returned, I pick up my magazine and flip back to the article on jobs and personalities. I shove Vaughn out of my mind and focus on my goal for the summer: if I can figure out what I want to do and set a plan in motion, maybe I can avoid law school. The thought of three grueling years of academics for a career I don't want makes my stomach roil. That my dad expects me to work for his firm afterward is gut-wrenching. Will more time away from my hometown make it easier to go back? Will pretending law makes me happy bleed into my cells enough for me to completely get over breaking the law and destroying the boy I loved?

"Saving the goods for Prince Charming?"

God, she never stops. I'm not *saving* anything for anybody, including a nonexistent Prince Charming, but the careless barb hits home anyway, because the goods *have* gone unused. I'm still a virgin by choice. Still feel promised to

Mason, because when our lives irrevocably changed we were madly in love with each other.

"Since I'm blessed with the joy of your company this afternoon, I take it you've had no luck finding a bartending gig," I say. "Hard to believe nobody's fallen for your sparkling personality."

She cuts me an annoyed—and dare I think impressed—glance. "Haven't started looking yet. I put a little savings aside, so I can kick back for a minute. But don't worry. I'm perfectly capable of standing on my own two feet. Something you'd know nothing about."

"You have no clue what I've had to deal with," I fire back, pissed that she thinks she knows what it's like to walk in my shoes. "Stop thinking you're the only one who knows life's not fair." Rather than wait for her to say anything else, I jump to my feet.

The swimming pool is freezing, but I'd rather deal with cold water than a cold sister. I've attempted a swim twice already and stepped down only to the fourth step, but third time's the charm. This time, I walk over to the deep end. I stare into the tranquil blue water. Just jump, Kendall.

Just.

Jump.

Laughter—deep, masculine laughter—floats to my ears, and I look up. Beyond my aunt's beautifully kept backyard and up to the patio next door, Vaughn and another guy have walked outside. My breath catches at the sight of him. Even from a distance he makes my skin heat, my heart stop, then start. A week without any contact has done nothing to diminish this unfamiliar tug toward him.

I watch him put his hand on the railing near their pool and turn his head in my direction. Our gazes collide. I think the guy next to him is looking at me, too, but I can't say for sure, because I'm stuck on Vaughn. Tingles break out over my skin.

There's something else I can feel. Or sense? It's weird, and my heart beats faster. *On three,* Vaughn is silently saying without moving a muscle. Encouraging me to go for it. I quickly drop my gaze and shake off the weird sensation.

I pull in a deep breath and on the count of three, I dive into the water. I swim underneath, fanning my arms out in smooth, even strokes, using my legs in short, leisurely kicks. It's blissfully calm, the weightless feeling, the quiet. I forget how chilly the water is and float the last few feet to the shallow end.

Breaking the surface, I take a deep breath. The sun is quick to warm my shoulders. I dip my head back to smooth my hair away from my face then step up the stairs out of the water. Dixie pays me no attention, so in an uncharacteristic move, I flip her the double bird. It feels good. And then it doesn't. Because Vaughn claps, having caught my rude gesture, I'm guessing. I immediately drop my arms and, without looking in his direction, hurry back to my chair. I didn't think he and his friend were still there, watching. Luckily, hedges block their view of where Dixie and I are situated. "I'm so embarrassed." I palm my cheeks to hide the pinkness I'm sure is there.

"Why?" Dixie questions as she cranes her neck to see where the applause came from. "Because your bikini turns transparent in water?"

My bikini is fully lined. I know she's trying to mess with me, and yet I can't help but check myself.

She resumes scribbling in her notebook. "Who's the hottie with Vaughn?"

"I don't know." I lift up the back of the lounge chair so I can sit against it, my legs straight out in front of me.

"Of course you don't," Dixie huffs in a tone that suggests my uselessness has reached a new benchmark. She doesn't even bother looking up.

I contemplate going inside the house to hang out with Snowflake and Google help wanted ads, but I'm not about to let my sister run me off with her toxic attitude. As of this moment, I'm over letting her bother me. The warm SoCal sun is glowing, the air is citrus-fresh, and I'm free to be who and what I want for the rest of the summer.

Settling more comfortably into my chair, we sit in silence that lasts until I hear a heavy knock, the white picket side gate unlatching, and a guy call out, "Hey, mind if we join you?"

I don't recognize the voice, but then I hear *his*. "It's Vaughn," he shouts, his voice deeper than the first, and a little hesitant, like it wasn't his idea to show up here. "And my friend Dylan."

Dixie and I look at each other. My eyes feel like they're about to cannonball out of their sockets. She's half naked, for God's sake. Her eyes, on the other hand, are inscrutable behind dark glasses. I don't hear the gate close, so I think the guys are waiting for the okay. "Do we mind?" I ask quietly.

"*I* don't mind," she says, sitting up and slinging the towel around her neck again. She's covered. Barely.

"We come with libations," Dylan shouts.

"Well come on back, then," Dixie calls in return. I remind myself this is our backyard and I can relax. Vaughn might make me nervous, but I'm in control here.

"Sweet Jesus," Dylan says, looking between Dixie and me. His eyes dart to Vaughn and I'm not sure what that's about, but I don't have time to ponder it, because then he looks back at Dixie and gives her a full-wattage smile that really is dazzling. She smiles back. It's not the kind that says she's impressed. More like she's clocking his cocky game from a mile away.

"Hey," Vaughn says to Dixie with a nod before he turns to look down at me. "Hi."

"Hi," I say softly.

"This is Dylan." He gestures over his shoulder with his thumb. "Dylan, meet Kendall and Dixie."

"Great to meet you both," Dylan says. He's holding a pitcher of what looks like margaritas in one hand and some clear plastic cups in the other. "Hold this for me?" he adds, deliberately handing the pitcher to Dixie.

She takes it, giving anyone who's looking flashes of the twins. Vaughn's not looking, and his lack of interest lifts my heart dangerously close to crush level. Dylan's a different story. He grabs one of the nearby cushioned chairs, the iron feet scraping the brick while he gets comfortable next to her lounge chair.

"That spot taken?" Vaughn says. He nods right next to me, and my pulse gallops.

I've thought about him a lot this week. A. Lot. I followed him on Instagram for a glimpse into his model life—and grinned like a fool when he followed me back. Most recently, he posted a couple of pictures from his photo shoot in Miami. I posted one of me eating a hot dog from Pink's Hot Dogs. (For the record, it wasn't as good as Mo's.) Our lives are completely different. His face is on display for millions to fall in love with. He hangs out with celebrities, travels, parties. I'm most comfortable in my pajamas, savor solitude, and sometimes feel like I carry the weight of the world on my shoulders. The very last thing I want is to be on people's radar. Once upon a time I dreamed of being in the spotlight, but not anymore. Part of the reason I gave up on acting is because I value my privacy. Call me a coward, but I can't handle having my mistakes splashed around for public consumption. It's not that I don't own them—I do—but they affect more people than just me, and I never forget that.

But right here, right now, it's just us, and all Vaughn wants is a place to park his super-fine butt. Next to me. "Have a seat," I say, patting the spot. He looks too good to be true in cargo shorts and a white threadbare T-shirt that's half tucked in the front. His light brown hair is finger-combed back from his face. Stubble lines his angular jaw.

He sits, his gaze sliding over me from head to toe and back up until his eyes meet mine. "Thanks."

"Ladies, my lemon margarita. There is nothing better on a warm day." Dylan hands one to Dixie. Pours another and offers it to me.

"Oh, I don't know. I can think of one or two things to do on a summer day that hit the spot better than a cold drink," Dixie says, innuendo clearly lacing her words.

"No, thank you. I'm good," I tell Dylan.

"I knew I liked you the second I laid eyes on you," Dylan says to Dixie.

Dixie laughs. "Everyone likes me when they first lay eyes on me. But fair warning, I don't play nice."

Dylan arches a brow. "But you do play." He turns his attention to Vaughn, moving his arm so the cup he offered me is now in front of his friend. "Here, bro."

"Thanks," he says. "But I'm good, too."

"Suit yourself. Means more for us." He raises the cup, taps it to Dixie's, and then downs half the contents like it's water. When he's done, he flashes another smile. "What do you think?"

Dixie takes a small sip. "Not bad."

I stifle a laugh. Dylan has no idea Dixie is an expert at making drinks. He leans over so he's in her personal space. "I can make it better. Want me to show you how?"

"Oh, would you please? Maybe while we're naked?" Dixie's delivery is so over-the-top there's no mistaking the mockery in her voice.

He scoots back and aims a grin at Vaughn. "Oh, I *really* like this one."

"Of course you do," she says. "You think you see 'fuck me' written on my forehead in invisible ink put there just for you."

"You mean it's not?" Dylan deadpans.

"How's the house-sitting going?" Vaughn asks me with a shake of his head.

"I haven't burned down the kitchen, so good."

"Hold up," Dylan says, eyeing the oatmeal raisin cookies on the table between me and Dixie. "Those are fresh baked?"

I pick up the plate. "Yep. Would you like one?"

"Hell, yeah." He takes two. I offer them to Vaughn. He also takes two, and I wonder if these boys ever get anything homemade.

"Fuck me, these are good," Dylan says, talking with his mouth full of cookie.

Vaughn nods and when he's finished chewing says, "They're fantastic. And I don't really like raisins."

I laugh. "Maybe I'll make you some chocolate chip ones."

"By 'you,' you mean 'us,' right?" Dylan says. The puppy dog look on his face makes it hard not to like him.

"No, I meant Vaughn," I tease.

Dylan feigns a sad face then reaches for the plate. "In that case, I'll polish these off now."

Vaughn leans over, his arm brushing my shoulder, his mouth at my neck, and little shock waves race across my upper back. "Dylan grew up on reservations and takeout."

"And you?" I whisper back.

"Pretty much the same."

"I hate to break up this little foursome," Dixie says with a glance at her cell, "but I need to head out."

"Where you rushing off to, Dix?"

"Word of caution, Dyl, the last guy who called me Dix couldn't use his for a week."

Dylan leans back in his chair and with a straight face

says, "Punish me, Dix."

Dixie stands and rolls her eyes. I suck in my bottom lip to keep from laughing and peek at Vaughn. He's staring at my mouth. So of course I look at his. His lips are full, the bottom lip a little more so, and I want to slide my tongue over it and then taste inside his mouth.

I quickly turn away. "Where are you going?" I blurt out. I need something else to focus on before I fall face first into my hot neighbor. I haven't wanted to kiss anyone since Mason. *Mason.* I picture his handsome face, his smile. What does he look like now?

"Not that it's any of your business, but I've got a guitar lesson." She gathers her towel against her chest with one hand while she holds her notebook in the other and slides her feet into a pair of black flip-flops.

"You any good?" Dylan asks, propping his elbow up on the top of his chair.

"I can hold my own."

"She sings, too," I offer. She's got an amazing voice. Not that I've heard it in a while. "You ever performed at an open mic night, Dix?"

I inwardly smile as Dixie presses her lips together. See? It isn't so nice being called a name you hate. I make a mental note to bake Dylan cookies ASAP.

"I have."

"Tomorrow night. Seven o'clock. Come to The Cabana on Sunset and let's see what you've got."

"Dylan owns the club," Vaughn supplies.

"I don't take orders. Especially from bar owners." Dixie twists around to go.

"I guess you're not as talented as you think you are," Dylan says.

Dixie turns on him. "Is that a challenge?"

"Let me be straight up with you. Yes."

She studies Dylan with an intensity I have no idea how to read. "I'll be there. And just so we're clear it's because I assume there's a purse for the winner."

"There is."

"Excellent. Bye, Vaughn. It was nice to see you again."

"You, too," Vaughn says as Dixie turns and walks away.

"What? No good-bye for me?" Dylan calls, but Dixie doesn't even pause, just waves over her shoulder. He tosses a grin at us. "Oh, yeah. She wants me."

Vaughn and I laugh at the same time. Dylan picks up the margarita pitcher and cups, then stands. "Shall we continue this back at our house?" he says. "Pick up where we left off before we came over here."

"Actually, I'm going to hang back for a few and talk to Kendall. I'll catch up with you."

"Kendall," Dylan says, "it was a pleasure meeting you. Don't be a stranger. We don't bite." Then he winks and adds, "Unless you're into that kind of thing."

I give him a closed-mouth smile and a polite, "Pleasure to meet you, too," while praying he doesn't see how out of my element his teasing makes me. Would Vaughn bite me? Where? And since when do I get a secret thrill from the prospect?

Vaughn turns so we're looking squarely at each other. "Looks like you made another friend."

"You think?"

"I do. I've known the guy a long time. He's cocky as hell, but underneath all the arrogance, he's one of the best people around." The sound of the side gate banging shut echoes around the pool.

Aaand…I'm alone with Vaughn. I reach under the chair for my cover-up and slip it over my head. "What did you want to talk about?"

His lips part slightly as his gaze rakes over my body.

My cover-up is completely see-through, and his blatant appreciation raises the temperature a thousand degrees. "Are you busy tomorrow night?"

"No."

"Great. Let's go to the club together."

Like a date? The suggestion/invitation—whatever it is—sends quivers up my arm and puts fireflies in my stomach. I discreetly suck in a breath.

I haven't felt this kind of thing since high school. My friends and I used to say the boys we crushed on in our small town didn't put butterflies in our stomachs; they put fireflies because our faces would glow when we thought about them. I look down at my lap before I embarrass myself by glowing.

I can't seem to stop this attraction to him, and if I'm reading his body language right, he's attracted to me, too. I close my eyes for a second to focus on my pounding heart. My head can talk all it wants about accepting things that can't be changed and moving forward, but the heart is a different organ. My heart doesn't care about logic. It's caged in a prison of its own making, stubbornly locked up. I can't figure out how to set it free. And until I do, I shouldn't be thinking about a date or a kiss with someone else.

This awareness between us may feel good, and deep down I may want to explore it more, but I can't. I'm not ready. I'm out of my depth.

"Or not," he says when I fail to give him an answer. "I just thought I'd be neighborly."

Oh. Disappointment floods me. My own fault for taking too long to answer him.

I press my lips together, jump to my feet, and slide around to the back of the lounge chair. My fingers curl around the backrest to help steady me. "I, uh, need to head inside to do some reading."

"Reading? What kind of reading?"

"Boring law school stuff," slips out of my mouth before I can think about it.

He stands, his eyes traveling over my suddenly sensitive skin before meeting my gaze again. "You're in law school?"

"Not yet. I'm starting this fall, but there's some recommended summer reading." That I can't believe I'm even peeking at. Routine is hard to break, though. And so is the promise I made to my dad. Hot guy versus Law 101 should be a no-brainer, yet I'm doing what I do best. Keeping my distance. Keeping things safe and steady, under control.

"I admire your dedication."

I shrug. "Thanks."

"If you decide you want to go tomorrow night, let me know. I'll drive you."

"Oh, um, okay. Maybe."

Vaughn takes a small step closer. "Look, if this is because of what happened the other night, you don't need to worry. I don't make a habit of drinking and driving. You're safe with me."

But I'm not. And not for the reasons he thinks. Reasons that scare me because they're new and unexpected and I don't know if I want to feel them.

"I do want to, but I'd rather meet you there," I say firmly, gaining my composure back.

He once again studies me with an intensity that is unnerving. I'm so lost in his stare that I don't notice he's moved forward to trace his finger down my arm until I quiver. "Fair enough. But I'm going to prove you can trust me." He pulls out his cell. "Can I at least have your number in case anything changes?" I give it to him without a thought then stand there for a good five minutes after he's walked away to contemplate what he just said.

Vaughn wants a next time.

My caged heart rattles the bars.

Chapter Eight

Vaughn

"No offense to Dylan," Matt says as we approach the entrance to The Cabana, "but this place is everything I hate about clubs."

"Why?" I reach for the simple metal handle on the understated cedar-plank door tucked into the street level of a post-modern office building on Sunset.

"It's pretentious."

I open the door, raise my brows, and make a point of looking around. "What makes you say that? The velvet rope? The big-ass bouncer in a headset working the door?"

In fact, there are none of these things. There's not even a street number or awning to signify you've arrived at your destination. You just have to know. Which is why it's pretentious.

"I don't need some bullshit exclusivity to feel special."

Just inside the door, the first hostess spots us and waves us past a small group of people—mostly guys—waiting to pay the steep cover. I lead the way down a narrow hall and toss him a grin. "How about now?"

"Nope. I don't need a comped cover charge to make me feel special, either."

The hallway empties out onto something truly special—a huge open-air configuration of wood and glass cantilevered above one of the best views on the Sunset Strip. The night sky and the lights of Hollywood provide a sparkling backdrop to what looks like a rich guy's patio party. Beautiful people pack the bar, mill on the decks, and lounge on low, oversized ottomans. Those with the means or the connections occupy seating areas of silvered teak and white canvas.

Another hostess appears to welcome us to The Cabana before escorting us across the crowded main deck and up a couple steps to one of the VIP enclaves opposite the bar, but with a prime sightline to the stage. Before retreating she lifts the RESERVED sign from the table, points out the bottle service menu, and promises a server will be over soon.

Matt scans the menu and then tosses it to me. "I definitely don't need an eight-hundred-dollar bottle of Ace to feel special."

"Lucky for Dylan and the other investors, you're in the minority." The place is hopping for a Sunday night, and most of the cabanas are occupied by thirty-something dudes springing for top-shelf cocktails to impress a highly curated guest list of twenty-something girls.

My cabana-mate leans back into the deep-cushioned comfort of our L-shaped sectional, crosses his arms, and stares at the stage where open mic night is in full swing. A comedian from Boston riffs about how everyone here is all sugar-free, soy-free, gluten-free. Back home he couldn't get a blow job to save his life. Here all he has to do is slap an "organic" sticker across his balls and people line up.

It's his big finish. Most of the audience groans. A small

contingent of Boston's buddies cheer him offstage like he's the next Adam Sandler. Matt shakes his head. "What's wrong with a pool table, a jukebox, Coors on tap, and a couple flat-screens over the bar tuned to ESPN?"

Just then a trio of girls stroll by. One of them tosses her hair over her shoulder and sends him a smile. He sits a little straighter.

"So you're telling me there's *nothing* about this place you like?" I challenge.

"Huh?" His gaze drifts back to me. "All right. Fine. It's got a nice view."

"Nicer than what you find at a place with a pool table and the game on over the bar?"

"I wouldn't say that, but"—something on the other side of the club catches his eye—"it's a damn fine view."

I look to see what captured his attention, and my gaze snags on long, slender legs displayed to perfection in a short white lace skirt. Legs my deviant mind has imagined wrapped around my waist more than once. My eyes track upward. Slowly.

Kendall's hair flows to her shoulders in loose, tumbling waves, the ends skimming the lacy edge of her strapless white top. The white plays up the platinum highlights in her hair and does amazing things for her sun-kissed skin. Although she's trying to be inconspicuous in her out-of-the-way corner, she practically glows. The girl to her left doesn't help. Amber occupies that barstool, a flag of color and similarly superior genes in a little red sundress and black cowboy boots. They're both facing the stage. A quick glance down the bar tells me Matt and I are not the only guys who notice them. An instant and proprietary heat surges through me. In some secondary part of my mind I realize Dylan's approaching the table, but I'll catch him later. "Be right back," I mutter, and head to the bar.

I'm halfway there when she sees me coming. She smiles before she catches herself. Graces me with an uncensored, utterly uncalculated reaction, and for as long as it lasts I feel like the only guy in the room. She locks it down as I move closer and watches me with a cautious look that lets me know I'm still at the audition stage as far as she's concerned.

"Hey, neighbors," I say as I draw up beside her, just to emphasize we're not mere acquaintances. She's wearing the pendant I gave her, and I see that as an encouraging sign. "An invitation from management has its privileges. We've got a cabana"—I gesture toward the spot—"reserved for Team Dixie."

Dylan's there now, with Matt, and he waves us over.

Kendall aims a questioning look at Amber, who answers with raised brows that answer, *Isn't this why we're here?*

"Come on." Taking their hands, I help them from their barstools and guide them across the crowded patio to our cabana. As we walk I realize Kendall's not wearing a skirt after all, but thigh-skimming shorts in a lacy fabric. A zipper runs from just below her shoulder blades to the small of her back. It's all one piece. The sporty, sexy look works for her… and me. I imagine us alone on *my* patio, her hands braced on the railing while I lower the zipper and reveal more of her smooth, tanned back. As long as I'm imagining, I envision she begs me to keep going, and I do—until I reach pale skin never touched by the sun. Then I kiss every satiny inch. I can practically hear her calling my name in a breathless voice.

"Vaughn?"

The voice in question fills my ear now, because I've slowed my steps. She has no way of knowing how the soft prompt grabs me by the balls. Matt and Dylan stand as we approach, and I do the introductions.

"Quite a place," Amber says as she scoots to the middle of the long side of the sectional. "We don't have clubs like this in Kansas."

Matt takes the seat next to her, closest to the edge. Dylan drops in on her other side. I settle Kendall into the corner and take the spot next to her.

"We lucked out with the location," Dylan says as if the space fell into his lap rather than required months of negotiations with the building owners, but I detect a hint of pride in his tone. "If you're going to open a club in L.A., might as well embrace the things L.A. does best, right? Perfect weather, amazing views, a casual vibe, and—"

"Overpriced drinks," Matt inserts.

"We can't all live on domestic beer. Expand your horizons, dude. Besides, when you're sitting at the owner's table, drinks are on the house." Dylan signals a cocktail waitress. "Ladies, what can I get you?"

"I'm a cheap date," Kendall says. "Just water, please."

"Same," Amber pipes in. "I drove."

I haven't had a drink since yesterday afternoon, and frankly, a beer sounds good, but Kendall's refraining, so I say, "Make it three."

"Water? Seriously? Did I interrupt an AA meeting?"

"I'll have a beer," Matt says. "Domestic."

"He'll have a Heineken," Dylan tells the server, and then orders a seven and seven for himself.

Amber asks how we know each other. Matt and Dylan begin tag-teaming their way through the story any one of us could tell in our sleep.

"So Mastermind here"—Matt jerks a thumb at Dylan—"decides we ought to make a break during nap time because the ice cream truck stops at the park across the street every day and we need to get in on that. We can be gone and back before anybody notices."

"Nobody's going to notice you have ice cream?" Amber asks.

"We were four. We didn't think it through," Dylan acknowledges. "I had five bucks burning a hole in my pocket, and I knew the gate code. That's as far as I'd gotten. The teachers were chatting, so we snuck out to the play yard and climbed the slope to the back fence."

"Vaughn was the smallest of us, back then, so he was supposed to squeeze through the fence and then come around to the gate, punch in the code, and spring us," Matt explains.

"A perfect plan," Dylan adds.

"Yeah, except I couldn't squeeze through the fence."

"You mostly could, after you took my advice and streamlined your wardrobe. I solved 90 percent of that problem."

"Yeah, a 90 percent solution that left me stuck in a fence, naked."

"Oh, no..." Amber's show of sympathy doesn't quite hide her amusement. Kendall doesn't even pretend not to laugh.

"You weren't *naked*," Dylan corrects. "You had your Spiderman underwear on. And how is it my fault you lodged that big coconut you call a head between the slats?"

"What happened?" Kendall asks.

"He started to freak, so we tried to work him free," Matt continues. "I grabbed his arm. Dylan pulled his head, and—"

"And this ungrateful little punk pushes me down the hill," Dylan supplies, eyes on me.

"You were breaking my neck, motherfucker. I told you to stop."

"Anyway, Dylan rolls down the hill and 'passes out.'" Matt makes air quotes around the words.

"I had a concussion."

"You had a bruise, Humpty. Meanwhile, I'm the last one standing, so I have to man up and get help. A trend that continues to this day, since Mastermind likes to snooze through any accountability whatsoever, and Pretty Boy usually ends up in his underwear with a bunch of ladies fussing over him."

"You're the hero." Amber smiles up at him.

"Always." He grins back at her.

"Could I trouble you for an act of heroism and ask you to point me in the direction of the ladies' room?" she asks.

He slides out of the seat. "I'll show you."

"Hey, if it weren't for me, you two losers would never have any fun," Dylan says as Matt leads Amber away. Then he mutters, "Oh, fuck," and practically vaults over the table. "Back in a sec," he says before he cuts through the crowd to a pair of girls making their way toward our cabana. I didn't even notice them, but very little of what happens at The Cabana escapes Dylan's notice. For sure not the arrival of two of Becca's girlfriends who side-hustle as a walking pharmacy. He can't have them dealing shit in here. Not unless he wants to spend the foreseeable future with vice cops and DEA crawling up his ass. But he's also smooth as ice, which is why they're all now standing together laughing. Rather than blocking their path, it looks like he's just really excited to greet them. The guy can muster up some convincing acting skills when he needs to.

"You know, you don't have to hang out here with me..."

Very convincing acting skills, apparently. I turn to Kendall. "I'm exactly where I want to be. They're Dylan's friends." I throw him under the bus without hesitation.

The tall brunette beckons me over with a smile and a wave.

"You sure? Looks like they're your friends, too. I can fend for myself until Amber gets back."

She sounds indifferent, but her expression doesn't quite match her tone. The casual smile tries to tell me she's cool either way, but her eyes? Her gaze clings to me like she's hoping I don't leave.

I'm not going anywhere. I rest my arm along the seat back and prop my ankle on my knee. "I'm not Dylan's wingman. He knows why I came here tonight. Matt knows. I'd venture a guess even Amber knows. You're the only one who doesn't seem to know, so I'm going to spell it out for you."

She holds up her hand. "You don't owe me any explanations—"

"Kendall"—I take her hand and thread our fingers together—"I came here tonight to be with *you*."

Those guileless blue eyes narrow. "Why?"

The one-word question sounds like a challenge, and I'm more than up for it. "Because I like you. Because we're neighbors. Because members of the Speed Racer Live Action Movie Fan Club need to stick together. There aren't very many of us."

"True."

"And because you bake the shit out of oatmeal raisin cookies, and now I'm driven to see if this thing between us could lead to…you know…"

Golden eyebrows practically disappear into her hairline.

"…chocolate chip cookies."

A smile accompanied by a little laugh tells me I've passed her test. "I guess that *might* be arranged."

I know an advantage when I hold one, so I keep talking. "Besides, fate brought us together. Who are we to question the magic?"

She laughs again. "I hate to burst your bubble, but I don't believe in fate. My aunt's invitation to house-sit brought us together."

"And you were available. That's fate."

Her smile fades and gives way to a frown. She sighs and pushes a hand through her hair. "Not exactly. More like a chance to—" Her voice cuts off, like she caught herself before she shared something she didn't mean to.

"A chance to what?" I gently prod. She can't leave me hanging.

"Think."

Five little letters can carry some serious weight. Every ounce of it lands in the center of my chest.

"Kendall…"

She pulls her hand free and drops it to her lap. "Sorry. It's not really as deep and dark at it sounds."

"Explain it to me." I may come off like a guy who has no worries, but I know a thing or two about deep, dark thoughts.

"I'd rather—"

"Don't say 'not' because I'm not letting you off the hook," I interrupt. Somehow we took a left turn into a minefield. This conversation stresses her out, but I want to fix it. I pick up her hand, interlock our fingers again, and hope that simple gesture of support removes some of the pressure. The house lights dim a notch, as if to help me out. *No such thing as fate, huh?*

"I wanted to be here instead of home for the summer before I start law school," she says, devoid of emotion.

Ahh. It's a parental thing. I get that, too. "Say no more." I squeeze her hand. "And good call. Spending the summer in the city of dreams is the perfect way to blow off steam before buckling down for three years of cutthroat paper-chase."

She looks at me for a long time, and my gut tenses. I don't know why, but before I can figure it out her gaze shifts. The server appears with our drinks. Matt's close behind. When she sets them on the table he drops a twenty on her tray as a tip and slides into his seat. "Where's our host?"

I glance back to where Dylan stood a couple minutes ago, but the girls are gone and so is he. "Duty called."

"Duty done," Dylan says, and bounces up the steps. "Scoot in, bitch. Where's Amber?"

Matt scoots a couple stingy inches and takes a sip of his

beer. "I left her at the head of the line for the ladies' room."

"Well, damn. Hopefully she's back soon. Dixie's up."

Sure enough, a smattering of applause breaks out as the spotlight follows a solitary figure to the center of the stage. She sits on the single stool, settles her guitar in her lap, and adjusts the microphone. Then she dips her chin and looks out at the crowd. The light catches her blue eyes. "Oh fuck," she says with a smile. "Not another girl with a guitar." The room quiets fractionally and a few people laugh. So far she's funnier than the comedian.

Dylan whistles loudly and yells, "Go Dix!"

She glances right and then left. "At this moment we're all tortured by the same questions. Can she sing? Can she play?" The observation earns her a few more laughs. "Let's put those to bed right now."

She props the guitar a little higher in her lap and launches into the opening chords of something rhythmic and bluesy. Two quick strums followed by the reverberation of a longer, lower chord, and then a repeat. It's nice. She can play. A hum of conversation resumes as people comment or try to name the tune. Then a voice ambushes the guitar, and six simple strings can't contain the rage of longing, lust, and despair Dixie unleashes as she laments the love on her brain. Conversation—hell, everything in the room—stops. All eyes fix on the stage. Her voice is amazing, the kind that raises the tiny hairs on my arms. The kind that could win *America Rocks*. Her gaze moves downward as she adds quiet, subtle notes from the guitar and proves she's got talent there, too. Beside me, Kendall whispers, "She's even better than I remember."

"She's great," I whisper back. Dixie owns the shit out of the song and the room. A few people break the quiet of a pause with whistles and claps, but quickly quiet so we can hear everything she's got. Her fingers dance over the guitar strings and motivate some couples to do the same.

Kendall gently sways in her seat. My mouth finds her ear. "Dance with me."

She shakes her head before she stammers. "That's okay."

"Okay?" I gesture to myself. "Five years of dance lessons, Kendall. Hip-hop, ballroom, and for reasons I'll never understand, tap. Trust me, it's way better than okay."

Her teeth press into her bottom lip, a second passes, then another, before she nods. She's still reluctant, but I'll do my best to take care of her. I pull us to our feet, lead her down the stairs, and wrap my arms around her waist. With no good alternative, she props her arms on my shoulders and clasps her hands at the back of my neck. She's a little stiff at first, but I find the beat and move us to the slow tempo. She falls into rhythm with me after a few seconds, and her body relaxes against mine. The heels put her at an ideal height. Our hips line up. Her breasts rest against my chest. I press her a little closer, because I can't resist, and she doesn't resist, either. She stares at my throat for a while but finally tips her head back and looks at me.

The song flows around us, and the room disappears.

"Hey," I whisper as I run my hand over the bare expanse of her shoulders.

She shivers. "Hi."

"Want to know a secret?"

"Sure."

"Last year I helped set the record for the longest Conga line. I was in Miami for a shoot and nearly 12,000 people Conga-ed."

Her eyes sparkle with amusement. "How fun, but not very secretive."

"It's a secret from Dylan and Matt. If they found out, they'd give me shit forever."

She chuckles. "I've never been in a Conga line, but I am

pretty good at the moonwalk."

I grin. "I'm going to need proof."

"Maybe someday."

"I'm adding it to my Summer Adventures with Kendall list. Chocolate chip cookies and verification of moonwalk skills." This girl brings out the easy, unworried side of me, and I like it.

She lets out a breath. "I actually haven't danced since high school."

Before I can ask her why, the last notes fade, the lights come up, and the room erupts in applause. Dixie smiles, says "Thanks" into the mic, and strides off the stage.

Kendall pulls her phone from the pocket of her shorts and bites her lip as she reads the screen. "Amber wants me to meet her outside. I better see what's up." She sends me the beginnings of a *see-you-around* smile.

"I'll go with you." I make the proposal over the noise of the standing ovation—like everyone in the place is endorsing my suggestion—and take her hand to lead her through the press of bodies. Amber will need a minute to work her way through the crowd, and I'll get some time alone with Kendall. Maybe enough time to convince her to let me drive her home? And maybe, once she's in my car, I can convince her to let me do more? I'm getting way ahead of myself, I know, but my chest still tingles from the weight of her breasts, her fingers feel right threaded through mine, and the sway of her hips as she walks the darkened hallway to the exit makes me imagine her walking into my bedroom. She turns and gives me a shy smile over her shoulder, and I wonder if she overheard my thoughts.

Or maybe she's having thoughts of her own? I'd love to know what's going on in her mind. I want her, but it's more than a knee-jerk physical reaction to long legs in short shorts, or blond hair streaming over bare shoulders. I want *her.*

The girl who brags about moonwalking but hasn't danced in a while, who can make a split-second decision to rescue a neighbor, but needs the entire summer to think. The girl who's off to law school in the fall.

But she's here for now, and if she put me at the top of her Summer Adventure list, I'd happily dedicate the next few months to making her very glad she did.

Will she let me? Her eyes find mine as I hold the door open and she steps out into the warm Hollywood night. I think she might. Not because I'm the guy on the Times Square billboard. She saw past the illusion of picture-perfect Vaughn Shaughnessy about five seconds after tackling me, and for some reason she's still looking. As we move toward the sidewalk, she slips her hands into her pockets and brings her shoulders up toward her ears in body language that says, *So…here we are. I want to talk about where we could go.*

We move to the edge of the sidewalk to avoid blocking the door, but it's not quite ten p.m. on a Sunday night, so the sidewalk is pretty much ours. A young guy in a red vest loiters by the valet stand, staring at his phone. His eyes drift up to check Kendall out.

I don't blame him. She's fucking luminous. Gold from the streetlight rains down on her hair and gilds her skin. Yet another unfamiliar territorial impulse takes root in my gut. I want to punch this jerk just for looking at her.

Instead I give in to an admittedly unevolved urge to stake a claim. I close in, crowding her until she's backed up against a parking meter, and I'm blocking her from his view.

Something winks at me from just above the tempting line where flesh disappears beneath lace, and my focus drops to the diamond in the center of her pendant. I trace my fingertip along the chain, touching the smooth skin of her chest at the same time, sending any bystanders a clear, if not strictly truthful message: this is mine.

Kendall shivers as my finger draws closer to the pendant nestled in the vulnerable little dip demarking the start of her cleavage, and I know without glancing at her that we're both watching my progress. I'm sure she's got something on beneath the silky top with its delicate lace edge, but whatever it is doesn't hide much, because her nipples rise against the fabric. Her breath comes out in an unsteady rush. My throat tightens as I fantasize about scraping my tongue over one of those stiff little peaks. Imagine the sensation of her nails scouring my scalp. Savor the vibration of her soft, appreciative moan.

I cup her jaw and tip her face to mine. Her eyes stay lowered and locked on my mouth. Her hands come up to wrap around my wrists.

"Kendall?"

"I…I can't." She closes her eyes and turns her face away. "I'm sorry."

I rest my forehead against her temple for a second and let the disappointment subside to acceptance. Then I take a step back and put my hands in my pockets. "Sorry wasn't what I was going for, but, since you are, the apology should probably be my line. Did I misread—?"

"No." She meets my stare squarely. "It's not you. It's… me." As soon as the cliché leaves her mouth, she groans. "Oh, God. Erase. Rewind. Delete. I can't believe I just said that."

"Said what?"

We both give a small smile.

"It really is me. I… It's complicated, but you didn't do anything wrong, and you definitely don't owe me an apology. I had fun tonight. More fun than I expected, thanks to you. I guess I got a little swept off my feet."

"Then we're even," I joke. "You swept me off my feet before we even said hello." Immediately I wonder why I opened my big mouth and mentioned the fucked-up first impression I made.

"It's not often I get to show off my superhuman strength."

I appreciate her returning the joke, but beneath all the banter, I'm confused. What makes the attraction between us complicated? Because the way she was looking at me and responding to my touch? Nothing about that felt complicated. I'm trying to find the right way to ask without coming off like some douche who can't take no for an answer when the club door swings open with a whisper, followed by the unsteady clomp of boots on concrete.

"Hey. Oh, sorry. I didn't mean to interrupt."

I turn to see Amber searching through her tiny purse for her valet ticket. Her face is pale and coated with a sheen of sweat that's left the hair at her temples damp and her mascara smudged.

Kendall moves around me, all thoughts about our moment seemingly gone. "What's wrong? Did something happen?"

Amber lets out a breath and hands her ticket to the valet. "I'm okay. Just got overheated in there and"—her eyes dart away—"a little queasy. This is what I get for eating day-old pizza for lunch."

"I'm sorry," Kendall says.

She waves away her sister's concern. "I'll be okay. I wanted to tell you I'm heading home. There's no reason to cut your night short, though, if you've got another way home." Her gaze jumps to me.

"I can drive you both," I offer, because I hate the idea of Kendall slipping away from me with all the unanswered questions like a roadblock between us. All I know for sure is she's definitely not sticking around. They may not be the closest siblings on the planet, but she's not staying while Amber heads off on her own, looking like death.

"No."

The word comes out in stereo from both sisters, loud enough to be heard over the purr of Sally's Jaguar pulling to the curb.

Amber offers a wobbly smile. "I know it's only a couple miles, but I don't know if my stomach's going to cooperate for the entire drive. I really, really don't want to be the girl who throws up in front of Vaughn Shaughnessy."

"You wouldn't be the first—"

"I'll drive us home," Kendall insists. She's in guardian angel mode as she walks to the driver's side and holds out a tip for the valet. But this time it's her sister she's looking after.

I help Amber into the passenger seat, close the door, and then lean in the lowered window. "Feel better soon."

"I will," she promises.

I glance over at Kendall. "Good night."

"'Night," she says around a small, apologetic smile before pulling away.

I stand there, rooted to my spot, watching the car's taillights disappear into the stream of traffic on Sunset. I'm not sure what just happened between us, but one thing is crystal clear. Kendall's not playing hard to get.

She *is* hard to get.

Chapter Nine

Kendall

"Ohmigod! This is excellent," Brit says, her face filling the screen of my phone. "I'm proud of you, K. Last time we talked I wasn't sure you'd put yourself out there."

"I don't know what I'm doing," I tell her, more confused than ever about Vaughn. Sunlight streams into the kitchen. Flour, butter, sugar, blueberries, and my secret crumbly topping make a mess of the counter.

"What you're doing is moving on, and the next time Vaughn touches your face or slides his fingertips anywhere on you, you're going to kiss the bejesus out of him. Got it?"

"It's not that—"

"Easy? Yes it is." Her argument is easier to swallow with the compassion in her big brown eyes. "You're single, K. He's single. There is no reason not to have a summer fling. Take it from an expert, he is into you." Her eyes soften even more. "It's time you let yourself off the hook for what happened with Mason."

She's been telling me this for years, but no one can absolve me but me. Memories and feelings, good and bad, are a powerful bitch to deal with.

I continue to plate the blueberry muffins I baked this morning when I couldn't sleep, caught up in thoughts of Vaughn's hands on me.

I want them on me again.

Everywhere. My body is on fire just thinking about him holding my waist while we danced. Goosebumps rise on my skin when I relive the sensation of his fingers grazing my neck as he sought the pendant practically nestled between my breasts.

"You're blushing," Brit says. "Hallelujah, there is a guy out there who can steal your resolve."

He's a thief of more than that, stealing my decision, my composure, and what I thought was best for me. Still. I'm just here for the summer, and I've never been the kind of girl to have a fling. Throwing caution to the wind comes at a cost, I've learned. A high one, and I've already incurred and inflicted more than I can handle in one lifetime.

"Maybe..." I relive his touch, his smile, our rapport... "Maybe there is." Temptation, for the first time ever, lives next door, and whenever I look into his eyes, nothing is normal for me.

The oven timer *ding*s, signaling the next batch of muffins is done. "I say you take some of those muffins over to him this morning," Brit suggests.

"You think?"

"Do it. Now, before you talk yourself out of it. I've got to run, literally, or I'll be late for work again, but text me later and tell me how it went, okay?"

"Okay."

"Promise me you're going right to his house after we hang up."

"Promise."

"Okay. Love you!"

"Love you, too."

Promise me. Growing up I was a huge Winnie the Pooh fan. I still am, actually. For our six month anniversary, Mason gave me a framed picture of Pooh and Piglet with the words:

Promise me you'll always remember:
You're braver than you believe,
and stronger than you seem,
and smarter than you think.

It's my favorite quote. I lean on the kitchen counter, close my eyes, and say the words again in my head. I was already in love with Mason, but I fell even harder for him that night. A piece of my heart will always be his.

"I can do this," I tell Snow, who is asleep under the kitchen table. Permission. Courage. A promise I can keep to my best friend.

I took off quickly last night, flustered by Vaughn's attention and anxious to get Amber home, so this is a good way to reconnect.

Two minutes later, I walk up Vaughn's driveway with a plate of warm muffins. The closer I get to his front door, the faster my pulse races. *Chill, Kendall.*

Dancing with him flashes through my mind again, the pounding of my heart as our bodies lined up. Even though the club was crowded it felt like we were the only two people in the room. For the few minutes we were pressed together I was so lost in the moment I forgot about my past. Wrapped in Vaughn's arms, it didn't feel like a betrayal. It felt right, like the first step toward whatever comes next.

I'm almost up the drive when I hear a car behind me. It's a black convertible Mercedes, and an older man is driving. He parks, hops out of the car, and raises his sunglasses so they sit on top of his head. “This is private property.” He’s dressed in a suit and tie and carries a definite air of impatience.

“I know. I’m here to see Vaughn.”

“Who are you with? Do you have an appointment?”

His tone is gruff, his stance intimidating. Worse, I don’t fully understand what he’s asking. “Who am I with?” I look around the otherwise empty driveway. “Myself?”

“Who reps you, or who do you rep?” He snaps, and hands me a card. “I’m Vaughn’s manager. Any requests need to go through me.”

That explains his terse manners. His gaze sweeps over my heather gray T-shirt dress and flip-flops, assessing me like this is an audition. By the frown on his face I’d say I don’t make the cut. What a jerk. “I’m not here on business,” I say, ignoring the card. “I’m a friend.” I turn to continue toward the front door.

“Not so fast.” He falls in step beside me, but his legs are longer and he turns on me. It isn’t threatening, but protective, and I guess I understand. He doesn’t know me. I could be a stalker. “We have a busy morning,” he says. “Is Vaughn expecting you?”

Shit. “No.”

“Didn’t think so. I’ll tell him you stopped by…” He trails off, eyebrows raised.

“Kendall.”

“His friend Kendall.” He says this like he doubts I’m telling the truth. He has no intention of mentioning me at all.

“Yes.” There is no way I’m getting inside the house, so I add, “Can you please give him these?” I thrust the plate in my hands forward.

He glances at the muffins like they’re poisoned apples.

“Please,” I repeat. His manners may be awful, but mine aren’t.

With obvious reluctance, he takes the plate. “Have a nice

day." He doesn't spare me another word or glance. He turns on his heels and strides away, his fancy black dress shoes clicking on the stamped concrete.

Wow. Guess I've been dismissed.

"Thank you," I call out before he slams the front door behind him.

What an ass.

My aunt's house is really quiet when I walk back into the kitchen, so when my phone rings a minute later, I startle and almost drop the glass bowl I'm rinsing. The only person who calls instead of texts is my mom, and, since we usually talk on Sundays, worry that something is wrong floods me. I grab the phone without looking at the screen. "Hello?" I say tentatively.

"Hey, it's Vaughn."

"Hi." I sit on a barstool for fear my legs aren't strong enough to keep me upright. Because holy jalapeno pepper, his morning voice is a little rough and super sexy, and I can't believe he actually called.

"Thanks for the muffins. They smell almost as good as you do."

My cheeks are on fire. And I'm shocked his manager actually gave them to him. "You're welcome. How are you?"

"Besides being pissed at my dad for sending my delivery girl home, I'm good."

"That was your *dad*?"

"Dad, manager, and self-appointed gatekeeper. I didn't know you were here or I would have put him on a leash."

"I could…" I'm about to say "come back over" but stop myself. His father is there for a reason, and he definitely wouldn't appreciate seeing me again. "…stop by later."

"How about this weekend? I've got a booking in Paris this week and my dad is driving me to the airport in a few, but we're having a barbecue Saturday afternoon. You and your sisters should come."

Me *and* my sisters.

"Umm…"

"Would it help persuade you if I said it was my birthday?"

"Is it?"

"Yes."

"How old are you going to be?"

"Twenty-four. I'm a Cancer. Which means I'm loyal, dependable, caring, and responsible. Convinced now?"

"Okay." It's not like we know anyone else around here or have an excess of party invites. And if something comes up, I doubt we'll be missed.

"Okay you believe me or okay you'll be here?"

"Both." How can I say no to his birthday? I don't want to say no. I'm just anxious, out of my comfort zone again.

"Great." I hear some rustling through the phone line, of clothes maybe. "I've got to go," he continues. "I'll see you this weekend. Thanks again for breakfast." He clicks off and I'd bet a million dollars I'm glowing like the sun on steroids.

"What's with your face?" Dixie asks, padding into the kitchen in her bare feet and a faded T-shirt that falls to the tops of her thighs.

"What's with yours?" I fire back.

She ignores my weak comeback and lifts a blueberry muffin out of the pan sitting on the counter. She breaks it in half, a tiny bit of steam billowing out. "I'm always happy when I'm five hundred bucks richer. Unlike you, princess, I actually have to pay my way."

The stone she threw lands in the pit of my stomach, but at the same time, I'm thrilled for her. "You won open mic night?"

"I did. You'd know that if you'd stuck around to celebrate with me and our hot neighbors." Her eyes meet mine, but the sharpness of her gaze has given way to something else.

Something she's not telling me. "How's Amber?"

"Bunkered. She went straight to her room when we got home, and I haven't seen her since. Maybe we should check on her?"

"One of us should." She takes a bite of the muffin. "I nominate you. People don't find me comforting."

I can't argue with that, but her brusque response doesn't quite hide the fact that she just expressed concern for our sister. She knows it. I know it. She knows I know it. Fighting a *gotcha* smile the entire time, I plate up a muffin before rounding the breakfast bar and heading out of the room.

I climb the stairs two at a time to check on Amber.

"Come in," she says after I knock on her door.

"Hey, how are you feeling?"

"Eh," she says from the comfort of her bed. She's leaning against the headboard, reading something on her laptop. Or she was. She minimizes her screen as I enter all the way.

"Need anything? I made blueberry muffins."

She shakes her head. "No thanks. Best keep your distance so you don't get whatever it is."

Sounds selfless, but it's a brush-off. We've lived under the same roof for two weeks. I went home with her last night. Whatever bug she's picked up, I've already been exposed to it, so she's trying to keep me away for her own reasons. "Do you want to see a doctor? Google says there's an urgent care a few miles away. Dixie or I could drive you."

"I will if I don't bounce back soon, but I'm already feeling a little better. Just tired. Right now all I really want to do is rest."

Hint taken. I leave the muffin on the dresser and escape her room almost as fast as I did the kitchen. Getting dismissed by Vaughn's dad who doesn't know me from Eve is one thing, but getting dismissed by my own sister stings—especially after I was there for her last night, but whatever. A couple of weeks together in Los Angeles hasn't suddenly made us best friends. I hurry to my room, change into better shoes, and slip out of the house to go for a walk. A solo walk. Snowflake is annoyed with me, but I'll take her out later. I've taken to long treks down the hill to search for help wanted signs in windows, grab a coffee, and let the sights and sounds of the city occupy my thoughts. On my dog walks, I tend to think about the fall and law school and how increasingly unappealing I find that life plan the closer it gets. The same trio of questions rotating in my mind…

When is a decision a fact that can't be undone?

Is it too late for me?

Can I convince myself to take a chance on change?

Chapter Ten

Kendall

Snowflake is walking me. Seriously. She is the leader and I'm the girl being pulled by her leash. It's crazy how strong she is. Determined. Even at ten o'clock at night. You'd think she'd do her business and be ready for bed, but no. Not Snow. She struts up the sidewalk like she's on a mission to save the neighborhood from nocturnal wrongdoings.

Her tenacity is a great Friday night distraction even though over the past week I've graduated from thoughts about my future to thoughts about the present.

And a certain guy next door.

When the sidewalk meets the end of his driveway, Snowflake's body shakes with excitement. She tugs harder on the leash, eager, it seems, to race to his front door. I look up the sloped drive to see if someone's home and find Vaughn walking toward us.

"Hey, neighbor," he says. He's wearing white-washed jeans, a black T-shirt that hugs his chest and biceps, and no shoes. And I think he's been drinking.

"You're back from Paris."

"Either that or I'm a hologram." He smiles. It's a slightly lopsided smile—as if his lips aren't fully on board with the command from his brain—and incredibly endearing.

I look around for signs of what's going on, but his house is quiet. Thankfully I don't hear the clanking of keys or see any in his hand.

"What are you doing?" I ask.

He comes to a stop in front of me and Snow. She goes berserk, twisting the leash so that I let go. "Hey, Snowflake." He bends to pet her and falls back onto his butt. She climbs into his lap and smothers his angular jawline in kisses.

"Were you going somewhere?" I ask.

He looks up at me, tired, and oddly vulnerable. "I was headed to your house," he says quietly.

Oh. I sit down on the ground next to him, lift Snow off his lap, and put her on the other side of me. "Stay." She huffs but drops to her belly, her little face atop her front paws. "What for?"

"For better company than another beer could provide." He lays back, eyes to the sky, hands laced behind his head, his knees bent.

"I'm better company than twelve ounces of fermented hops?"

The question pulls a laugh out of him. "It was imported, if that helps."

Now I laugh. "That makes *all* the difference." I lie down beside him. The ground is a little cool, but the air is warm, a slight breeze upping the humidity and carrying the scent of jasmine. The sky is overrun with stars hanging out with a half moon.

"Here." He sits up, reaches behind his neck to pull off his shirt, then balls it up to tuck under my head as a pillow. Dead.

I'm dead. His muscles flex as he resumes his position. I try not to stare at his ripped abs.

"Thanks."

"Welcome."

We stay like that, side by side in comfortable silence, for a minute or two. In the distance, I hear the faint sounds of traffic on Sunset.

"Can I trust you?" he finally says, like it's taken Herculean effort to get the words out.

"You can."

He doesn't move or speak.

"I promise."

"A story in *Variety* came out today about me being one of the people the *America Rocks* producers are considering to take over as host."

"Oh my God!" I turn my face toward him. "That's a really big deal. Congratulations." *America Rocks* is my favorite reality show.

"It's not mine yet, and according to Hollywood insiders the producers would be idiots to give me the gig."

"Why?"

He lifts his hand to tick off the reasons. "Model-turned-host works only if it's a fashion competition, I'm too young, I've got a not-totally-unearned reputation for partying, I don't have the right experience, and..."

I turn onto my side to look at him. My cheek is on the soft cotton of his T-shirt, and it smells like man and spice and everything nice. He remains in profile. "And?"

"I'm a second-stringer, even in my own family. My sister was the true star. This is just an attempt by my manager-slash-father to reclaim some of her glory, and"—he takes a deep breath before continuing—"and I know I have to get used to haters if I'm going to continue in this business, because they're part of the deal, but sometimes they hit really low."

My heart immediately hurts for him. I want to tell him he's a star no matter what happens with *America Rocks.* I want to ask about his sister, but I don't think that's what he needs right now. God, it sucks being picked apart like you don't have any feelings and judged unworthy. I know firsthand, and I never want to go through the ordeal again. But when it happened to me, the thing I appreciated most was a change of subject.

"So, I ate fried chicken and waffles this week and I didn't think anything could beat a New York City hot dog, but oh my God, was it good."

He rolls onto his side, props his head in his hand. His smile is crooked and raises goosebumps on my arms. "You went to Roscoe's."

"I did. And guess what else?"

"What?"

"I got a side of gravy to go with it."

His green-eyed gaze stops my breath for a second. "Don't look at me like that."

"How am I looking at you?"

"I don't know. Like you'd miss me if I walked away."

"I will."

Will. Not would. Because we both know my stay is temporary. I roll back onto my back, my head nicely cushioned thanks to him. "I'm sorry about the stupid story."

"Thanks."

"Did you go to college?" I ask out of the blue. I mean, I did just graduate, and I'm scheduled to start again in September so it's a valid conversation topic.

"I enrolled for a semester, but I started getting more bookings around the same time. Between shoots and travel, it was impossible."

"I imagine that's a cool education itself."

He's still on his side, still staring at me. I hope he doesn't notice the quick rise and fall of my chest as I continue to stare at the sky. "Yeah."

We're quiet once again. Out of my periphery, I notice him yawn. I'm about to tell him good night when he says, "Do you think if you could redo your bad days, it would make you a different person?"

His question makes me feel like I've been pushed out of an airplane without a parachute. I take a few freefalling seconds to contemplate what's he's asked. What I wouldn't give to erase the worst day of my life. To have Mason back. But am I changed because of it? I've felt shame and regret, and on some days my feelings have shredded my insides. Yet who I am is the same, I think.

I roll my head to make eye contact, but his are closed. "I don't know," I whisper.

"Me either."

"I should get Snowflake back." At the sound of her name, she perks up.

"All right. See you later."

"Should we walk you to your door first?"

The corner of his mouth lifts. "Nah. I'll get up in a minute. I'm good to make it inside."

"Thank you for the shirt." I kiss his cheek.

That gets his eyes to open. And once again it's like he can see right inside me. I hurry to my feet, picking up Snow's leash. "Happy almost-birthday."

I don't wait for a reply. I speed-walk away, feeling his attention on my backside. When I get to my room, I change into my pajamas, crawl into bed, and fall asleep with flutters in my stomach.

• • •

Saturday afternoon I hurry downstairs to head to Vaughn's

party. Halfway down I realize I forgot his gift, and I turn to get it but find Amber at the top of the stairs. She takes in my white crocheted slip dress and shell-studded flip-flops and fiddles with one buckle of the vintage denim overalls she's layered over a ribbed white tank top. They swim on her, so she's rolled the legs to mid-calf. Well-loved white Chucks cover her feet. "I thought it was a barbecue," she says.

I nod. "It is."

She fingers the brim of her KU blue and crimson ball cap. "Maybe I'm underdressed for an L.A. barbecue?"

"You're both *over*dressed."

I twist to find Dixie standing at the foot of the stairs, wearing a tiny red bikini top—the kind held on by a tie around the neck and one at the back—and ripped cutoffs so short the front pocket linings hang past the frayed denim, and so baggy they show off matching red bikini bottoms. She's holding a bottle of tequila and shaking her head like Amber and I are hopeless. "Get real, girls. Between the temperature and the drinks, everybody'll be in the pool in an hour."

With that pronouncement, she turns and strides to the door. The bikini is definitely a thong. I follow but glance back at Amber and murmur, "Don't take fashion cues from a girl dressed like a Baywatch extra." I glance down at my outfit and sincerely hope every other girl there isn't in a bikini. "Or one who might be trying too hard. You nailed it. You look cute and casual. And besides," I add as I pull the door closed behind us, "you're a ten-second walk back here for your suit if you decide to swim."

"You look great," Amber offers. "The dress suits you. It's summery and fun, but, you know"—she tips her head toward Dixie's all-but-bare back and gives me a grin of pure mischief—"still leaves a little to the imagination."

"Imagine this," Dixie says, and flips us the middle finger over her shoulder. "You're just jealous of my bikini."

Amber laughs. "Dixie, I may, on occasion, be jealous of your perky B cups, but I promise I don't envy the bikini." In a not-so-subtle aside to me she says, "I couldn't wear that thing even if I wanted to. I'd never get my boobs strapped into a triangle top."

Though we have different maternal genes to thank for it, we're in a similar situation in the boobage department. I give her a smile of commiseration. "Me, either."

"You two kill me," Dixie huffs. "Making everybody wonder, 'Will they or won't they?' is totally the *point* of wearing a triangle top."

Cars are parked bumper to bumper in the driveway next door. The steady beat of music beneath the ebb and flow of conversation confirm we're not too early. Both grow a little louder when Vaughn opens the front door.

"Hello, Birthday Boy," Dixie says, handing him the bottle of tequila.

He hears her, because he takes the alcohol, but his eyes are locked with mine. "Happy birthday," I say, then realize that damn it, I forgot his present. I'm about to tell him I'll be right back, but the way he's looking at me makes all my limbs forget how to work, and I'm frozen to my spot. Amber rescues me by murmuring, "Happy birthday from me, too," and handing him a small wrapped box she produces from a pocket of her overalls. "It's a Jayhawks bottle stopper. In case you have leftover tequila."

"Thanks." He spares a quick glance at my sisters. Then, with his eyes back on me, says, "Come on in."

Dixie goes first, and then Amber, because I'm still kind of stuck, but finally my feet get the memo and I step inside Vaughn's house for the first time. It's sleek and modern. Definitely some designer's idea of a bachelor pad, but not a reflection of Vaughn's personality if you ask me. I have this sudden flash of Becca standing by the low-slung leather sofa in some Armani/Casa showroom, saying, “This would be perfect for the living area.”

“Dix!” Dylan calls from a slider leading outside. “Get that sweet ass of yours out here and tell me what you think of my peach daiquiri. You too, Ginger.”

“Ginger?” Amber questions. “Since when am I Ginger?”

Dixie rolls her eyes. “Since birth. Come on.” She takes Amber’s arm and heads toward the epicenter of the party. It looks like a big crowd—heavy on the X chromosome—is on the back patio.

Vaughn leans forward to say something in my ear, but the doorbell rings and he pulls back. He hesitates for a second like he’s considering making a run for it and having whoever is at the door let themselves in, but his hosting duties kick in. “Give me a minute?”

I nod. He can have all my minutes.

The group of new arrivals looks like *High School Musical the College Years*, and Vaughn is quickly swept up into their momentum. He tosses me an apologetic glance and a one-more-minute signal with his index finger as he’s led away. I wave my arm to let him know it’s okay. It is his birthday party, after all.

Left on my own, I’m tempted to keep to myself and take a look around. I’m given no such luck when Dylan pops back into the house, notices me still in the entryway, and shouts, “Kendall! We’ve run dry. Bring your sexy self over here and help me make another pitcher.”

I laugh. He waits until I’m in motion, as if he knows better than to trust me, before he steps away. I come upon the kitchen to find him grabbing a bowl of fresh peaches. He tosses his free arm around my shoulders. “Let’s go, babe, you’re up next.”

We step outside onto a large redwood deck. The sun is low in a violet-crimson sky, but the air is warm and summery.

Dylan keeps hold of me until we reach a built-in bar with a blue-flecked granite countertop. "This is Kendall," he says to the friends gathered there.

"Hi." I give a quick wave. "Hellos" ring out in return.

The blender whirrs, and a minute later I'm handed a glass filled to the rim. Dylan says, "Here. Tell me that's not the best damn daiquiri you've ever tasted."

"I'm sure it's great. It's just that—"

"Come *on*, Midwest. It's Vaughn's birthday. You accepted the invite, which means you're duty bound to celebrate."

Even without hours of mandatory alcohol awareness classes under my belt, I'd recognize peer pressure, but it doesn't mean he's not right in his own convoluted way. This is Vaughn's day, and I am here to participate in the festivities. We're all adults, drinking at a party is a social norm, and I'm not driving. I can relax and enjoy a cocktail if I want.

"Cheers," I say and lift my glass.

The first thick, icy sip slides down my throat easily. It's sweet and tangy but super strong. I'll need to pace myself so I don't feel like I can't handle this.

"How'd I do?" Dylan says, grabbing a redhead walking by and bringing her under his arm. She giggles and snuggles against him.

"It's good," I tell him, but I don't think he hears me. He's got his tongue down the girl's throat.

"Hey," Vaughn says, coming up beside me. My body immediately relaxes and leans toward him. "Sorry about ditching you. I see you've got a drink."

"I do," I answer with confidence I don't entirely feel, but I want him to know I'm okay indulging in Dylan's specialty.

As if on cue, Dylan hands Vaughn a glass. How he poured while his mouth is still attached to the girl at his side, I don't know.

"Come on." Vaughn takes my hand—sending a ridiculous

amount of pleasure through me—and leads me to a sitting area where several party guests are lounging on a semi-circular sectional. Vaughn sits and tugs me onto his lap even though there's an available spot next to him.

He flashes a smile that is so beautiful my heart stops.

"Happy birthday," I say and lift my glass to clink with his.

"It is now."

I've never actually believed eyes could mesmerize, but there's no other way to describe my reaction to Vaughn's. The opaque green around his pupils lightens to a translucent shade as bright and rare as beach glass before deepening to a thin dark outer ring.

His gaze holds me hostage. I can't look away. Part of me is overwhelmed with panic, but another part of me is buzzing with euphoria I can't blame on the drink. I'm under the Vaughn influence, and I don't want the light-headed sensation to end. With Brit's advice on replay in the back of my mind, I want to revel in it.

"Thanks for last night," he whispers as I try to get comfortable on his lap and not spill my drink. Or let anyone around us notice my hand is shaking.

"You're welcome." And where should I put my arm? Around his neck or keep it wedged between us? He settles me closer, and I've no choice but to drape my arm over his shoulder. The side of my boob rests against his chest.

"Hey." He slants his mouth so it's right at my ear. "Relax. I've got you."

He certainly does.

But keeping calm is impossible. My dress is thin and I can feel him inside his classic-fit dark-blue shorts. I force myself to stop wiggling.

"How was Paris?" a girl asks from across the sitting area.

"*Bonne*," Vaughn tells her.

Talk continues after that to trips his friends have

planned over the summer. I sip my cocktail and listen to the conversation. Vaughn finishes his drink, puts his glass on the low round table at the center of the sitting area, and then rests his hand on my thigh, fingertips underneath the hem of my dress.

A bomb of arousal goes off in my body. I clench my legs together to stave off the tingles making their way between my thighs. My panties were already wet, but now I suspect there are more obvious signs of what he's doing to me. I'm sure a flush covers my cheeks and neck.

I scramble to my feet. "Point me in the direction of the bathroom?"

"I'll take you—"

"Don't be silly." I stop him from rising with a hand to his chest. "I can find it." I desperately need a few minutes alone to get my overactive hormones under control.

"There's one off the kitchen," he says.

"Great. Thanks." I hurry away, only to be stopped by Dylan at the built-in bar.

"Kendall! Hold up. Your sister says she can make a better daiquiri than me, and I need you to be the judge."

"Princess there doesn't know the first thing about a good drink," Dixie says from behind the blender without sparing me a glance.

"I don't know, Dix, she approved wholeheartedly of mine already, but if you want to chicken out..."

"You do know she's a bartender, right?" I ask Dylan.

"What?" He stares at Dixie. "You bartend?" She winks at him. "Pass me a taste." He beckons with his fingers, palm up, indicating he wants a drink right this second.

Dixie pours with a flourish and then slides the glass across the granite. Dylan downs a large gulp. "Fuck me, that's exceptional. You're hired."

"Wrong. I'm here to enjoy this party." To prove her point,

she tosses back a shot.

"I meant at The Cabana. I'm down a bartender and could seriously use your help."

She puts a hand on her hip, arches her brows. "You seriously can't afford me."

"Come by the club tomorrow morning and we'll talk." He takes another sip of his drink. "I can sweeten the deal with a fringe benefit."

"Dylan, I'm sure your benefits are impressive"—sarcasm coats her words like sugar on a daiquiri glass—"but I don't sleep with my boss."

"My benefits are legendary, actually, but I meant stage time, Dix. I don't mix business with pleasure, either. I was talking about a weekly gig in addition to bartending. However"—he shrugs and grins—"if you'd rather sleep with me, that's your call."

Her gaze cuts left. I track it to where Matt's standing against the rail, monitoring the exchange with a dark, broody look on his face. A muscle flexes in his jaw as he watches Dixie consider her options, and a random question pops into my head. Exactly *how* did Dixie and my hot neighbors celebrate her open-mic win last week?

Finally, Dixie pours herself another shot, clinks the glass against Dylan's, and downs it. "See you tomorrow at the club, boss."

People watching the exchange laugh and give Dylan shit about having his "epic" benefits rejected. Matt takes a long swallow from his beer before turning to brace his forearms on the rail and stare at the pool. I continue on my way. Undercurrents are flowing like riptides out there, but I can't tell which way they run. I'm too off-balance from Vaughn's dizzying scent and the imprint of his hand on my thigh. I enter the kitchen to take a moment to just breathe.

Ducking in an empty alcove, I call Brit for a quick pep

talk. She picks up on the first ring. "How's the party?"

"Good, but things are moving at warp speed."

"Things meaning hands all over each other?"

"His hands, yes."

"Kendall, it's okay. All of it is okay. You're entitled to have fun. Kiss a guy. Put your hands on him. Enjoy a summer fling. It's normal."

"I know."

"And if you don't go for it, you'll regret it."

She's right. I will. "Thank you for the reminder."

"Just call me Dr. Brit! Now go do everything I would."

I chuckle. "That could take a while. I'll call you later," I say in lieu of good-bye.

"You better."

I hurry down the hall, close the bathroom door behind me, and flip on the light switch. The small room is decorated with a wide sink console that has several drawers with an open shelf at the bottom. I splash some cold water on my sweaty palms, and feel some semblance of control come back. One daiquiri and I'm a tiny bit buzzed—just enough to relax and live in the moment. Am I ready for Vaughn? I'm not sure, but I'm drawn to him in a way I've never felt…with anyone.

A knock on the door spurs me to get moving. I open it wide. "Hey," a girl wearing a skimpy bikini top and tiny white shorts says. "You done? I really have to pee."

"All yours." I step around her into the hallway. My curiosity gets the best of me when I pass a half-open door. It's an office with a large desk, bookcase, chaise lounge, and—my gaze snags on a framed black-and-white portrait of a young woman hanging on the coffee-colored wall. I can't help but move closer. The shape of her face. Her smile. She reminds me of Vaughn.

"You found my hiding place."

I startle at the sound of his voice. I'm caught, but I'm

rooted to my spot, the picture keeping me in place. He comes up beside me, his arm brushing mine. The now familiar electric charge heats my skin.

"Sorry. I shouldn't have—"

"No worries. I don't mind hiding in here with you."

Sitting on his lap might throw my hormones into overdrive, but these kinds of comments are going to get me in real trouble. Vaughn is so much more than I ever expected. His sincerity and depth keep catching me off guard. I glance at him and get his profile, his attention focused where mine just was.

"That's my sister."

"The one you mentioned last night."

He nods. "Yeah. She died ten years ago." He turns his head and I look up into his eyes, hoping he sees how much I care. How honored I am that he shared that.

"I'm so sorry. What happened?"

"She was working out when she suddenly collapsed. By the time the paramedics arrived, she was gone. It turned out she had an undiagnosed heart defect."

I wrap my arms around his waist and squeeze. I'm not sure what more to say, but I want to comfort him. I can't even imagine how awful those days were, the years since. Parents aren't supposed to outlive their children. Siblings are supposed to have a lifetime together.

"She was a model, too, and she'd just landed her first major movie role and was ecstatic. She was poised to be the next big thing, and in the blink of an eye it was over. My parents were..." He shakes his head. "Devastated. Especially my dad. My mom used to joke that when it came to us kids, she was just an incubator, and that was especially true when it came to Andie. Dad managed her career from day one, so a huge chunk of his professional identity was wrapped up in her. They didn't just share a father-daughter bond. They shared goals and dreams." He shrugs out of my hold. "Andie always told me to enjoy having Dad as just a dad and not a business advisor controlling every aspect of my life, but I envied how tight they were. Then after..."

"After?" I whisper.

"After she died, Dad sank into a deep depression. He would sit in his study for hours, staring at the wall. That's when I asked him to manage me. And just like that he had a purpose again. Someone needed him. *I* needed him. The sad thing is, I always needed him. He just couldn't see it. It's like if he can't have the relationship on his terms, it doesn't exist. But his terms are...unsustainable."

I lace my fingers with his. He's staring so intently at his sister's picture, my chest aches for him.

"Andie knew. She warned me. I see that now. But back then I thought she didn't want any competition for star of the family, so I blew it off. I should have listened more closely."

"What was your favorite thing about her?" I want to end this conversation on a positive note before I lead him back to his party.

Vaughn reaches out and touches the picture, traces the smile that's basically a feminine version of his own. "My sister was the funniest person I knew. She used to do these dead-on impressions of our mom and dad—behind their backs, of course—and make me laugh so hard I couldn't breathe." A faint smile plays across his lips. "I haven't thought about that in a long time." He turns toward me. His eyes lose the faraway look as he absently tucks my hair behind my ear. "Thanks for asking about her." Then he leans down and brushes his lips against mine.

It's a simple thank-you kiss, inspired by appreciation, but chemical reactions don't take motives into account, and the chemistry between us has been simmering since day one. The boiling point is dangerously close. Before the first tingles subside, his mouth is back. Not a fleeting brush this time, but a small bite, followed by a slow, deliberate slide.

Long, dizzying minutes pass. Or maybe just seconds… I lose all track of time with his lips on mine and his scent fogging my brain. When he raises his head, I run my tongue over my bottom lip to steal a hint of his taste, and his eyes track the move. We stare at each other for several charged seconds. I'm hardly able to breathe. It's like he's sucked all the air out of the room. All that's left is his heat. His eagerness.

"Vaughn," I whisper just before his mouth crashes over mine.

His lips coax mine apart. His tongue sweeps into my mouth. I drown in the textures and taste of him. He dominates all my senses, and once again I'm swept up in something I can't fight. I don't want to fight. Vaughn's in my head, and he isn't going anywhere.

Without breaking the kiss, he lifts me up by the waist and sets me on the desk, nudges my knees apart with his hip and leans in between my spread legs. I feel his erection through his shorts. My dress offers barely any coverage below, but I don't care. Hot chills—is there such a thing?—race up my arms, down my back, and along the inside of my thighs.

Vaughn tastes like peaches and a hint of mint and I want to kiss him all night. I slowly uncurl my fingers from the edge of the desk and lift my arms to drape them around his neck. Bring him even closer. I arch my back, a silent plea for him to touch my breast, either one, just please hurry.

He groans against my mouth, and my wish is granted. He cups me like I'm fragile and rubs his thumb across my nipple. I'm pretty sure Vaughn can read any and every signal I give him. For a second my inexperience worries me, but when his hand slides down my stomach and slips under my dress to toy with the edge of my panties, I forget my amateur status.

This is really happening.

Chapter Eleven

Vaughn

I want to devour. I want to savor. I want to kiss Kendall until she's breathless and touch her through her clothes until she begs me to strip them away, but at the same time, I want to flip her around, drag her panties aside, and pump an orgasm into her so hard and fast all she can do is cling to my desk and bite her lip to keep from screaming my name. I'm damn near paralyzed by the competing urges, but then she sighs.

It's not a worried sigh, or a stop sigh. It's the kind of sigh a woman reserves for the first taste of imported chocolate. This sigh says she wants to enjoy every sweet moment. It slides down my throat and feeds the animal inside me made of greed and hunger just enough to stop it from running wild. I soften our kiss, brush my lips over one corner of her mouth, the other, and then use the tip of my tongue to tease the sensitive crevice. I'm doing my best to make her think about other sensitive crevices my tongue could tease and making myself insanely hard in the process.

"More," she murmurs. "I need more." She opens her lips wider under mine.

Just like that, the animal is straining the leash. I plunge headlong back into the kiss, mouth fused to mouth. With one hand on her jaw, I slide my tongue inside and taste every part of her I can reach. After one long, compliant moment, she surges forward and gives me the same treatment, her quick mouth trapping my tongue, sucking furiously as I withdraw.

"I can make you come," I whisper, slipping my fingers just inside her underwear. They're damp. Thirst prickles the back of my throat. "The way I just kissed you? I want to kiss your pussy just like that, until it's as wet and swollen as your lips. Keep kissing and licking until you come for me."

Her heart pounds next to mine, almost as hard and fast as my own. Her stomach quivers against my abs. I'm sure she can feel the ridge of my hard-on jutting against her thigh. There's no concealing it at this point.

"Right here, right now," I add.

"Okay," she breathes out.

Someone pounds on the door and she nearly startles off the edge of the desk. I keep hold of her, bury my face in her hair, while from the other side of the door, Dylan calls, "We've got a shitload of people out here, birthday boy, and you fuck like my grandpa. Have your private party later."

I groan and slowly withdraw my hand. Having a houseful of people who assume we're in my office, knocking out a birthday bang, kinda kills the mood. Also, it sends a message I don't want to send, to Kendall or anyone else. She isn't some random girl I snuck off with for a quick thrill. This thing between us might be temporary, but it's not random. In fact, the last status update from Kendall was *It's complicated,* and we should probably have a heart-to-heart about that *before* orgasms are exchanged, not after. Right now, however, the moment could use a little humor. I take a step back to give her some space, and say, "Two things. One"—I hold up a finger—"I'm going to kill my roommate. Two"—I extend a second finger—"I do not fuck like Dylan's grandfather."

She looks up from straightening her dress and smiles. "I really wouldn't know."

Where has this girl been all my life? I slide her hair over her shoulder and kiss the curve of her neck. "He's in his seventies and has a pacemaker; I'm in my prime and there's nothing wrong with my heart. Give me a chance later and I'll prove it to you."

"You're on."

Grateful she's cosigned for picking up later where we left off, I take her hand and lead us back to the party. Music is thumping. All around me, people smile, laugh, flirt, and talk, but I'm not switching gears so easily. It's not just because I was two seconds from spreading Kendall's legs and sucking the best birthday present she could possibly give me right out of her clit. We agreed on later, and I can deal with the anticipation. Talking to Kendall about my sister is what's thrown me a curve. I rarely mention Andie. Most of the time when people hear about a loss like that they murmur "sorry" and try to steer the conversation in a different direction fast, but Kendall didn't. She didn't treat it like a wrong turn into a dark tunnel and immediately look for a way out. She stuck around. She shined a light. And some of that light has stayed with me.

Everybody else is sipping drinks and enjoying the lingering traces of sunset. It's not quite an inner circle, but it's tight enough that I know at least one person in every three.

I see my agent's assistant, Molly, and her boyfriend. A few model friends I've worked with. A couple of Matt's classmates from the Academy. Matt sits next to Amber on the sectional, deep in a conversation. This is much smaller than some of our Saturday night blowouts, but I like the quieter vibe. No

Becca. No mood swings or illegal party favors. Everybody's chill.

Everyone except Kendall. I'm not sure why, but she's a ball of nerves. The fingers entwined with mine practically clench with tension. I'd like to call it sexual tension—a residual effect of Dylan interrupting us—because God knows I have plenty of my own to go with hers. But it feels like more.

Dylan nabs a fresh pitcher from the bar and then walks to the open end of the sectional and sits down. Two girls immediately bookend him, and he fills their drinks. My cell vibrates from the back pocket of my shorts. I've already received birthday calls from my mom and dad. I got a gift basket from my agent. Everyone else is *here*, but I pull my phone out anyway and glance at the screen.

A text reads, *Happy birthday, sexy!* It's from Becca.

I haven't heard from her since she left for New York, but she hasn't missed my birthday for the past five years, so the wish is appreciated. Maybe we can salvage a friendship from the shipwreck of whatever we were, moving forward. *Thx*, I text back and start to put my phone away. An immediate vibration stops me. I look at the screen.

I have a surprise for you.

Uh-oh. I don't want any surprises.

The phone vibrates with an incoming text. *Knock-knock!*

At the same time, the doorbell rings. Fuck.

Dylan sets the pitcher down and slides past me. "I got it."

I want to say, "Don't," but there's no point. I didn't expect Becca, didn't invite her, but as Kendall stares up at me with trusting eyes I feel exactly like the jerk I didn't want to be.

I hear the front door open. Dylan's voice carries. "Can I see your invitation?"

"I have an open invitation," Becca replies.

And then she swoops onto the patio, wearing a straw cowboy hat, lethally high-heeled sandals, and a sprayed-on gold tank dress. The clingy fabric certifies she's not wearing a stitch more than what we see. She spots me and ambles over, graceful despite the shoes. Kendall stiffens and tries to tug her hand away. I firm my grip. Becca's come-and-get-me smile fades as she notices Kendall and our linked hands. Her stride slows.

"Hey, Bec," My smile feels tight on my face. "Long time no see."

She tosses her hair, and her laser-white teeth reappear. "It has been a while. Happy birthday, baby." If she planned to plant a kiss on me, she adjusts on the fly and gives me a hug instead.

"Thanks. How did New York treat you?"

Her smile widens. We're on her favorite subject—her. "Like a queen." She gives a careless gesture with her hand. "Parties, parties, parties, meetings, meetings, meetings. I did the spread for *Vogue* and met with a director about a small but crucial role in a movie he's filming this fall. I'm headed to Milan next. You should come with."

"Good luck with that," I say, deliberately ignoring her request. At some point I know she and I will need to have a conversation, but not tonight. "This"—I put my arm around Kendall—"is my friend Kendall. Kendall, this is Becca."

"Hi," Becca breezes as she takes stock and tries to figure out whether she should recognize Kendall. "I feel like I've seen you before."

Shit. They have seen each other. The night I met Kendall for the first time. Shame makes the back of my neck hot. The last thing I want is that night brought up in front of everyone. I make a conscious effort to stop my leg from bouncing.

Kendall cuts me a brief don't-worry glance then shakes her head. "I don't think so."

Relief swarms my chest. She's got my back.

"Sweatbox Shred at 220 Fitness with that sadist,

Antonio?"

"No. Sorry. I don't sweat with sadists, and I'm just visiting for the summer. House-sitting for my aunt and uncle next door."

"Oh." The notion momentarily stuns Becca. "You're a student?"

"I was. I graduated from NYU this past spring."

"Nice. So what next?"

"Law school."

Becca shivers like the very idea chills her to the bone. "Sounds awful."

Kendall tenses and wiggles out of my hold. Rather than reply to Becca she turns to me. "I'm going to grab some water." Then she offers a perfunctory, "Nice to meet you," to Becca and walks away.

"Same," Becca calls to Kendall's retreating back before her attention jumps back to me. "Congratulations," she says quietly. "I hear you're now on the short list for *America Rocks*."

All I really want to do is shake her off and follow Kendall, but she can and will disrupt a party just to get attention, and I don't want to inflict her on everyone. "Thanks. How'd you hear?"

"Not from you, my so-called friend. You're a freaking vault." She slaps my chest a little too hard to be playful. "A little bird told me, and your dad confirmed when I called to find out about your birthday plans."

That explains a lot. Naturally my father would take it upon himself to invite Becca to my party. He's the one who introduced us several years ago because, in his words, "She's photogenic and she has a fan base, but she won't overshadow you." Touching, right? "Tell the little bird to be quiet. The producers will make an announcement once they've reached a decision."

Her shrug promises nothing. "Well, you know how little birds are. Is that Molly?" she asks, nodding to my agent's assistant.

"Yeah. Go say hi. Tell her about New York."

"I will." She takes a step in her direction and speaks over her shoulder. "After everyone leaves, I'll deliver your birthday present. Upstairs?"

I want to permanently pass on the present, but saying so right here, right now, is no way to finesse this situation, so I give her a noncommittal smile. "Not this year. Have fun in Milan."

She pulls a face, and for a second her eyes look anguished before she blinks, and I wonder if I'm seeing things. "I will." Then she makes a beeline toward Molly without a backward glance.

I scan the deck for Kendall. She's standing near the cooler with a bottle of water in her hand, looking out over the patio, but she senses my stare and glances at me. She packs a lot of messages into one simple glance. Messages like, *What the hell am I doing here?* And, *What the hell is she doing here?* And, *I want you, but I wish I didn't.*

I shove my hands into my pockets and send her a silent request for forgiveness. I'm suddenly ashamed I have someone like Becca in my past. Someone I used and let use me because it was easy—at first—and convenient, and I didn't want to make waves. It occurs to me I go to great lengths not to make waves. Be charming. Never let it seem like anything gets to me. I don't know Kendall well yet, but I know she's not like that. She's not putting on an act, and she has no ulterior motives. If she's with someone it's because she wants to be with him. Right now, today, she wants to be with me. That makes me special—and all the more determined not to mess up.

"You want me to get rid of her?" Dylan stands beside me,

speaking low. He looks toward Becca.

Right. As if that would go well. “Thanks, but no. As soon as she works the party and realizes there’s nobody particularly useful to her, she’ll leave.”

“Your call, man. It’s your birthday. Get yourself a plate.”

“In a sec.”

He nods and wanders to the long table at the far end of the patio where the food is set out buffet-style. The pool lights click on, as well as the landscape lights around the area. They put a soft glow on everyone. The music doesn’t quite drown out the hum of conversation. It’s relaxed. I take a long, deep breath and will myself to do the same. Then I head toward the girl taking up space in my head I didn’t know was available… until her. Manners force me to stop and be social when all I really want is to grab Kendall and take up where we left off in my office. Eventually I make it across the deck to stand beside her. She looks up at me and opens her mouth to speak.

“How do you take your burger?” I ask quickly because I’m almost certain by her expression she’s about to tell me she has to go.

“I’m not really hungry.” She twists the cap on her water bottle open, then closed. “Thanks for inviting me, but I should probably—”

“Stay and eat,” I interject, cutting her off. “Or at least keep me company? Come on, I’m starving. I take her hand, but she doesn’t move.

Instead she faces me, and I hear her next words before she even opens her mouth.

“Did you invite her?”

“No.”

“So…” She pulls her mouth into what she probably thinks is an impassive line, but all it does is make me want to kiss her lips until they soften and open under mine. “You have a surprise guest. I’m sure she’d like to spend time with you and…catch up or whatever."

"There's no whatever," I correct, and take her hand to lead her down the patio and around the side of the house where we can talk privately.

"Vaughn—"

"Shh." Once we turn the corner, I let her go. She leans against the wall and gazes up at me. "Look, I'm not going to lie. Becca and I have hooked up, but that's in the past. We've been friends for a long time, too, and that's not going to work anymore, either." I brace my hands on either side of her head and look her in the eyes.

"I didn't invite her." It's darker back here, but I can see her gaze dart over my shoulder and then drop to our feet. "I invited *you*. The only person I want to catch up with is you."

"Look, whatever is going on between us is…"

"Undeniable?" I suggest, because if she says "complicated" right now, I'll have to prove her wrong. So much for the heart-to-heart I promised myself we'd have. I'm not sure I can handle it.

She sighs. "Pointless is the word that springs to mind. We don't want the same things. We have very different goals."

"You don't know what you want," I point out. "You came here this summer to think." I'm not trying to argue with her, but these are words straight from her mouth.

She lifts her chin and stares into my eyes as if she's searching for something. "I can't do that properly if my mind's constantly on you."

"Has your mind been constantly on me, Kendall?"

I can't hold back my smile when she responds with a very exasperated, "Yes."

I don't have any magic words to make her let go of her worries and cut herself some slack. All I know is she's a good person, and she makes me want to be a better one. "Maybe right now you're not supposed to be thinking about anything but this…"

I kiss her.

She's rigid for a second, and then melts against me with a small sigh. I cup her jaw and take us both deeper. Her lips part for my tongue, and I lose myself in an addictive combination of peaches, rum, and Kendall. A big-brother voice in the back of my head wonders how much she's had to drink, but then her fingernails rake through my hair and big brother shuts up. She rises onto her toes and kisses me back with an urgency that tells me she doesn't want to think about this too much, either. Just go…go…go. And Jesus, I'm going, because her tongue's sliding over mine, and the soft scrape of her nipples against my chest brands me through her dress and my shirt. Next thing I know I've got my hand under her skirt, holding her tight little ass, lifting her higher as I kiss my way to her ear.

"I owe you an apology."

"For what?" She angles her face so her mouth finds mine. She rocks her hips, seeking, offering, demanding. It's all I can do not to tear her panties off and give us both some relief, but I want to give her more. She deserves more.

"I owe you an apology for not walking away with you back there, because it made you doubt. And that was wrong. It's you I want, Kendall. Don't ever doubt that."

Her hands fist in the front of my shirt and pull my mouth back to hers. This isn't something she wants to talk about.

"I'll show you." So saying, I back away.

"Vaughn—"

And drop to my knees.

"Vaughn?" All the impatience leaks out of her voice. She says my name like a breathless question. I can't help but smile.

"Yes?" I wrap my hands around her hips and lean forward to kiss her through the dress. Her body heat surrounds me.

I inhale so deeply I taste her in the back of my throat when I swallow.

Ten fingers sink into my hair and hold fast. "Wh-what are you doing?"

"Showing you how much I want you, so there's no room for doubt in your mind." I scrunch her dress up and kiss her again through silky white panties. Her eyes go huge, and then the lids drift down.

"Oh, God."

I lean in for another kiss. Her fingers tighten in my hair and her hips shift away, but the wall brings her up short. And I'm not easily discouraged. I put my mouth against her. "Tell me this is okay."

"It's oh…kayyy." The word trails off as I angle my head so my lips brush her clit. I slide my tongue lower, over her slick, wet panties. She gasps, and her hips jerk so fast I almost lose my grip on her, but then she comes surging back for more. I give her more, and more still. I'm just as desperate for this as she is. I'm delving everywhere now. Over the panties, under the panties—hard, fast, soft, slow—switching it up to drive her out of her mind. Her head's rolling back and forth against the wall, she's chanting my name and pulling my hair like she intends to rip it out in handfuls, and I can't get enough of the pain because it means she's beyond manners, or reserve, or her impressive self-control. Making Kendall go wild is my new goal. I want it to go on and on, but the way she's calling my name in ragged little pants tells me she's not going to hold out much longer.

"Believe me?" I ask and rim her with my finger.

"Yes," she says breathlessly.

I put my tongue to good use on the throbbing little spot that makes her moan and circle her opening faster. I want to be inside her when she comes. Just a couple fingers, so I can feel every flutter. Every spasm. I want her body hugging me with grateful abandon as I send her over. I push two fingers in deep…and she sucks in a hard breath. Not the good kind. The *holy shit, that hurts!* kind.

I immediately withdraw. "Are you okay?"

She scoots away from the wall and quickly readjusts her clothing.

"Hey," I say, and stand slowly so as not to freak her out. "Talk to me. I'm sorry if—" The rest of my sentence gets caught in the back of my throat because her eyes are brimming with tears. I'm confused and concerned until it dawns on me. She was so tight. Like maybe…*fuck*.

"Are you a virgin?"

"It doesn't matter. I just…I can't do this. I made a mistake."

"You don't need to be embarrassed. You just took me by surprise." Dammit. "Look, I can take it slower. Much slower—"

"No." The word comes out fast and a little hysterical. "It's not you. It's me. *Shit.* I can't believe I said that again."

But she's not laughing at herself this time. She's not laughing at anything. She's on the verge of crying. "I'm not the person you think I am. You think I'm good and…innocent. I'm not. Not in the ways that really matter. I've done things I can't undo, and trying to pretend I'm free doesn't change anything. I'm not free. I don't know if I'll ever be free."

Her words come in a torrent—painful and ragged like they're tearing her to pieces. "What are you talking about?" I keep my voice as calm and low as I can manage.

She wraps her arms around herself as if she's freezing on this eighty-degree night. "It doesn't matter. I have to go. Sorry I ruined your party."

"You didn't ruin anything. I'm sorry if I—"

"Stop. Please." She shakes her head. "Leave it alone, Vaughn. For both our sakes, just leave me alone." She turns on her heel and takes off.

"Kendall?"

She doesn't so much as pause. I want to chase after her, but I don't, because I can't bear to be the cause of the look in her eyes.

I don't understand what just happened. I don't know what I did wrong or how things went sideways so quickly. I know only one thing. Whatever she was trying to tell me matters. It matters a lot.

Chapter Twelve

Kendall

I step out the front door and down the walkway on a caffeine mission to the coffee shop at the bottom of the hill. Sleep once again eluded me last night, the culprit a birthday boy with the power to tie me in knots comprised of want, need, and curiosity that overrides my uncertainty. I hate the way I left things with Vaughn last night.

I acted immature. I am what I am, and I'm pretty sure he knew before he touched me that I didn't make a habit of hooking up. What Vaughn did was make me *feel*. Physical urges I haven't felt since Mason, but also emotions I'm not sure I'm ready to deal with. I've kept myself closed off from anything too intense for a long time, always in control of my body and mind, but Vaughn threatens my control without even trying. I can't write it off as a standard female reaction to a chiseled jaw and a billboard-worthy assemblage of abs, chest, and…ahem…other male attributes displayed to perfection in snug boxer briefs. NYU had its share of gorgeous guys who occasionally earned a second glance, but never a second date. What draws me to Vaughn runs deeper. He asks, "Can I trust you?" and I'm toast. I want to know his secrets, and that scares me. I want him to know my secrets, too, and that scares me even more, despite—or maybe because—sharing those secrets means giving up control. And losing control with him feels incredibly right. It gives me…hope. Hope that I can find happiness with someone again. Happiness with myself, too.

So just be with him already, right?

It's not that easy. His concern and patience last night when he discovered I'm still a virgin were very reassuring, but also stark reminders that he doesn't know all there is to know about me. If he knew *why* I was a twenty-two-year-old virgin, how would he look at me then? Would he still want me? Without knowing the answer to that question, I couldn't be with him. And that's all I could focus on in that moment—that I shouldn't be there, letting him assume I was some kind of good girl when I'm the furthest thing from good. I'd needed to escape. From him, from my past, from having choices Mason doesn't. I glance up at the light-blue sky, wishing for the thousandth time he and I had made a different decision that night.

With my sudden mood flip, I figured Vaughn would run for the hills. Only he didn't. Instead, he had the decency to be concerned. Five minutes after I ran home and into the sanctuary of a hot shower, Amber knocked on the door and wanted to know if I was okay. Vaughn had told her I was upset and asked her to check on me. It had taken another five minutes to convince her I had a skull-splitting headache and needed darkness and solitude to make it go away. I got out of the shower to find a glass of water and two pain relievers on my nightstand, which immediately made me feel guilty because I didn't really need them. I made a mental note to thank her this morning, but she was gone by the time I woke up.

I've made it as far as the sidewalk when I notice activity at the house across the street. Without thinking, my feet take me over there. Little girls are twirling around the front lawn in princess costumes, giggling. Their arms are spread wide, playfully bumping one another. A big blue plastic tub sits off to the side and overflows with tulle, colorful boas, magic wands, veils, crowns, and sparkly shoes. My fingers twitch. I stare as the mid-morning sun shines down on the dancing princesses like a spotlight, and I'm reminded of my own childhood when my friends and I dressed up and performed for our parents.

When nothing could touch us, and the applause from our "audience" echoed in my ears for days.

The tallest girl notices me and stops moving. She's wearing a Birthday Princess crown to go with her yellow gown. She looks over her shoulder at her mom, I'm guessing, sitting on an iron bench near the front door, then back at me. I smile, give a little wave, and because I don't want to come off like a creeper, call out, "Hi. I'm from across the street." I gesture to my aunt and uncle's house. "I was just out for a walk and noticed you guys playing. Happy birthday."

"Want to play with us?"

Her invitation surprises me until I watch her stare dip below my chin. I look down. Oh yeah. I'm wearing my black Kings tank top with a big silver crown on the front that my aunt sent me after they won the Stanley Cup.

"It's Kendall, right?" the mom says, walking across the grass.

"Right."

"Sally talks about you and your sisters all the time." She puts her arm around her daughter's shoulders. "Sally says Meg reminds her of you at this age." Meg does have my same coloring.

The young girl's eyes go saucer-size. "Do you like to play make believe?"

"I do," I say, unable to stop my smile.

"Cool. Wanna play with us?"

I absolutely do. I want to remember what it feels like to be free of all the thoughts clogging my mind and pretend to be someone else for a little while. I step onto the grass. "I'd love to."

"You can be Ariel."

"She's my favorite. How did you know?"

Meg grins with a shrug then takes my hand. Her fingers are chubby, her palm soft. "Come on. You have to get dressed up."

My dressing up entails a purple boa around my neck, a green one around my waist, and every bangle the girls own on my wrists. I love that I'm the lone throwback princess.

"All the girls are in a young ensemble group that meets twice a week," Meg's mom says. "This summer they're performing—"

"You can go sit down now, Mom."

I chuckle, remembering all the times I dismissed my mom when I was young, and am soon swept up in an elaborate story of princess sisters on a quest to find Ariel's long lost prince. It seems all the other princesses have their one true love already. Before I know it, I'm teaching them little things that my drama teachers taught me. Lessons to improve body awareness and creativity and how to throw their voices. We stretch our imaginations and laugh and twirl, and I'm having a great time.

I like this version of myself.

Something behind me grabs the girls' attention and I turn.

It's Vaughn.

My heart skips a beat. He's a hundred kinds of distracting,

wearing olive cargo shorts, a thin light-green T-shirt that stretches across his chest and shoulders, Nikes, and no visible socks. He smiles and the under-ten set beside me go all smiley in return. He's a freaking female magnet no matter the age.

Everything we did—he did—last night crashes into my mind, and despite my panic attack when I left him, I'm happy to see him again. By the sexy twitch of his lips and awareness in his eyes, I think he's glad to see me, too. No doubt my cheeks are flaming brighter than Red Hot Cheetos.

"Hey, neighbors," Vaughn calls out. "Is this a no boys allowed zone or can I join in?"

"You can be Prince Eric!" Meg shouts with excitement. The other girls squeal.

Stick a tail fin on me and toss me into the ocean, because I'm pretty sure I'd breathe easier under water than I am right now. Vaughn is coming closer, his focus solely on me, and my worries that last night would be the last time I saw him vanish.

"Hi," he says.

"Hi."

"Come on, Vaughn," Meg says, taking his hand. "You have to come over here."

I raise my brows at Meg's familiarity.

"What? A guy can't spend time with his neighbors? I'm not even her favorite. Matt's her favorite," Vaughn says under his breath before Meg pulls him away.

It's really hard to continue being Ariel and teaching the girls things with Vaughn's eyes on me. I can't concentrate *at all* and trip over my own feet twice. Plus, watching Vaughn interact with the kids is adorable.

Meg's mom shouts a five minute warning for lunch and my stomach growls, reminding me I've yet to eat today. Or get my coffee. When Meg announces it's time for Ariel to receive the kiss of true love from Prince Eric so they can live happily ever after, chills break out across every inch of my skin.

I lay down on the grass as directed by Meg, my head propped up with a pillow. Vaughn is instructed to kneel beside me and get busy. We both chuckle, and some of the tension I'm feeling melts away. With my eyes closed, I remember every nanosecond I've spent with him. His smell, his touch, his taste, his smile, his eyes. Eyes that don't just look, they see, and he wants to see me. My body has craved his from the moment we met, but it's more than a physical want. It's the way Vaughn makes me feel when we're near each other.

Desire alone can be fought. Add emotions and the battle grows a million times harder.

Vaughn's warm breath tickles my lips. My eyes fly open, and that's when he kisses me. It's soft, sweet, and oh so careful. Despite the way I left him last night—maybe even because of it—he still wants me, too.

The quick peck isn't enough, and it's crazy how much I want to pull him back to me. He takes my hand and helps me to my feet. The girls jump up and down and clap their approval. Vaughn takes a bow, so I do the same. We're bombarded with hugs before the girls skip away toward the house.

I walk over to the bin of costumes and take off my boas and bangles. When I turn around, Vaughn is watching me. "I wouldn't have taken you for a hockey fan," he says with that sexy, easygoing attitude of his.

"I'm not, really. It was a gift from my aunt." I stay where I am. Per usual with Vaughn, I'm not sure what happens next. I don't know how to do this anymore.

But I do know I owe him an explanation for my behavior.

We stare at each other. It's like an addiction the way our eyes can't stay off each other. I'm dying for him to make the first move. He does.

"Go out with me tonight," he says, taking steps closer.

The invitation catches me completely off guard in the best possible way. "Out?" This could mean a lot of things, and I need specifics. I'm so glad he didn't listen when I told him to leave me alone.

"I tried to skip a few important steps last night and almost shortchanged the both of us. I want to take you out on a date. I want to hold your hand. I want to talk and listen. I want to kiss you good night. I've got a list of wants, actually, but we'll start with that." He stops inches in front of me.

I swallow the gigantic lump in the back of my throat. Wow. Just wow. His admission makes my knees weak and my heart take notice.

"Do not ask me why, Kendall. Don't second-guess this or say there's no point. You and me? We're something. I aim to find out what we are. Unless you tell me no."

I shake my head, then nod my head, shit, I don't know what to do with my head. But the answer is yes. Yes, I want to find out, too. I want to trust him. With everything. My secrets. My uncertainties. My regrets. My virginity suddenly seems like the least complicated piece of it. "What time should I be ready?"

The grin he flashes steals any lingering doubts I have about my intentions toward Vaughn Shaughnessy.

Mostly.

I spend the rest of the day getting ready, starting with a long soak in the bath followed by a shower to shave, exfoliate, and wash my hair. After, I rub lotion all over my body and picture it's Vaughn's hands on me instead.

I wait for my renegade thoughts to bring guilt, but they don't, so I picture him kneeling in front of me with his tongue and fingers in my most intimate places, and I'm turned on. Restless and needy. I sit on the edge of the bathtub and spread my legs. I haven't touched myself in a long time. I've *never* watched, that's for sure, but the mirror across from me gives me a perfect view. And I'm suddenly curious. I'm seeing myself through Vaughn's eyes. I reach over and grab the vibrator Brit included in my summer house-sitting survival kit. With a push from my finger the device turns on, and I put it over my clit. The contact fires up all my nerve endings, lifts me to the brink of release within seconds, and I realize I've been hovering there since Vaughn dropped to his knees and put his mouth on me. I'm beyond overdue for an orgasm and can have one like this, but I want more. I need… I take my free hand and slowly slide a finger inside, imagining it's him. It's not the same. Not enough. I add a second finger and concentrate on the memory of him doing this—the way he circled, and then pushed deeper. I linger, repeating those motions, stroking and playing while I fantasize about him doing the honors. Experimenting in ways I wouldn't normally, but I think he might. I visualize him moving inside me, searching. Searching for…oh God, that spot right *there*, and then, holy shitnuts, I come so hard I sink to the floor.

Through the very last spasm, I picture Vaughn.

If my daydreams are this powerful, I can only imagine what the reality might be like. My entire body heats at the thought.

I stand and walk on shaky legs into my room. Clothes are strewn all over the bed, indecision still weighing on me. Last week I did some shopping, but I can't decide which of those purchases to wear tonight. Because it's on top, I wiggle into a short purple sundress, and then eye my reflection in the full-length mirror. It's summery and sexy in an understated way. Would the little black halter dress be better? I wish one of my sisters were around to offer an opinion.

As if I have my very own fairy godmother on speed dial, I hear a door slam, followed by footsteps on the stairs. I walk out to the landing to find Amber coming up, lost in thought.

Looks like unwelcome thoughts, judging by the way she's gnawing her lip and frowning into space. I apply the brakes and prepare to put my body in reverse. Now is not the time to hit her up with a fashion emergency.

But I'm not quick enough. She spies me. "Oh, hey." She slips the small bag in her hand into the outside pocket of her purse. "Didn't see you there." Her steps speed up as she approaches the landing, but then she pauses and looks me over. "Cute dress. That color's great on you."

The unsolicited compliment bolsters my courage. "You think?" I pluck at the skirt. "I'm trying to decide between this and a black dress."

"What's the occasion?" She heads toward my room.

"I'm going out with Vaughn." I double step to catch up with her, then almost plow into her when she abruptly stops.

She turns. "As in, a date?"

"Yes."

"Whoa." Her eyes go wide. "Really? Dixie insisted you'd taken some kind of vow of celibacy."

My sisters know I got into an auto accident with my boyfriend during my senior year, but no details. They don't know the whole situation.

"No vow," I say. "Vaughn asked me out and I said yes. As to where it leads…we'll see."

"Sure you want to stress the dress?" She walks over to my bed. "Underwear might be the thing to put the effort into."

"I'm not wearing any," I joke. But as long as she's here, I pick up the black dress and hold it in front of me. "Which one says, 'I dare you to find out'?"

Amber tilts her head and taps her finger against her upper lip. "The black one is all-out sexy, and makes your blond hair pop, but honestly?"

"Yes, please."

"I think it's a little too straightforward for you. I don't

mean that in a bad way. I'm just saying it's more Dixie than Kendall. You know?"

I do. I toss it aside and study myself in the mirror again.

Amber comes up behind me. "The purple plays up your eyes. Plus the keyhole neckline is unique and a little naughty."

"That's perfect for a first date, right?"

"You ask me this with a straight face after admitting you're not wearing underwear?" She turns her head and scans the few pieces of jewelry on the dresser. "Besides, this isn't really your first date. Open mic night was your first date. His birthday party was date number two. So that makes this date number three. As for the dress, I like it with these." She hands me the diamond drop earrings my parents gave me for graduation.

I take them from her and work them into my ears. Via the mirror, I smile at her. "Thanks."

"You're welcome." She grins back.

My gaze strays to my nightstand, and I spy the pills she left for me. "By the way, thanks for the painkillers. I didn't need them, but it was thoughtful of you."

She notices where my attention has wandered. "I didn't leave them."

Huh. "If you didn't, then that means..."

Amber lifts one corner of her mouth. "I guess Dixie's good for more than just *giving* headaches. I texted her last night and told her you had a migraine. She must have dropped them off."

"Well, that's certainly..." Mind-blowing? "...unexpected. They're probably not painkillers at all. They're probably poison."

She laughs. "Actually, I think having sisters around is growing on her. When I talked to Matt at the party yesterday, he told me after her open-mic performance, she got flustered when the guys told her we'd come to see her sing."

"Really? All I got from her was a snide comment about us leaving early and missing the real fun."

"Of course you did. She'd swallow her tongue before admitting the truth out loud, but we know better. She liked that we showed. The whole I-don't-need-anybody 'tude is a big, fat act. We all need someone sometimes."

"Dixie might be the exception to the rule. You have to admit she's got the don't-need-anybody act down pat." I close the clasp of a purple bead bracelet and jiggle my arm until it rests low on my wrist.

"She's had a lot of practice. Oh, pretty. The bracelet totally completes your outfit."

"Thanks again for your help."

"No problem. Have fun tonight." Her wide smile fades a notch. "But if you think you might have FUN-fun, make sure you're prepared. Dixie's probably got—"

"What do I probably have?" sister number three interrupts, stepping into my room and holding something out to Amber. "Besides your credit card. You left this in the car."

"*Gracias.*" Amber pockets the card before going on, "You probably have condoms. Kendall's going out with Vaughn tonight."

Dixie studies me for a moment before she digs around in the oversized bag hanging from her shoulder. "Since when did I become the freaking condom fairy?" she mutters.

My face starts to heat. "I don't need condoms. I don't sleep with a guy just because he asks me out. I think that's more your style." The last part comes out harsher than I intended, but we've strayed into very personal territory, and I'm not sure I'm comfortable going there.

Dixie looks at me like I'm nuts. "Even going by whatever good-girl checklist you use, this is a no-brainer. He's given you a classy gift." She drops a condom onto my bed. "He's spent the requisite amount of time getting to know you."

Another condom lands on my comforter. "He's springing for dinner." A third small foil square joins the others. "You're into him, and for whatever reason, he's into you, too. What are you holding out for?"

My face heats further under her scrutiny. Dammit, I should have just said "thanks."

Suddenly Dixie's eyes widen. "Oh. My. God. Is perfect princess Kendall a virgin?"

Her voice contains more shock than scorn, but it doesn't matter. Something inside me snaps. I pick a condom off the bed and hurl it at Dixie. "I am *not* perfect." The small missile bounces off her shoulder. I hurl another. "I'm nobody's princess." This one hits her chest before falling to the carpet. "And the reason I'm still a virgin is because…" All at once tears are choking me. Somewhere in a different part of my brain I see Amber and Dixie staring at me like I've suddenly started molting, and in a way I have.

"…of Mason." The facade I've hidden behind for the last several years cracks apart, and I'm not sure what's going to emerge.

"Are you two still together?" Amber asks. "I didn't realize."

I shake my head, swallowing the bitter taste in the back of my throat. It's time for me to set the record straight. That I *want* to share the truth is a huge step, one I'm not going to second guess. "We had plans that night to lose our virginity."

"Prom, right?" Amber says. "Same night you guys got in the accident."

Again, I nod. "What you don't know is that we'd both been drinking, I was the one driving, and he never…h-he never fully woke up."

For a long moment there's not a sound in the room except my labored breaths. Then Amber murmurs, "Oh, Kendall." She takes my arm and guides me to the bed.

My legs give out and I drop down. She sits beside me.

"Hold up."

I wince at Dixie's words and impatient tone. She stands in front of me and crosses her arms. "You've been blaming yourself for what happened to Mason this whole time?"

I blink away tears so I can pull her into focus. "I was the one driving his truck."

"You were both drinking that night, right? Why did you get behind the wheel of *his* vehicle?"

"He…" I sniff and wipe my nose as memories play through my mind. "He said he'd had more to drink than me."

"So you both made the choice to roll the dice. You both took the gamble. End of story."

"It's not that simple," I answer automatically.

"I didn't say it was simple. But it's the truth," Dixie retorts. "He got into the car, knowing the risks, and he owns that choice. It's not all on you. Neither of you should have driven anywhere, but the fact that you were behind the wheel doesn't make you the only one who made a crappy decision. I never met Mason, but if he loved you half as much as you apparently loved him, he wouldn't lay all the blame at your feet. He wouldn't want you to stay tied to him like this and deny yourself a personal life as some useless penance."

I'm too stunned to respond. Dixie doesn't usually give a flying fuck about my feelings. She wouldn't waste a single breath on absolution. Not for me. But she's a big believer in owning your own shit, and she's the first person to call me out for taking on Mason's. Would he blame me? I like to think he wouldn't, but if he could see himself now? I don't know.

"You made a mistake." Amber says. "You drank too much, and you made a mistake. And yes, sometimes mistakes affect other people even when you meant no harm. But Kendall, everyone makes mistakes."

I sniff again and wipe my cheeks. "Not like mine."

"No," she quietly agrees. "Not like yours, but..." A long inhale tells me she's working up to something. "I know what it's like to make a reckless decision that ends up having long-term consequences you never intended."

"What do you mean?" I ask.

"Nevermi—"

"Amber," I plead. "If you really don't want to keep going, I understand, believe me, I understand, but I'd like to know what you were going to say."

She blows out a breath then speaks to the floor. "I spent my whole college career focused on my studies. I had my eye on graduate school, and I refused to get distracted. While other people went to parties, I went to the library. All the effort paid off, because by the time I started my last semester I'd already been accepted to grad school. I had my housing, financial aid, and scholarships lined up. After my last final I decided to celebrate. I went out, drank way too much, and hooked up with some guy I'd never met."

"I call that a typical Friday night," Dixie quips.

"Yeah, except the condom fairy didn't visit me that night and now..." She reaches into her purse, digs into the drugstore bag, and tosses a pill bottle onto my comforter.

I read the label upside down. Vitamins. P-r-e-n-a-t-a-l vitamins. What the what?

"Holy shit." Dixie takes a step back, her focus dropping to Amber's stomach. "You're pregnant?"

My gaze zooms there, too, while my thoughts scatter like leaves in a windstorm. Finally, I catch one. "Did you tell the father?"

"I don't know who he is. We didn't exchange names." She covers her face with her hands. "I have a vague memory of long, dark hair and a goatee, but that might be Captain Morgan. I went to the bar with my roommate. She says we parted ways around midnight, and I stumbled into our apartment around two. Were it not for the Uber charge I wouldn't even know how I got home."

"Are you going to—" Dixie breaks off, and then starts again. "It's totally your decision, and I make no judgments, but are you going to keep—"

"I'm having the baby," she whispers. "What happens from there, I haven't decided yet, but I have some time to weigh those options." She drops her hands, and I can see the resolve in the set of her chin. "That's why I can't go home. My mom and stepdad wouldn't understand. Being pregnant outside of marriage goes against their beliefs. I'm an adult and this is my call, but"—she lifts a shoulder and lets it fall—"I shouldn't live under their roof if I'm not prepared to abide by their rules."

"You don't have to explain," Dixie says. "I moved out of my mom's house the minute I turned eighteen. So they don't know?"

"Not yet. I've told only Aunt Sally, who immediately insisted I spend the summer here." She glances at Dixie and then me. "And now you two."

Dixie crouches until she's eye level with Amber. "Whatever you need, you know you're not in this alone, right? You've got Aunt Sally, Uncle Jack…"

"And us," I add, placing my hand over Amber's fist.

"And us," Dixie agrees, and stacks her hand on mine.

Chapter Thirteen

Kendall

Twenty minutes later, I've almost wrapped my head around the conversation with my sisters. "Sometimes things happen for a reason," I say to the framed picture of my aunt and me on my nightstand just before the doorbell chimes. I double-check the condoms are in my handbag then hurry downstairs. Stopping in the entryway, I tell Snow to chill before I smooth my hands over my hair, catch my breath, and steel myself against the visual orgasm that is Vaughn Shaughnessy.

When I open the door, though, the mental cold shower fails. He is so much hotter in person. Snow obviously agrees, because I swear the excited noise she's making sounds like a purr.

"Wow," he says, raking his eyes over my sundress. His gaze lingers on the keyhole at my chest. It's a rather large keyhole. "This is going to be harder than I thought."

"What?"

"Nothing," he fires back. "You look amazing. Ready to

go?"

"Yes, thanks. You look amazing, too." And effortlessly gorgeous from every angle. I close the door behind me.

It takes only a few minutes to arrive at our destination, a cute restaurant just off the beaten path. The hostess greets Vaughn like he's a regular and leads us to a table. As usual, his nearness clouds my head. My pulse races.

The room is dimly lit and decorated in rich, dark colors. Our small corner table with a bench seat is semi-private. I sink into the pillows at my back as I look over my menu. When the waiter stops to take our order, we both ask for steaks, his with fries, mine with a baked potato.

As the waiter retreats, Vaughn turns to me. "So, you're a virgin."

I almost choke on a swallow of water. "'Fraid so," I manage, and set the glass down.

"Virginity pledge?"

"No." It's so far off base I actually smile. "Is this your idea of interesting dinner conversation?"

He's utterly complacent as he shrugs. "I'm interested. Very interested. Religious reasons?"

I shake my head. "No again."

"Just haven't met the right guy?"

My smile wilts. We've reached a conversational cliff. The next step is going to be a doozy. I tip my head to the side and look him in the eye. "You sure you want to know?"

He takes my hand. "I'm sure. You can tell me anything, Kendall. You can trust me." Then his expression kind of freezes, and his fingers squeeze mine. "Shit. I'm a dumbass. Somebody hurt you."

Once again, his concern makes me feel like a fraud, but this time I have to speak up instead of running away. "No. Nothing like that. *I* hurt somebody." My chin trembles, and there's a painful clog in my throat, so instead of elaborating,

I pinch my lips together and wipe the corner of my eye with my free hand.

"Tell me," he whispers.

I'm not sure if it's a question or a request, but the patient words push us closer to the point of no return. Even though I'm terrified he won't be there when I land, it's a risk I'm ready to take. If I keep holding Vaughn at arm's length he'll definitely back off. There was a time I never shied away from people, and I miss that girl. If I tell him the truth he'll either think I'm an awful person and this will be the last time I see him, or…

He'll understand.

"I was seventeen when I got a DUI," I say quietly.

His breath hitches before his hold on my hand tightens. The gesture gives me the courage to continue before I lose my nerve.

"It was after prom. My boyfriend, Mason, and I were both drunk—everybody was, not just us, and maybe that made it harder for us to realize how wasted we were. We never should've gotten in his car, but we'd made these big, romantic plans to spend the night at a hotel and finally, you know"—I clear my throat—"commit to each other in the one way we'd been saving."

"But it never happened."

He's falling with me now, and I'm sorry for it, but there's no way to shortcut the distance or soften the impact. We're going to go all the way down, we're going to hit hard, and afterward, things won't be the same. "I can still feel the vibrations moving up my arms and through my body as I tried to handle the steering wheel, tried to keep control of his truck so it wouldn't spin out. I'd taken a curve in the road too fast, distracted by Mason's hands on my body and his voice in my ear urging me to go faster. I was too drunk to question my actions. The radio was blasting, the big V-6 engine roaring, and yet I heard this strange silence between my mind whispering *Oh shit*, and Mason yelling 'Look out!' Sometimes when I close my eyes I can recapture the sickening weightless sensation just before we plowed into a tree, but the moment of impact remains a blackout." My breathing seesaws as guilt and pain lance through my chest. "All I remember is a rain of sticky glass particles pelting my face."

"Jesus," Vaughn says so softly I barely hear it. He wraps his arm around my shoulders and brings me closer, turning his body so it forms a barrier between me and the rest of the restaurant. Not just to comfort me, I realize, but to shield me from the curious stares of other diners. He thinks he knows where this fall from grace ends, and he's gallantly trying to protect me. He doesn't know, but I'm beyond grateful for his attempt. It puts him in a small, trusted circle. My parents protect me. Brit protects me. But most of the people Mason and I grew up with judged me—some silently, some loudly, almost all without a shred of mercy. I could never go through that again. It's one of the reasons I don't go home often or stay more than a few days.

I guess I've been silent for too long because Vaughn whispers, "Mason?"

"He didn't have his seatbelt on and went through the windshield." A tear trickles down my face. Vaughn gently wipes it away with the pad of his thumb.

"I'm so sorry."

He thinks we've hit bottom, and I'm bizarrely tempted to let him believe it, but the truth is we're still falling. "Me, too. I'm sorrier than I can ever express, but..." And down we go. "He didn't die. He suffered severe brain trauma. He's still breathing, but otherwise unresponsive." The tears start to fall more heavily, because I hate this part the most. Seeking escape, I turn away from Vaughn and lean my forehead against the wall. "We were supposed to go to college together, get married, work together, and have babies together. We had it all planned out."

The arm around my shoulder gently pulls me into the safe harbor of his chest. "You loved him."

"I loved him so much. A part of me always will, and it's like an anchor around my heart."

Vaughn's regard is tangible, like he's realigning all this new knowledge to piece together my past. Prom…hotel room…my virginity…my hesitation to get involved with him.

"I understand," he says with tenderness I'm not sure I deserve. "When was the last time you saw him?"

This is one of the toughest things for me to accept. "I saw him in the hospital briefly after the accident." I close my eyes to block the worst of it. "I wasn't supposed to. I had broken ribs and a concussion, but I needed to know how he was. People kept saying, 'He's alive,' without meeting my eyes. I couldn't take it anymore. I had to see for myself, so I snuck down the hall to ICU. Apparently the nurses found me screaming and crying hysterically in his room. They had to sedate me. After that neither my parents nor Mason's wanted me to see him. Everyone thought it would be…damaging."

"I get that," he says quickly. "But now, after this much time, it might help—"

"His parents still aren't open to it. His mom says he wouldn't want me to see him the way he is now, and he deserves to be remembered as young, vital, full of life. She's protecting him. And in a way, me, too. I want to remember him looking strong and vibrant in his football uniform, his jeans and T-shirts, his tux that night. I can't blame her, but—"

"But you don't have closure. That weight you feel around your heart, that anchor? It's not him. It's you. This is your life. You're in charge of charting your course, and you have to decide when it's time to let go."

I nod, because deep down I know he's right. It took a

suspended license, sixteen months of community service, three years of probation, mandatory alcohol awareness training, and hours of therapy to get me to this truth. "The last four years have been one long, slow exercise in letting go and learning to reach out again. I let go of the dreams I shared with Mason. I let go of my hope for forgiveness from our old friends, who wouldn't look me in the eye but whispered behind my back. Eventually I let go of self-hate and bitterness, which weren't getting me anywhere but were hurting the people who love me a great deal. I reached for ways to make my life meaningful. I reached for New York and college. I reached for new friends and new goals."

"And you succeeded," Vaughn says.

I'm proud that he thinks so. "Mostly. There are things I'll never fully let go of. Regret will stay with me always, and it should. Some of the goals I'm reaching for don't feel right for me anymore, but to please my dad maybe I need to give them a chance. And then there's the whole virginity thing."

Our meals arrive, and I'm grateful for the distraction even though I can't eat a bite. Vaughn's been beyond understanding, but it's time to let him off the hook. "Thanks for listening to all of this, but we can go if you want. I'm sure it wasn't the date you imagined."

Vaughn shifts just enough to allow us room to eat. "I imagined getting to know you better. I don't see how we do that without honest conversation." He slides linen-wrapped utensils my way. "Thank you for confiding in me."

Relief I didn't anticipate washes through me, leaving my head light. To hold myself together, I unroll the utensils and cut into my steak. "I wanted you to know me—ugly parts included—before things between us got too…friendly."

"Are things between us going to get friendlier?"

"I don't know," I admit, but something inside me flutters at the prospect. It could be panic.

"Can I ask you one more thing?"

He can ask me anything at this point. I literally have nothing left to hide. "Sure."

"Is 'the whole virginity thing' something you're trying to hold onto, or let go of?"

This question, off another guy's lips, might compel me to slap his face and say, "I just shared my most painful secrets with you, and you're trying to figure out whether you have a shot at getting laid?" But the concern in Vaughn's eyes as he searches my face tells me it's the exact opposite. *He's* trying to figure out what *I* want. He's putting me in charge of how… *ahem*…friendly we get. He'll play it my way. A new lump forms in my throat, and I take a sip of water to ease it before answering. "I think, for a long time, it was something I held onto out of love, loyalty, or guilt—probably a combination of all three—but it's difficult to say for sure because nobody really tempted me. Until now."

His quick smile assures me that last part went straight to his ego, but then he tips his head and strokes his thumb along my cheekbone. "Maybe you're tempted now because you're ready?"

Or maybe I'm tempted because it's him? Attraction is one thing, but a man who listens without flinching while I unpack more emotional baggage than he could possibly have bargained for? I could really fall for him.

I place the fork on the plate at the wayward thought and lean away. "Yes, I think so. But I'm here for the summer." Getting too attached will just break my heart and, given the delicate state it's still in, that's a mistake I can't afford. Time for a reality check. "And we're on very different trajectories. You're destined for fame, be it from *America Rocks* or something else, you're going to get there. I would never want that spotlight to somehow spill over onto me. I can't hold up to it, and I can't do it to Mason, my parents, or his. I need my privacy."

"Kendall, I would never tell anybody the things you told me tonight."

I clasp his hand. "I know you wouldn't, but as your career takes off, your fans will be curious about your life. Especially who you're *friendly* with. The media will do their best to feed that curiosity."

Vaughn breaks eye contact to motion to the waiter for our check. "Right now, this summer, I can keep things on the down-low. Even friendship. I promise."

The coil of tension inside me loosens. I finger-comb his hair back from his forehead and can't help giving him a smile. "Friends for the summer?"

"Friends forever," he corrects, and adds a wink. "Down-low for the summer. You up for a movie or something?"

I love that he doesn't want our date to end, but after getting so little sleep last night, I'm tired. I also know myself. I need some time alone to process everything. Sharing Mason with him has left me feeling a new kind of vulnerability.

"I'm actually pretty wiped. Another time?"

"Absolutely."

We talk about less charged topics on the drive home—things I like about Los Angeles, things I miss about New York, and whether one is required to root for "da Bears" when one attends school in Illinois. We're laughing at each other's Chicaaaago accents by the time he parks in my aunt's driveway. He's out of the car and around to my door before I release my seatbelt. His bigger, stronger hand takes mine to help me out. Our fingers remain comfortably entwined on the short walk to the front door.

"Thank you for dinner," I say. "I'm really glad we talked." The words aren't exactly the right ones given everything I've revealed. But specific, more meaningful words would be too much. They'd put too much pressure on both of us.

He releases my hand and, rather than step forward to give me a kiss good night like I think he will, he takes a step back. "Me, too."

I refuse to read anything negative into the distance he's putting between us. Tonight was intimate enough without adding anything physical, and I know he doesn't want to pressure me on "the whole virginity thing." Still, I can't stop myself from leaning forward and going up on tiptoes to kiss his cheek. "Good night."

He lets out a long breath, the only indication I have that separating is equally hard for him. That he wants more, but he's taking my *another time* to heart.

"Good night, angel." He backs up another step. Then another and another, his eyes never leaving mine.

When he pauses, I think maybe he's changed his mind about a more serious kiss, but he doesn't retrace his steps. "You busy Saturday night?"

"I don't think so."

"Come to dinner at my house."

"I thought you didn't cook."

"I have a few skills. Trust me to get it right." One corner of his mouth curves up into a very wicked smile. "What have you got to lose?"

The question puts a tremble in my stomach. We both know exactly what I have to lose. "Okay."

"Seven?" he asks, as if any woman could say no when he uses that grin.

"Seven." I watch his retreat, waiting until I hear his car start before I slip my key in the lock and turn the handle. Once inside, I press my back against the thick wood and let out a long, uneven breath.

Hello, virginity? It's me, Kendall. I know we've been through a lot together, but I think it's time to give you up.

Chapter Fourteen

Vaughn

There are worse ways to spend a Tuesday afternoon than on the terrace of a suite at The Peninsula. I've been to the posh Beverly Hills hotel before, for parties and events, but this is the first time I've been here for work. Sitting on a cushioned chair under a shady awning surrounded by two beautiful women might not look like work, but I'm five hours into day two of a music video shoot for the first single from last year's *America Rocks* winner's debut album, and I can personally attest to the fact it is work.

I'd like to think being cast for Laney Albright's video means I'm a lock for show host, but it doesn't work that way. The *America Rocks* producers don't oversee the recording side. They partner with a major record label, and it's the label who finances the album, videos, and associated music promotion stuff. To separate things by another degree, the video production company is a completely independent entity, so it's not like an *America Rocks* casting director put me in this chair. At least not directly.

All that acknowledged, we're not going to waste the chance to build more speculation. The shoot has wrapped, but I'm sitting next to Laney and across from entertainment reporter Kit Hoover from *Access Live* because my deal includes participation in a "behind the scenes of Laney Albright's upcoming video" interview. It's all part of a carefully crafted plan devised by the label's PR team, my publicist, my agent, and my dad. I've got a head full of talking points, including Laney's album—which is awesome—what it's like to work with her—also awesome—and some generic responses regarding how I feel about my chances of becoming the new host of the show. I've been coached on how to deflect any questions that stray too far off topic, plus my dad's hovering unobtrusively out of camera range "in case things go sideways."

As if I'd let that happen. I've been interviewed before. Not by such a high-profile outlet as *Access Live*, but I know how to offer up a charming version of no comment. My job is to smile, project energy, and make the interview exciting.

And it is exciting, but as I listen to Laney tell Kit how thrilled she is with the album, and how she can't wait to share it with all the fans who supported her throughout the competition, my mind starts to wander. It drifts to the same place it's been drifting since I found myself on the receiving end of a driveway tackle—Kendall. I'm still digesting everything she confided during our date the other night. So much about her finally clicks into place. One painful event explains why such an intrinsically outgoing person hesitates to get too close, why such a smart, beautiful girl would hole up in her aunt and uncle's house all summer if left to her own devices. I know it wasn't easy for her to talk about what happened. If I could take away all the suffering and give her back the life she expected, I would. But I can't change the past. All I can do is try to understand what she's been through…what she's going through. In some ways I do. I understand what it's like to stare into a mirror and ask why fate had to fuck with the person I loved? Why not me?

I also understand there's no answer to that question. What is, is. She's here, she's whole, and she's doing her best to come up with a purpose for her life, but I can do my damndest to show her she deserves happiness while she's at it. Starting with—

"Vaughn, tell us…" Kit's voice breaks into my thoughts. "Is there any truth to the rumor you and fellow model Rebecca Bismark are"—she pauses a beat to draw out the anticipation —"engaged?"

I nearly choke on my tongue, and her smile turns coy. Questions about my personal life are technically off-limits. She's not the first reporter to lean in with her best guileless expression and test the topic, but she *is* the first to suggest there's a rumor about Becca and me. Hmm. Wonder who started that? I shoot a quick glance at my dad, but he's leaning against a pillar, scrolling through his phone.

"We're friends," I say easily, even though the reply feels slippery in my mouth. "I've known her for years." I lean back in my chair and offer the camera a loaded smile. "But I'm not involved with anyone." Strangely, those words leave a sour aftertaste on my tongue. Or maybe I owe that to two days of people handing me lemon water?

Kit laughs as if we're coconspirators and cups a hand behind her ear like she's listening to something distant. "I think I just heard a huge sigh of relief from our viewers."

We wrap the interview after that, I pose for a group shot, and then heave my own mental sigh of relief when the production assistant pops her head through the French doors and confirms I'm good to go.

Dad saunters over and claps a hand on my shoulder

as we move from the terrace to the suite. "Great job with the interview. You handled yourself well, and once it airs, your face and name will be even more firmly connected to *America Rocks*."

"Thanks. Just so you know, I've got this." I strive to keep my irritation locked down, because the middle of a suite crawling with crew is no place to get into a family squabble. "You don't need to babysit me."

"I can see that, but I wanted everything to go perfectly so..." He shrugs. "An abundance of caution beats a lifetime of regret. Trust me on this."

My irritation bubbles over into frustration. How do I combat logic like that? I don't know, but it's time to try. "Dad, I need to—"

"Hey, how about we grab a bite in the bar and go over the schedule for the rest of the week?"

"I'm familiar with the schedule." Tomorrow I fly to Vegas to host a couple pool parties at the Hard Rock. I've done it before. It's nothing to stress over. I fly home late Friday night. Saturday is all mine, and I'm spending it with Kendall. If things go according to plan the same can be said for Sunday.

"I added a few additional things, including one for this evening."

"Without running them past me?" Jesus, I'm losing control of my life.

"That's what I'm proposing to do right now," he fires back. "Look, Vaughn, everything over the next few days is nuts-and-bolts stuff. It's important, but it doesn't keep you in the national spotlight—a spotlight burning brighter than ever thanks to Nigel's *private* meeting with us on the patio of The Ivy. Letting it fade is a missed opportunity, and you didn't get to where you are now by missing opportunities, but it's going to take more than a couple social media posts from Vegas to sustain the interest. My job is to keep the thunder rolling.

Nigel and John expect us to do that. They're watching to see if we can."

I run a hand through my hair and take a deep breath to retrieve my calm. I don't appreciate being ambushed rather than consulted, but putting broken manager-client dynamics aside, I know he speaks the truth. "Okay. Let's talk in the bar." Actually, it's probably ideal, I realize as I check my watch. It's not quite five. The bar won't be crowded yet, so I can have the I-love-you-but-you-need-to-back-off conversation without a PR coordinator weighing in. "Let me change and then I'm ready."

"I need to check on something downstairs. Meet you in the bar?"

"Deal."

It doesn't take long to wash up and trade out the interview-ready Tom Ford jacket, aged jeans, and white T-shirt provided by the stylist for my black-and-gray Henley and black jeans. It's not exactly a huge transformation, but it feels like slipping back into my own skin.

I shake hands, pose for a couple pictures with the crew, and I'm out of there. I get an elevator to myself and check my phone as I ride down to the bar. Nothing urgent. I upload a funny shot from this morning to Instagram. One of the stylists swooshed my hair into a faux-hawk and I'm giving the whole thing a right-eyebrow-raised, WTF look. It won't get as much love as a shirtless shot, but my core followers will appreciate the candid glimpse of the day.

I'm still focused on my phone as I step out of the elevator, which might explain why it takes me a moment to locate the source when I hear a female voice call, "Vaughn, baby, are you done for the day?"

I look up to find Becca breezing across the gleaming marble atrium toward me, backlit by Southern California sunshine spilling through the glass doors of the hotel's main entrance. She's got a couple shopping bags on her arm and her sunglasses doing secondary duty as a headband to keep her hair away from her face and highlight those cheekbones. A gauzy gray sundress with little black accents skims her torso and flutters around her calves. Between her cross-lobby greeting and her young Gisele looks, several heads turn in our direction. When she reaches me, she rests her body against mine, wraps her arms around my neck, and plants a kiss on my lips. "Hey."

"Hey." I step back because I feel like I'm in a scene where I never got my script. Hell, we're even dressed picture perfect in complementing tones of black and gray. "Um…what are you doing here?"

She links her arm through mine and laughs. "I'm here to see you, silly. I'm joining you for a celebratory drink."

"We're celebrating?"

"Yes. I got that movie role I auditioned for when I was in New York! And you're still in the running for *America Rocks*, despite all the naysayers. Let's get a table in the bar, and I can give you a proper bottoms up."

Pun intended, her look assures me. I ignore that for the moment, because I'm still confused, but I do offer her congratulations and go along as she starts moving us toward the bar. "How did you know where to find me?"

Her brow wrinkles at my question as we walk into the paneled and mirrored bar decorated like a nineteenth century gentlemen's club. "Aren't you happy to see me?"

Rather than answer, a lead weight sinks in my stomach. I glance around. Where the hell is my father?

We approach a table in the center of the room—optimal for seeing and being seen—and I spy Kit, a cameraman, and another guy sitting at the bar. Kit gives me a "gotcha" smile and taps one of the guys on the shoulder.

Awesome. I acknowledge her with a head nod that says,

What? I told you she's a friend.

As we settle into deep leather chairs, Becca's pretty eyes look slightly bruised at my silence. I reach across the table and give her hand a quick squeeze. "Thanks for being here. I didn't know you were back in town."

She shrugs. "I wanted to surprise you."

"Mission accomplished." I look over her shoulder to see where the hell my father is.

"He's not coming," she says. "You've got me instead."

Our eyes meet and hold, and for the first time I realize I'm not the only person my dad likes to manipulate.

"We've fed the media the authorized crumbs." She pauses while a waiter delivers an apparently preordered bottle of champagne, pours two glasses into long crystal flutes, and leaves the bottle nestled in a silver bucket brimming with ice. When he retreats, Becca twirls the stem of her glass between her fingers and looks at me like I'm the center of her universe. "Now it's time to give them something less authorized to chew on. Vaughn Shaughnessy and Rebecca Bismark…are they or aren't they madly in love?"

I lean back in my chair and wish we didn't have to have this conversation in public. "I've already told them we're not."

"Are you sure about that?" She tips her head to a coy angle. Her foot finds mine under the table, and she runs her toe up my shin.

"Bec." I pull my legs under my chair as I rest my forearms on the table and lean toward her. "I don't want to pretend with you anymore."

"But I'm about to break big. Same for you. If we play this right, combining our momentum will give us both an extra boost. And…"

"And what?"

"Nothing." She lifts her glass and clicks it to mine. "To us."

I down my glass in one long gulp and place it carefully on the table before saying, "There is no us," I reiterate. "Not for public consumption."

"And privately?" Uncharacteristic vulnerability laces her words, but I honestly don't know if it's authentic or an act.

"You don't need me there, either. Not anymore."

She crosses her arms, studies me. "Well, it's not really up to us, is it?"

I frown as my dad's words from earlier this evening replay in my mind. *I added a few additional things, including one for this evening.* I'm going to strangle him. My phone buzzes as that lightning hot thought singes deep into my brain. The screen fills with a text.

Enjoy the champagne. We'll catch up tomorrow.

Fuck strangling him. I am definitely going to fire my dad.

Chapter Fifteen

Kendall

Today's walk finds me veering off Sunset and exploring side streets lined with trees and trendy shops. In New York City, I walked everywhere and loved it. I loved navigating the crowded sidewalks, catching threads of conversations over the steady rumble of traffic, following the scent of the flower vendors, or the seduction of a luxurious window display. A small blessing, I often told myself, attending college in a place that didn't require I drive anywhere.

Walking in L.A. is obviously very different, but the destination remains the same—a personal sanctuary built from fresh air and the head-clearing simplicity of putting one foot in front of the other. One of my mom's favorite phrases floats through my mind. "One step and deep breath at a time."

I've been replaying last weekend over and over in my mind, one minute feeling more honest and in control of my life than I've felt in a long time and the next worried I've fallen into a false sense of security. There's nothing wrong with either emotion, I tell myself. Don't second-guess. Go with the flow.

My cross-trainers continue to eat up the sidewalk, and my mind adds an encouraging little mantra. *One step...one deep breath...one step...*

The *ding* of my phone interrupts, and I take it from my back pocket to find the screen lit with a text message from Vaughn.

Hey baby. U up?

I laugh and type out a reply.

A hookup text at ten-thirty in the morning? That's pretty cheesy.

I'm in Vegas. I've lost all track of time. What are you doing?

Walking along Sunset. Checking out the shops. Maybe find a job.

Gonna buy yourself something sexy?

Ha. All I've got on me is my phone and ten dollars earmarked for Starbucks. *If you consider an iced coffee sexy, then yes, I am.*

Yep. Sexy.

I laugh again. *You have a strange definition of sexy.*

Three dots appear and linger on the screen. His response is taking a little longer this time.

Are you going to hold it firmly in your hand? Put your lips over the tip of the straw and use suction until your mouth fills?

Suddenly the mid-morning sunshine on my face feels a little hotter, and I'm glad I have the sidewalk mostly to myself. A naughty impulse compels me to reply, *I'm going to go slow. Make it last as long as possible. Savor every drop until it's completely drained.*

The three little dots appear again, and I'm practically holding my breath to see his response. Was I too smutty? Not smutty enough? I'm new to sexting.

Holy $#!@. I just had a long-distance…iced coffee.

Glad you enjoyed yourself. Pride makes me sassy.

I enjoy YOU. Looking forward to Saturday.

Me too. Have fun in Vegas.

I'd rather have fun with you. Later Kendall. He ends with an iced coffee emoji.

I slip my phone into my pocket and peek into a clothing boutique. The reflection staring back at me catches me off guard. The girl in the glass wears a secret smile.

The Vaughn effect. They ought to create an emoji for that.

But he's done more than just put a smile on my face. He helped me confront a huge obstacle keeping me in my untenable limbo.

Me.

Mason didn't push my heart into a holding cell and hide the key. He couldn't do it even if he was the kind of guy who would want to—which he isn't—because I'm in charge of my heart. It's mine to give, and it finally dawned on me that I can give it many times, in many ways. Love's not a finite thing. I don't have to retrieve what I've given, or give back what I've taken, in order to move on. I just have to be ready to give again. There's freedom in that realization, and I close my eyes to absorb the weightless sensation. I'd hoped to get unstuck this summer and am grateful for the assist.

Who knew the guy hanging in Times Square would become my friend-slash-unknowing therapist? Not this girl. And now he's poised to become more.

One step…one deep breath…

My stomach hears my thoughts and rumbles to remind me I want a pastry with my coffee, so I pick up my pace again. I sniff the air and can practically smell the blueberry muffin I've been craving almost as much as I crave Vaughn. *Gah.* I can't even think about food without Mr. Tall, Charming, and Sexy intruding.

The stores transition from retail to business offices as I continue my walk, and when I pass signage for an attorney, I'm hit with a stab of nostalgia. As much as I dread law school, I do miss my law firm internship. Not the legal aspects, so much, but I miss being busy with work and hanging out with the other interns.

Distracted by the recollection, I turn the corner and bump right into someone. *Oomph.*

"Oh my God, I'm so sorry," I say to the woman whom I've literally knocked off her feet. She was already kneeling, so she didn't have far to go. By the time I crouch down she's already back on her haunches, so I help pick up the flyers strewn all over the ground. "Are you okay?"

She waves away my concern. "I'm fine, just klutzy. I'm sorry I'm practically taking up the whole sidewalk."

I study one of the flyers. It reminds me of a Matisse painting, the colors vivid and bright, and drawn if I'm not mistaken, by a child. Bold black typeset tells me there is an art exhibit happening courtesy of Art In Progress.

Once we've gathered all the papers, we stand. The woman is maybe ten years older than me with deep brown eyes and dark hair pulled back into a high ponytail. "What's Art In Progress?" I ask, handing her my pile of flyers.

"Thank you." She adds them to her stack inside a small box then adjusts the strap of the messenger bag hanging over her shoulder. "AIP is an organization that helps people in need through art." She nods to the storefront behind me. "This is our studio."

I turn to see the words ART IN PROGRESS beautifully etched in gold lettering on the window and different pieces of art on the other side of the glass. Twisting back around, I notice a car parked at the curb, the trunk open, and several boxes marked AIP.

"Do you need some help?" I ask.

"Would you?" she asks with gratitude and relief. "It's just me this morning, and I'm running late, as usual."

"Sure." I grab two boxes and follow her inside. The space is large with hardwood flooring and dark painted walls. Framed photographs, sculptures, and a piano decorate the area. I put the boxes down near a reception desk, and we make one more trip to her car.

"Thank you so much," she says, wiping her hands down the sides of her jeans. "I'm Candace, by the way."

"Kendall. It's nice to meet you." I take a closer look around, my gaze drawn up to the ceiling, and all the air whooshes out of my lungs. Somebody's painted a cross between a rainforest and outer space up there. "Wow," I murmur.

Candace tilts her head back. "It's amazing, isn't it?" she says with awe. I bet no matter how many times someone looks up, he or she always feels like they're standing on the edge of the world, about to jump into a heaven of living color.

I drop my chin and take one of the flyers. "Can you tell me more about this place?"

"I'd love to. Would you like a tour?"

"Sure."

"We were founded twelve years ago with the goal of using art as therapy and offering a safe place for young people grappling with various types of challenges to share their creativity with others." She leads me down a hallway and I'm shown a room filled with musical instruments, then a room overflowing with canvas and easels and paints, and then another one with a puppet theater and garment racks filled with clothes. By the time we walk through French doors to a small outdoor theater underneath an open tent, I'm officially in awe.

"Wow. Inspiration lives in every nook and cranny of this place."

Candace laughs. "Inspiration lives up here." She taps her temple. "Our mission involves finding the right ways to unlock it. We provide workshops in Music and Movement, Fashion and Design, and Visual Arts, which includes film, theater, painting, and photography. Leading experts designed our programs to support adolescents going through difficult life changes by offering creative tools and mentoring to help them assess and express their emotions, gain perspective, and reclaim power over their responses to the challenges they face."

As we return to the lobby area, I smooth my hand along the wall. Maybe I can absorb some healing just by being under the roof of this really cool operation.

"Are you a nonprofit?"

"Not exactly. We're a not-for-profit organization." At my frown, Candace continues. "Meaning our founder generously funds our operation and any profits, or donations, go back into the organization. Anyone who needs our help receives it at no cost."

I read the flyer in my hand. The art exhibit is next week. "This is open to the public?"

Candace plops down in a chair behind the desk. "It is." Her phone rings from inside her bag and she raises a finger. "Excuse me a minute," she says as she pulls out a notebook, eyeglass case, an apple, sunscreen, and her wallet before grabbing her cell in victory. "Hello?"

I stroll around the room to give her some privacy, but easily hear her side of the conversation. Someone named Tiffany quit to go backpacking in Europe with her boyfriend and yes, the timing is terrible, but Candace placed an ad with an online employment company this morning, so fingers crossed she'll have a new assistant by week's end. She goes on to talk about an upcoming workshop, some other business points, and dinner plans for Saturday.

A nanosecond after she's said good-bye, I spin around to face her.

"Sorry about that." She looks up from the desk, rubs the side of her forehead like she might be getting a headache.

Maybe I can help her with that. "You're hiring?"

She gets to her feet and comes around the desk, giving me a more thorough inspection. "An assistant coordinator, yes."

"I'd love to apply for the job," I say, feeling for the first time like this is a job I'd actually like.

"Okay. How about I interview you right now?" She glances at her watch, obviously not thinking too hard, either, and I'll take it. "I've got a few minutes if you do."

"I've got all day."

She gestures toward a red velvet couch and we sit. "Tell me about yourself," she says.

So I do. Mostly. It turns out she graduated from Columbia, so we immediately have four years in New York in common, as well as favorite restaurants. She's easy to talk to and, while my work experience is limited to my internship, I did volunteer as a camp counselor during my first two summers at NYU. I enjoy working with young people, I have strong organizational skills, and I can empathize with those emotionally struggling for one reason or another. I don't go into any detail, but I do share that I'm still dealing with a traumatic event from *my* past. The biggest detriment to my qualifications is my temporary status in L.A.

"Given that my last assistant called me from the airport to tell me she was running off to Europe with her boyfriend, you're providing me a lavish amount of advanced notice," Candace says. "And in all honesty, I'm a little desperate with the exhibit a week away, so how about we give it a try?"

I don't even attempt to keep my smile from being too big. "I'd love that." Oh my God, I have a job. And it has nothing to do with law!

Candace has me fill out some paperwork, we agree I'll start tomorrow morning, and then she's rushing out the door to an appointment and I'm hurrying to buy myself some celebratory breakfast. I've got a ton of questions for her, realizing belatedly that she didn't tell me much of anything about the job. That's okay, though. When I get home I'll do some online research so I'll have an even better understanding of AIP.

Something she said while giving me the tour comes back to me. "We use art to help improve and enhance physical, mental, and emotional well-being."

My heart gives a little sway.

Sounds perfect.

Chapter Sixteen

Vaughn

I flick the silver lighter Dylan gave me for my birthday and touch the flame to the tip of a white pillar candle set in a curvy glass container. Once the wick ignites I step back and take stock. This patio has served my housemates and me well for hanging out and throwing the occasional pool party or barbecue, but as far as I know none of us have attempted to use it as the setting for a romantic dinner. Now I wish I had some experience to draw from, because I don't want to forget anything.

Have I?

As I look around I run through my mental list. Music? Check. Candles? Check. Privacy? Check, check. Matt's spending the weekend at his mom's house in Alta Dena, teaching his youngest sister to drive. Dylan's at the club until at least three a.m., but his timetable doesn't matter because his downstairs master bedroom has a separate entrance, and he uses it whenever he comes in super late—or early, as the case may be. Either way, Kendall and I have the place to ourselves tonight, which is key no matter how things play out. I want her to know I took my promise seriously. I know how to be discreet. I can protect her privacy. Our privacy.

The flame from the candle I just lit draws my attention to the low, round table on which it sits. I centered the table in front of the sectional so we could relax, eat, and talk out here where it's secluded, but not closed in. The pool lights add a nice boost to the glow of the candle. The sun won't set for another hour or so, but I squint and try to picture the scene at dusk. Should I have gotten her flowers? I bet she likes flowers. On the other hand, I don't want this whole thing to come off like some cheesy *Bachelor*-style rose ceremony.

It has to be flawless but honest. I told Kendall to trust me to get it right, and she did, but now her trust has planted an unfamiliar crop of nerves in my gut, because of who she is and everything she's been through and…because of the sex.

Ironic, right? I have a fuckton of experience when it comes to sex. Fun sex, friendly sex, dirty sex, and occasionally impersonal sex. I'm not saying I'm proud of this—though for the most part I'm not ashamed of it, either—but I'm not used to feeling this unsure of my moves.

I want to give her excitement. I want to blow her mind. I want her to know she's special. She's not a random hookup, or a career tactic, or a fuck buddy. I'm not entirely sure what she is, but I know I need to earn the trust she's offering. I want every detail she sees from the moment she walks in my door to tell her I'm going to take care of her.

My phone vibrates. I reach into the pocket of my jeans, hoping to God Kendall's not calling to cancel, and get a burst of relief followed by a flare of resentment when I see it's my dad. I consider letting him go to voicemail, but he can be relentless. Ultimately, my life will be easier if I just take the call.

"I can't talk now," I say into the phone, opting to own the conversation from the outset and keep it short.

"This won't take long. I know you leave for the Armani shoot Friday morning, but I got you on the VIP list for Laney Albright's album release party this Thursday. My assistant will send you the details and passes."

The guest list for Laney's highly anticipated debut album will be heavy on *America Rocks* brass, possibly including Nigel, which makes the tickets a big score. Dad's good at those, and I'm fine playing along with this part of the business. Better yet, I'll actually enjoy the music, but I'm more interested in the one detail he slipped in without much fanfare. "Passes, plural?"

"You and a guest. Becca's more than willing, naturally, but—"

"No…" Before I can tell him it's out of the question, and why, he continues.

"I'm thinking the same thing. It might be better to keep people guessing, and there are some bigger names interested in being your date for the event. I'm going to reach out to a few people—"

And there it is. The part of the business I don't appreciate at all. He's my manager, not my matchmaker, and people aren't commodities. "Don't bother. I've got a date." Kendall.

Several beats of silence meet my statement. "What are you talking about? Who?"

"None of your business. I'm twenty-fucking-four years old, Dad. I'm entitled to run my personal life without your sign-off."

"A public appearance is *not* your personal life. You're there as Vaughn Shaughnessy, the most obvious choice for the new host of *America Rocks*. Who you hang on your arm for these people to see? That's a career decision, which makes it my business."

I glance at my watch. Shit. Kendall will be here any minute. I do not have time to finish this pissing contest with him. "I've got it handled."

"You can't show up with some pretty young nobody who caught your eye at Dylan's club. I need to check her background. Having a fake ID and a fuck-me smile might work for The Cabana, but it's not going to cut it Thursday night. She needs to be…appropriate. Not jailbait or some aspiring porn star."

"She's not underage or a porn star." Claws of a tension headache dig into my skull. "She's twenty-two. Just graduated from NYU."

"Is she trying to break into the business?"

"No. She's house-sitting for the summer." A knock at my door has me heading inside.

"A house-sitter? I don't see any point to this, Vaughn."

He wouldn't. "I've got to go. Thanks for the tickets." I end the call, toss my phone on the narrow table in the entryway, and open the door.

And there she is, on my doorstep, stealing my breath in a sleeveless black dress that hugs her curves. Her loose hair looks even blonder against the dark fabric. Her skin seems even more golden. The diamond in the pendant I gave her winks at me from its enviable position guarding her cleavage. And last but certainly not least, a slit runs high up one thigh—high enough to make me wonder if she's wearing anything under the dress.

I wipe my palms on my jeans. "Hi."

"Hi." She breathes the word and offers me a little smile. Awesome. We're both nervous.

My nerves might explain why I'm just realizing she's holding a gift bag in one hand and a plate covered in aluminum foil in the other, although the slit in her skirt is more likely the culprit. "What's all this?" I take the plate off her hands.

She looks up at me from beneath a fringe of lashes. “You wondered if this thing between us could ever lead to chocolate chip cookies.”

The pink invading her cheeks fires my blood. Just to see her blush harder, I say, “I meant it as a euphemism.”

“I know,” she teases, but her cheeks do, indeed, turn a shade closer to red. “And this”—she raises the bag—“is the birthday present I forgot to bring you.”

“You didn’t—”

“I wanted to.”

I want to kiss her. In hello. In thanks. To acknowledge this constant energy between us is something new for me, too. I lean in and plant one on her lips, keeping it quick, and mostly innocent, because I don’t want to come on all hot and heavy first thing, but when I draw away, a sugary, vanilla flavor hits my tongue. Her lip gloss. Without really planning it, I come back for another taste. She inhales quickly just before I settle my mouth over hers, and the involuntary, breathless little sound excites me in a way a calculated moan never could. My free hand cups the back of her head, and next thing I know I’m delving deep, and the sweetness of Kendall supersedes everything. Her fingers are in my hair, her scent in my head, and her breath in my lungs.

A voice in the back of my mind reminds me I’m trying to be a gentleman tonight, and I’m standing at my front door with a plate of cookies in my hand, jumping her like some hard-up perv who’s after only one thing. I ease back. She closes her lips around my tongue as I slowly withdraw, and I feel the slick tug of her mouth all the way to my cock. Now I’m the one dragging air into my lungs, struggling for control. Her hand slides from my hair to my jaw. I rest my forehead against hers, and, after a few seconds, open my eyes and fall into two clear blue oceans.

Worried I’m looking at her like a lion stares down a

gazelle, I drop my hand, muster up a smile, and straighten. "Did I mention you look beautiful?" The compliment puts another flush in her cheeks and earns me a self-conscious laugh.

"You, too."

I take her free hand and lead her inside. "Thanks. Just for that, you get one of these fresh-baked cookies my neighbor made me." This is mostly me wanting a cookie and not wanting to be rude.

"I actually already ate a few, so those are all for you."

I steer her toward the kitchen, put the plate down on the counter, and peel back the tinfoil. "If you insist."

"Open this first." She puts the gift bag in front of me.

Why I'm keyed up about what's inside, I have no idea. Maybe it's because I can't remember the last time a woman I dated gave me something besides liquor or a blow job. I lift out the tissue paper then reach my hand inside to withdraw a men's woven leather bracelet. It's black, double corded with a slipknot, and it's fucking awesome.

"I thought, since you got me something to wear, I'd get you something to wear, too," she says softly.

I slip the buttery soft leather onto my wrist. "I love it. Thank you." It takes everything I've got not to kiss her again. I resist because I need to take this slow, and when I put my mouth on her, I lose sight of that goal.

Her gorgeous smile tests my willpower. "You're welcome."

I snag a cookie to give my mouth something to do besides lust for her. "Holy shit, these are insane."

"Thanks. I'm glad you like them."

No blush this time. She's comfortable accepting certain kinds of praise. For some reason I miss the pink cheeks. I want to see them again. "Oh, I like the way you bake, Kendall, but you have other talents I like even better."

She arches her eyebrows. "Oh, really?"

"Yeah." I put half the cookie back on the plate and then lean against the counter and face her. "For starters, I like the way you kiss."

Victory is mine. Color stains her cheeks, but she seems to own it more easily now. "The kissing must be a natural talent, because I can promise you I have way more practice baking."

My dick twitches thinking about the extent of those natural talents, and the practice I'm ready to give 100 percent to, but not yet. I cover the cookies with the foil. "I'm going to hide these from my roommates, otherwise I'm liable to get none, and then we'll start on the culinary masterpiece I slaved over."

"You slaved over dinner?"

"Don't even get me started. I dialed the caterer. I explained the occasion. I pored over an endless menu of options and made tough decisions like which two sides should accompany the entree." I stow the cookies away in a bottom drawer underneath a clean dishtowel, and then pull a large bottle of water and a couple platters out of the fridge. She takes the water from me before I lead the way out to the patio. "Then I had to supervise the setup by diligently standing aside and staying out of their way. I'm fucking exhausted."

Her lips quirk as she puts the water on the table and settles into the sectional. I take the spot beside her and feel my mouth stretch into an answering smile. She arranges her legs under her, folds her hands in her lap, and eyes me. "Exactly how did you explain this occasion?"

"You know"—I shrug, deliberately casual—"the standard, deflower-the-beautiful-virgin-next-door dinner."

She chokes out a laugh before clearing her throat. "Do they list that one between corporate event and family reunion?" Her hand hovers over her upper lip to hide her grin.

"Yep. Lucky number seven."

"So I assume we're having...a hard sausage sampler?"

"Please. I would never be so obvious. I believe the theme of tonight's menu is Things You've Never Tried Before." I pick up the bottle of water and pour her a glass. No booze tonight. I don't need it. Don't want it.

She raises an eyebrow and glances at the appetizer tray. "I hate to break it to you, but I've had berries, bread, and cheese before."

"Fine." I spread one of the cheeses on a slice of bread, top it with a raspberry, and hand it to her. "What *haven't* you had before?"

"Um...frog legs," she says around a bite. "And sex. But I've never much wanted to try frog legs."

"Got it. No on frog legs, yes on sex." Jesus, I like this girl. I'm not sure I'll be able to keep to my side of the sectional while we eat.

"That would be my preference."

"Noted." I pick up a strawberry from the tray, hold it out to her, and enjoy the feel of her soft lips against my fingers as she closes her mouth around it. "Let's talk about that."

She swallows. "All right."

"I was thinking we should drill down on the act—so to speak. What have you done? How far have you gone? What did you like? What didn't you like?"

Another strawberry disappears between her vanilla-flavored lips. I fight an urge to chase it with my tongue because I want to hear what she says. I want to know. I don't want to move too fast or make another misstep. Mostly, I don't want to cause her any pain.

"What have *you* done?" She rests her head on the cushion and looks over at me. "How far have you gone?"

Shit. I really hadn't planned on getting into a game of "I Never" with her. When it comes to sex, there's very little I've never done, but that fact suddenly strikes me as sad and sordid. "I want to make it good for you, Kendall. That's why I ask."

Her smile returns, just a bit challenging. "And I want to make it good for you. It's been four years since I've done anything sexual with a guy. But before that, Mason and I did everything except have intercourse. I'm not without skills, they're just rusty."

Mention of Mason reminds me of how important tonight is. "I don't want to hurt you." There. I said it. So much for finesse.

"I don't think you need to worry about that."

"Because…?" I've never had a candid conversation like this with a girl before, but it's necessary. I won't cross any line she doesn't want to cross.

The color rises in her cheeks, but she returns my stare straight on. "Because I didn't hurt myself the other day when I was thinking about you and taking care of business solo-style."

"Only once? That's it? I must be in the hundreds by now, starting with the night we met."

"You passed out the night you met me."

"Okay, the morning after. I woke up with a vision of you in my head, and a hard-on so unstoppable I nearly came all over the sofa." At this moment, images of Kendall going solo-style fill my mind, and now my throat's dry and my cock is like granite, but I want to hear more, so I down some water and lean closer. "What did you imagine me doing to you while you were taking care of business?"

Her eyes drop to my mouth, and then to my lap. "There are a couple different scenarios." She leans her head to the side and trails her hand down her neck. "They all get the job done—"

"Your favorite."

"You first."

"Okay. You wander onto my deck," I say without hesitation. This is an often-played scenario and, if she wants to hear it, I want to share it. "It's night. The pool lights are on, and they guide you here. You're wearing a robe, but you slip it off as you approach the water, and you're naked beneath. I'm in the shadows, and I don't know if you see me or if you think you're alone, but you stop at the edge of the pool and stare at the water for a minute while the breeze has its way with you. I stay where I am, breathing shallow and gripping my dick through my jeans as I watch your nipples tighten. You bring your hands up and run your fingertips over them. Your eyelids droop and you bite your lip, and I wonder if you're imagining me touching you. I decide you are, since you're standing at my pool, and I think about stepping out of the shadows, but I don't. Not yet."

This session of true confessions is having a painfully predictable effect on me, but I don't care, because I can't take my eyes off Kendall. Pink cheeks, parted lips, she's hanging on my every word. As I watch, she crosses her legs and shifts forward. I nearly die.

"Then you dive in, and I step to the opposite end of the pool. I can hardly walk. I want you so badly every step tortures me, but the sight of your naked body gliding under the water tortures me even more. A couple lazy strokes, and you break the surface right at my feet. By the time you see me there I'm already closing in on you. I grip your wrists and haul you out of the pool. Water's streaming off you, and you're probably a little cold, but I don't care because I'm on fire—every fucking inch of me. I hold you against me. You're cool and smooth and sleek. I'm touching you everywhere, but I can't get you close enough, fast enough. Maybe I'm moving too fast, because you wriggle out of my grasp and walk away. You walk to the railing, wrap your hands around the top bar, and then shoot me this look over your shoulder—a look that says I've got to do more than just show up and grab you."

Kendall's hands rest near mine on the table. I wrap my fingers around her wrist. Her pulse is pounding. I feel the echo of it in my head. My chest. My aching balls.

"What do you do?" Her voice is barely a whisper.

"I walk over to you and stand close but don't touch you anywhere. When you shiver, I sweep your hair aside and kiss the back of your neck. Just that. My lips on your skin. I kiss my way down your body, inch by inch. I stop often. I take my time, until you're gripping the rail and squirming under my lips. Then I turn you around and kiss my way back up. I taste every part of you. You're screaming for me now, and I let you scream, because my body's screaming, too, and why should it suffer alone? But I give you only my mouth, working you with my lips and tongue until your breath hitches, and your body stiffens, and you come in a sweet, heavy rush. I catch you before your legs give out and lift you onto the railing. I tear my jeans open, part those long, endless legs of yours, and finally, finally drive into you. You're tight, and wet, and still quivering from the first orgasm, and it's more than I can take. I fuse my mouth to yours and fuck you like my life depends on it. You're wrapped around me, holding tight, with your heels digging into my thighs and your fingernails raking my ass. This time your scream flows straight into my throat, vibrates down my spine, and into my balls. Then your body hugs my cock, I call your name, and come in one long burst that drains me, body and soul."

I look down at our hands. Mine's still around her wrist, but somewhere in the course of the story, she clamped her fingers around my wrist, too, the leather bracelet she gave me pressing into my skin. Now she lets go and tugs herself out of my grasp. Then she gets to her feet.

Shit. Scared her off with my raunchy jack-off fantasy. I drop my head and listen to the click of her high heels on the deck. I expect to hear a rapid tap as she descends the steps, but it doesn't come. The noise stops abruptly.

"Vaughn?"

I look up to find her standing at the rail, holding onto the topmost bar and looking over her shoulder. Her gaze locked on me.

Chapter Seventeen

Kendall

Sexy fun. That's what tonight's about. I haven't stopped thinking about Vaughn. Haven't stopped wanting him. Even from across the patio, he weaves a seductive spell, and I want his dirty story-telling mouth all over me. That he's fantasized about me the way I've fantasized about him is a huge turn-on. We've flirted all week via text, and I knew while getting dressed that tonight I wanted him to be my first.

"Yes?" he answers, rising to his feet. I like the predatory gleam in his eyes.

Instead of replying, I turn my head, and before I can talk myself out of it, start to shimmy out of my dress. He's set up this little scenario, giving me the impetus and direction I needed, and I plan to deliver. I sway to the sultry music pouring out of hidden speakers and slowly bare my body to him, exposing my back, my ass, my legs. When the material reaches my ankles, I carefully step out of it. I'm left in a black G-string with a tiny pink bow at the top of my butt and my fuchsia sling-back pumps.

A breeze coasts over my skin, turning my nipples into aching points. I grip the railing in anticipation of Vaughn's approach.

"You are fucking gorgeous," he whispers in my ear. His warm breath and raunchy compliment send a hot shiver through me, and suddenly I'm languishing in the sexiest moment of my life. His smooth jaw brushes my neck, but otherwise he doesn't touch me.

Still, his nearness penetrates all my senses. I hear the echo of his words in my mind. I inhale the scent of his aftershave. The realization he took these measures to captivate me turns me on a little more.

"Thank you," I say.

Touch me, I almost add, but don't. Because I can feel him standing right behind me, and the anticipation sparks like a palpable thing. I can practically hear his heart beating strong and fast in his chest, feel the rush of his blood and the heat of need building, and through all that I sense his restraint. The rush and the heat and the need thrill me, but so does his control. My confidence grows, not because of his composure, but because of mine. I own this. I am strong, sexy, desired.

But it's hard to hold still, knowing he's fully clothed, and I'm next to naked, and he's looking his fill. Prickles of awareness tighten my skin. The moment stretches. When I don't think I can hold out another second for him to touch me I say, "What are you waiting for?"

"I don't want to rush. Well"—he laughs—"I do, more than you could possibly know, but I'm not going to, because this is like my first time, too."

Mutual first times. That's how this was supposed to happen for me, but…it didn't. I swallow the emotion his words stir up. There's no place for my past here. This is about the here and now. About Vaughn and about me.

"*Puh-lease*," I say to add levity to our situation. "It's probably not even your hundred-and-first time."

"It's the first time I've been someone's first. I take the privilege seriously. So yeah, we're going to take it slow. You're going to tell me what you want, and when you want it—how hard, soft, deep, long—and I'm going to give your beautiful body every single thing you ask for. Deal?"

Thank God he can't see my heart flailing around like I've swallowed a hundred happy pills. How is it possible to feel cherished and desperate at once? I nod. "Deal."

"So tell me, Kendall. What do you want?"

My mind whirls with the possibilities. I may not know what it's like to have sex, but I know what need feels like, and I'm feeling a whole new level of it right now. I throb between my thighs. My nipples ache from the light caress of the breeze. "I want you. I want everything. And I want it now."

He lets out an unsteady breath I find strangely reassuring. This conversation is taking a toll on him, too. "That leaves things wide open. Tell me to stop if I do anything you don't like."

"I don't like that you're stalling," I tease. I'm ready for action. Lots of it. I push the momentary thought of his experience with countless girls out of my head. Right now, I'm the one who gets to reap the rewards of his skills.

"You call it stalling; I call it seduction." He kisses my shoulder, and my panties grow wetter.

His lips are warm and soft, the contact firm, as he presses kiss after kiss along my shoulder, but his mouth slowly turns hotter and hungrier as he progresses. It's the only part of his body on me, and it's electrifying.

He drops kisses across my upper back to my other shoulder, then slowly tracks down my spine, his lips parting and openmouthed devotion raining down my flesh. I quiver. My breathing speeds up. His tongue flicks out, but it's not exactly a lick, more like a promise. A promise of what's to come, and I immediately think about him tasting me, sucking on my clit. Laving me until I can't hold anything back.

I squeeze my thighs together, because I'm not quite wanton enough to spread my legs in invitation when I'm exposed like I am. The memory of Vaughn's fingers inside me, my dress bunched around my waist, panties pushed to the side, is a heady one, and I clench my thighs again to offset the pleasure the reminder stokes inside me.

I'm close to coming, and we've just gotten started. How wasteful would that be?

His mouth lands on the tiny bow of my panties, his teeth tug the lace that runs along the cleft of my ass. I wiggle as his tongue plucks it like a guitar string. The scrap of material covering my new wax job rubs against my folds. My legs shake.

"You like that?"

"I…" I can't answer because he does it again, tugging infinitesimally harder, and I can't stop myself from bending forward to give him better access.

"Yes or no," he prompts. His breath flutters over my skin and even though it's warm tonight, I feel goose bumps rise.

"Y-yes. I like it…" Then he licks down my ass crack, and I stop breathing.

My hands slide off the railing and reach for him—to stop him or pull him closer, I don't know.

Vaughn takes hold of my waist and spins me around. He's on his knees, his jeans undone, his shirt gone. For a moment, all I can do is drink in his tan, toned male beauty. It's not hard to see why his chiseled pecs, speed-bump abs, and twin ridges of muscle cutting in at his hips grace a big billboard, but reality is even more overwhelming, not to mention a little intimidating. Then I spy a thin strip of woven leather encircling his wrist. The birthday present I gave him.

Seeing my gift on him reminds me this isn't some perfect stranger. This is the man who thanked me for confiscating his car keys, and slow danced with me in a crowded club, and listened—held me close and really listened—while I told him my deepest secrets. This is Vaughn, and just like that my hesitation evaporates. I want to see more. I want to hook my fingers into the loose waist of his jeans and drag them down. I want him naked. I want to see. Touch. Taste.

Our eyes connect. I lick my lips and prepare to speak, but he beats me to the punch.

"I've had your scent in my head for days." He leans in, his lips hovering close to my lacy panties, and inhales deeply. "Like a craving. I can't wait to put my mouth here again."

Yes. Yes!

"But we're taking it slow, so first…"

He kisses up my side, licks my belly button, skims his lips all the way to the bottom swell of my breasts. Without thought, I run my fingers through his hair. He groans and rises to his full height before tilting his head and crushing his mouth to mine.

My body turns liquid as he delves between my lips and subdues my tongue. I wrap my arms around his neck, press our bodies together.

As fast as he claimed my mouth, he abandons it, leaving my tongue tingling and my lips burning for more. I'm about to protest when he palms my boobs and rubs his thumbs over my nipples. The peaks tighten even more under his attention. Without looking up he says, "Jesus, Kendall. You're stunning." He traces the line where my tan transitions to the paler skin always covered by my bikini top. "Beautiful," he murmurs. "You're the most beautiful thing I've ever touched."

Although the words sound impossibly sincere, my mind rushes to rebut them. Even if I didn't know he'd touched truly flawless girls—models and pop stars and actresses, oh my—

he's definitely touched himself. But then our gazes lock, and the look on his face threatens to overwhelm me. I haven't recovered when he bends his head and takes my nipple into his mouth.

I gasp as he works me with his lips and tongue while gently, and then not so gently, pinching my other nipple. The double assault is pleasure so sharp it's nearly pain. I arch my back, seeking more, but he pauses.

"Too hard? Too soft? Tell me how you like it."

"Not sure yet." I manage a quick breath. "Better try again."

His smile flashes for an instant before his mouth and hand switch places. I bite my lip to stop myself from actual begging. He tastes every inch of my torso—at least it feels like he does—before his mouth lands on the inside of my thigh. His fingers hook the strings at my hips, and he inches them down while he drops wet kisses so close to my sex I can barely keep still.

"By the way," he says, slipping my G-string around and off my shoes. "Those pumps are sexy as hell. Mind leaving them on?"

I shake my head. I'm standing naked in front of Vaughn Shaughnessy.

He's going to fuck me against this railing.

I'm afraid to blink for fear I'll wake up from this dream.

He takes his time looking at me—all of me—like I'm a treasure map or a rare gemstone. Like I'm something special. And in this moment, it feels true. With Vaughn kneeling before me and brushes of pink and gold painting the sky as the sun sinks below the horizon, I feel aglow with possibilities.

"Kendall," he finally says, "are you ready to spread your legs and give me another taste?"

I can't speak, but I manage to inch my thighs wider.

He takes this for the yes it is and leans in, his long fingers wrapped around my thighs. I squeeze his shoulders and watch as his lips make contact. He kisses me there with the same devoted hunger he used on my mouth. His tongue is warm and wet as he circles my clit.

I do my best not to squirm even as my muscles tighten. I'm on sensory overload, about to detonate. Nothing has ever felt this good. Vaughn licks, sucks, devours, and I'm soaking wet, his upper lip glistening with the proof. The sight makes me so hot, I whimper in response.

"You like that?" His low voice caresses my sex.

"God, yes. Don't stop."

He places the softest of kisses against my center. "Just my mouth, or are you ready for more?"

"More." The word tumbles out. "I want more."

I feel him smile just before he slides a finger inside me. Unlike the night of his birthday, this time I'm not nervous. Not conflicted. I'm so ready, and accept him with a soft moan of pleasure. He circles and strokes for a moment before carefully adding another finger. I'm just starting to feel the strain of being stretched to capacity when he groans against me. The vibration is like a massage, relaxing every muscle in the vicinity. The pull subsides and then dissolves into even more pleasure. He feels it, or knows it, because he works me inside and out with abandon. I'm lost completely to him. I move. I writhe. I ride his fingers and buck against his tongue. I taste sweat on my upper lip. I hear the erotic sounds of his mouth moving hungrily over me, his fingers filling me. That's all it takes for the pressure building inside me to break into a thousand glorious pieces.

My breath catches and my heart revs as I chase every swirling, glowing fragment of my release. He doesn't let up until my legs are about to give out.

"I've got you," he says, tightening his supporting grip and raining kisses along my thigh.

Yes he does. I sigh and watch him move to suck, then kiss the flair of my hip. My stomach muscles quiver anew. It's impossible to put into words what the sight of his lips on my body does to me.

When he lifts his head we both look at the red mark blooming on my skin. He offers me a wicked grin. "Vaughn was here," he whispers.

Before I can say something crazy like, "Feel free to stop by anytime," he takes me in his arms and lifts me onto the railing.

For a second the cold metal stings my unprotected ass. But when Vaughn captures my bottom lip in his mouth, a hot shockwave races down my spine, and the chill vanishes.

The hard ridge straining the front of his jeans presses snugly against the part of me he's just turned into a playground of nerve endings. I moan into his mouth, our tongues stroking, as one of his hands leaves my waist and cups the back of my head to deepen the kiss. My heart is still pounding from my orgasm, I taste myself on his tongue, and delicious tension starts to build inside me again. He kisses me like he can't get enough. I run my hands over his back.

We're both breathless when he breaks away to pull a condom out of his back pocket and push his jeans and boxer briefs down to his knees.

My eyes widen as I take him in. He's big and thick and for a second I worry this might hurt more than I anticipated. He can only be so gentle. Whether he does it smooth and fast, or slow and by degrees, at some point that big, thick cock is going to go all the way inside me.

"You look so fucking gorgeous right now, shining brighter than the sunset, but if you'd rather go to my room—"

"No. This is perfect," I say to his cock.

He laughs, but it sounds a little pained. "You want to touch me first? Inspect the goods before you decide?"

Without answering, I wrap my hand around his dick. He twitches under my touch, and I swear he grows even bigger as I rub up and down.

"Fuck me, Kendall, please. Any way you want. I'm all yours."

I look up and meet his half-lidded eyes. A flush tinges his cheekbones. The sight staggers me and makes me bolder at the same time. "Think I could get you off with a few more strokes?" I slide my thumb over the head of his cock before fisting him just a little tighter on the downward slide. He's smooth, but rugged. Hot and hard…he shudders from my touch…it's powerful.

A groan rumbles around in his chest. "You could make me come by blowing *on* it. Is that what you want?"

"I want you inside me," I confess. It's true. There's a sharp, empty feeling in my core and right at this moment the pain of not having him is worse than anything.

"Thank God." His gentle hand brushes mine away. He rolls the condom on then steps between my legs and once again takes my bottom lip between his teeth. His fingers find my center to part my folds and a second later he's guiding himself inside.

I wrap my arms and legs around him and hope he doesn't feel me tremble. Because it's not fear, it's gladness that it's him—this generous, gorgeous, disorienting man—taking me somewhere I've never been before.

He enters me slowly, keeping to his word not to rush our first time. The head of his cock slips inside, then inch by inch he pushes in farther. It's exquisite. Intense. My body stretches to make room for him, but I feel my muscles pull taut, impeding his progress.

It's not enough to hurt, more like a twinge of uncomfortable pressure—a small warning that something's going to have to give if we keep going.

He cradles my cheek with his palm. "Breathe."

Our eyes connect as I abide by his wishes. Then he thrusts—all the way home this time—and forces the air out of me in a gasp. A muffled gasp, because he seals his mouth to mine and swallows it.

For so long just the thought of sharing this part of myself with someone brought on pain and guilt, but right now I'm overcome with different feelings. Feelings too strong for words, too overpowering to leave room for anything else except Vaughn. He grinds his hips against mine, creating the most incredible friction ever. Eager for more, I grind right back. I'm completely absorbed in him, in *need* of him.

He withdraws a little, and then surges into me again, and again. Harder. Faster. The friction starts to burn, but the burn doesn't hurt. It's addictive. I dig my heels into his thighs. Hold onto his ass. Hold onto the sensations he's building in me.

Our kiss is a wild collision of lips and tongues. Our teeth click. He breaks away to kiss my jaw, the spot just below my earlobe. Bundles of hot, tangled nerves coil inside me.

I take a breath as he buries his nose in the hollow of my neck. "Do you like it? Do you like having me inside you?"

"Yes." I twine my arms around his head and rock my hips to bury him deeper. "I can't get enough."

"I planned to fuck you slowly," he whispers, his voice huskier than I've ever heard it. "I don't want to be too rough with you." His deep inhale tells me he's struggling to get a hold of himself. He smiles against my throat, and adds, "Not the first time."

I'm on board with multiples. He can captain me all night. I tighten my hold on him. His thrusts turn more rhythmic, no less enthusiastic, but measured…strategic. And, yep, it's an excellent strategy. I *love* having him inside me.

Before I can question the verb I just chose, he moves his hands to my ass next, so I'm seated in his palms, and tips my hips a little. I moan out loud. His cock feels even longer, and thicker, and strokes an entirely new spot. A rush of warm tingles descends on me, and I realize everything I felt before was just a ghost of what's coming. And I want it. Desperately. I grind against him and pant-gasp-sob through a second orgasm I swear he wrings right out of my soul.

"Fuck," Vaughn mutters. His body goes rigid, he pumps into me one more time, and then my name falls from his lips—breaking a little between the syllables—like he's completely lost in *me*.

I've never liked my name so much as in that moment.

He stays seated deep inside as we slide down from our high. I press my lips to his collarbone, luxuriating in the salty taste of his skin. I may have just given him a piece of me, but he's given me something in return: freedom.

Plus, two amazing orgasms I'll never forget.

He lifts his head and touches his nose to mine. "You okay?"

"Mmm-hmm. You?"

"More than okay." His grin is positively deadly. It should be illegal for someone to have a smile like his.

Fireflies do a break dance in my stomach; a warm flush spreads over my skin even though I try not to read too much into those words. He can't possibly mean I rocked his world like he just rocked mine.

He tucks a strand of hair behind my ear. "I have to warn you, I could get addicted to your pussy. Touching it. Kissing it. Fucking it." His lips find a vulnerable spot by the corner of my mouth. "How much touching, kissing, and fucking do you think it can take?"

Oh my God, his words alone are going to make me come. I open my mouth to say something equally sexy, like, I can take as much touching, kissing, and fucking as he can dole out, and then…

His stomach growls. "Ignore that," he says between kisses to my neck. "I have more important appetites to satisfy."

"Hey now." I tip my head to give his lips free range. "Did you or did you not invite me over for dinner *and* sex?"

"You're right. I did. Can you eat while I touch, kiss, and fuck you?"

"I don't know…" I trail off when his mouth roams into a ticklish zone. "It might present a choking hazard."

"Fair point." He straightens and gives me a raised eyebrow and a smile made for temptation. "Sure you want dinner now?" As he asks, he moves inside me once—as if he really *is* addicted and hates to abandon his new favorite thing—but before he can do anything more, his stomach rumbles again. Loud.

We both laugh, then I say firmly, "Dinner. Afterward we'll see about more touching, kissing, and fucking."

"Promise?" He phrases it as a question, but his smirk is too much. He's a bad, bad boy, and he knows it. With one hand holding the base of the condom and one pressed almost protectively against my body, he gently pulls out. I miss his warmth immediately.

He picks up my dress and panties. When he hands them to me, his knuckles brush mine. Electricity skitters up my arm. Our gazes collide. I break eye contact first so we can right ourselves before sitting back down at the table. I'm pleasantly sore and have a hard time hiding my happiness, the corners of my mouth pulling up no matter how hard I try to keep my face neutral.

What just happened between us was magical. I've had years to imagine what it would be like to lose my virginity, and this far exceeded my dreams. Vaughn's touch, his taste, his smell, flooded my senses, keeping me rooted in the single most intimate moment of my life. That we talked while we moved with each other heightened our connection. We may have just fucked, but it was more than a simple fuck. For that, I'll always be grateful he was my first.

Vaughn steps over to the barbecue island to wash his hands in the small sink. He returns as I finish dressing and laces our fingers to lead me back to the sectional. He motions for me to sit first then takes the spot beside me. Energy continues to crackle between us as I spread some cheese on a slice of bread and take a bite. Wipe a crumb off my lip. Catch him watching me.

"I have some exciting news," I say.

"Tell me."

"I got a summer job."

He makes a face in surprise, still managing to look incredibly hot. My body temperature spikes for a second, remembering the feel of him inside me.

"You're looking at the assistant coordinator for Art In Progress, it's this fantastic…" I babble for several minutes about the organization and what I've been up to since starting work there two days ago.

When I finally stop to take a breath, Vaughn leans over and presses a soft kiss to my lips. "You're amazing. Congratulations."

"Thanks."

"You said the art exhibit is on Wednesday. Are you doing anything Thursday night?"

I pop a cheese square into my mouth. "Are you asking me out on another date?"

"I am. I've got passes to Laney Albright's album release party, and I'm hoping you'll go with me."

My stomach tightens. A public date with the next possible host of *America Rocks* to celebrate last season's winner is like walking down the street with a boa constrictor around my neck. All eyes will be on us. I twist the stem of my glass and try for a smile. "That's really nice of you to ask, but I can't."

"You have plans already?"

"No. Honestly, and no offense, but I'd rather not be seen with you in public." Tonight, I took a huge step away from trapped, conflicted Kendall. I'm moving forward. I need to keep moving forward, but I also want to keep my personal life private.

His eyebrows lift. "No offense, huh?"

"I'm sorry. That came out wrong. What I meant was you're a celebrity, and with that comes media attention. I like to stay under the radar."

He takes my hand in his. "There will be a lot of other high-profile people there. I'm not the main attraction." His thumb rubs over my knuckles. "But I do have to go, and I leave town for a photo shoot Friday morning. I really want to spend time with you while I can. How about we skip the press gauntlet and sneak in?"

The soothing gesture of his thumb lowers my defenses, as does the subtle reminder our time together is limited. But still…"I know I sound paranoid, but all it would take is one picture of us on social media for people in my hometown to start rehashing my past, except this time their comments could find a broader audience. A part of me is always afraid of that kind of exposure. I'm not just worried about myself. I would hate for Mason and his parents to be put through it."

"I understand, but I swear it won't be an issue. This is an exclusive event, not a media free-for-all. Inside coverage of the actual party will be limited and focused almost entirely on Laney." He turns my hand over, traces his finger across my palm. "I can't see the future, but I don't need that power to know nothing will happen Thursday night except we'll listen to some new music, dance, schmooze a few of the *America Rocks* producers—if they show—and hopefully congratulate Laney. It should be a fun event, but it will be infinitely more fun if you join me.

"Besides," he adds, as if he doesn't know I'm already a big puddle of yes, "how can you leave Los Angeles without attending a Hollywood VIP event with your good friend Vaughn?"

Is that the turn we've taken? Friends—good friends—with temporary benefits? It rings a little hollow, but it also puts my concerns into perspective. I'm not a permanent part of Vaughn's life, and he's not a fixture in mine. So, is there really any harm in experiencing the excitement of his world for a few hours? "Okay."

I barely get the word out before his handsome face is inches from mine. His lips graze the shell of my ear. "Great. I'll pick you up at six."

"On one condition. You come to my exhibit on Wednesday."

His grin is blindingly white. "Deal. That takes care of Wednesday and Thursday, but right now I'm more interested in tonight. I hope you're okay with staying over, because I'm not done yet," he says. "Not by a long shot."

Dizziness fills my head and without any hesitation I say, "I'm not done, either."

Chapter Eighteen

KENDALL

The pillow underneath my cheek is soft like cashmere. So are the sheets covering my naked body, and I want to stay in this spot forever. I'm warm, snuggly, and—I take a deep breath—surrounded by the smell of fresh laundered—maybe even new—high-thread-count cotton *and* him.

Vaughn.

Vaughn with his skillful hands, multitalented mouth, incredible stamina, and decided disposition to make me feel special. After having me on the patio, the rest of our naked time was spent covering every surface in his room, moving through intimate positions that made me blush. And I may be a novice, but when he moved with slow, purposeful strokes inside me, our gazes locked on each other, I felt more than just a physical connection.

I blink my eyes open.

I'm not falling for him or anything, just extremely satiated.

Sunlight slips inside the room underneath the partially opened curtains covering the floor-to-ceiling windows. Last night Vaughn had wrapped me in his arms and shared points of interest lighting up the cityscape beyond the glass. When a shooting star had twinkled across the sky, we'd both caught the show. He'd said, since we saw the star together, we should make a wish together.

"Aloud?" I'd asked. "How will it come true, then?"

"I already got my wish tonight, so anything else is a bonus," he'd whispered in my ear. It had tickled. In places besides my earlobe.

"Okay. What should we wish for?"

With his chin resting on my bare shoulder, he'd let out a deep breath. "Nude Mondays."

"Be serious!"

"I am. Think about it. Everyone hates Mondays. But if clothing was optional, I bet it would become everyone's favorite day of the week. Better than Friday." Then he'd kissed the slope of my neck and we'd stopped talking.

I roll over now to smooth my hand across the spot he left vacant sometime this morning. Before we'd fallen asleep around two a.m., he told me I could sleep in as late as I wanted. He had to meet up with his trainer for a trail run at nine. I giggled when he made the cutest face and said he'd cancel, but doing so last minute meant a follow-up workout that would leave him sore for days.

Speaking of sore, I'm achy between my legs. An ache I'll gladly suffer again and again. I smile at the reminder of the amazing night I had.

His bedside clock reads 10:07. Ten. Oh. Seven. I can't remember the last time I slept so peacefully for eight hours straight. The Vaughn Effect is officially at maximum-strength potency. Sighing, I sit up, keeping myself covered. It's then that I notice a plate on the nightstand, holding two of the chocolate chip cookies I brought last night. Beside it is a pink blossom that looks suspiciously like one of Aunt Sally's carefully tended damask roses standing tall in a drinking glass half full of water. Propped against the glass is a plain white notecard with my name scrawled across it.

I fall back onto my pillow with the biggest grin ever in the history of grins. He carefully planned last night, but this? This is spur of the moment. If Vaughn keeps this up, my heart doesn't stand a chance.

Heart? Uh-uh. Good friends with benefits, remember?

Of course I remember. But I roll out of bed anyway, dress quickly—sans panties, since I can't find them—and then sit at the edge of the comforter and bite into a cookie. Sex multiple times obviously leaves a girl with an appetite.

My eyes stray to the rose. It's in full bloom, and I can't resist touching one velvety petal. Yes, there's a whole bush full right next door, but Vaughn picked this one for me. Picturing him sneaking over to steal a flower puts a smile on my face. A little naughty, a lot charming, and totally Vaughn. He's showing me all his sides even though I don't think he's aware he's doing it.

And the note reads as follows... *Kendall, has anyone ever told you that you sleep like an angel? You do. A sexy angel. Next time I promise to wake you properly. ~Vaughn*

I read his words several times before tucking the note into my handbag. I don't have the words to describe the joy they bring me. With my shoes and purse dangling in one hand and the flower in the other, I slip out his front door.

Dixie and Amber are sitting side-by-side at the breakfast bar when I walk into the kitchen. They both stop mid cereal spoon to their mouths when they see me. Even Snowflake looks up from chewing her dog bone to check me out. I swear she nods her head in approval.

"Looks like someone had her cherry popped," Dixie

says.

I'm pretty sure cherry describes the color of my cheeks. I put my things down on the counter and stand across from them.

"Pretty flower," Amber says.

"Yes," I say in answer to both their observations.

A beat of silence passes and then the three of us start giggling like…well…sisters. Don't get me wrong. I have no delusions about us being best friends. But there's a connection here. One I hope we can continue to cultivate.

"So? How was it?" Amber asks, pushing her bowl of cornflakes to the side.

"Amazing," I breathe out. "All three times were amazing."

Amber lets out a victory whoop and throws her arms in the air like her team just scored the winning field goal. "Three times, Miss Dixie. Pay up!"

Dixie makes a face. "Yeah, yeah, yeah. I owe you twenty bucks. As for you, princess"—she points a finger my way, but I see a definite grin lurking beneath her sore-loser expression—"there's a fine line between glowing and gloating. He's hot. He's good in bed. Enough said."

As if mere words could stop me from glowing or gloating. But for once the old nickname doesn't sound like an insult. It's lost its bite because now I've done something she can relate to. Possibly even respect. But more importantly, I respect *myself*. There will be only one first, and I chose a guy who viewed that as an honor. When he looked at me, it was like no one else existed.

My stomach flutters at the memory. "Enough said? So you don't want to know he was super-attentive? Or that he wiped out my insecurities thirty seconds after I walked through the front door? Or he made me laugh as hard as he made me come?"

"Just don't fall for him," Dixie says around her last bite of cereal.

"I won't," I quickly say, and disavow all knowledge of the little voice in my mind that whispers *it's a lie*. I can't listen to that voice, and I have no plans to share it with my sisters. Brit is waiting for my call, so she'll remind me I need to figure out my own life before thinking about a relationship with someone. She's beyond excited about Vaughn and me having a good time together, but she's also sensible. Cautionary when it comes to getting too attached when I'm the temporary neighbor and he's got goals that collide with mine.

"Gotta shower," I say to cut off any more discussion from either Dixie, Amber, or the whisper in my head. I scoop my stuff up off the counter and take the stairs two at a time to my room. Once inside, I close and lock the door. I strip off my clothes. In the confines of the cream-and-white tiled shower, my muscles and mind relax under the hot water.

I know what I'm doing, right? And what I'm *not* doing. This is my summer of self-discovery, and Vaughn is an important and unexpected part of it. Being with him released me from the burden on my heart. Mostly. The next step is accepting law school. There are lots of things I can do with a law degree besides practice law. That I can't think of what those are isn't cause for concern. I'll have three years to figure it out.

The thought hurts and helps at the same time.

• • •

"Good morning!" I walk into Art In Progress on Monday with two iced coffees, one silly grin over memories of my first dirty text, and a gigantic breakfast burrito for Candace and me to share. "I brought sustenance." She's been working overtime to get ready for the exhibit, and as the kick-ass assistant I am, I support her efforts with caffeine and carbs.

She looks up from behind the reception desk to give me a quick smile. "Bless you."

"Is everything okay?" More lines than usual crease her forehead. I hand her a coffee then slide a chair over to the desk. I pull the warm burrito, already cut in half, out of the brown bag. The smell of egg, cheese, and cilantro wafts to my nose.

"I just hung up the phone with Josie. She has the stomach flu," she laments.

"Josie?"

"Our art teacher. She was supposed to teach a class this morning. The kids are putting the final touches on their paintings for the exhibit."

"You don't have anyone who can substitute?" I take a sip of my drink.

"Not on such short notice. And I'd do it, but I've got a list a mile long of things to get done before Wednesday and have a meeting with our publicist in an hour and then the framers are coming to start framing the artwork and the lighting company is after that and then the photographer—"

"Did you forget you've got me?" I ask, not the least bit offended I seem to have been overlooked. Two days together is hardly enough time to put me at the forefront of her thoughts.

Candace lets out a deep breath. "I'm sorry. I did, kind of. You have no idea how happy I am that you're here."

"Tell me what you'd like me to do today and I'll do it. You have no idea how happy I am to be here, too."

"How do you feel about teaching?"

"Done." I peeked in on a music class last week and I'd venture to say "teaching" is a loose term. The students are afforded a lot of creative freedom, and they seem to thrive on it. Guidance might be a better term than teaching, and I can do that. I've done my fair share of paint-by-numbers.

"Whatever angel sent you to me, I'm very grateful." She pulls back the paper covering her burrito and brings the stuffed tortilla to her mouth. "Thank you."

"I could say the same to you."

She tilts her head to consider me. She hasn't asked me to elaborate on the traumatic event I mentioned to her when we met, but I'm certain she's thinking about it now. If she'd asked me last week, I probably would have declined. But today, I'm okay with it. Actually—I put my burrito down—I'd like to tell her.

"When I was seventeen, I made a huge mistake and got behind the wheel of my boyfriend's car after winning a game of 'Who's more sober?' Unfortunately, as it turned out, we both lost. I hit a tree and suffered minor injuries, but he went through the windshield." I talk for another minute, appreciative when Candace doesn't look at me with pity or disgust. She doesn't judge. She asks a few questions like, how long before I stopped having dreams in which Mason miraculously recovered and life went back to "normal"? A couple of years, I tell her, and in saying so, realize it's true. The life I'm living nowadays feels "normal." My hopes and dreams spring from who I am and where I am now.

When she wants to know if there's any salsa in the takeout bag—as if a kick-ass assistant like me would neglect to bring salsa—just like that, we fall back into comfortable conversation, talking about the list of things that need to be done in the next forty-eight hours. The more we discuss, the more excited I get. I can't wait to show her what I'm made of. I've never shied away from hard work.

At ten o'clock my summer class starts. "Hi everyone, I'm Kendall, and I'll be overseeing your class today. How was your weekend?"

"Good," they return.

"I can see you're just about done with your paintings and have put a lot of hard work into them." I walk between the four teenagers sitting on stools in front of easels. The theme for the exhibit is "The Power of Us," and on each canvas is the artist's unique rendition.

"Would you please introduce yourselves?" I ask.

"I'm April."

"Javier."

"Brooklyn."

The fourth student, a boy whose light brown hair is bisected with a scar several inches long, doesn't say anything.

"His name is Will and he doesn't talk," April tells me.

"That's okay," I say, a sharp pang stabbing my heart. Not pity, but concern. For the first few days after the accident, I barely spoke a word. It was easier for me to keep things bottled up inside. "Can you hear me, Will?"

He nods.

I ache to know all of the stories in this room, and maybe with time I'll get to hear them. April, Javier, Brooklyn, and Will look to be around sixteen or seventeen, close to the age I was when I crashed Mason's car. I'm not sure I believe in fate, but if my aunt hadn't asked me to house-sit for the summer, I wouldn't be standing in this room right now, trying to hear these kids and trying to help them.

"It's nice to meet all of you," I say. "Your artwork is beautiful." It truly is, but I stall in front of Will's piece, awe overcoming me. He's chosen to use charcoals instead of watercolors like the others, and the depth and detail are amazing. The drawing depicting three young girls playing with a large black-and-white dog is so lifelike it's as if I could reach out and touch them.

Are they girls he knows? Sisters? Friends? Will's focus is fixed firmly on his picture, his shoulders hunched in concentration. Whether from his memory or imagination, it's remarkable and tugs at something in me. My eyes see the girls as Dixie, Amber, and me, bonded in a way we never were at that age, but maybe are heading toward now. Seeing it leaves me a little sad about our past but hopeful about our future. I have no idea how much Candace is charging for these works of art, but I want to buy this one.

"Where's Josie?" Brooklyn asks.

"She has the stomach flu." I resume walking around the easels, impressed by each picture. The talent varies, but that's not what this is about. It's about the artists pouring out their feelings, and that mission is accomplished—in the colors, shapes, shades, and clarity.

April stops painting. "Will she be okay for the exhibit?"

"I'm sure she'll try her best to be here," I say, moved by the concern. This group may be here because they need emotional support, but that hasn't stopped them from caring about someone else.

I could easily pull up an easel and join them.

• • •

The house is dark when I get home. I flip on the lights and try not to trip on Snowflake, who is underfoot and barky about being left alone in her big, comfortable house with her millions of dog toys. I scoop her up and fuss over her as I make my way to the kitchen for something to quickly curb my major hunger pains. Luckily, the kitchen just happens to be Snow's favorite room in the entire world, so she settles in my arms and switches from annoyed bark to excited bark. "Are you hungry, girl? Me, too. And unlike one of us, who has three live-in servants to see to her meals, I'm running on half a breakfast burrito, which is way under my normal calorie intake." Not that I thought much about food today. I was having too much fun substitute teaching and helping to prep for the art show.

Still holding Snow, I open the cupboard where Sally keeps the dog treats, dig out one shaped like a fish, and let Snow inspect it. She approves by biting off the tail. Great. I put her down with her feast and scan the room. The plate of chocolate chip cookies is right where I left it on the kitchen counter. I peel back the clear plastic wrap and take one of the remaining two, only to hear a greedy whimper at my feet. I shake my head at Snow. "No. This is *my* treat. That's *yours*," I say, and use my foot to point at her biscuit. Then I bite into the cookie. Snow grumbles and then turns tail, takes her biscuit, and runs off.

As I eat both cookies, my thoughts stray to Vaughn and the smile on his face when he devoured the ones I brought him. I've probably smiled a dozen times today thinking about his killer green eyes and the words that come out of his sexy mouth.

Licking crumbs off my fingers, I notice a lined piece of paper with writing scrawled across it. I reach over. *Snow has been walked and received her "good walk" treat. Don't let her con you into giving her another.*

Oops.

Dixie and I are at the ArcLight for a movie. Text if you're home before seven and want to join. A & D

I glance at the digital clock above the stovetop. It's seven fifteen.

I'm not too disappointed but wish I'd known sooner so I could have tried to meet them at the theater. Looks like it's a turkey sandwich then bed for me. Just as well, since tomorrow will be another insanely busy workday. My lips twitch in anticipation.

I startle when there's a knock on the kitchen door. It's Vaughn. And oh my God, is that a pizza box in his hands?

"Hi!" I say, opening the glass door and trying to act like

he isn't the best thing since, well ever.

"Hey. Pizza delivery." He gives me a quick kiss on the mouth before striding inside.

The pie smells delicious, but he smells better. Which is crazy given my love of carbs, but apparently I'm not the only one who notices because Snowflake charges into the kitchen to bark with joy and dance around his feet.

I don't blame her. "Thank you. I'm starving."

He puts the box down on the counter, and I notice things Snow will never properly appreciate, like the way his T-shirt stretches across his broad shoulders. The guy is dangerous coming or going. And I'm hungry for more than food now.

"Me, too," he says, turning to look at me. My legs go weak at the blatant hunger in his eyes.

I think he wants more than pizza, too.

"What kind did you get?" I manage to perch on a barstool without flinging myself into his arms.

"I wasn't sure what your favorite toppings were"—his gaze bounces around the kitchen—"or who else might be joining this pizza party, so I took the safe bet and went with cheese only."

"Dixie and Amber went to a movie, so it's a pizza party for two. And I love just cheese." *And you.*

Whoa. So not an appropriate thought. I lift the box lid and give Vaughn a slice before taking my own. He pulls a chunk of crust from his piece, shows it to Snow, and then tosses it into the hall with a "Go get it, girl!" before I can say, "No! She's already had two treats." Oh well. Off she goes. I'm in such a hurry to stuff my face and hide my affection for him anyway, that I burn the roof of my mouth.

"Ow. Ow. Ow." I fan my hand in front of my face. "It's *hawt*." I need to chill out. It's normal for friends to feel attachment, so I don't need to burn my tongue off in order not to accidentally blurt out something inappropriate.

"How about we slow down, Speed Racer, plate our food, and take it to the couch?"

I nod. Then watch as he takes care of everything, including glasses of water and napkins. I follow him to the family room where we sit facing each other on the sofa. There is no end to how long I could stare at him.

"This is really good. Thanks again," I say.

"Welcome. I'm glad our timing worked out." His attention hasn't strayed from me for even a second, his eyes keeping us connected and making my body heat. He's a pretty intense friend. Just saying.

"How did your final audition go? It was today, right?"

He runs a hand over his smooth, angular jaw. "It went well, I think."

"What did they have you do?"

"Another actor and I were put into a room and thrown a bunch of scenarios, like this person is going to move forward, this person is not, this person is a great singer, and then we had to improv what we'd say."

"You are a smooth-tongued devil, Vaughn Shaughnessy. I bet you slayed every single one of their scenarios."

"I must have done okay because then they called me into a room by myself and said, 'The judges just tore a performance to shreds and the contestant's father passed away two weeks ago, go.'"

"Oh my gosh, that's horrible. What did you say?"

He scans the room like he's looking for the answer. "I—um—I said bravery takes different forms, and tonight you showed us one of them. Getting up here, continuing to compete, made a whole lot of people really proud of you. They're rooting for you to come back strong next week."

Smooth-tongued doesn't begin to cover it. "How did you come up with something so perfect off the top of your head?"

"I don't know. I tried to say what I'd want to hear if I was the contestant."

"You nailed it."

"I hope so. The new set is sick, by the way. Regardless of what happens, maybe I can get you in to take a look around."

"Can't say no to that." Pizza sauce smudges the corner of his mouth, so I wipe it away with the pad of my thumb.

He puts his plate on the coffee table, and waits for me to finish my bite before taking my plate and placing it atop his. "Can I get you to say yes to my next question, too?"

We lean toward each other. It's slow-motion torture. It's also safe to say I will agree to all his requests. And that's a fairly frightening realization, especially considering I thought all the scary parts of this…whatever this is…were behind me. They're not, though. Each step I take with Vaughn is new and leads down an unmapped path. Are there landmines here? Do I care? "What's the question?" I mutter.

"Put this on me?" Somehow he's produced a condom packet in his hand.

Oh my. If this is a landmine, I will gladly throw myself on it. Lifting my brows and fluttering my lashes, I ask, "Anywhere in particular?" We inch closer.

"Considering it's extra large, there's only one place it will fit."

I laugh. I can't help it. Any more than I can help how I break eye contact to glance down at his lap. And then my eyelids flutter. I can't believe he's hard—full-mast hard—and we've yet to really touch since his quick hello kiss. I'm immediately turned on knowing I do this to him. "Wow. You must *really* like pizza."

"Pizza I can take or leave, but you I've got to have. Now."

"Right here? On my aunt and uncle's couch?"

His naughty smile doesn't quite protect me from the unadulterated longing in his eyes. "I've had a dirty fantasy about you and this sofa for several weeks now."

Now I do, too, but there are big gaps between my fantasies and my actual know-how. “I've never—”

“You've got this, sweetheart.” The naughty smile softens into something that matches the look in his eyes and destroys me completely. “You've got *me*.” Our noses touch and then…

We can't get our clothes off fast enough. Hands seeking, roaming, tugging off shirts and unzipping jeans. Mouths fusing, tongues tangling, teeth nibbling. When Vaughn gently bites my lower lip, I feel it in my breasts and between my legs.

I'm naked and flat on my back seconds later. He straddles me, offers me the condom.

I pull my hand back as if he's holding out a blowtorch or a scalpel or something else I'm not qualified to handle. “I don't want to accidentally mangle anything. I like it too much to hurt it.”

He laughs—a little strained—and places the rolled latex on my palm. “I'm hurting already, Kendall. The only way you make it worse is by not touching me.”

Well, when he puts it like that…

I lift the condom and place it like a cap on the blunt smoothness of his crown. Sensing my nervousness, he talks me through rolling it over his long, thick member. His penis is a work of art—an erotic masterpiece of strength and sensitivity. Sliding my hand along the length awakens a complex and powerful string of nerves running from my fingertips to my core. I'm wet and ready.

“Perfect,” he whispers before he props one of my legs over the back of the couch and the other over his shoulder. His fingers find their target to test my readiness and then he's thrusting inside me in one smooth stroke. “Fucking perfect.”

It is.

His hands slide to the back of my neck to bring my mouth to his. His kiss is firm. Hot. Possessive.

It's everything.

Chapter Nineteen

Vaughn

"I can't believe I let you talk me into this."

Kendall's breathless words are barely louder than the patter of water against tile. "Showering?" I ask innocently as I skim my soapy hands up her shoulders. "Don't you do it every day?" My fingers find and massage tight muscles at the base of her neck.

Her eyelids droop and the back of her head hits the tile with a muted thump. "Not with a *guy*."

After a farewell knead to her now loose neck I slide my hands down the slopes of her breasts and give her nipples a playful pinch. "Hey, I'm not just *a guy*."

"Okay, a neighbor…"

"Neighbor? That's how I rate?" Determined to make her pay for the deliberate slight, I run my fingers along her sides.

She jerks and shrieks. She's ticklish. Holy crap is she ticklish. Knee raised, body curled, eyes tightly closed ticklish. Charmed and, well, victorious, I go to town, prepared to fully exploit this situation. "Say 'You're the best neighbor ever, Vaughn.'"

"Can't…growing up there was Suzie Gilmore, and she had…in-ground trampoline. Vauuuuuuughn!"

"Say it." I dig in at her sides, between her ribs. Her attempt at self-defense bounces harmlessly off my shoulder. "Say it or I show no mercy."

"Ahhh! Vaughn, I swear to God—"

"Try again," I encourage, and walk my fingers down to her waist.

That's when a palm cracks across my ass. Desperate. Unchecked. Loud.

It doesn't hurt, but the impact of wet skin on wet skin reverberates in the small space.

Her eyes pop open. "Oh. My. God. I'm so sorry."

I lean in and nuzzle her neck. "Not me. C'mon baby. Do it again."

She pushes me away with an exasperated laugh. "Get off of me and let me see the damage." Laugh or no, I can tell by the way she bites her lip that she's more concerned than she needs to be. I turn and look over my shoulder as we both watch a red palm print appear on the comparatively pale skin of my ass cheek. At the sight of the mark, the very pleasant semi I've sported since I snuck into the shower turns heavy.

"Does it hurt?" She dances fingers over the zone of impact and my erection surges to full, painful attention.

"No," I say quickly. "And yes, just not how you mean." But I don't move. I keep letting her caress the tender spot because I like the hot stain of her hand on my skin. I like the concern in her eyes, as well as the hint of I-can't-believe-I-did-that. Every soothing sweep of her fingertips across my ass has a direct and inversely proportional effect on my cock. It's throbbing for equal attention. Each finely diffused droplet of water that rains down on it becomes a separate punishment.

Kendall's lips brush my earlobe. "Would you like me to…?"

"What?" Did that thick, inarticulate noise come from me?

"…kiss it better?"

Before I can fully process the question, much less respond, she's on her knees behind me, and…"Jeeesuuuuus." I grip my aching cock in a rough, but incredibly necessary hold while Kendall's soft lips meander over my ass. They trail, gentle as a feather, stopping occasionally to press firm little kisses against my heated skin. Every nerve ending she touches seems to have multiple direct counterparts all along my shaft. I run my hand over it, tugging at those phantom sensations.

Her mouth moves again. She kisses lower.

I feel the tingle of it all the way to my balls. My tugs grow harder. Hard enough to lift the boys.

The next kiss involves a quick, spearing dart of her tongue, and my harsh curse bounces off glass and tile.

"Uh-oh," she says from behind me. "Does something else hurt now?"

I've created a monster. Despite my agony, I feel a smile stretching my lips. "God, yes. You don't know the half of it."

With hands on my hips she urges me around and then takes in my predicament with wide, serious eyes. "I can see there's quite a bit of swelling. Should I kiss this better, too?"

I get lightheaded at the thought. "Would you?"

She nods seriously, but then offers a tentative smile. "Where would you like me to start?"

"My balls," I say automatically, because I'm pretty sure if I release the chokehold I have on my dick I'll come.

But then. God. She places a chaste little kiss on one. *God.* The other. I'm breathing fast and shallow. She swirls her tongue, leisurely and thoroughly. My free hand sweeps her hair away from her face. "*Jesus*, Kendall."

When she leans back on her heels and looks up at me she's breathing shallow, too. "What about under here?" Her fingers slide over my white knuckles. "Does it hurt here?"

"It's killing me," I answer honestly, "but I don't know if I can..."

My words dissolve into the steam, because Kendall simply unwraps my fingers and moves my hand aside. I brace both on the wall in front of me and dip my chin to watch her slowly run her tongue from the base of my cock to the flare of the head.

"Better?" she asks without actually lifting her lips, because she knows damn well it isn't. My breath explodes around us in ragged pants.

"I think I'd better give this some attention, too." Her fingers dance over the tip. "Maybe one little kiss?"

I grab my pounding erection with one fist and manhandle it down until the tip points directly at her evil, cock-teasing mouth. "Yes, please."

She does. Another of those tiny, chaste, annihilating kisses, and for a haphazard second I don't know if I'm going to groan until my lungs deflate, pass out, or come. Possibly all three.

"I think it's going to need more TLC, Vaughn." That's all the warning I get before she closes those lush lips around me and takes me deep. In seconds my legs burn like I've run an ultra marathon, but it's the strain of standing still that slowly wrecks me. My muscles are receiving rapid-fire messages from some primitive part of my brain, commanding my hip flexors to move. But I can't. I have to be a gentleman.

Do not fuck her mouth.

Do not.

Fuuuucck.

I can't stop myself from looking down, watching my cock

disappear between damp lips a shade darker now that they've been roughed up from the friction of working me over. I don't remember letting go of the wall, but suddenly my fingers are sinking into the wet silk of her hair.

She makes an eager noise and follows the subtle pressure on her scalp that I didn't even mean to assert. She takes me deeper.

"Kendall…"

A little deeper.

"Kendall, baby, don't…

Deeper still, and then suddenly, she's not taking anymore, she's receiving. I'm *giving.* Glutes thrusting, hips rocking, head of my cock invading and retreating from the soft haven at the back of her throat while I hold her head just where I need it. Through the haze of an impending orgasm I look down and see her, beautiful and somehow…proud…knowing she owns this moment. She owns me. Then she closes her eyes, tips her head back one crucial degree, and swallows. I watch her throat work, and I'm lost. I come in a shuddering, groaning torrent. I come in her throat. Her mouth. On her tongue. When I finally realize what an impolite load I'm spending, I try to withdraw, afraid she'll never volunteer the privilege of her mouth again, but she clamps her hands on my ass and nuzzles closer like she craves every last drop.

I hope to God she does, because I'm too far gone to do anything but give it to her. Seconds, hours…potentially days later I watch my wrung-out dick slide from her lips. She runs the tip of her finger along the corner of her mouth, and then looks up at me. There is no mistaking the triumph in her smile. "Say, 'You're the best neighbor ever, Kendall.'"

I drop to my knees and pull her into a soggy embrace. "Best neighbor ever." My surrender comes out bouncy with laughter. "You win. You win all the things."

"I feel like a winner," she whispers, and runs her fingers

through my wet hair.

I pull her face close for a kiss. "That makes two of us."

• • •

Ever have those rare and mysterious spans of time where every pitch life throws in your direction, you knock that fucker right out of the park? Players call it a streak, and some do crazy shit to keep it going—don't shave, don't cut their hair, tap the bat against the sole of the right cleat, the left cleat, and then the outside corner of home plate exactly three times before assuming the stance. Whatever it takes.

That's my life right now. I'm on a winning streak, except I'm maintaining it effortlessly. Becca texted me she's over "us." Anonymous Hollywood insiders might be bashing my chances of being the next host of *America Rocks*, but the fan reaction has been overwhelmingly positive, and that can be a game changer in and of itself. To top it off, my dad has finally picked up on my frustrations with him and given me some much needed space. He refrained from hovering at the sidelines of an interview I did over the first part of this week, and, more importantly, he hasn't tried to meddle in my personal life.

Which brings me to the best part of this streak—Kendall. I love spending time with her. And no, that's not a euphemism for "banging her like a screen door in a hurricane," as Dylan cynically suggested when our paths crossed at the house and I told him I was on my way out to hang with her. Don't get me wrong. I love her body—the feel of her, the taste, the uncensored way she reacts to the things I do to her—but with Kendall, sex is only one facet, as opposed to the primary objective. Hell, I don't even know if there *is* a primary objective. All I know is with Kendall, I feel more like myself than I have in a long time.

Public parking sucks tonight, but I finally find a spot to pull into that doesn't require a permit. I jump out of the car and hurry down the sidewalk toward the art gallery. Thanks to a meeting that ran long, traffic, and typical south of Sunset parking challenges, I'm much later than planned.

I pass a furniture store with a window display featuring a cushiony white sofa. Innocuous as it may be, it serves as a trigger. The kind that transports me to the night I laid Kendall out on my neighbor's wet-dream of a sofa, hitched her long legs high, and then sank into her again and again while she gasped my name, and…okay, these kinds of memories are going to get me arrested for walking a public street alone on a Wednesday evening with a depraved grin on my face and a hard-on that won't quit.

I adjust my khakis and my thoughts, but the grin persists, because now my mind jumps to last night in my bed, when I pretended to wrestle her off me after she snuggled close and wedged her cold toes between my calves. Next, I flash to standing beside her in the kitchen early this morning, brewing coffee and making her laugh at my attempts to seduce her with a whisk I didn't even know we had while she flipped slices of egg-drenched bread in a pan. We froze when Matt walked in all geared up for another day at the academy, took stock of us—Kendall menacing the front of my sweats with stainless steel cooking tongs while I tried to whisk my way under the T-shirt she borrowed. "There goes my appetite," he muttered, before he walked out. We laughed so hard we had to hold each other up.

I can feel a residual smile curving my lips as I turn onto a side street and search for Art In Progress. It's not hard to find. A small crowd loiters on the sidewalk in front. I pick up my pace for no other reason than I can't wait to see Kendall. She's talked about this job, the kids, and this place enough for me to know she's excited about tonight's exhibit. And I'm excited for her. I know any job can seem shiny and bright after only a handful of days, but I wonder if she realizes she's never sounded even a tenth as excited about getting her law degree as she has about AIP.

I keep a neutral smile in place as I walk past the mix of teens and adults gathered out front. Recognition flashes across a face or two, but this isn't my night, and I don't want to steal attention, so I ease through the door. There are even more people inside. It's a decent-sized space, but nonetheless at capacity. The hum of conversation echoes in the well-lit room, along with soft background notes from a dark-haired guy playing a piano. Because I'm scanning the crowd for Kendall, it takes me a moment to notice the art. Photographs, sketches, and paintings decorate the dark-toned walls. Sculptures bask under spotlights. And then there's the ceiling. Shades of blue and green swirl above, tinged with yellow, purple, orange, and red. It's like an ocean. A sunset. A galaxy of color designed to shower inspiration down on all of us.

Duly inspired, I renew my effort to find my girl. *My girl.* I falter for a moment. The thought of her being mine is disconcerting. Not because I don't want to be with her. I do. So fucking much. But I can't promise I won't unwittingly hurt her. Ultimately, my career is my main focus; it's what I've strived for. But then I see her standing at the far end of the room, and I selfishly forget about everything but wanting her. Needing her.

She's in conversation with a kid who looks about sixteen and a middle-aged woman with similar features. Kendall's not facing me, but as if sensing my attention she turns her head, and her gaze collides with mine. My smile expands at the same time hers fades, and for a moment I'd swear she looks at me like I just sucker-punched her, but I don't get a chance to confirm my impression because she turns back to her conversation.

What the…?

Yes, I'm forty minutes late, but she knows I was tied up in my meeting; I sent her a text as soon as it ended, telling her I was on my way. Is she bent because I wasn't here when the event started? That doesn't make any sense, either. She told me the show would last two hours and I should come by whenever. I stare at her from across the room, and I can tell by how she rubs the side of her neck that she feels my regard, but she doesn't turn.

Fuck it. I'm going in. I walk over to her. Not fast, not slow, but directly so there's no doubt of my destination. The two people she's speaking with look my way as I near, acknowledging my approach. Kendall? Nothing.

"Hey," I say, not bothering to hide my confusion, even though airing my uncertainty with an audience probably isn't the best move.

"Hello," she replies, her tone cool and professional. "Vaughn, this is Bonnie and her son Will."

I exchange greetings with Bonnie and get a shy nod from Will.

"Are you one of the artists?" I ask Will, while taking measure of Kendall from the corner of my eye. She keeps her focus on the teen.

Will nods again. Okay. I get it. Speech isn't his thing.

"Do you have work on display tonight?"

He inclines his head and points, indicating the framed sketch of three girls playing with a dog that I noticed on my way in. "The charcoal drawing? That's yours? Dude"—I offer him my fist for a bump and he gives me one—"that piece caught my eye."

The boy blushes and shrugs. His mom squeezes his shoulder. "We're very proud of his work."

"I can see why," I answer sincerely.

"Oh," Bonnie exclaims. "There's Josie. We want to say hello before we head out. It was nice meeting you, Kendall." She expands her smile to include me. "Vaughn."

"Nice to meet you, too," Kendall replies, and you'd never guess by her smile that there's a single thing bothering her. But I know. "Will, I'll see you Friday."

He offers a wave before they walk away. I turn to Kendall. "What's wrong?"

Her body language answers with a resounding *everything*. Her back is straight, her arms crossed, her figure a long, contained column in a midnight blue pantsuit and complicated silver heels. "Nothing I can get into right now. I'm working. If you want to wait until I'm done here, we can talk then. It's entirely up to you."

"I'm sorry I'm late."

"I know. I saw your text."

Someone passes behind me. Kendall lifts her chin in greeting and takes another step away from me. "Excuse me. Another artist and her guests just arrived. I need to welcome them."

Now I step back, too, because as much as I hate the brush-off, her point is valid. I don't want to do anything to jeopardize this opportunity for her. "I'll find you later," I say, and walk to the nearest wall to stare blindly at a group of watercolors. I won't hover. I won't crowd. But I will damn well wait her out. I do covertly watch her in action. Any casual onlooker would see an outgoing, radiant woman with a knack for putting those around her at ease. Only someone who's taken a crash course in the nuances of Kendall Hewitt would detect the tension in her shoulders or the determined set of her smile. When our gazes clash from across the room, I force myself to focus on the art, not on dissecting what I might have said or done to put the wounded look in her eyes.

I take my time walking through the exhibits and end up

meeting Candace, Kendall's boss. She's a bouncy woman with genuine enthusiasm for what she does. It's clear she could talk about Art in Progress all night, but the event is winding down, and her sharp look says she recognizes I haven't hung around all evening strictly for the exhibit, no matter how worthwhile the cause. She turns, catches Kendall's attention through the thinning crowd, and waves her over. The reluctance in her strides confirms my impression she's been stalling for the last half hour.

"Kendall, thank you so much for your help tonight. I don't know what I would have done without you. But now"—Candace glances at her watch—"you're officially off the clock. Take this handsome fellow and hit the road."

"I can stay and help clean up. I don't mind—"

"Nonsense." Candace swats the suggestion away like a pesky fly. "You came in early to set up. The rental company will deal with most of the cleanup, and we'll tackle the rest tomorrow. Go. Shoo. Thank you and good night."

"Okay," she says through a forced smile. Her eyes dart to me. "I have to get my purse from the office, and I'm parked in back."

"I'll walk with you," I say, and gesture her to go ahead. We're silent while she leads us down a narrow hall, past some workrooms, and into a small, utilitarian office. I shut the door behind me and watch her retreat to the other side of the desk.

"Sorry I was late," I say softly, and walk around the desk to ease into the space beside her.

"I told you it's fine." She retrieves her purse from a lower drawer and straightens. "No explanations necessary. I mean, we're friends enjoying a casual summer thing, right?"

Those stiff words put my back up all over again. Right or wrong, *my girl*, floats through my head again. "Casual? What part feels casual to you?" I lean in so our faces are only inches apart. "When you gave me your virginity? When we had breakfast this morning after spending the night in my bed?" The office is private, but even so, I speak low so my words go directly into her ear. "When you had my dick in your mouth?"

She pushes me back. "We didn't have any rules or make any commitments. You're free to do what you want, and I'm free to—"

"Hold on," I interrupt, because my go-with-the-flow default setting is about to blow, even though I know it's not fair. She was a virgin. This world is new to her. Of course she wants to travel in it. Experience more. It's not her fault the idea makes me want to punch a hole through this wall. My winning streak is about to come to a crashing end, but I'm not letting go without a fight. "Maybe we didn't spell out the parameters of 'us,' but when did we decide this is *casual*?"

"You decided." She corrects. "About the time you went on a date with Becca."

I'm clueless. "What are you talking about?"

She pulls her phone out of her purse, taps a button, and points the screen at my face. I have to ease her hand back six inches before I can focus on a photo of Becca and me leaning across a table at The Peninsula.

Shit. We're right there in color-coordinated glory on Becca's Instagram feed, along with the caption "Missing my boo."

"That picture was snapped over a week ago, and it wasn't a date." There's nothing to do here but be honest, even if it puts my dysfunctional relationship with my father front and center. I *want* to level with her. "My dad set it up ambush-style on the last day of filming Laney's music video to feed the gossip sites something juicy. I didn't know she was going to be there. We shared a toast over her landing a movie role, and she tried to talk me into being a publicity couple. I said no. The end."

She lowers her hand and looks away. A muscle quivers in her throat. "It doesn't matter…"

I cup her jaw. "It matters to me. I don't feel *casual.* I don't want casual. I want you. I don't care if this is just for the summer. I don't care if you're eventually going to law school to get on with your life. For the duration, I'm yours." I inhale deeply and add, "And you're mine."

Her breath hitches, and I wonder if I'm about to be kicked in the balls for coming off like a domineering asshole.

"This was before last weekend?" *Before we had sex*, her eyes say.

"Yes." I wrap my fingers around her wrist. "Yes, but it wasn't before I started to realize I was—" Caution urges me to take stock of my words, but I don't want to. I want to let them out. She deserves to have them no matter what she chooses to do with them. "Kendall, it wasn't before I realized I was into you. And if it counts for anything, I've told my father he can't just—"

"Me, too."

The two words cut through my sloppy arguments. "What?"

"Me, too," she repeats, and closes her hand around mine. "I'm into you, too. I feel like this thing between us is…I don't know…special."

"It is," I interject, but she shakes her head to silence me.

"But I'm not adept at reading the signals. Maybe you spend the weekend with all your dates? Maybe snuggling under the covers and sharing showers and cooking breakfast only feels special to me because I've never done it before?"

"It feels special to me, too. Believe me, Kendall. I might be a lot of things, but I'm not a liar. I haven't done this before, either. When it comes to this"—I point to her and then to me—"we're both virgins."

She spears her fingers into my hair and pulls my face

close. "I believe you," she says before she presses her lips to mine.

Relief courses through me. I dive into the kiss. I don't know where we've landed, exactly, but it's somewhere beyond the reach of manipulated photo ops and unspoken emotions. Wherever we are, it feels vital.

Chapter Twenty

Kendall

Laney Albright has the kind of rhythm and New Yawk swagger that makes it impossible to keep still when she sings. My hips are wiggling, my shoulders are swaying, and right behind me, standing so close our bodies keep grazing, is Vaughn. At every point of contact, sparks of awareness flare. Then recede. Flare. Recede. It's maddening in the best possible way.

It's a good thing he can't see my face because it's no doubt glowing pink with adoration.

Tonight is crazy. The past *week* has been crazy. My ordinary life has changed in ways I never imagined. The hope I held deep down for things to change may have included a guy, but not one like the tall slice of heaven now putting his hands on my hips.

Instantly, my head, my heart, my tummy are all fluttery. These feelings swoop in regularly, so I should be used to them. But I'm not.

We move to the music, the beat a mix of electronic and hip-hop. I've been acutely tuned in to Vaughn since the second he knocked on my door and took my hand to lead me to his car. My air space is entirely filled with him whether we're driving, sneaking into an album release party or getting our groove on. There may be a couple hundred other people here with us, but I don't see any of them.

I glance to my right. Except for him. Justin Timberlake is five feet away. He's new to *America Rocks* this season, taking over as a judge. He shook my hand, which means I may never wash it again, and couldn't have been nicer when we were introduced. Being in the roped-off VIP section definitely has its perks. Thankfully, Justin has soaked up 90 percent of the attention. While girls have definitely noticed Vaughn, they haven't approached. A couple of people wearing press lanyards are on the other side of the venue, a safe distance away.

Muted spotlights circling the stage give the event space on Hollywood Blvd. an intimate feel. The friends and fans here for this special night are singing along with Laney as she belts out her most recent hit. Also across the room is a seemingly endless upscale bar, the glass from liquor bottles and tumblers fracturing the stage lights into twinkles of blue, green, and gold. Outside, massive video screens overlooking the street and sidewalk play a constant loop of Laney's appearances and songs. In the lobby is a lounge with couches and portable shelves filled with shoeboxes from tonight's sponsor, Adidas. Laney is known for the custom rainbow-striped sneakers she wears—no matter the outfit—and so tonight everyone in attendance is getting a pair.

The music continues to thump loud enough that I can see people's lips moving, but I'm not sure if any sound is actually coming out. Not until Laney holds the mic out for the audience to fill in the refrain.

When the song ends, the crowd goes wild. Laney gives a shout-out of thanks then brings her hand to her face like she's covering her eyes from the sun. "Vaughn Shaughnessy? You out there?" she asks, her vowels drawn out long as the Brooklyn Bridge.

"That's my cue," he whispers in my ear, having prepared me ahead of time—but only this morning. I almost changed my mind about coming, knowing he was going to take the stage. Since Vaughn is featured in Laney's music video she thought it would be cool for him to be the one to emcee a quick Q and A. Vaughn agreed—mostly to appease his dad after Vaughn told him he wasn't going to do the velvet rope photo op. I didn't like being the reason Vaughn stayed under the radar, but he assured me it wasn't a big deal.

Not for the first time, I wonder if I might get in the way of his career.

I'm the reason Mason didn't get to follow his dreams, and it would kill me to be the reason Vaughn missed an opportunity.

Vaughn makes his way to Laney, the girls in the audience squealing like crazy and high-fiving him as he passes. He hops up onstage and strikes up an easy conversation with the pop star that has everyone laughing and sighing. Vaughn is a natural, so at ease in front of an audience. He will absolutely win the hearts of America if he becomes the next host of *America Rocks*. He may even outshine the contestants. I wonder if he sings?

I look over at Justin again. He's wearing a baseball cap to keep a low-ish profile. Tonight is about Laney, and it's sweet that he's here for her. Vaughn told me Justin is one of the producers on her debut album.

"The album drops Tuesday. Any special plans?" Vaughn asks into a microphone.

"Just chilling with friends."

"What time should I be over?" Vaughn teases.

"I want to come!" someone in the crowd shouts.

Laney smiles before Vaughn quickly says, "We'll all be with you in spirit."

Gah. The *America Rocks* brass are crazy if they don't hire Vaughn.

"Thanks, everyone," Laney says.

"You guys ready for one last song?" Vaughn asks the room. A resounding "yes" is the answer. Laney recaptures the audience's attention as Vaughn returns to me with a megawatt grin on his gorgeous face. "How'd I do?"

"Fantastic." I lift up on tiptoes to kiss him.

He wraps his arms around my waist, pulling me closer. "What do you say we make our escape now while all eyes are on the stage?"

"I like that idea." I silently pray no one catches us.

Fingers laced together, we stop in the empty lounge to grab a pair of the complimentary shoes. An Adidas rep asks our sizes, bags our swag, and we're about to be on our way when a tall, good-looking man wearing jeans, a tight black T-shirt, and a five o'clock shadow approaches. "Vaughn Shaughnessy, are you sneaking out without saying hello?" Whoever this person is, he has a very nice British accent.

Vaughn releases me to shake hands with the man. "Nigel. It's good to see you again."

"You, too. I had a call with John earlier today to get caught up on a few things. Your name came up more than once."

"That's...good?"

The older man laughs. "All good, although he complained your schedule is bloody hard to work around. Almost as bad as mine. I hear you're off to San Francisco tomorrow for a photo shoot."

"Gotta go where the work takes me."

"I appreciate that ethic." Nigel's attention shifts to me. "'Course a smart lad makes sure he's not all work and no play."

"I'm sorry," Vaughn says. "This is Kendall. Kendall, this is Nigel Cowie, the executive producer of *America Rocks*."

"It's nice to meet you," I say. "I'm a huge fan of the show."

"Lovely to meet you, and thanks for watching." He gives me a kind smile, earning my regard right away, then returns his focus to Vaughn. "Great job onstage."

"Thank you." Vaughn threads his fingers through mine once again. I squeeze his hand to convey, *Woohoo! Nigel Cowie said you did a great job!*

Nigel's gaze dips to our linked hands like he can hear my inner thoughts. Am I thinking too loud?

"I won't keep you," he says, his tone amiable.

"I'm glad we ran into you," Vaughn says. "Enjoy the rest of the night."

"Likewise," Nigel replies.

The second Vaughn and I are outside in the warm summer air, I say, "He really likes you."

"You think?"

"Yep."

"I tried to play it cool."

"You were the coolest of cool."

"There's a *cool* bar around the corner." Vaughn's smile is anything but cool. It's hot, and it's getting me hot, too. "Are you up for something to eat?"

"Sounds good," I say.

He opens the door to Lost Property Bar, allowing me entry first. With his hand on the small of my back, he leads us to a round open table in the back. He pulls out my chair before sitting across from me in the low-lit, sophisticated bar. I hang my purse over the chair back and relax into my seat. I've got the best view in the place right in front of me.

Dressed in a fitted mesh-trim T-shirt the same shade as his eyes, his light brown hair effortlessly sexy, and a playful bend to his lips, Vaughn is ridiculously appealing.

"Whatever you do," he says, putting our shoe bags down before leaning his elbows on the table, "don't tell Dylan we came here instead of The Cabana."

I laugh. "I can hear him now. 'You went to that fucking dive instead of my place? What the hell is wrong with you?'"

Vaughn cracks up. "You sounded just like him."

"I'm good with voices. Want to hear my James Corden?"

"He's only my favorite late night talk show host, so yes."

"He's my favorite, too!" Okay, so now I really want to impress him. I clear my throat. "Hey, man, you left your guitar at my house last night, so I've got it here, but I'm going to be late for work now."

"I don't know why listening to you imitate a male late night host is sexy"—Vaughn takes my face in his hands—"but I need to make out with this exceptionally talented mouth now." The split second his lips meet mine I open for him. Every kiss is better than the last. Every taste makes me forget everything but us. Our tongues slide against each other, our lips meld. I'm helpless to stop the tiny noise of approval that sounds from the back of my throat. Vaughn kisses me harder in answer.

After a minute—or maybe ten, I've lost track of time—someone's chair scrapes against the floor, reminding us we're necking in a bar. We pull back at the same time. Vaughn's eyes stay glued to mine as he gets comfortable in his seat again. The intensity that arches between us feels magnetic, and I'm ready to dive into another kiss. Screw privacy.

"Let's order before I drag you out of here." He picks up the small menu left on the table just as the waitress arrives. Vaughn orders me a lemon drop martini when I tell him I want something fruity and not too strong, and an iced tea for himself.

"You're not having a drink?" I ask.

He shakes his head. "I'm good without it."

"Iced tea for me, too, then," I tell the waitress before Vaughn and I order a few different appetizers to share.

"Laney was incredible," I say. "I'm glad I came tonight."

He reaches across the table for my hand, runs his thumb across my knuckles in a gesture I'm getting way too accustomed to. This time it's the same hand JT shook. My hand is currently the lottery winner of body parts. "Thanks for risking being seen with me."

"You can thank me later."

"Oh, I plan to. Numerous times."

I press my thighs together, his promise a direct link to *there*. "It was fun getting a glimpse of you in action. I really hope you get the hosting job."

"You've been privy to more than a brief look at my moves, baby," he says in a low, playful voice.

My body perks up further, a flame inside me stoked by his flirting. "*Shut up.* You know what I mean. You're a natural onstage."

"Thanks." Sliding his hand back and resting his forearms on the table, he twists the bracelet I gave him around his wrist. Without thought, I reach for my necklace and rub my fingers over the pendant. "You know, you're a natural, too."

I frown in confusion.

"At helping people, lifting others up, and supporting a cause. Last night at the art exhibit I watched you engage the artists and their families. You knew every student by name. You knew their projects and said something special, something personal, about each one. You took efforts to make them feel proud of their work."

The compliment is like sunshine after six months of rain. "They should feel proud. We sold every piece and raised close to twenty-five thousand dollars."

"That's fantastic," he says. "Congratulations."

"Thanks. I'm on cloud nine that I got to be a part of it." I gather my hair and pull it over one shoulder. "Hey, I've been meaning to ask you, can you sing?"

His mouth quirks up, and my female parts hum. "Not at all. You?"

"Not even a little."

"So you and I should definitely team up for the next karaoke night." He leans back and crosses his arms.

"It's always better to get laughed at *with* someone."

"That's my theory." Vaughn's brilliant green eyes, the ones that intimidated me when we first met, sparkle with a one-two punch of warmth and desire. It's impossible to remain unaffected when he looks at me like that.

"What was the first concert you went to?" I ask, fiddling with the hemline of my dress.

"Coachella." A look of nostalgia turns his one-in-a-million face into a one-in-a-billion piece of chiseled art. Vaughn is so much more than what people see on the outside. "It was the tenth anniversary of the music festival, and I went with my sister. Andie had been before so knew all the ins and outs. I think we both slept a total of eight hours in three days. It was awesome."

"Who did you get to see?"

He runs his fingers through the hair at his temple. "Paul McCartney, The Cure, Morrissey, The Crystal Method, The Black Keys, Thievery Corporation, Amy Winehouse, and a bunch of others. Every one of them was epic. What about you? First concert? Wait. Let me guess." He studies me like he can read my mind, so I think about a baby giraffe to throw him off.

"Destiny's Child," he says after hardly any deliberation.

My mouth drops open. "How did you know?"

He has the decency to look surprised—for all of one second—before he laughs. "Sheer brilliance on my part."

"More like sheer luck," I fire back.

"That, too. Plus you were humming 'Bootylicious' the morning I came by to apologize and get my keys."

Was I? I honestly don't remember, but my heart skips a beat over the fact that he tucked away such a small detail. The waitress arrives with our drinks. "Your food will be out in a minute," she says.

Vaughn waits for her to step away before he sends me a sly smile. "And you are, by the way."

"I am what?" I ask with my glass halfway to my lips.

"Bootylicious."

My face heats as I take a long gulp of iced tea, and another hip-hop classic pops into my head: Nelly's "Hot in Herre." Yep, I'm ready to take off all my clothes with Vaughn again.

• • •

"Keep your eyes closed," Vaughn says softly.

"I am." I squeeze his hand tighter, hoping I don't trip over my feet on our way to his bedroom. The house is quiet, making me acutely aware of my own breathing. "Have I mentioned I hate surprises?"

"Only twice since we walked through the front door, but too bad."

I hear the creak of a door then sense brightness. The door clicks shut. Vaughn lets go of my hand.

"Can I open them now?"

"Not yet." His warm breath fans my face, so I know he's standing right in front of me.

"*Vaughn.*"

"Patience, beautiful." He gently grips my shoulders and turns me around. "This is so you aren't tempted to peek.

Give me thirty more seconds."

"*Ohh-kayyy.*"

He rustles around his bedroom, giving no obvious clue to what he's surprising me with. When he'd asked me to stay the night with him, I'd immediately said yes. When he'd said he had something for me, I'd said bribery wasn't necessary. He'd laughed. God, I want to listen to his laugh every single day.

"All right. It's ready. Turn around and open your eyes."

I'm a little disoriented as I attempt a one-eighty, but I think I'm looking toward his bed. Maybe he's sprawled out naked? Ready and waiting for me to do whatever I want with his body? My legs shake at the thought before I blink the room into focus. I am facing his bed, but it's not Vaughn leaning against it. My breath catches.

The drawing of the three young girls is propped up with pillows. Will's painting is here!

"Oh my God."

Vaughn smiles. "Surprise."

"How did you...when I went to..." I walk closer, my adoration moving from the picture to Vaughn. "I was secretly hoping to buy this and was disappointed when I found out someone had already purchased it. How did you know?" I hadn't told anyone how much I loved this piece of artwork. I wasn't sure what the protocol was and didn't want to hurt anyone's feelings by buying one student's work over another.

"I watched you."

I shift my gaze back to the lifelike dog being held in such a loving way by his owner. Vaughn's words thrill me *and* make me nervous. It's been a long time since a guy has paid such close attention to me.

I'm reminded of Mason and the Winnie the Pooh quote he gave me, and the guilt that still lingers deep in my heart rises closer to the surface.

Vaughn traces a finger up my bare arm. "I watched you

from across the room when you stood in front of this drawing like you were seeing two friends. I bought it for you right after that and asked Candace to keep it a secret."

"Thank you. I love it."

"I love this." He touches the corner of my mouth. "It looks good on you."

"What? My lip gloss?" Am I still wearing any? My breath catches in my throat for some crazy reason.

"Your smile, Kendall. I love seeing you smile."

Tears sting my eyes. I fling my arms around his neck and kiss him. He kisses me back with equal enthusiasm, but eases away too soon and smooths his hands down my hair. "You know, Nigel had an excellent idea tonight."

I blink, trying to follow his sudden shift in conversation. "Did he?"

"Uh-huh." He leans in and kisses me again—just one firm kiss—before adding, "He said a smart lad finds a way to mix some fun with the work. It just so happens you're my favorite type of fun. Will you make me a smart lad, Kendall?" He follows that up with another, longer kiss, which only succeeds in scrambling my brain.

When my mouth is mine again, I do my best to respond to his question, even though I don't understand what he's asking of me. "I'd do anything for you—"

"Fly to San Francisco after work tomorrow," he says quickly. "Spend the weekend with me. My shoot may take up most of Saturday, but you can come along, or enjoy a spa day at the hotel, shopping in the city, or a little of everything. Saturday night and Sunday will be all ours. We can sight-see, or order room service and spend the entire time in bed. Whatever you want. Just don't make me go two long days without this smile."

He touches the corner of my mouth and I realize I've done it again. I'm grinning and completely unable to say no to this man. “You are a smart lad,” I manage, before he kisses the rest of my acceptance right out of my smiling mouth.

Kissing leads to shedding clothes. Naked bodies leads to twisted sheets and salty skin.

Not to mention a perpetual smile.

If only it could last.

Chapter Twenty-One

Vaughn

Crawling out of bed at the crack of dawn doesn't normally bother me, even after a late night, but this morning it flat-out sucks. Instead of turning off the alarm I set just in case my internal clock failed, I want to hit snooze, snuggle against the warm, soft woman by my side, and wake us both up little by little. I want to roll her under me, slide into the place she's warmest and softest, and watch her eyes flutter open. I want to see the hazy blue turn crystal clear as her pupils tighten to pinpricks while dawn breaks across the sky and her orgasm breaks over me.

Surely I can spare ten or fifteen minutes out of my morning without risking my flight? I'll see her tonight, but right now my body thinks the idea of spending the better part of a day away from Kendall sounds like the worst kind of torture.

Then again, her body might have its own definition of torture. Like getting prodded out of sleep by a relentless dick that had its way with her more than once last night. I lift my head off the pillow and look at her. Sometime during the night we curved ourselves into mirror images of each other. She sleeps on her stomach with her face turned toward me, hair tumbling over her eyes, lips slightly parted…and slightly red around the edges from my mouth, my teeth. Did I mention my relentless dick? One of her hands rests on my pillow. One knee touches my hip.

Her breathing remains deep and even. Using a fingertip, I move her hair away from her face and trace her cheekbone. No change. Not even a twitch of an eyelid. She's out.

Her swollen lips reclaim my attention. The ripe look has my dick drilling into the mattress, but I'll bet this isn't the only place she's swollen this morning.

Instead of leaving her cursing your name every time she moves, how about you let her get some sleep? I squeeze my eyes closed, bite my lip, and try not to groan out loud at the sensation of my cock dragging across the sheet as I crawl out of bed. I console myself with thoughts of us riding the cable car to Fisherman's Wharf on Saturday night, buying her a tacky tourist sweatshirt and a clam chowder in a bread bowl because she's cold, then taking the path through the park to Ghirardelli Square. She'll choose her favorite varieties of their world famous chocolate, and back at the hotel, I'll feed them to her in between orgasms.

Kendall stretches into the empty spot and lets out a contented sound from somewhere beyond the veil of sleep.

I should take a picture of her like this and text it to her later so she understands the heroic effort I mustered up to leave her alone. But a certain part of me liked the sound of her sigh too much, so now I've got a shower date with my soapy fist, as well as a flight to catch. I'm one step toward the bathroom when I hear the front door open and close. I almost ignore it, except I know Matt leaves the house before the sun rises, and Dylan would use his private entrance at this hour. Who's here?

I find last night's jeans in a pile of Kendall's and my clothes and tug them on before heading downstairs. My bare feet don't make any noise, but the same can't be said for the leather soles of the mystery visitor's shoes. I hear the footsteps echoing on the hardwood in the direction of my office. What the *hell*?

I push the door open in time to see my father take a seat behind the desk and fish for something in the inside pocket of his suit jacket.

"Dad? What are you doing here?"

His head jerks up. "I wanted to speak to you before you left. In person," he adds as he withdraws an envelope.

I don't like the grim look on his face or the Houston-we-have-a-problem tone of his voice. "What's up?" I sound calm, but my mind is already busy rewinding last night's party to figure out what's wrong. Nothing springs to mind. The evening went perfectly. "Did something happen?"

"No, thank God. But I urged you to let me make sure you invited someone appropriate as your date last night." He tosses the envelope at me. "Kendall Hewitt is *not* appropriate. I get that you thought she came with some kind of neighbor stamp of approval, but she has a skeleton buried in her closet, and my investigator didn't have to do much digging to unearth it."

I'm stunned. Not by the so-called skeleton some investigator included in a report. I'm stunned that my father did a background check on my neighbors' niece because she attended an event with me. The invasion of her privacy slices like a knife. Words fail me.

Dad, not so much. "Luckily Ms. Hewitt managed to fly under the radar last night. Your publicist got a few texts for details, but we're responding with 'a friend.'"

"I know all about Kendall's past. She told me before I—"

"What the *fuck,* Vaughn? I gave you the benefit of the doubt and backed off, but Christ almighty. Are you trying to torpedo your career? How could you be so reckless with your reputation after all the time and effort we've invested into getting you where you are? Her drunken crash left her boyfriend in a motherfucking coma—"

"He's not in a coma," I say lamely. "He's just... unresponsive."

"Oh. Well that makes it *aaaall* better." He shoves his hands into his hair and scoffs at the ceiling. "Forget everything I said. I'm sure America will fall head-over-heels for a nice Midwestern girl who evaded a felony murder conviction on a medical technicality." He drops his hands and shakes his head. "Of course you don't understand. You don't have kids. I hope you never see one of yours *unresponsive*, but if you did you'd know you could never forgive some criminally careless party girl for leaving your child worse than dead while she merrily goes on with her life. Out of all the girls in L.A. this is the one you chose to link yourself with?"

"Nobody's merrily gone on with anything." I slam my hand on the desk, surprising us both. "Kendall's struggled to find a way to move on. It's been more than four years, and she's still working her way back."

My dad shakes his head. "You have some ludicrous idea there's an expiration date on something like this. There's not. Do you honestly think America's going to find nobility in her struggle?"

I don't know how to respond. If they knew her, if they heard her speak, they would. But presented like my father serves it up? No.

He leaps on my silence. "Right now we need to do damage control before there's any real harm done. I've got a call in to Rebecca's manager. I'm thinking a rendezvous in

San Francisco." He starts to pace behind my desk. "You two meet up for a romantic dinner at...fuck, I don't know." He pivots and paces back. "Whatever the hot place is right now. I'll give a local reporter there the heads-up, and they'll get it on camera."

"Dinner with Becca in San Francisco is *damage control*?"

"Not dinner," he snaps as he turns to pace back the way he came. "A bended knee proposal. That will blow everything else off people's radar, including Kendall Hewitt. Crisis averted and a new wave of positive publicity for you to ride right into your first season with *America Rocks*." He stops behind the desk—*my* desk—absolutely certain of his authority. "There are drawbacks, of course. I don't know how her movie will do, but we can keep the engagement in place until the hiatus, and then reevaluate." He's talking to himself. I might as well not even be in the room. That I'll go along with whatever he plans is a foregone conclusion. "We don't want to tie you up indefinitely if it doesn't make sense."

"No," I say softly. I want this hosting gig more than I've wanted any other professional goal I've set for myself. But not like this.

Apparently he interprets the single word as my agreement to his strategy, because he doesn't even pause for breath, simply pulls his phone from his jacket and starts tapping the screen. "I'll reach out to Becca's manager and get the ball rolling. Order a parting gift for the girl next door, let her down easy—"

"It's not necessary," a soft voice interrupts from behind me. I turn to see Kendall, the color drained from her cheeks, standing in the doorway. She's wearing her dress from last night and an expression on her face that says she's heard everything.

My dad curses under his breath. "Look, sweetheart, I'm sorry if this all sounds calculated, but we're in a calculated business."

"No." I turn and face my father, my finger pointed at him. "You don't talk to her." I tap my finger to my chest. "You talk to me."

Turning quickly back to Kendall I add, "And you *listen* to me. Not him. Me. Everything you just overheard? I'm not doing any of it."

My father barks my name, but I hold up a hand to silence him without taking my eyes off Kendall. For some reason my statement puts a weary smile on her face. She folds her arms and leans a shoulder against the doorframe. "You're not going to let me down easy?"

"No. I mean..." I drag in a deep breath because dammit, this is an unfair situation—to both of us. "I'm not going to let you down at all. I don't need damage control—"

"I do." The smile turns sad as she pushes off the door so she's standing on her own two feet. "You're strong, Vaughn. You're so close to perfect it hurts just to look at you sometimes, but I've got imperfections—big ones—and they're mine to keep. Defending myself against scores of people I don't know?" She shakes her head, a little desperate now. "I'm not up to it. I may never be."

I take a step toward her. "It wouldn't be like that."

"It would be exactly like that," my father insists.

"You're fired."

"What?"

"Vaughn..."

"No." I cut them both off before everything spins further out of my control. "You need to get out," I say to my dad. "You'll always be my father, but as of this minute you're no longer my manager."

"Don't, Vaughn. Your dad is trying to protect you."

"I don't need protection from—"

"I can't do this." Kendall backs up, like if she exits the

office everything will suddenly snap back to normal. Like *she's* the destabilizing force, instead of me, or my father, or our fucked-up relationship that I should have found the strength to fix a long time ago.

"This isn't your fault," I assure her.

"Maybe not, but I didn't think things through when I started seeing you. Spending time with you felt so good, I forgot about the outside world enough to ignore the consequences. I mean"—she lets out a hollow laugh—"there weren't supposed to be any consequences, right? We're temporary. Something fun for the summer before we went our separate ways. This thing between us was special because it wasn't complicated. Neither of us signed up for complicated."

"Fuck sign ups. Kendall, I *care* about you."

"I care about you, too. But it's not enough. Or maybe it is, and this is where we end things, caring about each other enough to let go."

"Stop. Stop right there because that's bullshit. Fuck anybody who thinks our personal lives are any of their business."

"If you care about her, you'll listen to what she's saying," my father mutters as he rounds the desk. "You might think I'm too prone to expect a crisis and too cold-blooded in the way I choose to avert them. Maybe I'm too protective of you. But this time, Vaughn, your reputation and career are not the only things at stake. The young lady has risks, too. Risks best mitigated by getting in front of the story at just the right moment, picking precisely the right outlets and interviewers to tell your side. Doing it correctly is a goddamn tightrope act, and one slip can mean the media chews you up and spits you out. Are you prepared for that?"

I want to answer, "Hell yes. Make the calls now," but he's not asking me. It's Kendall he directs the question to, and she's pale as a ghost at the very idea of discussing her most devastating experience with strangers.

“I have to go.” She’s already in motion. “I’m sorry.”

I start to go after her, but she turns tearful eyes to me and freezes me to the spot with four little words.

“I don’t want this.”

Chapter Twenty-Two

Kendall

Actions speak louder than words.

All morning, I can't get the thought out of my head. The trite phrase is like an incessant knock on a door that can't be opened. One monumental teenage mistake and it doesn't matter what I might say or how sorry I am. Not that I would ever excuse my actions. I take full responsibility for driving under the influence. But to be judged so harshly without the slightest possibility of understanding cuts to the bone.

This has always been a private matter. I mean, not private, private, obviously. I grew up in a small town. Everyone there knew what happened. Everyone formed opinions, a few of them compassionate, but most of them hurtful, and they *knew* me. They *knew* Mason. The thought of random strangers knowing my business makes it difficult to breathe.

But knowing this about myself–knowing my limits–doesn't help lessen the hollow ache in my chest. This isn't only about me. It's about Mason and his parents. My family.

And it's about Vaughn. The single worthwhile thing I can do right now is make sure his reputation stays intact. If it's not *America Rocks*, it will be another show, I've no doubt of that. Which means I have to let him go, because as much as walking away from him hurts, harming him in any way—even by association—would hurt worse. I've been there. Done that. With Mason.

I'm crushed, despite all the lip service I paid to this thing with Vaughn being strictly temporary. This morning's shower consisted of one giant cryfest. I thought I'd cried him right out of my system by the time I'd dressed and dragged myself to work, but nope. I dry the corners of my puffy red eyes with a tissue then stare at my reflection in the bathroom mirror. It's not me I see, but Vaughn's father's outraged face. I hear him tell his son, *You have some crazy idea there's an expiration date on something like this. There's not. Do you honestly think America's going to find nobility in her struggle?*

The last thing I want is to damage Vaughn's reputation and career because of his relationship with me so, ironically, this puts me on the same side as his father. How he found out about the accident, I don't know. I was a minor. My record sealed. It feels so incredibly *awful* to have someone pry into my personal life because...what? He wants only the best for his son. Someone who offers advantages, and enhances his image, and I'm not that girl. My actions have doomed me in his eyes and will no doubt ruin me in others, too.

I toss the tissue into the trash and wipe at my cheeks with the pads of my fingers. I should have called in sick today. It isn't a stretch. I feel battered from the inside out, infected by something I can't shake, and vaguely contagious. Touch me at your own risk.

"Kendall?" Candace says from the other side of the door. "Are you okay in there?"

I close my eyes. "Yes. I'll be right out." Swallowing the

emotions thickening the back of my throat, I pull myself together.

Candace is waiting for me when I step into the hallway.

"Sorry about that. So where were we?" I walk around her, embarrassed by my moment of weakness when she asked if I'd had fun at the album release party last night, and I'd made a run for the bathroom rather than discuss Vaughn.

I sit at the side desk in the reception area while Candace resumes her spot behind the welcome workstation.

"I'm guessing from your reaction that something happened with your boyfriend?"

"He's not my boyfriend," I'm quick to correct. "Just a friend, and can we talk about something else?" *Anything* else.

"All right. How about making your job permanent?"

My jaw drops. "*What?*"

"I know your plan is to attend law school, but I'd be remiss if I didn't let you know how much I value having you here and wish you would stay. I think we make a great team, and I sense you do, too. You're fabulous with the kids, and they feel comfortable with you. I'd love to design a class for you, love to get you more personally involved in art therapy, and of course continue to have your administrative assistance. You're far more organized than I am." She smiles. "Sold yet?"

"I don't know what to say."

"Say you'll think about it?"

I'm at a loss for words. I break eye contact to look around the room, at this special place that in a very short time has come to mean something to me. This is exactly what I wanted. A viable alternative to law school.

"You've mentioned your aunt and uncle are here, but know I am, too. The job is yours when summer ends, if you want it."

I'm going to cry again. Damn it. That she sees such potential in me lifts me from the low I've struggled with for the past few hours. I'm not a liability here. I have value. Not in spite of my past, but *because* of it.

All of a sudden, I know what I have to do. "Thank you for having so much faith in me. I think a trip home will help me sort things out. Your belief in me means a lot, but I need to have a couple of face-to-face conversations to figure out if I can pursue this opportunity without feeling guilty or letting anyone down. Is it okay to take the rest of the day off if I can get a flight?"

"Absolutely."

I stand, walk over, and give her a hug. "Thank you."

"You're welcome. Whatever decision you make, you've connected with the students here and for that, I'm grateful."

She couldn't have said anything that would have meant more to me. A human connection—that's what we all crave, isn't it?

I reserve an early afternoon flight so have zero time to go home first, which is fine, since the last thing I want is to risk a run-in with Vaughn. He's texted me, asking to talk, but I haven't responded yet. I need time to get my thoughts organized.

An Uber picks me up from the studio and forty-five minutes later, I'm at the airport, anxious to get in the air and unplug for a few hours. I call my mom from the terminal to let her know I'm coming home. Her excitement overshadows her concern with my last-minute decision. I've got plenty of clothes still in my bedroom closet and can stop at a drugstore for toiletries. Next, I text Brit to give her a quick update.

Everything has come to a head. Called things off with Vaughn, and Candace offered me a job. Am flying home for the weekend to talk to my parents…and Mason hopefully. Will FaceTime with you later to tell you everything.

She immediately texts back.

Sorryations! That's sorry + congratulations. I need ALL

the details. Wish New York wasn't so far away, but you've got this. Love you.

Thx. Love you, too.

Finally, I call Amber to tell her I'm flying home for the weekend and why. She wishes me safe travels and then shouts—across the room to Dixie, I imagine—what I'm up to. Dixie yells back, "About fucking time, princess."

I wholeheartedly agree.

• • •

I step outside into warm, noisy, fuel-smelling air and find my mom leaning against her car (parked illegally) in the pick-up line of the airport. The second our eyes meet, she's moving toward me with open arms. "Hi, sweetheart. It's so wonderful to see you." She wraps me in a tight hug. "How was your flight?"

"Hi, Mom." I hold on to her, the warmth of her embrace the comfort I need after four hours spent thinking about my life. "It was good."

She pulls back, her hands on my upper arms, as she studies me for a long moment like I'm the best thing she's ever seen and she wants to fix whatever is troubling me. "I've missed you."

"Missed you, too." Our weekly phone calls could never replace being together in person. We've always been close, and my eyes grow heavy with emotion. It's not that I share *everything* with her. She is *my mother.* But the hard things, the things I'm afraid to say out loud, I know I can tell her without fear of being made to feel small.

"That you left Los Angeles in such a hurry tells me we have a lot of catching up to do. Come on."

We get in the car, leave the bustling Chicago airport and setting sun behind us, and begin the hour-long drive to my small Wisconsin hometown. The distance gives us plenty of time to talk.

"How are things with Amber and Dixie?" Mom asks. That's one of the amazing things about my mom. She cares deeply for my stepsisters because they're important to my dad and me.

"Getting better every day. We're finally finding some common ground and that makes it harder for them to hate me."

"They never hated you." She has to say that. It's in the Mom rulebook. For my whole life, she's talked me down from my difficulties with my sisters. Sometimes she succeeded. Sometimes she didn't.

"Mom?" I need to tell her my main reason for visiting before I lose my nerve and before I can continue to talk about everything else.

She glances at me. "Yes?"

"I want to see Mason."

Mom gives a shaky breath as her chest slowly rises then falls. She keeps her attention on the road, one second, then another ticking by. "I knew this day would come, but I have to ask, is this about Vaughn?"

She doesn't know all the details of our relationship, but she's smart and can decipher my phone voice like nobody's business, so she knows he and I are more than friends.

"This is about me taking charge of my life. Closure is important, and I never got any where Mason's concerned. He didn't get any, either, and if he needs something from me, too, I want to give it to him."

She reaches over to squeeze my hand. "Sounds like it's time to find out."

"Do you think Carrie and Brian will allow me to see him?"

"I don't know, honey. He's getting weaker, according

to the last update I got from Carrie. They added a second caregiver for nights. But we can drive over there and ask."

My mom has always supported me with the tenacity of a bulldog, but I need to do this on my own. "I appreciate the offer, but I think I'll call Carrie and ask first. I don't want to show up unannounced."

"Their number is still the same," Mom says.

I call Mason's mom. She's surprised to hear from me, yet also understanding after I tell her how I've never stopped loving Mason, but that the time has come for me to move on, and I can't do that without seeing and talking to him. I want him to hear my voice. I want him to know he'll always have a place in my heart. She sniffles over the phone line, which makes me choke up, which makes my mom tear up, and it's like our emotions are finally set free. They say time heals all wounds, and I'm grateful when Carrie says she and Brian are home for the night and I'm welcome to stop by.

After I hang up, Mom and I don't talk, but she reaches for my hand and doesn't let go. I appreciate her silent understanding. Sometimes everything that needs to be said is done so without words.

The quiet also gives me time to mentally prepare. I'm scared to see Mason, worried I might react in an unkind way. I remember with vivid detail how he looked in the hospital. A thick white dressing around his head, his face bruised and swollen. He was unable to communicate or move, save for the brief shifting of his once vibrant brown eyes. I'd bitten my lip to keep from shrieking, only to lose my shit in the next second.

"Hey," my mom says, pulling me out of my recollection. "One step and deep breath at a time." She comes to a stop in Mason's driveway, the house a mere two blocks from my own.

I wrap her in a hug. The saying has always been her motto. Her way of reminding me to stay in the moment, recommended for everything from stage fright to performance anxiety before a tough algebra exam, to seeing my ex-boyfriend for the first time in years after my reckless action left him profoundly and irreversibly injured.

"Want me to come with you?" she asks.

Reaching for the door handle, I lightly shake my head. "I'd rather do this on my own."

"Okay. I love you." She wipes the corner of her eye. "I'm proud of you."

"Thanks."

Before I've even stepped onto the porch, Carrie opens the front door, and it suddenly feels like things are moving too fast—the world, my blood, my thoughts. I fight to hold my ground, put one foot in front of the other, while every instinct inside me screams to turn and run. What if this is a terrible idea? What if Mason stares at me with vacant eyes, or worse, opens his mouth and screams, "You did this to me!" like some kind of horrible miracle? Worse, and far more likely, what if he's an unrecognizable shell of a person, hooked up to tubes and wires, and I'm the one who freaks?

"Kendall," Carrie says with such hesitation my heart splinters. There was a time she greeted me with open arms.

"Hi. Thank you so much for letting me drop by like this."

She nods before leading me into the house that was my second home while Mason and I dated. Familiarity wraps around me. Everything looks the same. But like Carrie, Brian greets me like if he blinked and I disappeared, he'd be okay with that. "Hi, Kendall."

I chew on the inside of my mouth. I will not cry in front of them.

We make small talk and, while strained, Carrie and Brian's ambivalence toward me thaws as I share details about my life and look them both in the eye to say how often I've thought about Mason. How things he said and did live in my memory and continue to shape me in so many ways. He mattered. He'll always matter to me. I don't know if it's the passage of time, or my sincerity, or both, but when Carrie steps forward to hug me, it's a turning point I feel deep in my bones.

"I gave Mason's caregiver the night off so you two could spend time alone together."

"Thank you. And, Carrie, I'm sorry—"

She holds up her hand. "You know what? You've apologized over and over again, and I think maybe it's time I apologized to you."

I shake my head. "You have nothing to be sorry for."

"I do. I was—I am—selfish when it comes to Mason, and I didn't realize how much it would affect you, keeping the two of you apart. You took a risk calling me, and I'm glad you did."

I press my lips together, unable to speak.

"Mason wouldn't want anybody's sorrow as his legacy. Especially yours. So for that, I am sorry it took me a while to get here." She pauses outside his half-open door, puts her hand on my forearm. "Nothing has really changed since you saw him in the hospital," she says softly, "but Brian and I believe he recognizes voices, so talk as much as you want."

"Okay," I murmur, overcome with emotion. Carrie walks away, not the least bit hesitant to leave me to enter Mason's room *alone.* I almost call for her to come back, but instead I push open the door, my pulse racing and my body shaking. The moment I see him, tears trickle down my face. Cuts and bruises no longer mar his handsome face, but otherwise, he does look much the same.

And also different. Or maybe it's me who's different. I've grown out of my seventeen-year-old self. But he's thinner. Frailer. More like a boy. While I've been maturing into womanhood, he's been reverting.

I sit in the chair beside his bed, glad to find his eyes open. "Hi, Mason. It's me." His eyes briefly flit toward me, and I choke out a sob. Whether or not he truly understands I'm here, I'm convinced he does. And I'm determined to make up for my absence, starting at the beginning.

"I can't tell you how much it means to me to see you. I'm sorry it's been such a long time, but please know not a day has passed that I haven't thought about you. I've missed you so much, but before I tell you all the things I want to share, I want to apologize. I'm so sorry about the accident. I'm sorry for crashing your car. I'm sorry I drove when I shouldn't have." I let out a slow breath then swallow.

"And I'm sorrier than you will ever know that you were hurt." I brush the hair off his forehead with a gentle touch. I wish more than anything he could respond, but decide to take his silence as acceptance.

"I went to NYU like we planned. Mom and Dad tried to gently push me in a different direction—NYU was too far away, too closely associated with you, but I insisted. In truth, I wasn't ready to abandon our plan. A part of me hoped for a miracle. Hoped you'd somehow recover and join me. All would be forgiven and we'd live happily ever after just as we'd always envisioned." I pause to wipe away new tears. "But that miracle wasn't in the cards, was it? Instead, I learned how to face a reality I hated, which was its own kind of miracle. I learned how to reconcile regret with forgiveness. I learned to let go of things I couldn't change no matter how desperately I wished to and move forward in a way that would make you proud…

"The summer after my sophomore year I got an internship at a law firm, which pretty much meant there was no going back on law school after that, at least in my father's eyes. I know it's not what we dreamed about, but I stopped acting after the accident. It wasn't the same dream without you there…

"I didn't really keep in touch with anyone from our group of friends. Sarah reached out and we texted each other a few times. I know, right? The girl who tried numerous times to break us up had the decency to see if I was okay. I hear she and Davis are dating now…

"I graduated at the top of my class and was accepted to the University of Chicago for law school. To say my dad's ecstatic would be an understatement. He's got the next several years of my life mapped out. Graduate with top honors, join his firm, and earn some kickass nickname so everyone knows I'm a force to be reckoned with. All good things, but my heart isn't really in it…

"So my aunt hatched the perfect plan to get Dixie, Amber, and me together this summer. Amber is definitely nicer to me than Dixie, but now that we're older, we're figuring out how to get along better. We *are* getting along better, and I'm hopeful…

"I still have the framed Winnie the Pooh quote you gave me. I kept it on my nightstand in college and you can bet when I move into my own place, it will always be on display. I treasure it, so thank you again for giving it to me…"

There's a knock on the open door. "Kendall?" Carrie says.

I look over at her.

"Just wanted to check on you. Your mom called when you didn't answer her call or text."

I reach into my purse. "I forgot to take my phone off airplane mode. Sorry. I'll text her."

"No worries, but—"

"Oh my gosh. It's eleven o'clock?" I've been talking nonstop for three hours.

"It is," Carrie says around a weary smile. These past hours have no doubt been hard on her, too.

"I'm sorry I kept you up. I had a lot I wanted to tell him." I notice I have two more texts from Vaughn before tucking my phone away. "I'll say good night and then head home."

"Sounds good. Brian will drive you."

"That's okay. I can walk." I did it all the time when younger, and our gated community is safe even at this hour. Before she turns to go, I jump to my feet and hurry to hug her. "Thank you so, so much for letting me see him," I mumble.

She squeezes me back. "You're welcome."

When I return to Mason, his eyes are closed, so I focus on the rise and fall of his chest as I speak. "I have to go now. Sorry doesn't begin to cover what I feel, but I think you know that. You know, because if we were to change places, I'd know. I'd know it was a terrible, unfortunate accident and never blame you. And I wouldn't want you to punish yourself. I'd want you to move forward and live your best life. I'd never begrudge you that." I wipe under my runny nose. "Thanks for being the best boyfriend a girl could ask for. You were everything to me and I'm really glad I got to see and talk to you tonight. Please know you'll forever hold a special place in my heart, and I'll always love you." He makes a sound. It's small and incoherent, but it's the most beautiful utterance I've ever heard.

"Good-bye," I whisper, dropping a kiss on his forehead as I stand to go.

On the walk home, a sense of peace settles in my soul. Mason will always own parts of my heart—the first boyfriend part, the first kiss part. First love. But he won't be the last, and that's okay. He loved me, too. He wanted me to be brave, and strong, and smart. He'd want me to live my life.

A light breeze tousles my hair. A full moon lights the sky. Fireflies perform acrobatics in my periphery. I pause on the sidewalk to reminisce about kissing him under the trees, picnicking on the grass, and laughing and chasing each other with Super Soakers. We shared so much, and for that I'm grateful.

My parents are asleep when I get home. I change into a nightshirt, use the new toothbrush Mom left out for me, wash my face, and crawl under the covers of my bed. My phone is almost out of charge when I pull up Vaughn's texts. *I hope you're okay*, his last one says. *Please let me know.*

I remember now that he's in San Francisco. That he'd wanted me to join him there. His concern—even when working out of town—hits me in susceptible places. I should make a clean break where he's concerned, for both our sakes, but there's nothing clean about letting him worry. *I'm okay. Flew home for the weekend. Thanks for checking.*

Three tiny dots immediately wave back, and just like that I discover it's possible for a heart to soar and sink at the same time. I wasn't expecting an immediate response.

Talk tomorrow? It's late there and you're probably tired.

Exhausted is more like it. Now that I'm cozied up under my down comforter, I'm minutes away from falling asleep.

I don't think that's a good idea, I text back. Understatement of the ages. It's like tearing fresh stitches from a deep wound.

Tomorrow, angel.

Two little words bring back the soaring, sinking sensation. I refuse to jeopardize his career, but—my willpower at an all-time low, I put my phone aside—I'll find the strength to stand firm tomorrow. My eyes droop closed in an instant, and my mind wanders back to this morning and replays every horrible second of the conversation between Vaughn and his dad. The next thing I know sunlight streams through the slats of the shutters on my window and I blink awake, unsure of what the day will bring.

Chapter Twenty-Three

Kendall

The smell of homemade waffles lures me into the kitchen. I pad into the room to find Mom at the stove and Dad at the square wood table reading the newspaper. "Good morning."

"There she is." Dad puts down the paper and stands. "Get over here and give your father a hug, Kenny."

"Hi, Dad." I walk into his arms, his familiar scent always comforting.

"How was your visit with Mason?" Mom asks over Dad's shoulder.

"Incredibly special…and incredibly difficult."

Dad gives me an extra hug, then releases me and returns to his chair. "Important things often are."

"Do you need any help?" I ask my mom, not wanting to go into any further details. This morning I have something else on my mind.

"Nope. This next one is for you. Have a seat." I sit in my usual spot across from my dad and eye the maple syrup, berries, and powdered sugar sitting in the center of the table. My dad's plate is well used already.

"How's California?" he asks.

I pop a raspberry into my mouth. "Great." Not counting yesterday morning, which I've decided to strike from my testimony.

(Yes, I just sounded like an attorney. Being in the same room as my dad does that to me.)

"Your sisters?"

Dad narrows his focus directly at me. He thinks he can read me like I'm on the witness stand, and oftentimes he can, but I've had practice over the years, and if there's something I don't want him to see, I'm good at hiding it. My sisters are a topic I'm willing to share openly, though. The hope in his eyes makes it hard to hold anything back where they're concerned. He loves them.

"Dixie is planning to stay in L.A. She's bartending and pursuing her music career. She played one night at an open mic and won. She was fantastic. She's still wild and bold and doesn't give a crap about what anyone thinks of her.

"Amber is staying in L.A., too. She's starting a program to get her masters in speech therapy in the fall. I think she'll probably stay with Aunt Sally and Uncle Jack for a while because…" *She's pregnant.* It hits me then that my dad is going to be a grandfather. That is a really big deal but not something for me to tell.

Dad raises his eyebrows at my trailing off.

"I don't think she's on the best terms with her mom and stepdad, and you know Aunt Sally, she loves having her family with her." Did that sound plausible? What one has to do with the other, I don't know, but he seems to have bought it.

"They're being nice to you?"

Mom puts a waffle down on my plate. I inhale the scent of cinnamon and nutmeg. "Nicer," I say, emphasis on the *er.*

Dad doesn't look satisfied, so I add, "We're adults and behaving like it for the most part. You don't need to worry about me." I pile all the extras onto my waffle.

"I'll always worry about you," he says.

I shrug as I stuff a bite of food into my mouth. The explosion of flavors is soooo good.

"And them," he adds before he glances away for a moment, lost in thought. It doesn't take a genius to see he misses his two oldest daughters.

Maybe before summer is over, I can convince my sisters to give their father a chance at a better relationship.

"I spoke to Lou Adler about you this week." Dad takes a sip of his coffee, his attention back on me and a proud tone in his voice.

The name doesn't sound familiar. "Should I know who that is?"

"Lou is the deputy dean at the University of Chicago, a scholar, and sure to be your favorite professor. She's looking forward to meeting you."

"Louella and your dad go way back." Mom lets half a waffle slide off her spatula and onto Dad's plate. She retrieves the other half for herself and sits down to eat.

"He goes way back with everyone," I say. If you don't know Michael Hewitt then you aren't from around here. Plus, his judiciary reputation crosses state lines.

"Are you saying I'm old?" Dad teases, cutting into his next helping.

"I think you just did that all on your own." I smile at him.

"See that, Sherry, she's already got the makings of a brilliant attorney."

Ugh. I didn't say anything lawyerly or brilliant, but that's my dad. I put my fork down. It's time to bring up my doubts about law school. Test the waters to see how disappointed he'll be if I change course entirely and stay in L.A. to work for Art in Progress. Am I foolish to even think like that? I've been accepted into one of the most prestigious law schools in the country. My future is guaranteed if I follow the path I've started down. I *could* grow to love law. I could do a lot of different things with a law degree—a lot of positive things.

I could put up the good fight and attend the University of Chicago like planned and then take the world by storm. Turn my father's dream into mine, too.

"Mom mentioned you've been volunteering at a gallery?"

My dad's question startles me out of my thoughts. "Actually, it's a lot more than that, and I'd like to tell you about it."

The shrill ringing of the house phone prevents me from saying anything further. Hardly anyone calls that number, so we all pause a moment. Mom's eyes meet mine for a quick second before she's on her feet to answer the call. "Hello?" she says.

Slowly, Mom turns her whole back to me. Her hand grips the edge of the counter. Her shoulders slump. When she speaks, it's so quiet I can't decipher what she's saying.

Something is wrong. She's displaying the classic signs of bad news. Worry numbs my senses. I shiver and can't stop.

Mom hangs up the phone. She scoots her chair beside mine so we're touching, then takes my hand in hers. "Mason passed away this morning," she says softly.

I had a feeling that's what she was going to say. The numbness intensifies as I sit there, quietly suffering through a piece of my heart breaking. Mason is gone. He's gone, and if I hadn't visited him last night… If I hadn't gotten to apologize, to talk to him, tell him how much I miss him and that he'll forever be a part of me, I would have missed my chance and been even more devastated than I am right now.

Was he waiting for me? Sticking around until I got a chance to tell him good-bye?

"He passed away peacefully in his sleep, honey."

Silent tears stream down my face. Mom wraps her arm around me while Dad moves to my other side and does the same. "He's going to a better place," he says.

I nod, too torn up to speak. The person who for a long time meant more to me than anyone, who helped shape me into the person I am today, is gone. I wiggle my nose and suck in my bottom lip, but it doesn't help. The tears fall in earnest.

My parents hold me while I cry. Right after the accident, they were furious, torn up inside. Beyond saddened by my actions. They'd taught me better than that, hadn't they? But they still loved me, and they stuck by me no matter what. Even when so-called friends wanted nothing to do with me, or people I'd known all my life looked away when I walked into church, or the grocery store. It softened the blow slightly, that they found it in their hearts to forgive me. It was a gift I never took lightly.

Dad gets up to grab me—and Mom—some tissues. When our sobs finally quiet, we talk about what comes next. Funeral arrangements will be made, so I decide to extend my stay. As hard as it will be, there's no way I can leave without seeing him laid to rest. I ask my mom if I can borrow her phone charger then head upstairs to shower. I stand under the spray until the warm water turns cold. The rest of the day goes by in a blur.

Sunday morning I wake up and don't know what to do with myself, so I cook. Banana muffins, lasagna, chicken parmesan, and Mason's favorite, peanut-butter-chocolate brownies. The recipes allow me to lose myself in the ingredients and measurements.

Dad passes through the kitchen on his way to a golf game. He mentions something about law school, but I don't really hear him.

By late afternoon, I'm drained. I collapse onto my bed

to close my eyes for a little bit. When my phone rings, I know who it is without looking. I didn't answer his calls yesterday, too upset about Mason and worried I'd ugly cry in his ear. I *think* I'm ready to have a conversation now, so I pick up on the third ring, noting I'm right about the caller. "Hi, Vaughn."

"Hi."

I squeeze my eyes shut at the sound of his voice.

"How are you?" he continues. "I was worried when we didn't connect yesterday."

"I'm… Mason passed away yesterday." I curl into a ball. It's the first time I've said that aloud. I texted Amber and Dixie this morning with the news and to let them know I wouldn't be home until the end of the week.

He lets out a miserable sigh. "I'm so sorry. Did you get a chance to see him?"

"Yeah. I spent a few hours with him on Friday night and Vaughn, it was"—tears prick my eyes but I blink them away—"so comforting to talk to him and finally get closure."

"I'm sure it meant a lot to him, too."

"I wish I'd pushed to do it sooner." My whisper is soft and thin, like a worn cloth polishing an old regret until it gleams anew.

"We all do things at our own pace. If you'd gone earlier, you might not have been ready for everything you needed to say."

"True," I say quietly.

We're both silent for several seconds. "How are you?" I ask, remembering my manners.

"I'm okay. Missing a certain blond, blue-eyed angel."

It's so tempting to lean into those words. Let them support me and give me strength when I feel a little lost. It's reassuring to be missed. Cared for. Especially after the events of the past two days. It's beyond tempting to confess I miss him, too, but I'm stronger than that.

Into my silence he asks, “So, when are you coming back?”

“I—I’m not sure. Mason’s funeral is on Tuesday and I’m going to stay a few days beyond that. Candace was nice enough not to fire me when I texted her I needed the week off.”

“Dude, let’s go!” someone—Dylan I think—shouts in the background, and suddenly I realize he’s not at home like I initially assumed. He’s out and about, living his life. “Sorry,” he says. “Dylan got his dad’s skybox, and apparently Matt and he are going to have aneurysms if we’re not in it by the time they throw the first pitch.”

“Don’t miss anything on my account.” I mean it in relation to so much more than the game. I mean it in relation to his life, his career, all the wonderful new opportunities the future will bring his way. Including, no doubt, a girl who will effortlessly pass the dad background check and make Vaughn so smitten he never thinks about the girl he befriended the summer before he became a huge star.

“I’ll call you tomorrow, but Kendall, I’m here if you need me sooner.”

For a moment I can’t speak for fear of saying something that gives away how much I want to be with him, kiss him, make love with him until the world stops and it’s just us. Finally, I manage a very choked, “Okay. Thanks.” We disconnect, and my poor heart aches again from the strain of another small good-bye.

Chapter Twenty-Four

Vaughn

I place my size tens on the stenciled yellow footprints, cross my wrists over my head, and let the body scanner do its thing. For about five seconds I'm an island of stillness in a sea of constant motion, separate from the conversations, loudspeaker announcements, and general chaos of LAX.

When the TSA technician waves me forward, I offer her a quick "Thanks" and walk to the end of the conveyor belt spitting out a steady stream of carry-on bags and plastic bins full of electronic devices, wallets, keys, and other personal paraphernalia. My stuff has cleared the screening tunnel but not the plastic barrier designed to keep all us impatient passengers from grabbing our shit right out of the mouth of the X-ray machine. Over the ambient noise of people and technology, I hear the distinct and familiar sound of my ringtone. It's only a bag and a bin away, but the older woman in front of me struggles to lift her carry-on off the conveyor, which creates a momentary backup.

"Can I help?" I question while bringing the wheeled bag down for her.

"Thank you." She beams her appreciation as I extend the retractable handle and spin the luggage so it faces her.

"No problem." Leaning past her, I take my sunglasses and ringing phone out of the bin.

"Don't want to miss a call from your girlfriend?" she teases.

I smile and shake my head while noting the unfamiliar number flling the screen of my phone. "No girlfriend, I'm afraid. She won't have me."

"Well, then, you'll just have to work harder to change her mind."

"That's my plan," I reply, and shoot her a thumbs-up at the same time I hit the button to take my call. "Hello?"

"Vaughn Shaughnessy?" A woman with a crisp British accent asks, and I immediately picture Miss Moneypenny sitting behind a tidy desk at MI6, wearing a phone headset.

"Yes." My gut tightens for reasons I can't attribute to lifting my carry-on bag off the conveyor.

"Please hold for Mr. Cowie." I hear a faint click and then music flows into my ear. Laney Albright's first single now competes with an amplified security reminder about unattended bags.

Holy shit. This could be it. This could be "the call."

I'm almost to my gate and halfway through the next Laney Albright song when it cuts off mid-verse and a familiar voice says, "Hello, Vaughn. Nigel here. Have a minute for a chat?"

"Of course." I stop at the perimeter of the waiting area for my gate, take a deep breath to steady my nerves, and swipe my damp palm along the leg of my jeans.

"You sound like you're North Bank Lower at Emirates, with Arsenal closing on the goal."

"Sorry." I press the phone to my ear. "I'm at the airport, about to get on a flight."

"Ah, well, there you go. I'll keep this short. Vaughn, fancy being the new host of *America Rocks*?"

I close my eyes for a moment and do a mental lap around the terminal, shouting and high-fiving everyone in sight. "Yes. Sure. I would absolutely fancy that."

"Brilliant. We're of a mind then. The casting team, the judges, the test audiences—hell everyone you auditioned for, including John and myself—unanimously agree you're the right fellow to welcome America back to its favorite show."

"I'm ..." *Honored? Grateful? Stoked beyond words?* "I appreciate this opportunity, Nigel. I won't let the show down."

"Not a worry. We talked with a lot of people in the course of making our decision, and everyone called you hardworking, easygoing, and a total professional. You've got your ego in check and your head on straight. The term '*hawt* AF' came up a bit as well," he adds, managing a decent twang. "Whatever that means. Nobody will explain it to this crusty old codger."

A laugh escapes me. Even though I suspect he's joking, I duck the explanation. "I think it means my ego just got out of check."

"I don't believe it. Not for a second. Speaking of seconds, I know yours are limited. Let me run through the next steps before I wish you bon voyage."

"That'd be great." I glance at the gate. "They haven't started boarding yet."

"I'll be brief. Can't have you getting stern looks from the steward. We'll reach out to your agent next and send over contracts. She and our lawyer will bat that around a few times, just to be sporting. Meanwhile, our PR folks will work with you and yours on a press release and some other publicity. Once we all sign on the dotted line, we'll pull the trigger on the announcement. Until then, though—"

"Not a word. I understand," I assure him, although I feel like my unstoppable smile might as well be a neon sign that reads I GOT IT! "Other than my agent, my publicist and my—" I almost say "my manager," but catch the words before they tumble out, because as of Friday morning I don't have a manager, and I haven't spoken with my father. "Other than them, I won't discuss this with anyone."

"Thanks. So, business or pleasure?"

"Sorry?"

"Your flight. Is it for business or pleasure?"

Some of my triumph dims as the cloud of Kendall's loss—the whole Kendall situation, really—floats back to the forefront of my mind. "Technically, neither. A friend of mine—you met her, actually. Kendall Hewitt. I don't know if you remember, but I introduced you at—"

"Laney's party. Of course I remember Kendall. I very discreetly—because I am discretion itself after two martinis—suggested you invite her along for your weekend of work." He chuckles. "Took my advice, eh?"

"Unfortunately, no. She recently lost someone who meant a lot to her. A friend she grew up with. I'm taking a few days to be with her. Offer my support. It's a difficult time."

"I'm sorry to hear that. Would you convey my condolences when you see her?"

"Yes. I—"

"I best let you go. I don't say so often, but there are a few things more important than *America Rocks*, and you're onto one right now. Safe travels. We'll be in touch."

"Thanks," I reply at the same time a gate attendant announces preboarding for my flight. A few minutes later I'm staring out the window of seat 3C, caught in a weird emotional limbo. The rush from Nigel's call has calmed to low-grade euphoria. I can't share the news with anyone at the moment, so even a limited round of thank-yous and congratulations with my inner circle will have to wait until I deplane. Meanwhile, another part of my brain is working overtime to figure out exactly how I carry off this uninvited visit I'm making. I have Kendall's home address from Dixie, so I could just show up on her doorstep and tell her I'm there for her if she needs me. Some might consider that an ambush, though, so maybe I should call first? *Hey, I just happened to be in the neighborhood and wondered if you needed my emotional support, or missed me, or are open to revisiting the topic of "us"?*

My cell rings again, reminding me I haven't toggled to airplane mode yet. They're still boarding the main cabin, so I pull my phone from my pocket and glance at the screen. It's my father. Apparently good news travels fast. My low-grade euphoria rises a degree, and I figure I have enough time to take the call and thank him before I'm wheels up, because he deserves massive credit for helping make this happen. Basking in our achievement might provide the right foundation for rebuilding the father-son part of our relationship.

"Hey Dad. I take it you heard—"

"I saw it."

The short reply, delivered in his terse tone, effectively cuts my words off. "Already? I didn't think it would happen this fast."

"You *knew* about this?"

"I learned, like, ten minutes ago. Nigel called to tell me—"

"Goddammit. *Nigel* knows about this?"

Okay, we're definitely not on the same page. A cold fist squeezes my gut. "What are you talking about?"

"I'm talking about a video someone uploaded of you stumbling around intoxicated at the end of your driveway after parking your car in the motherfucking hedge. The lighting sucks and the sound is lousy, but it's definitely you. And if I'm not mistaken, Kendall costars in this candid documentary currently elevating CelebrityDrunkCam channel to trending status on YouTube. Jesus Christ, Vaughn. What the hell were you thinking? Your mother and I have already buried one child. Don't you dare put us through that nightmare again."

For an endless moment my mind spins like a tire in mud, fighting for sufficient traction to follow what my father's saying. Then, slowly, his words sink in and form treads strong enough to propel my thoughts forward—straight into a brick wall of consequences so huge I can barely measure them. The first brick hits me directly in the heart. "Kendall..." Shit. "Kendall wants her privacy."

"Nobody's going to tag Kendall. She's not the drunk celebrity," my dad points out, "and her back is to the camera most of the time. I assumed it was her based on the totality of the circumstances."

A tiny fraction of the pain in my chest subsides. He's probably right. Whoever took the video—it had to be Becca or her friend—wouldn't know Kendall's last name or be concerned about figuring it out. I'm the target. Me. Because I didn't want to keep up with our charade? I knew she could be manipulative, but this is...*fuck*. The next brick in the wall of consequences lands heavily in the pit of my stomach, because the opportunity I worked hard for, and won, is no doubt about to be withdrawn thanks to shady revenge tactics from someone I once called a friend. I should be off-the-chain furious, but right now I just find the whole thing sad. "I haven't seen the video. Until you told me, I didn't even know there was a video, but I promise you the situation wasn't what it looks like."

"Let me put it in focus for you, Vaughn. To your mother and me, it looks like you don't give a shit about us or what it would do to us if something happened to you," he says bluntly. "To a random viewer it looks like you got trashed and lost control of your car. In case none of that matters to you, I've got one more. To the producers of *America Rocks*, it looks like a whole lot of risk they don't need. Risk you have a judgment problem, potentially a substance abuse problem, and a propensity to ignore the law and endanger yourself and others."

Guilt and an oversized brick of self-pity threaten to pile on, but I deflect these and use the rubble to construct an architecture of truth. "I do give a shit about you and Mom. I lost Andie, too. I felt the pain, too, and I saw what it did to you. I've spent *years* trying to distract you, most of all, from that pain, so do me the favor of knowing me well enough to believe I wouldn't throw everything away intentionally. I did drink too much that night, but I didn't get behind the wheel. I went for a walk. Bec…" Right now I want to rat her ass out so bad, but there's no point. Her word against mine, unless I drag Kendall into it. And I won't. "Someone else decided to go to a club, took my keys without my permission, and made it as far as the end of the driveway, nearly running Kendall and me over in the process. I would have ended the night in a body bag if not for Kendall, because the person driving my car didn't—"

"Was it Dylan?" my dad asks, with a real crack in his voice. "I know it's not Matt, and I'd give Dylan more credit, but that kid has a reckless side."

"Not Dylan. Not Matt." I look around to confirm nobody's paying attention to my end of this conversation. "It was Becca," I relent. "Either Becca or her friend recorded and uploaded the video. Perfect timing to wreck my career, because Nigel called me less than fifteen minutes ago to tell me I had the job."

An extended, presumably shocked silence greets my revelation. Finally, my father clears his throat. "Why would she do this?"

"Jealousy? Spite? Because I told her it was time for us both to move on."

"I thought she understood how this business works."

A flight attendant catches my eye and signals for me to end my call.

I nod. "Dad, this business involves *people*, not chess pieces. When you manipulate them to further your own ambitions, can you really act surprised when they turn on you?"

"I don't know. Maybe not. Perhaps I'm guilty of tunnel vision where you're concerned, but it doesn't change the fact that you earned the hosting job. This bullshit bad press doesn't have to cost you your shot. We just need to get ahead of the scandal and overtake it with our narrative before it has a chance to do any damage. I'll place a call to Nigel to explain everything and convince him to give us twenty-four hours to resolve this to their satisfaction. The video doesn't show you driving—or even in the vehicle—so he should be able to grant us that much. Hell, we can accomplish a lot of damage control in half that time. An interview with a major media outlet—Kit from *Access Live* will jump all over this. You tell the real story. Kendall will corroborate, and…"

I feel his fervor through the phone, and it's so fucking tempting to grab the lifeline he's holding out to me, but… "I can't."

"What?"

Just saying the words calms my racing pulse to a steady, purposeful rate. The flight attendant returns, and this time she's not fooling around. Me and another asshole in the row ahead of me are getting serious stink eye. "I can't do anything about this right now. I'm sitting on a plane about to pull away from the gate, talking to you on borrowed time. Once I hang up I'm out of the loop for at least twenty-four hours."

"Get off the plane. Whatever you've booked, this is more important."

"No." The certainty calcifies in my bones. "Kendall needs me. She didn't plan it, and she didn't ask me to be there for her, but she needs me right now, and I'm not going to let her down, because I..." The words "I'm in love with her" nearly tumble out, but I bite them back, because Kendall deserves them first. "I've got to go, Dad."

"Wait." I hear his long exhale, followed by a silent moment while he struggles to choose the right words. "Being there for Kendall is more important to you than fighting for *America Rocks*?"

"Yes."

Silence.

Another deep breath follows, and I imagine him loosening the knot in his tie. "All right. I understand. It's your call. Do what you need to do."

He's letting me make this choice—not that he has any other option unless he can teleport me off a plane—but still. Progress.

I disconnect and switch my phone to airplane mode. The flight attendant starts her safety spiel. I close my eyes, exhale slowly, and release my grip on the goal I held in my hand for a whole fucking minute.

The plane backs away from the terminal, and it's like I'm backing away from my dream. At this very moment, though, there's something—make that someone—more important than a job. Nigel said as much. He told me there are some things more important than *America Rocks*, and I'm onto one of them. Kendall. She matters, because I'm in love with her. She's my priority.

I hope to God I can convince her I should be hers.

Chapter Twenty-Five

Kendall

Early Monday night the doorbell rings. Mom is wrist deep in homemade pizza dough while I shred cheese so I quickly wipe my hands with a paper towel and go to answer it. Swinging the door wide, I can't believe my eyes.

"Vaughn?"

He lifts his aviator sunglasses to his forehead. "Hi." He smiles next, making my pulse trip over itself.

I lean against the edge of the door for support. "What are you doing here?" Now I know why I hadn't heard from him. He was flying the friendly skies and no doubt making all the flight attendants' and passengers' day from his mere presence.

"I thought maybe you could use some extra support at the funeral tomorrow."

Wow. This is one of those surprise moments life has up her sleeve that I'm both happy and confused over. Despite the uncertainty between us, Vaughn is here, standing two feet in front of me, offering his support. He didn't have to be here. Not at all, yet he chose to be. This is better than the "I'm just a boy standing in front of a girl…" *Notting Hill* moment. This is a supreme gesture, one that presses pause on our debatable relationship.

Does this make my decision about where or if he fits in my life more difficult? Heck yes. But deep down, I'm bowled over by his concern and thrilled to see him.

Something of my inner monologue must show on my face because his smile falters.

"I should have checked with you first." He takes a backward step, adjusting the duffel bag hanging off his shoulder.

"What? No." Now that he's here, a greedy part of me insists on clinging. I lunge at him, wrapping my arms around his waist and pressing my face to the crook of his neck. His scent is familiar. Soothing. I breathe it in like I'm oxygen starved. "Thank you. Thank you for coming all this way." This will probably make a final good-bye even more painful, but I'll deal with the fallout later. The fact that he's made a gesture like this overwhelms me to the point that I'm incapable of gathering a single defense.

He tucks a finger under my chin to lift my face to his. The soft kiss he presses to my lips makes my legs weak. "I had to come. I couldn't stand not being here for you."

"How did you know where I live?"

"Dixie hooked me up with your address. Then she told me she'd have my balls if I so much as blinked at you the wrong way while you were dealing with Mason's death. I think she's starting to take her sister status a little more seriously."

"Maybe so." I take his hand. "Come inside. My mom and I are cooking. I'll introduce you."

"I should warn you right now, moms love me."

I roll my eyes but inwardly smile. I close the door behind

him, put his bag on the hardwood floor next to the entry table, and note he's dressed a little less casual than usual with a light green collared button-down that turns his eyes emerald. "I'm pretty sure everyone loves you," I say over my shoulder.

Something flashes across his face, but as soon as it's there it's gone. He opens his mouth to respond, then closes it, thinking better of it, I guess. And proving that while we can tease each other, our situation is also fraught. Right now it's too easy to say the wrong thing. We arrive at the kitchen just as Mom calls out, "Who was at the door?"

"Mom, this is Vaughn. Vaughn, my mom, Sherry."

Her eyes bug out of her head when she looks at him. I'm not sure if it's because of the things I've told her about him or because she's surprised. Probably a combination of both.

"Hello," he says. He starts to extend his hand then notes her hands are full of flour as she rolls out the pizza dough and drops his arm. "It's a pleasure to meet the mom of one of my favorite people."

"The pleasure's mine." Mom takes the two of us in before settling a questioning gaze on me.

"Vaughn came for Mason's funeral."

"For Kendall," he corrects, and sends me a patient look. "I know tomorrow is going to be tough."

Mom washes her hands at the sink and shoots me a look that says, *He's a keeper.*

She misses my, *Yeah, but I can't keep him,* look because she wipes her palms down her apron then steps toward Vaughn and hugs him. "Thank you." She pulls back. "That means a lot. We're making pizza for dinner. Would you like to stay?"

"I would."

Jeez. Slow down there, Mom. Dinner with the family puts me in more danger. It means my mom and dad will get to know Vaughn directly. And vice versa. Stories will be swapped. Laughs shared. It's one thing for my parents to hear about Vaughn from me, where I own the flow of information. Quite another for them to bypass me and form their own bonds. I try to catch my mom's eye before this spirals further out of my control, but there's no stopping her when she's in Mom mode.

"Where are you staying tonight?" she asks, resuming cooking duties while unknowingly sending my pulse into a tailspin.

"I thought I'd grab a room at the nearest hotel."

"Nonsense. You'll stay here. I'll make up the guest room."

Vaughn laces our fingers together. "Thank you. I appreciate that."

And now things are definitely, irretrievably beyond my control.

The hand holding does not go unnoticed by Mom. "How are you at slicing tomatoes?" she asks the guy currently in possession of more than my hand.

"Umm..."

I glance at him and out of nowhere, I laugh. Only my mom would look at Vaughn Shaughnessy and think, "Sure, he's easy on the eyes, but can he slice tomatoes?"

"Vaughn's more of a takeout kind of guy." I release his hand and slip around the counter to get back to grating cheese.

"Today he's the tomato guy. Come on, I'll demonstrate."

It's surreal standing in the kitchen of the house I grew up in with my mom and Vaughn and talking and laughing while we make pizza. I sneak peeks at him constantly, admiring the quick, genuine smiles he offers my mom as she not-so-subtly pumps him for personal deets.

"Kendall tells me you live next door to Jack and Sally. Did you grow up in Los Angeles?"

"Born and raised."

"Any brothers or sisters?"

"*Mom.*"

"It's okay," Vaughn says, finished slicing the tomatoes. "I had a sister, but she passed away several years ago."

"I'm so sorry." Mom touches his arm in comfort.

"Thank you." A beat of silence passes. "How about you? I'm not sure which side of the family Aunt Sally is on?"

Mom grins and launches into our family tree. I'd like to hide behind a giant oak right about now, but I grin, too, and bear it. Thankfully, our tree isn't all that big, and he's already met almost half of it. Mom puts two pizzas in the oven just as my dad walks into the room.

I make introductions, and then, since Mom has a green salad ready to go, the four of us sit down at the table to start eating.

Dad doesn't waste any time getting to the bottom of my relationship with Vaughn. "I take it you and Kendall have gotten to know each other well." It's a fair question considering I've never told anyone outside of family and Brit about the accident and Mason.

"Vaughn's been a true friend." I don't need my dad to know exactly how deeply we're involved.

"She's been a better one," Vaughn says easily, going along with my friendship description.

Dad gives a nod of acknowledgment. "Did you talk to any of your old classmates today?" he asks me. "Jim Baker's daughter is starting law school in the fall, too, you know."

"I did not know."

"You two should touch base before school starts."

I run my fork through my salad. "Maybe."

"Kendall is going to make an incredible attorney one day," Dad tells Vaughn.

"I've no doubt she'll be incredible at anything she chooses to do," he says. His eyes bounce from my dad to me. Hold.

They're saying everything he respectfully won't say out loud. *Choose what you love.*

Sometimes that isn't an option. What is that saying? *Do what you have to do until you can do what you want to do.*

Whatever decision I ultimately make about my career, with Mason's funeral tomorrow, I'm too emotional to think too deeply about it now.

Mom pulls the pizzas out of the oven. I'm grateful we polish them off over simple conversation. When finished, Vaughn and I do the dishes. I show him the guest bedroom and bath. While he's brushing his teeth or whatever, Mom corners me in the hallway.

"I won't bug you for all the details now, but I need the whole scoop after he leaves."

"I've told you—"

"Don't even," she interrupts with a wave of her hand. "I can see the way you two look at each other, and I've heard the sound of your voice for weeks when you've talked about him on the phone. You two are in love."

"*What?* No we're not."

"Do not lie to me, Kendall Hewitt."

I rest against the wall with a sigh. Oh my freaking God. That can't be true, can it? "You think he loves me?"

"He flew all the way here to be with you, sweetie. What do *you* think?"

"I think our lives are going in completely different directions."

"That may be true, but ask yourself this: is your life going in the direction of your dreams? You gave up one dream after the accident. I'd hate to see you settle for something that means more to your dad than you."

I'm floored by her intuition, even though I probably shouldn't be. I can't hide things from her like I do my dad. She's always seen right through me. "I don't want to disappoint him."

"He could never be disappointed in you."

But he could. After the accident, when he took care of all the legalities on my behalf, I overheard him use those exact words with his law partner. I'd let him down, and if it had been anyone else in the car with me, things could have gone very differently. Carrie and Brian didn't push the district attorney for a harsh sentence—a big saving grace for my father's efforts to shield me from maximum penalties.

The guest bedroom door opens and Vaughn steps out.

I abruptly lift away from the wall. "Hey. Want to watch a movie?" I ask him. It's the first thing to come to my mind.

"Sounds good."

"Good night, you two," Mom says with a smile. "Breakfast is at eight. We'll leave for Mason's service at nine."

"Okay. Thanks," I say.

"Thank you again for having me," Vaughn adds.

As soon as Mom rounds the corner, Vaughn scoops me into his arms. He holds me for a long time, his chin on top of my head, his hand rubbing up and down my back.

"I can hear you thinking, Kendall. Stop worrying. Stop feeling like you have to draw a line so we both understand the boundaries. I'm here because I wanted to be with you. That's all we have to say. For now."

There's a big conversation hidden in those two little words, so "for now" I'm going to tiptoe around them, but still speak from my heart. "I'm really glad you're here," I say into his shoulder.

"I am, too. Your mom makes the best damn pizza ever."

I manage a smile. He's trying so hard to lighten the seriousness of the situation. I still can't believe he hopped on a plane to be with me for the funeral. His flight back to L.A. is in the afternoon. He's traveled all this way for less than twenty-four hours because he cares about me.

And if you truly care about him, you'll cut him a clean break before he gets back on that plane.

"If you think her pizza is yummy, you should try her spaghetti and meatballs."

"Anytime," he replies, and I realize my attempt to keep the mood light came out like an invitation, or at least a possibility. "Vaughn, I didn't mean—"

"Shh. I know what you meant. We're letting that be for now, remember?"

I do, and then I don't, because he leans in, cups my neck, and kisses me. Softly at first, full of tenderness and comfort. But the kiss turns hotter the second he parts his lips, because I slip my tongue inside, lured by the solace, yet immediately swept up in the need. Tonight he tastes like the best Italian dish ever, and I could live off his kisses forever. His hands find my waist. He slants his head to angle my mouth right where he wants it. For several mindless minutes we make out in the hallway, lost to everything but each other. I almost forget I can't handle being with him in the public eye, and he can't risk his future on a girl with my past.

Sobering at the thought and the fact that we're devouring each other in my parents' home, I pull away.

"Umm…I think I'd better just go to bed."

He runs his hand over my hair, brushing it back from my face. "It's going to be okay," he says before kissing my forehead.

I study the little furrow not normally on his forehead. "Are *you* okay?"

"I'm fine. I'll see you in the morning."

Something tells me he's not, not at all, but he turns before I can question it.

• • •

A few marshmallow clouds hang in the light blue sky as we stand at Mason's burial site. White folding chairs are situated in two rows for family members. Beautiful multicolored flower arrangements from the service adorn the short ends of the plot.

It's my first funeral, and I hate it.

The pretty exterior does nothing to dull my inner pain, but I guess the warm summer day is better than rain.

As some unseen device lowers Mason's casket into the ground, I cling to a memory of the two of us lying on towels at Big Foot Beach State Park, laughing as we tried to sculpt sand castles that kept collapsing, but really we didn't care because we were content just hanging out together.

When the casket is released, a whimper slips through my pressed lips. I can't imagine what his parents are going through right now. Vaughn squeezes my hand. He hasn't let go of it the entire time we've been at the cemetery. He's kept me standing when more than once I've wanted to crawl.

Mom takes my other hand, laces our fingers together. If not for these two people on either side of me, I'm not sure I would have been brave enough to remain here.

Mason's passing has drawn a huge crowd to pay their condolences. Practically everyone in our small town knows Carrie and Brian, knows what happened that tragic night. Nobody's blatantly pointing or shooting me dirty looks, but I once again feel like a pariah.

My gaze lands on Sarah standing beside Davis. They got engaged a few weeks ago, and as happy as I am for them, I know we'll never be friends again. I think that makes me normal. Beside Sarah is Taylor. Taylor was the gossip queen in high school, and judging by the rumors she shared during our brief conversation, still is. Next to her is Willow Baker. Jim's daughter can't wait for law school and definitely wants to connect there. I simply nodded in response, grateful when another friend interrupted us in order to meet Vaughn.

I take that back. I'm grateful Vaughn is with me, but not thrilled with the attention he's garnering. The people my parents' age aren't interested in him, but Mason's and my friends from high school are an entirely different matter. Glancing across the burial site, they're huddled together and trying to covertly snap pictures of Vaughn with their cell phones. Prior to the service, when I'd made the effort to say hello to everyone, the overwhelming response had been excitement at meeting the guy from the magazine ads and music videos.

This is a funeral. Honoring Mason and expressing sympathy to his family should be top priority. Instead, Vaughn is a distraction I didn't think about. The hairs on the back of my neck rise. I look up and catch Carrie's eye. As expected, grief pulls at the lines of her face, but what isn't expected is the irritation. She cuts a glance to mine and Mason's old friends, then back to me. The message is clear—the twenty-somethings are more interested in Vaughn and my relationship than paying respects to her son. Her displeasure hits me like a punch in the throat.

"Hey," Vaughn whispers in my ear.

I turn my head to look up at him.

"You all right?"

"I've been better."

He brushes his thumb over my cheek. "Have I mentioned how strong you are? How brave? You're here today when most people in your shoes probably would have chosen not to attend."

"Thanks for saying that."

"It's the truth."

As much as I want to forget this day, I won't. I'll remember the way Vaughn took my sadness and softened its edges with tenderness. I'll remember how hard it was to keep my heart closed off when he understood it so well. He knows what it feels like to lose someone, and while my love for Mason and Vaughn's love for his sister are very different, the experience of loss forms another bond between us.

"You won't mind if I remind you a few more times, will you?"

"No." How could I? It's not lip service. His sincerity is tangible.

The moment the burial concludes, I tune out the rampant whispers from my peers and approach Carrie and Brian to apologize for any disturbance Vaughn and I have caused this morning.

Carrie doesn't mince words. She asks us to leave. It's crushing and expected at the same time. I fight back tears when I once again give her my condolences.

My legs shake as I say good-bye to my parents, telling them there's no need for them to rush. I'll see Vaughn off and then meet them at home.

"I'm really sorry my being here caused a problem," Vaughn says. He wraps his arm around me, bringing me close to his side. I hear and feel his misery. It wasn't his intention to upset anyone. I know that.

I also know I can't keep doing this. "Me, too," I say, sorry that when I say good-bye to him this time, I will stand by it for both our sakes.

Chapter Twenty-Six

Vaughn

People mill around in the distance, talking in small groups or slowly making their way to their cars and saying the kinds of things people say at times like this. “Such a beautiful service,” or “He’s at peace now.” Yes, and hopefully, but my guess is funerals are for the living rather than the deceased. I know the person I’m most concerned about is standing right in front of me, looking pale and tired.

I don’t want to add to Kendall’s burden. I didn’t come all this way to cause more stress during one of the most difficult times in her life. I sure as hell didn’t intend to turn a memorial service into a fucking photo op and watch a grieving mother hold Kendall accountable for the bad behavior of grown-ass adults who can’t keep their curiosity in check during a funeral for one of their own. But that’s how it went down, and now the Town Car’s engine idles in time to the seconds ticking off in my mind, reminding me I’m running out of chances to turn “for now” into “for keeps.” Hell, I don’t even know if she’s still coming back to California.

I wrap my arms around her and slowly pull her close until our bodies touch. She doesn't resist, but she holds herself stiff for a moment, then sighs and relaxes into me. Her arms link around my waist and tighten in a quick, almost desperate hug. "Thank you for being here. I don't know how I would have made it through without you, but…"

No buts. I tighten my arms when she tries to ease away. "You would have made it through the same way you made it through everything that came before this—with honesty and courage." Before she can argue I kiss her. A little hard, a little possessive, because I need to make sure she *feels* the truth of my next words. "But here's the thing. I want to be with you. Not just for this trying time, but for all the times. It's kind of a permanent thing. My heart is yours. I need you to know that."

She pales further, which I didn't think was possible, and shakes her head. So much for not adding to her stress.

"I don't… I can't take it, Vaughn. As much as I want to, at the end of the day your father was right—"

"My father was out of line. He has been for a long time, and I've finally gotten him to wake up to it. We've talked. Our relationship has been broken for years and one phone call won't fix it, but he knows I'm not going to accept things the way they were. I'm taking control of my life and career."

"He's just trying to protect you."

"I don't need protecting. Not anymore. And never from you." I pause to let that sink in. "You're my brave, fierce guardian angel."

"I'm not." The denial is instant and breathless. She starts to pull away, then changes her mind, grasps my shoulders, and tries to give me a shake—which is pretty much like a butterfly trying to shake a tree, but I sense her rising panic. "I'm none of those things, because the idea of my past mistakes being splashed around for public consumption terrifies me. Mason's death doesn't erase my mistake. It doesn't protect his parents from the nightmare of seeing their deepest tragedy served up as entertainment, like what happened today. It doesn't shield you from—"

"I don't need shielding, but I can do right by you and the people you care about. You would have to trust me to make sure it wasn't a nightmare. That's all, Kendall." I hold her stare, attempting to sway her through sheer force of my will. "Just trust me. Let me be *your* guardian angel."

Smooth hands link at the back of my neck. She rises to her tiptoes and slams her mouth against mine, and then holds on like I'm the only solid thing in her world. For a second I think I've won, but then I taste her tears on my lips. "I c-can't," she whispers when she draws back. "Please don't text or call. It's too hard. Good-bye, Vaughn."

Feeling her move away from me is like relinquishing a limb or a vital organ. It's oddly soundless, considering how deeply I feel my insides tear. I watch her leave through a haze of pain. I can't slay this dragon for her. I do understand the stakes. I already paid my own at the hands of the media, and they were pretty fucking steep—I got a text from my agent last night confirming *America Rocks* rescinded their offer—but I paid that price willingly, because being with the woman I love in her hour of need was more important than fighting to keep a job. It hurts knowing she doesn't care enough to fight for us, too, but I can't make her trust me.

The driver coughs into his fist to get my attention. "We need to head out now if you want to make your flight."

Right. Numbness sets in as I ride to the airport. I'm on autopilot through the terminal and the flight. My body is present and accounted for, but my head's somewhere else. It's back in Lake Geneva, standing on a path at a cemetery, replaying the conversation with Kendall and wondering what I could have said, *should* have said, to convince her we're worth the risk. Should I have told her I lost the *America Rocks* job? I didn't, because she had enough sadness to deal with. She didn't need mine. Especially when it doesn't fundamentally change anything. I'm not going to quit pursuing my professional goals because one fell through, which means for Kendall to be with me, she has to be 100 percent sure that if her past comes to light, she can trust me to say and do the right things to protect her and the people she cares about.

I still haven't figured out how to prove I can do this by the time I'm wheels down at LAX, but when the *ding* sounds, signaling it's okay to take phones off airplane mode, mine's in my hand, automatically checking to see if I have a text from Kendall. My heart doesn't want to give up on us.

Kendall hasn't reached out, but my phone's been busy while I've been out of the loop. Several of the social media icons are dotted with tiny red circles containing unexpectedly high white numbers considering I haven't posted anything in a couple of days. A quick scroll through Instagram tells me what's up—photos of Kendall and me at the funeral with accompanying text that holds nothing back. I'm tagged, and Kendall, along with reference to the accident and speculation about us. Same show on Facebook and Twitter.

My phone slips from my sweating palm before I can check my text messages. *Fuck*. This is bad. The likelihood of someone besides my dad identifying Kendall as the girl in the YouTube video just got a lot higher, except now Kendall's backstory will be attached. Her worst fear is forming like a tornado on the horizon, and there's no containing it. Not when the posts are coming from the personal accounts of people in her hometown rather than a tabloid. I shouldn't have gone to the funeral. I should have realized this could happen. If my father were standing beside me right now he'd be saying, "I told you so," in his most infuriating voice. My heart pounds in my ears. I want to hurdle seats and push my way off the plane, but I bank the impulse and scoop my phone off the floor. I can't undo this. And I probably can't stop the story from making the jump from social media to mainstream media, but I can make sure I don't add to the damage. I can provide Kendall some shelter from the harshest elements of this storm. I love her, and I need to protect her, even if she ends up hating me for what's happened. I quickly search my messages, looking for the one person I know can help me do what I have to do. He's there. My dad texted twice. The first is consolation. *Nina told me America Rocks withdrew their offer. I'm sorry. You earned it, and it's their loss.* I thought I'd mentally accepted this outcome, but an avalanche of new disappointment tumbles through the hole in my chest where my heart used to be and lands heavily. His next text is hours later, obviously in response to the social media activity. Instead of the "told-you-so" I predicted, the message simply says, *Let me help.*

Am I certain he knows how to dial back his ambitions and support me rather than direct me? No. But he wants to help, and I want to give him the chance. I'd like to feel like my dad has my back—as a dad—not as someone orchestrating my every move. We'll see.

I call. He picks up on the first ring, and he listens without interruption, which is a major change. Within seconds he's up to speed, including how I want to handle this situation. Instead of trying to talk me out of it, he tells me he'll meet me at my place so we can get to work. He's endeavoring to get behind my decisions, not make them for me, and that's a distinction I appreciate. Even in the middle of a shitstorm.

He's also genuinely good at crisis communications. He knows who to call and how to get the message out. I'm calmer just for having run through it with him, I realize, while retrieving my bag from the overhead compartment.

He's not trying to take over, or tell me to do this thing his way or the sky will fall. The sky is falling no matter what we do, it's just a question of whether we can get it to land in the least impactful place.

When I open the front door for him ninety minutes later, he gives me a hug. "Thanks for letting me help with this, Vaughn. I know Kendall's important to you. I get that now."

"She is." I pat his shoulder a little awkwardly—we've never had the most demonstrative relationship—and lead him to the office. "Thanks for stepping up."

I take a seat behind the desk and gesture my dad to one of the chairs on the other side. Last time he stood where I am, perhaps unconsciously taking the power position, while I faced him from the subordinate side. It's not lost on me that the tables are turned this time.

His decision to investigate Kendall's past and deem her unacceptable isn't what we're here to talk about, but it still sticks in my craw, so I can't stop myself from taking the detour. "You're not the least bit tempted to tell me we could have avoided all this if I'd just listened to you?"

He takes off his suit jacket and sits. I don't know what he dropped to rush to my side, but based on how he's dressed I'm guessing it was business. "No. I overstepped where she's concerned. I've just…" He studies me as he considers his words. "I'm not sure when I started to see people as potential problems simply because they hadn't come vetted through me, but I did. The easy answer is because you're my child and I want to protect you, but there are other, less admirable factors, I'm afraid. Ambition. Positioning. It's easy to lose sight of what's important because you're too focused on what's strategic."

"Like Becca? She was strategic?"

This pulls a dull laugh out of him. "So much for protecting you, huh?"

"Dad, I'm not a child. I'll always appreciate your expertise, but I don't need protection."

He nods. "I know. In my head I know that. In my heart? Well, the heart of a parent is a complicated thing, especially when you've lost one child."

And there it is. He lost, and I've been trying to make up for it ever since. I take a deep breath and calmly say, "I'm also not Andie. I know you loved her. I loved her, too. And I know you two were extra close, but I can't defer running my own life just to give you a sense of purpose and the illusion of control."

"I know. The ironic thing is Andie and I butted heads about this all the time. She wanted more say over the direction of her life and career. But after she died I second-guessed every bit of freedom I gave her. She should have been seeing a specialist. That trainer she used wasn't qualified to take on clients with her condition. How could I have let it happen?"

"You didn't *let* it happen, Dad. You didn't know. Nobody knew—"

"I was her father. I should have known, for Christ's sake!"

His raised voice echoes off the walls before the silence rushes in, all the louder after his outburst. The shock in his expression tells me he's kept that guilt locked up for years.

"You can't protect someone from everything." I keep my voice low but sure. "That's not living. Living comes with inherent risks. The trick is to make sure you're taking the right risks for the right reasons."

He stares at me for a long moment. Finally he clears his throat. "For you, this is the right risk, and Kendall is the right reason?"

I look him straight in the eye. "Even if it drives another nail into the coffin of my career, this is the right risk. Even if nothing I do changes Kendall's mind about taking a risk on *me*. But it means a lot to know I'm taking this risk with you on my side."

"Always," he says with gratifying speed. "If I haven't mentioned it lately, I love you, and I'm always on your side. I meant what I said about supporting your decisions rather than making them for you. I'm on this."

"Thanks, Dad." For the first time in a long time, the sentiment is heartfelt.

• • •

The morning following the funeral, social media posts concerning the event have gained almost as much notice as the video. My publicist is working overtime to field calls on both. Neither Kendall nor I are being given a break, but I'm sick to my stomach to see she's being dealt the bigger blow. I'm ashamed of the pedestal women are putting me on, cutting me slack when I'm the one who dragged Kendall—unintentionally—into this media freak show.

It's killing me to keep my distance from her. My fingers itch to dial her number or text her to say I'm sorry for bringing her deepest fear down on her. I'm thankful she's got her parents while at the same time mad as hell I'm not the one there to shoulder her pain. She asked me to stay away, and I'm abiding by the request, but she didn't ask me to keep my thoughts about her to myself.

Hence, Plan B. Will Kendall watch? If she does, will anything I say change her mind? I don't know. All I know is I've got to give this my best shot. She deserves nothing less.

Sitting on a comfortable couch on the set of *Access Live*, I watch a tech adjust studio lights while a makeup artist does last-minute touch-ups to ready Kit for the camera. Thanks to my dad's connections, she was more than happy to set up an interview today. Although she's been as congenial as always, I know she's not going to pull any punches once the camera starts rolling. She's got me in the hot seat, she's done her homework, and if there's dirt to dish she's going to make sure *Access Live* gets the first and biggest shovelful.

Makeup finished, Kit looks up and gives me a smile. "We ready?" she asks to the room in general. The segment producer responds in the affirmative, and seconds later we're rolling. She does a short intro spiel and then lobs me a softball question about how it feels to be part of last week's number one most viewed music video.

I tell her I learned the news midway through a photo shoot in San Francisco, when Laney called me screaming a bunch of stuff they'd have to bleep if I quoted her word for word, but she was really excited and very cool to share the credit with me. I'm pleased people liked the video and stoked for Laney, because her first single is amazing, but it's just the start. The rest of the album is going to blow peoples' minds.

"Can we look forward to seeing you in more videos with our newest *America Rocks* winner?" Kit asks. Her smile and twinkling eyes invite me to divulge things we both know I'm not at liberty to discuss.

"You'll have to wait to see," I say with a smile.

"Vaughn, we're terrible at waiting. After receiving that good news in San Francisco I understand you traveled to a small town in Wisconsin." Kit tips her head slightly, and adds, "Was that for a new video by any chance?"

Obviously no, and she's well aware, but this is her way of leading into the real reason for this interview. I imagine when the segment airs, this is where they'll flash one of the internet pictures of Kendall and me embracing. "My visit to Lake Geneva was personal," I respond. "I went to support my friend Kendall, who lost a close friend after a long battle with injuries following an accident."

Kit nods, her normally perky expression serious. "Your friend Kendall Hewitt, who was driving while intoxicated when she crashed the vehicle and inflicted severe brain trauma that ultimately killed her passenger, Mason White."

I nod. "She made a terrible mistake at seventeen, and it had tragic consequences. It's an all too common mistake, statistically speaking. According to the most recent reports from the National Highway Traffic Safety Administration, over a third of fatal motor vehicle crashes among people aged sixteen to twenty involve alcohol, and that statistic doesn't change much for drivers over the age of twenty. Ever heard the saying 'There but for the grace of God go I?'"

"Of course."

"Nobody got much of God's grace that night when two teens climbed into a car after attending prom, but Kendall's spent every day since then ensuring nobody else makes the same mistake while she's around. Including me."

Kit leans forward. "She stopped you from driving under the influence? That's an interesting statement, especially considering I recently viewed a video that appears to show you in a drunken exchange with a woman many speculate to be Ms. Hewitt, after losing control of your vehicle."

And this is where they'll cut to the YouTube video. I own up to *my* mistakes, no sugarcoating. I explain our story, to the extent I can. My lawyer has weighed in on things like how I can't say Becca stole my car while intoxicated and almost killed me without risking a defamation lawsuit. Plus she contacted me, genuinely distraught, and assured me she didn't release the video. Her friend did, in a sick way of supporting Becca over our "breakup." So instead, I explain that an unidentified person or persons helped themselves to my car and took a joyride down my driveway, nearly hitting me before losing control, stalling in a hedge, and abandoning it—which sounds like a load of crap, but it's the best I can do. I explain how Kendall risked her life to prevent me from getting run down. How she confiscated my keys when I tried to get behind the wheel to move my car. How by doing that, she reminded me there is no situation where it's okay to drive under the influence. I finish by saying, "I can't know why fate put her in my path that night, but I'm forever thankful to Kendall for being there."

"She was your guardian angel," Kit says.

I couldn't have asked for a better response. "Absolutely. And it goes beyond me. She's fought hard to find meaning and purpose for her life. She volunteered during college. After graduating, she accepted a position working with traumatized youth. She finds ways to quietly contribute every day."

I pause for breath and then stare at the camera. "What she *didn't* do was seek any of this current attention. She's a private person. She didn't ask me to attend her friend's funeral. I made that decision on my own."

"Why?" Kit asks.

"Because when someone you care about is going through a rough time, it's hard to keep your distance. But if I'd realized my presence would put her in a spotlight I knew she didn't want, I would have tried harder to stay away. Not because I think she should hide her past or be ashamed of the woman she is today, but because I try to respect her wishes. I admire her, I'm really proud of her, and…well, I love her."

The segment director and production assistant practically high-five over my on-air confession. Kit flashes a smile so wide it's blinding. "Oh my goodness. Is Vaughn Shaughnessy off the market?" she asks.

I can't muster up a smile of my own, because my response is completely serious. "I'm hers for the taking, but the ball's in her court."

Chapter Twenty-Seven

Kendall

"You look miserable."

"I am miserable," I say to my mom. I'm curled up on the couch, watching cooking shows on mute because the hosts are way too cheery for me today. I like to see the food, though. Not that I've got much of an appetite.

"Don't move," Mom says.

"No problem." I've been in this position for most of the morning. It's bad enough I can't shake the look of hurt on Vaughn's face when I told him good-bye, but then last night I discovered my social media accounts blowing up. More than one old friend had posted pictures of Vaughn and me at the funeral along with horrible, hurtful captions. The kinds of things I wanted to keep secret. I can't get the pictures and narrations out of my head. Can't believe my peers could be so cruel.

Before going to sleep, I turned off all notifications and seriously thought about closing my accounts, but then it occurred to me that by running away, I'd be letting the haters win. I'd be letting them run me off. I've already suffered consequences I wouldn't wish on anyone, and it's *them*, not me, at fault this time.

If there was any lingering doubt in my mind about belonging in my hometown or anywhere near it, it's gone. I don't want any part of small-minded people and assholes with nothing better to do than talk crap behind someone's back. I tossed and turned in bed for hours, hiding under the covers like that would make it all go away.

It won't.

I have no idea if the internet is still buzzing with gossip about us. I can't bring myself to look. I can't bear to know if the publicity about my past has hurt Vaughn's chances with *America Rocks,* but I don't have to consult any screens to know it hasn't helped. This proves what I—and his dad—feared. Being around me isn't good for his career. That's the gist of the stories spreading all over the place like I'm not a real person with real feelings.

I wipe at my eyes, thinking back to our good-bye when one second I was telling myself to resist him and the next I was telling myself to pull him closer. To never let him go. All relationships are tethered to pasts, and dealing with a difficult one is a lot easier with someone by your side.

By my side is a hazardous place for someone like him, though.

"Here we go," Mom says, holding a wooden tray with iron handles in her hands. She sets it down on the coffee table. "Two steaming mugs of hot chocolate, marshmallows, and chocolate chip cookie straws."

"My favorite," I say with gratitude.

"It's always on hand, and I think today is a perfect day to indulge." She places a straw and a giant marshmallow into one of the cups and passes it to me. "It's okay to be upset, sweetheart, but maybe this will help a little."

I take the mug in both hands and sniff the bittersweet scent. "It does. Thanks."

Mom lifts her drink. "The people who matter, honey, know the person you are and would defend you until their last breath if asked."

"I know."

"And intelligent people know to take what they read on social media with a grain of salt."

"Maybe."

"No maybes. How anyone would think it's okay to give an ounce of respect to the kinds of comments being shared is ridiculous."

Comments claiming I brought Vaughn Shaughnessy to my ex-boyfriend's funeral to show everyone I'm hot shit, living in Cali, sleeping my way to the career I always talked about. There are people calling me a drunk and worse. Comments warning Vaughn to drop me before I hurt him, too.

My mug shakes in my hands.

Mom steadies me with a gentle touch and helps me put the cup back on the tray.

I sniffle for the thousandth time. "It's hard to ignore all the horrible things people are saying."

"But not impossible. Tune it out with the things you know are true in your heart, and if that doesn't work repeat after me…"

I sink back into the couch. "One step and deep breath at a time," we say together.

"This is another opportunity, you know," Mom says.

"For?"

"For showing what you're made of. For setting an example and using the mistakes you've made to help others. You've got a platform, too, and when you rise from this shitstorm like I know you will, admiration, not animosity, will follow you."

A breathless laugh escapes my tight throat. My mom never uses bad words, which means she is super serious and there is no room for argument.

Not that I want to. My past is out there now, and all I can control is how I let it affect me. I straighten. "You're absolutely right."

"I usually am." Mom playfully bumps my shoulder.

I hear a door open followed by loud footsteps, Dad's fancy black loafers tapping the floor. "Hello?" he calls out.

"Hey, honey," Mom calls back.

Dad enters the family room with his briefcase in one hand and a pie box in the other.

"What are you doing home so early?" Mom asks.

"Don't get upset," he says, his attention on me, "but I got word there were a couple of reporters lingering out front. I got rid of them and also had a craving for harvest apple pie."

"*What?*" My entire body shakes. I look toward the window.

"Hey," Dad says. "Eyes on me."

I'm about to hyperventilate. Or have a heart attack. Maybe both. I wave my T-shirt away from my stomach. Is it hot in here?

"Kendall."

I swallow the emotion lodged in my throat then find my dad's fierce blue eyes. "They're gone and won't be coming back. I made sure of it," he says. "You're safe."

It's like déjà vu. He said similar words after the accident. And he was right. He's got my back, like always. I breathe a small sigh of relief as he gets comfortable on the couch. Mom goes to the kitchen, I'm guessing for plates, napkins, and forks.

"Thank you," I say, my voice a little rough.

"You have nothing to be ashamed of, you know." Dad opens the box to my favorite pie. "You made amends for your actions years ago, and again with Mason a few days ago. And you handled yourself with dignity at the funeral. You're strong enough to deal with anything that comes your way."

"I second that," Mom says, returning and dishing us each a piece of pie.

We're quiet for a minute while I absorb my parents' support. I have paid for my mistakes. I've suffered, learned to make the best of my situation and believe in myself again.

My dad clears his throat, and then says, "So, I got an interesting call today from—"

"Dad," I interrupt. My timing isn't perfect, but his pep talk is the impetus I needed to tell him how I feel. After everything he's done for me, I owe him the truth. "I don't want to go to law school." The weight dragging my shoulders down floats up to the ceiling like a helium balloon poked with a pin. The pressure of pretending it's what I wanted drifts away with the scent of apples, butter, and cinnamon.

Mom blesses me with a tiny but proud smile. Dad stares at me like I've confessed to murder. It's true in a way. I've killed his dream of having me join his firm.

I hold my breath, waiting for him to say something. This isn't a surprise to my mom, but it is to him. I've never so much as mentioned having any doubts. My bad. He's my father and I know deep down he wants what's best for me. Especially today, with all the scrutiny I'm dealing with. No way can he possibly object. Right?

"Now or ever?" he asks.

I press my hands into the couch cushion while forcing myself to maintain eye contact. "Ever. I'm sorry."

"Is this because of Vaughn?" he asks, his voice tight.

"No. Not at all. I've had my doubts for a while, and it took this summer to make me realize my dream job isn't an attorney. It's working with young people who are grappling with various challenges and emotional hardships. I know a thing or two about guilt and pain and self-loathing, and I love working at Art in Progress. Their goal is to use art as therapy and offer a safe place for kids to share their troubles with others, and in so doing, heal. I've been offered a full-time position there."

Dad runs a hand down his dress pants. "You can help people as an attorney, too, you know."

"I know. But it's not the same. And I'd like to start now rather than three years from now."

"You want to stay in California."

"Yes."

"Not because of the boy."

I almost scoff. He's definitely not a boy. "No, not because of Vaughn. I want to do this for me, Dad. I *need* to do this. I fell into a job that makes everything I've been through feel useful, and the thought of giving it up hurts."

Mom takes my hand, squeezes.

Dad seems to be absorbing my announcement with a measure of reluctance, his jaw firm, his eyes narrowed. I guessed he wouldn't be overjoyed by my decision, but I'd like his support, if not his approval. It's time to appeal to the non-lawyer part of his brain.

"I also want to continue building the bond Amber, Dixie, and I have forged. I think we're on our way to being real sisters, and I don't want to lose that by living halfway across the country."

He scrubs a hand over his cheek. "You know I won't object to that. But I can't help you the same way if—"

"I don't need your help, Dad," I interrupt. "I mean, I did today, but moving forward, you just said so yourself that I've got this. I may *want* your help sometimes, but the decision should come from me."

"I worry—"

"You'll worry no matter where I am or what I'm doing. I

need to do this. I think this is the path I'm supposed to take."

The room is silent for several beats.

"How about we defer for a year and revisit the possibility in the spring? It never hurts to have a backup plan in case you change your mind."

"Okay." I won't change my mind, but if the compromise means I have his acceptance, I'll take it.

Mom sighs with relief and digs into her pie. Before Dad takes a bite he says, "I'm proud of who you are, Kenny."

"Thanks, Dad."

"And no matter what, I love you."

"Love you, too." I take a bite of my food, relief flooding me. I'm so relieved I won't be starting law school in the fall. "What was the interesting call you got today?" I ask, remembering I cut him off with my announcement.

"It was from Vaughn's publicist."

I choke. "What did she—or he—want?"

"She wanted to let me know they were handling things on their end and were very sorry for the attention Vaughn's presence at the funeral created. She said she and her team were available should we need anything."

"Wow," I mutter.

"That's so considerate," Mom says.

"Before hanging up she told me Vaughn was doing an interview with *Access Live* today."

"I love that program," Mom says.

What kind of interview? Did he get the hosting job? On autopilot, I reach beside me for my phone then remember I left it upstairs—turned off. I've missed Vaughn more than I thought possible, and I'm incredibly antsy for any glimpse of him. Nothing would make me happier than to see he's the new host of *America Rocks* and that this whole funeral fiasco hasn't hurt him.

"I'm going to run upstairs and see if I can catch it." I

hurry out of the room before my parents say anything—or Mom wants to watch it with me.

Once I get to my bedroom, I climb onto my bed, lean against my headboard, and turn on the television. Luck is with me. The show is about to start. The program opens news-style with discussion on different celebrities. I tap my fingers on my leg. Chew on my bottom lip. Finally they preview the interview with Vaughn, coming up after the commercial break.

Which is taking forever. I bring my hand to my mouth, bite my nail. I've never bitten my nails in my life, but apparently it's time to start.

Finally, Vaughn appears on screen with Kit. I like her. She's always bubbly and sincere and I relax slightly, thinking Vaughn is in sensitive hands. They begin talking.

Oh. My. God.

The interview isn't about him being the new host. It's about me. I stop breathing when Kit says my name and what I did to Mason. The crushing blindside has my finger on the remote to turn off the interview. But then the camera cuts to a close-up of Vaughn, and I'd swear he's also stopped breathing. I watch his lips move, but don't hear what he's saying.

I use the remote to rewind the past several seconds.

Vaughn defends me. His voice is calm. Definitive.

A video is mentioned. It plays on the screen. Holy crap. It's from the night I met him. How in the world…?

Vaughn comments on the recording, shares what happened, and opens himself up to professional damage by not denying much of anything as far as his own behavior that night. He sings my praises. He continues with basically telling everyone I saved him in more ways than one and to back off the funeral speculation.

Then he tells everyone watching he loves me.

I think I maybe levitate off the bed, his words pure magic. I'm lighter than air and ready to float right back to him.

He ends with, "I'm hers for the taking, but the ball's in her court."

The program moves to the next segment. I turn off the television and power on my phone. I need to get in touch with him. He could have chosen to ignore the video, to not dignify it with a response, and yet he spoke up. To help me. To reach out to me and do right by me, even when I told him to leave me alone. I've been an idiot.

A gazillion notifications fill the screen on my cell. I swipe to open and find four text messages. I check those. They're all from Amber and Dixie, sent to our group chat.

Holy shit. Did you see Vaughn's interview?

Hellllooooo...where the hell are you? Please tell us you saw Vaughn on national fucking television.

L.A. is two hours earlier so they obviously watched the show live.

Princess, if you don't text back, I'm going to break something.

Ignore her. She just hates not being in the know.

I text back *Just watched it.*

My phone rings. It's Dixie. "Hey," I say.

"Hi. How are you?"

That she asked speaks volumes, but I've learned when it comes to her it's best to pretend she doesn't really care. "I'm shocked. Blown away. My heart has never pounded so hard."

"Well, I thought you might like an update."

"Okay."

"Dylan just stopped by. Vaughn got the job as *America Rocks* host, but when that video hit YouTube, they took back the offer."

My whole body sags, every muscle aches. He must be devastated. "Who released the video?"

"Nobody knows."

Except me. I know. Or at least, suspect.

"I'm coming home." I disconnect with a quick goodbye, my mind a massive highway going in several different directions. Vaughn has continually put me first, and it's past time I did the same for him.

His getting, then losing, the job as host is bullshit. I need to fix it *then* claim his heart.

My story is out in the open now. Since last night, I've hated that. But I don't have to. I can welcome it and use it to help others. One comment flits through my mind. The only one I should remember, rather than all the negative ones. Why is it so much easier to let harmful opinions bother us, rather than allow good ones to lift us up? *Kendall,* @blakedreams had written, *you're not alone. I got a DUI at 17, too, and lost someone. It gets easier, I promise.*

I wish none of my past leaked, but it has. And if I don't tell—or better yet, show—Vaughn how I feel about him, I'll regret it for the rest of my life.

I quickly change out of my pajamas, text Dixie an apology for hanging up on her, and hurry downstairs. I have a plane to catch.

• • •

The next morning I wake up back at my aunt and uncle's house, the bedsheets in restless disarray. It took some deep thinking, but I've got a plan. Operation Vaughn Rocks is set in my mind despite the false components to it. I'm not comfortable lying, but desperate times call for desperate measures. I'll apologize to everyone later.

"Knock, knock," Dixie says, entering my room.

"Morning," Amber says from behind her.

"Hi." I sit up, unsure why tears are tickling the corners

of my eyes. "I'm happy to see you." That's probably why. I'm home. These girls and this city are my home now.

They sit on my bed. "Don't go getting all sappy on us," Dixie says, observant and unsentimental as ever.

"I'm not." I so am. Talk about an emotional few days.

Dixie leans back like my feelings are contagious, but I see the truth in her eyes. She's glad to see me, too. "We came in here for an update, not a heart-to-heart."

"I can do both," I say, and launch into discussion on the funeral, the media, my parents, and Vaughn. "Am I making a mistake?"

"No," Amber is quick to say.

I bring my legs up and cross them, waiting for Dixie to weigh in. It hasn't always mattered to me what my sisters think, but this summer has brought us closer; their opinions mean more now. And whether Dixie admits it or not, I know she cares about me.

"I'm the Queen of Mistakes," she says.

"Meaning?" I ask.

"Meaning where would we be without making them?"

I certainly wouldn't be here. *Things happen for a reason* may be a cliché, but I'm a believer. I like the person I am sitting on this bed with the two girls who mean so much to me. Saying good-bye to Mason, forgiving myself, telling my dad my truth, all major steps to helping me move toward the future I'm meant to have.

"Not that I think you're making one now," she adds.

"Thank you," I say with a sigh before spilling my plan to help Vaughn.

"That is badass," Dixie says.

"Ditto." Amber nods her head.

I'm relieved they don't think me crazy or out of line. I eye the alarm clock. It's only eight. I've got a few hours before it's showtime.

"In other news," Dixie, says. "Dylan told Amber she looked uptight and offered to loosen her up."

"He was trashed," Amber points out. "And despite the charming offer, a hard-partying club owner is the last thing I need in my life right now."

I drop my gaze to her tummy. "How are you feeling?"

Amber scrunches her nose. "A little better."

"Well enough to sit on a dick? Or has that not kicked in yet?" Dixie smirks. "A girl I worked with back home got knocked up and I shit you not, she was horny all the time."

"Great. Can't wait." Amber sinks into the comforter and closes her eyes.

"I know what we're getting her for her birthday," I say to Dixie.

Dixie fist-bumps me. "With extra batteries."

"On that note, I'm going downstairs for breakfast," Amber says.

"Right behind you." Dixie stands, looks over her shoulder at me. "You coming?"

"A little later. I've got to shower and practice my accent."

Chapter Twenty-Eight

Kendall

I give a silent prayer for success and forgiveness as I dial my phone. It rings once. Twice…

"Nigel Cowie's office," a woman with a sharp British accent says.

Please let this work.

"Hello, this is Laney Albright. I'm so sorry to bother you, but I forgot where Nigel and I are having lunch today?" I deliver the words in my best Laney impersonation. I've drawn out my vowels, dropped my *R*s and pronounced *D*s instead of *T*s.

"I don't have you on his calendar."

"It was last minute. I'm…heading out of town this afternoon, so he told me to swing by and join him, but I forgot the name of the restaurant."

"Did you try his cell?"

"He didn't pick up." *Please, please, please just give it up, lady.* I sound exactly like Laney, if I do say so myself.

"Lunch today is at Tesse Restaurant."

"Right. Tesse," I repeat just to be sure I understood her. She *hmms* her agreement. I thank her, hang up, and quickly Google the restaurant. It's on Sunset, not too far away. Yes!

This may be considered stalking, but it's purely selfless, so that has to wipe out any inappropriateness. At least that's what I tell myself as I drive to the restaurant. When I get there, I take a peek inside. Mr. Cowie is seated at a table with two other men.

Rather than bother them—I do have some scruples about this—I wait outside on the sidewalk. There's no shade, so within minutes, sweat trickles down my sides and I wipe at my forehead. Lift my arm to shield my face from the bright sun. I hope my perspiration isn't visible through my yellow sundress.

It feels like forever, but is probably more like twenty minutes, when the three businessmen exit the restaurant and step under the umbrella for the valet.

"Mr. Cowie?" I say on my approach. When his attention turns to me, I continue. "I'm sorry to bother you, but I was hoping you had a minute?"

"Kendall, is it?"

"Yes." I'm relieved he remembers me. Or maybe I should be mortified because of all the recent media attention. Either way, I've got some things to say to him.

"Excuse me, gents," he says to his companions.

"Thank you so much," I tell him, grateful when he gestures for me to follow him back into the restaurant. I'm really doing this.

We're immediately seated at a table for two. Nigel makes a motion with his hand to indicate we shouldn't be bothered. "I expect you've got something on your mind," he says.

"I think you made a mistake."

"In regards to?"

"Vaughn Shaughnessy should be the next host of *America Rocks*. As you may remember, I'm a huge fan of the show and have watched it since the beginning. When Vaughn told me"—Nigel's thick brows reach his hairline—"*confidentially* that he was being considered for the new host, I couldn't have imagined anyone better. I don't know if you saw his interview…" I trail off, hoping to collect some intel before I keep going.

"I didn't see it live, but have since received and viewed a copy from his publicist. I'm bloody sorry, by the way. For your loss."

"Thank you." I look away for a moment in order to keep my composure. "I need to tell you Vaughn wasn't completely honest in that interview."

Nigel's eyebrows rise again. "Is that so?"

I nod. "He blamed an 'unknown person' for driving his car that night."

"Yeah, the old 'unknown person' culprit. Unfortunately, that's not terribly convincing, given there's nobody else in the vehicle. What's shown is you taking his keys and leading him away. If you're here to tell me it was him after all—"

"It wasn't him," I interject. "That's not what he lied about. He lied when he said he didn't know the driver. I can't say why he chose to keep her name out of it, but a woman named Rebecca Bismark took his car without his permission, and after nearly running us down in the driveway, she laughed like it was a big joke and walked away scot-free. I'd lay odds she's the source of the video, but that part I didn't witness firsthand."

Nigel regards me with an unreadable expression. Am I making any headway? I'm not sure, but I've got to keep trying.

"What I *do* know is Vaughn isn't a risk or a liability. He's one of the strongest, most reliable people I've ever met. The person who released that video wanted to portray him in a false light to hurt him, and if you don't give him back the job, then she wins. I don't want her to win, Mr. Cowie. She's not a nice person."

He holds his jaw in his hand. "No, I reckon she isn't."

"She's rubbish."

That earns me a grin. He reaches his arm across the table to shake my hand. "I'm delighted you came to see me, Kendall."

"Thank you for hearing me out."

"The pleasure was mine."

"I, uh, need to tell you I called your office and pretended to be Laney Albright so I could trick your secretary into telling me where you were having lunch today."

He throws his head back and laughs before getting to his feet. I stand as well. "Brilliant strategy," he says.

"I'm glad you're not mad."

We walk toward the front of the restaurant. He opens the door for me. "As long as no one is hurt, the things we do for love should never be criticized."

I look down at the sidewalk in an attempt to hide my blush.

"Valet ticket?" he asks me.

"I'm around the corner."

"Until we meet again, then."

What does that mean? I hope it's that he's changed his mind about Vaughn. "Okay. Enjoy the rest of your day." I spin, put one foot in front of the other. When I round the block, I let out a breath so big it could probably knock someone over. Thankfully, no one is close enough.

I'm not sure my Hail Mary plan has worked, but I'm pretty positive it didn't do any further damage.

Rather than head straight home, I drive to Art in Progress to tell Candace I'd like to accept her job offer.

"I'm thrilled," she says, giving me a hug.

"Me, too. I was worried with all the recent attention that you may have changed your mind."

"I put very little stock in crap like that. What matters to me is the person who looks me in the eye and is brave enough to tell me her truths. Our students are going to learn a great deal from you."

"Yes, they will." I can't wait to learn from them as well.

"We'll talk job specifics tomorrow morning. Be here at ten sharp."

"I can't wait. Thank you."

My stomach grumbles as I leave the gallery, so I stop at Pink's Hot Dogs. The line is a dozen or so people deep, but a hot dog smothered in onions and relish sounds too good to pass up. I eat it in the car with the air conditioning blasting.

I return home midafternoon, noting with a mix of nervousness and joy that Vaughn's car is parked in his driveway. I hurry into the house to brush my teeth—no girl in her right mind should profess her love to the guy of her dreams with onion breath—and change into my gray V-neck T-shirt dress and washed denim chucks. The outfit says *cute but not trying too hard.*

"Hey!" Amber catches me before I rush out the front door. She's wearing a bathing suit. Her sunglasses sit on top of her head. Snowflake rushes past her to say hello.

Darn it. So much for a stealthy enter and exit while my sisters and Snow were out in the backyard. Not that this is a secret. It's just I can't wait another minute to see Vaughn.

"How'd it go?" she asks. "Did you get to speak to the producer guy?"

I bend to pet Snow. "I did. I think it went well." Rising, I thumb over my shoulder. "I'm going next door to talk to Vaughn. Catch up with you later?"

"Yes. And good luck."

"Thanks."

Snow tries to leave with me. "Not right now," I tell her, gently nudging her away from the door with my foot. She doesn't take the hint. "Amber! Will you call for Snowflake?"

"Snowflake! Come get a treat!" she shouts from the kitchen.

At the word "treat" Snow darts off so fast she practically leaves her little pink hair bow floating in the air behind her. I disappear just as quickly, striding toward Vaughn's house. I slow to a walk as I start up his driveway. Goose bumps pop up on my arms in anticipation of seeing him. I think about all the things I want to say. But then an engine turns over, taillights blaze bright red then white, and his car starts to move.

For a split second I'm transported back to the first night we met. The memory is short-lived, though, because this time the car is carefully backing out, and when I wave my arms in the air and shout, "Hey!" the Rover immediately stops. The engine clicks off. The driver's side door opens. And the hottest guy I've ever seen climbs out. His come-closer-if-you-dare eyes latch onto mine as we slowly walk toward each other.

I dare. From this moment on, I will always dare with him. "Hi."

"Hi," he says. "I heard you were back." His gaze touches on every part of me, lighting a fire in the pit of my stomach.

"I'm glad I caught you, but do you need to be somewhere? I can come back–"

"Now's good." The gap between us shrinks further. "I was just going to the florist."

"The florist?"

"To buy you flowers before I walked over to see you."

We're maybe five feet apart now. Four feet…three feet… two. We stop, arms at our sides, and stare at each other. The way he looks at me steals my breath.

"You wanted to see me?" I manage to ask. The little speech I had planned drifts right out of my head. I try to hang on to the threads, but it's hard to think straight when Vaughn takes my hand in his. I glance down at our entwined fingers. His hand is so much bigger than mine, yet we fit like we were molded for each other.

He leads me to the grassy slope beside his driveway and plants us under a palm tree. We sit side by side, not quite touching.

"I just got off the phone with Nigel."

"Oh?"

"He had an interesting meeting today."

"Really?"

Vaughn takes my chin between his thumb and finger and turns my face to his. "The flowers were going to be a thank-you. You went to bat for me."

"It was nothing."

"It was everything."

"You've done so much for me, Vaughn, and I haven't thanked you nearly enough. You've fought for me from the start, and it was time I fought for you. When I heard you'd gotten the job and then lost it, I had to do something. You're selfless, you speak from your heart, you're perceptive, and *America Rocks* needs you as their host."

"Nigel agrees."

There's a moment where everything stands still as those words sink in. A second later, I tackle hug the next host of *America Rocks* and knock him flat on his back. "Yay! That's fantastic. Congratulations!" I kiss him all over his face, capturing his smile against my lips, swallowing his laughter with my own.

He rolls us over, careful to cushion my landing with his palm spread across my back. Looking up at him is better than looking at a double rainbow. Better than gazing at a sunrise.

Better than a sky full of the brightest stars in the galaxy.

"Thank you," he says.

"There's nothing I wouldn't do for you."

"Really?" He's half teasing, half asking. I get it. He needs confirmation of where I stand.

I'm about to answer when Snowflake comes barreling across the lawn, yapping away like we're hiding her favorite bone and she's bound and determined to retrieve it.

Vaughn scoops her up and returns to a sitting position beside me with Snow in his lap. "Hey, girl. Your timing sucks."

I sit up. "How did she get out?"

"It's not the first time. I think I know where she escapes from. Come on. I'll help you close it up." He moves to stand.

I stop him with a hand to his arm. "Wait."

This moment right here is one I will never forget: our eyes locked, the air still, the only sound our beating hearts. "There's nothing I want more than to be there for you. I'm sorry I got scared. I'm sorry I let you walk away like I did." I take his hand in mine. "I love you. I love you so much I can't imagine my life without you in it."

Vaughn smiles. It's big, bright. *Mine.* It rearranges my molecules. Makes me feel safe. Cherished. "Are you putting the ball back in my court, Kendall? Because I'll warn you now, I'm keeping it."

I smile in return. "That's exactly what I'm doing. What you said on national tele—"

He kisses me. It's lips and tongues, love and passion. I feel it everywhere, but most of all, in my heart. He pulls away way too soon. "You're staying in L.A.?"

"Yes. This might sound weird, but I've found myself in the things that matter most," I say. "Art in Progress. My sisters. *You.*"

Another full-watt smile lifts his mouth, lights his face, and renders me momentarily speechless. He puts Snow on the grass, gets to his feet, and lifts me up, spinning me around with my feet flying behind me.

"Vaaaauuuughn! Put me down!"

"No way. I'm not letting you go ever again."

"Okay," I say as he slows and eventually lowers me so my feet touch the ground. True to his word he doesn't release me.

"I love you, Kendall. For the girl you were, and the woman you are."

"Thanks for being patient with me."

"Always."

"Thanks for being mine."

"Easiest thing I've ever done. And"—he kisses me—"something I will never take for granted."

I smile. "I feel the same."

"What do you say we take this mutual admiration society to my bedroom?"

"I say that sounds great."

Snowflake barks. Vaughn and I laugh.

"How about my bedroom?" I ask.

"I don't care where we go as long as I've got you to myself for the rest of the day."

"That can be arranged." We hold hands and lead Snow home.

"My life is about to get a lot more frenetic," he says. "But no matter what, my priority is you. I can't promise to shield you from everything, but we can keep our private life private. We don't have to—"

"Hey, let's take it one day at a time. I don't need to hide anymore, even though I do like the idea of keeping things private."

"We will then."

"I have no doubt. You're my someone, Vaughn. The person I want to share everything with. The person I want to treasure and protect and who will treasure and protect me in return. I wasn't ready before, but I am now. As it turns out, I've had someone at my back this whole time."

He stops our strides and cups my cheeks. "Always." He kisses me softly on the mouth. "You had me at 'Look out!' you know. I kept looking at you and thinking *this* girl. She's your soul mate. Don't fuck it up. Promise me you'll always be mine."

"I promise."

We kiss again, then tucked under his arm, we make our way up the driveway and toward something…more. We're walking toward our future. No holding back. No shying away. I'm no longer stuck in my past. I'm no longer distracting myself from living life to the fullest. I'm in love. With Vaughn. And more importantly, with myself again.

Acknowledgments

Big THANK-YOUs to:

All the usual suspects at Entangled—Stacy, Liz, Heather R., Curtis, Holly, Riki, Nancy Cantor, and the rest of the team.

Our readers—to the extent you don't overlap, we hope you do now! We know your free time is precious, and we appreciate you spending some with Kendall and Vaughn.

To our families for their support of a year's worth of weekend coffee dates and joint writing sessions.

To Social Butterly PR for helping spread the love!

To Nicola and Sandii, our unbribed beta readers, who disproved the notion that one gets what one pays for.

And last but not least, thanks to each other. Couldn't have done it without you!

Acknowledgments

About the Author

When not attached to her laptop, *USA Today* Bestselling Author Robin Bielman can almost always be found with her nose in a book. A California girl, the beach is her favorite place for fun and inspiration. Her fondness for swoon-worthy heroes who flirt and stumble upon the girl they can't live without jumpstarts all of her story ideas. She is a 2014 RITA Finalist, loves to frequent coffee shops, and plays a mean game of sock tug of war with her cute, but sometimes naughty dog, Harry. She cherishes her family and friends and loves to connect with readers. You can sign-up for her newsletter here: http://bit.ly/1E140Y4

Samanthe Beck lives in Malibu, California with her husband, their young son, a furry ninja named Kitty, and Bebe the trash talkin' Chihuahua. When not writing fun, contemporary, melt-your-Kindle sexy romances for Entangled Publishing's Brazen imprint, she searches for the perfect cabernet to pair with Ambien.

Also by Robin Bielman

the Wherever You Go series

Talk British to Me

Lips Close to Mine

Too Hard to Resist

the Kisses in the Sand series

Keeping Mr. Right Now

Blame It on the Kiss

The Best Friend Bargain

the Take a Risk series

Worth the Risk

Risky Surrender

His Million Dollar Risk

the Secret Wishes series

Kissing the Maid of Honor

Her Accidental Boyfriend

Wild About Her Wingman

Yours at Midnight

Also by Samanthe Beck

the Tropical Temptation series

Dirty Games

the Compromise Me series

Compromising Her Position

Hard Compromise

Compromised in Paradise

the Love Emergency series

Emergency Engagement

Emergency Delivery

Emergency Attraction

the Private Pleasure series

Private Practice

Light Her Fire

Falling for the Enemy

the McCade Brothers series

Lover Undercover

Falling for the Marine

Wicked Games

Best Man with Benefits

Discover more New Adult titles from Entangled Embrace...

Until We're More

a *Fighting for Her* novel by Cindi Madsen

Chelsea is the best friend I've ever had. Ever since she left, I've been a wreck, focusing only on keeping my family's MMA gym afloat. But now she's finally back, and things are weird between us. By weird, I mean I can't stop thinking about her in *that* way. Even stranger, I'm pretty sure she's feeling the same. And this time, I'm not going to stop fighting until we're more.

Once Upon a Player

a *British Bad Boys* novel by Christina Phillips

When my mum gets sick, I volunteer to fill in for her and clean some hot jock's penthouse. I've heard all the rumors about him, so the plan is get in, clean some toilet bowls, and get out. After my last experience with a "sports hero," I'm done with that sort of guy. Unfortunately, spending time with Lucas Carter is dangerous. He's so charming, but I can't let myself forget––once a player, always a player.

Full Count

a *Westland University* novel by Lynn Stevens

If I want to keep playing baseball, I need a tutor. I don't know what—or who—I expected, but it sure as hell wasn't Mallory Fine. Quiet, a little intense, my kind of gorgeous Mallory Fine—who hates baseball and any guy who plays it. I tell myself this is only a tutoring relationship, but I'm a liar. Mallory might be a challenge, but so is getting back on the ball field and I'm determined to make that happen—no matter the cost.

Without Words

an *Under the Pier* novel by Delancey Stewart

Firefighter Roberto DeRosa's career is over. After an accident leaves him struggling with words, communicating with people is difficult, but Dani Hodge has a way of seeing through the walls he's put up, and being with her makes him want to try.

Printed in the USA
CPSIA information can be obtained
at www.ICGtesting.com
LVHW090227100624
782789LV00022B/131

9 781093 291438